RAGE AND D

The bastard had sliced clean through her shirt. One millimeter more and she ... bleeding ...

"Lesson one," Cullin said. "Watch the man wielding the blade ..."

He smiled in pure masculine satisfaction.

Ari whispered a curse.

His gaze dropped to her mouth and the fire flared in his eyes. He grabbed her by the hair and fastened his mouth on hers. She tasted exotic spice and the faint trace of salt. Fire shot through every fiber to her core, urging her to melt into him. Before she could rouse the least bit of bracing rage, he released her. She wiped a sleeve across her mouth as much to erase her mortifying lack of alacrity—she should have shoved her blade through his chest—as to obliterate the feel of his lips on hers.

"Lesson two," he said. "Never offer what you cannot afford to lose."

ELISE

Thank you so much for stopping to visit at

RT 2011

ENEMY WITHIN

MARCELLA BURNARD

BERKLEY SENSATION, NEW YORK

THE BERKLEY PUBLISHING GROUP
Published by the Penguin Group
Penguin Group (USA) Inc.
375 Hudson Street, New York, New York 10014, USA
Penguin Group (Canada), 90 Eglinton Avenue East, Suite 700, Toronto, Ontario M4P 2Y3, Canada
(a division of Pearson Penguin Canada Inc.)
Penguin Books Ltd., 80 Strand, London WC2R 0RL, England
Penguin Group Ireland, 25 St. Stephen's Green, Dublin 2, Ireland (a division of Penguin Books Ltd.)
Penguin Group (Australia), 250 Camberwell Road, Camberwell, Victoria 3124, Australia
(a division of Pearson Australia Group Pty. Ltd.)
Penguin Books India Pvt. Ltd., 11 Community Centre, Panchsheel Park, New Delhi—110 017, India
Penguin Group (NZ), 67 Apollo Drive, Rosedale, North Shore 0632, New Zealand
(a division of Pearson New Zealand Ltd.)
Penguin Books (South Africa) (Pty.) Ltd., 24 Sturdee Avenue, Rosebank, Johannesburg 2196,
South Africa

Penguin Books Ltd., Registered Offices: 80 Strand, London WC2R 0RL, England

This book is an original publication of The Berkley Publishing Group.

PRINTING HISTORY
Berkley Sensation trade paperback edition / November 2010

Library of Congress Cataloging-in-Publication Data

Burnard, Marcella.
  Enemy within / Marcella Burnard.—Berkley sensation trade pbk. ed.
    p.   cm.
  ISBN 978-0-425-23685-7 (trade pbk.)
  I. Title.
  PS3602.U759E64   2010
  813'.6—dc22   2010022419

PRINTED IN THE UNITED STATES OF AMERICA

10 9 8 7 6 5 4 3 2 1

ACKNOWLEDGMENTS

Special thanks:

To my beloved husband, Keith, whose patience, faith, and support know no bounds.

To my family for rooting for me, for talking up my book at every turn, and for not disowning me over that faraway look I'd get in my eye whenever a story started playing in my head.

To my longtime friend and cohort, Dr. Kurt "Spuds" Vogel, Lt Col, USAF (ret) for keeping me rooted, if not in the probable, then at least in the outer reaches of the vaguely possible.

To Dawn Calvert, Darcy Carson, Carol Dunford, DeeAnna Galbraith, Melinda Rucker Haynes, and Lisa Wanttaja, a great group of writers, mentors and, best of all, friends.

To my editor, Leis Pederson, and to my agent, Emmanuelle Alspaugh, for helping me tell a better story.

To the members of Feline-L whose wide-ranging backgrounds and interests allowed me to ask the most obscure questions and receive cogent answers.

Last but certainly not least, my sincere thanks to Eratosthenes, Autolycus, Cuillean, and Hatshepsut, my feline snoopervisors, lap warmers, keyboard walkers, and reminders that no matter how large looms the deadline, there's always time to play.

CHAPTER

1

※━◦❀◦━※

SUN glinting off the barrel of a gun stopped Captain Ari Idylle dead in her tracks. She cursed under her breath. A perimeter guard? Three Hells. No one on her father's science expedition knew how to stand guard like that. She eased off the trail, shifting her thought processes from research scientist to military operative.

Three short, insistent beeps startled her, kicking her heart into high gear before she realized it was the guard's ident badge transmitting.

"Captain," the guard muttered. "Incoming."

"Affirmative. Scanning."

She didn't recognize the voices of the men tracking and possibly trying to capture her. That meant someone else controlled her father's ship.

Sucking in an alarmed breath, Ari shucked her backpack and jacket. Draping the coat around the pack of carefully stowed viral specimens, she backed up as the shimmer of a teleport beam locked onto the ship's badge pinned to her jacket. The bag and coat vanished.

She took to her heels, recalling every ounce of training she'd ever had, and slipped into the cool forest.

What had happened? She'd left her father and his four crew members cataloguing botanical oddities two days ago. Fear squeezed the breath from her. Did her father and the rest of the crew still live?

She halted and listened. Nothing. It didn't mean that she wasn't being tracked. Only that she couldn't hear anyone tracking her. She swore again and angled back to the ship, sliding between massive, thorny tree trunks. Whoever these people were, they knew she'd have to get close enough to assess the situation.

Breathing hard, she scaled a rocky, fern-studded rise and lay belly down in the brown and red fronds. The sun sat midway down the sky. She had four or five hours of light left. Ari fished for her binocs, parted the ferns, and peered into the clearing where the *Sen Ekir* sat, hatch open, equipment and specimens still sitting in the shadow of the ship's belly. Except for the absence of scientists, the scene looked so normal she could almost believe she'd imagined a stranger's voice answering to "Captain."

Another glint of sunlight on metal and she suddenly saw the man stationed in the bushes opposite the hatch. A sniper. Spawn of a Myallki bitch. Who the hell were these guys, and what did they want with a science ship? She put the binoculars down, careful to avoid any telltale flash of light on glass. She drew her little snub-nosed pistol and desperately wished for an assault rifle and scope. Her tiny, short-range gun was useless against snipers, but Armada Command had taken her guns when they'd taken her command and sent her on a forced sabbatical.

She let the ferns slide upright in front of her and blew out a shaky breath. Nothing ventured, nothing gained. She keyed the transponder embedded in the skin behind her left ear.

"*Sen Ekir. Sen Ekir*, come in."

"Well, well, well," a masculine voice drawled. "If it isn't our wayward scientist. Your father's worried about you."

"Identify," she demanded, ignoring the sudden hope speeding her pulse. Just because he'd mentioned her father didn't mean he was alive.

"Why don't you come on down and find out?"

"Ident."

"What do you want?" he countered, his melodic voice dropping into a coaxing, seductive tone that sent a shiver through her.

Ari swallowed hard. She'd just placed his musical accent. He was Okkarian. Had he proven that the mythical voice talents of his race were fact? She shook off the thought and wiped a hand over her face.

"I want a Wrate Leaf burger, a nice char on the outside, the inside still white and tender. With real guacamole, not that crap they make in the chem lab on Rackora. And an ice-cold pint of the darkest Porter this side of the Three Hells," she said.

Silence.

"I'll settle for my father on the squawk."

The man laughed softly. "Alexandria Rose Idylle. I'd been told you don't have a sense of humor."

"You have me at a disadvantage," she noted.

"I like it that way," he said in a whisper thick with innuendo. "Stand by."

Blotting sweat from her forehead, she sighed. She still didn't know anything she could use.

"Alex?"

Her breath caught. "Dad. Status."

Her father's laugh sounded forced. "Screwed six ways to Sunday. The ship's been commandeered. The four of them caught us unaware. No one takes science ships. We . . ."

"Casualties?" Ari smiled. Trust Dad to tell her how many bogeys she had to face.

"None."

"Repairs?"

"Complete. Except that someone's scrambled my command codes. What in the Three Hells were you thinking, locking me out of my own ship, Alex?"

She didn't answer. They both knew what she'd been thinking, that she couldn't trust anyone farther than she could throw the *Sen Ekir*.

"SOP, Dad," she growled. "Could we put a cap on the trade secrets, please?"

The captain's voice cut off anything her father might have said. "You know what I want you to know, now. So how about we talk trade?"

And he knew far more than she wanted him to know. She whispered a curse. She shouldn't have bothered. Thanks to the damned transponder, he heard.

"You want the code fixes," Ari surmised.

"No," he said, relish in his tone. "You. In trade for your father's life, all their lives."

Dismay drove ice through her. She shivered. He wanted her? Why? She shoved speculation aside. First things first.

"Secure the crew and my father off ship," she countered. "I'll give you the decode."

"You. Or they die."

She rested her forehead on her arms. Damn it. She should have known that half a dozen different enemy governments and criminal organizations would come looking for her. She'd been captured and imprisoned by the Chekydran. Humanoids in Chekydran captivity didn't live long, but she'd survived. Her own government kept asking how. Why shouldn't everyone else? Who was the pirate who'd taken her father's ship working for? Shaking her head, she swore again. Her friends and family were in danger because of her. The captain had her by the short hairs and he knew it.

"I'll take your answer, now. And your weapon. Not necessarily in that order."

Ari heard the click of a safety being cycled off a gun. Then she realized. She hadn't heard him via her transponder. She'd heard him with her ears. Damn it all, he'd used the distraction of her father to get the drop on her. And she'd let him. She rolled over in a flash, bringing her gun to bear, and stared up the barrel of a slim-line Autolyte 49-G modified assault rifle. Illegal. Highly illegal.

Golden eyes glared down the barrel at her. Unruly chestnut hair fell across his forehead. He was tall, his body lithe with a hint of long, lean muscle beneath bloodstained, ripped, and singed freighter-brown fatigues. She noted visible bruising on one prominent cheekbone and the shadow of a beard on the carved plains of cheek and jaw. The arrogance, intellect, and skillfully masked pain in his face tripped her internal alarms.

The man wasn't simply dangerous. He was a weapon. A lethal, tempered work of art.

"Give me the gun," he commanded, edging forward and kicking her booted foot out of his way.

Her grip sagged, and Ari belatedly registered the thread of power he'd tucked into his order. Fear gripped her as she fought the compulsion to obey and failed.

He took the pistol from her limp hand. "Get up."

No ring of control in that instruction. She rose, watching for any lapse of attention, any mistake she could turn to her advantage. He didn't make any.

"Hands on top of your head," he commanded. "Lace your fingers. Turn around. You wouldn't be hiding anything from me, now would you?"

He sounded hopeful. She braced herself, but his pat down was swift, efficient, and thoroughly professional.

"Turrel. Secure. Inform Daddy his little girl's coming home."

"Aye, Captain."

"A Wrate Leaf burger?" the captain said, amusement in his tone. "If you're a scientist, I'm the Ykktyryk king."

Too few teeth and definitely not reptilian. Ari bit her tongue to keep from saying it aloud.

"You can put your hands down. Turn around," he ordered. "Slowly."

When she glanced at him, he gestured her down the hill with a jerk of the rifle. She trudged past him. He grabbed a handful of her shirt and rested the barrel of the rifle against her back. Steering her by the scruff of the neck and the pressure of the gun, he ushered her toward the ship. They passed his perimeter guard.

She frowned and looked long at the guard's blue-black face. Chilly violet eyes watched her pass. A Shlovkur. Official word had it that a race-specific plague had exterminated the entire population. Interesting. Almost as interesting as the fresh blood on the man's face and the fact that when he fell in behind them, he glanced uneasily over his shoulder. They feared someone, or something, other than her.

She felt marginally brighter.

If they were on the run, how had they gotten to the tiny world her father and his crew had been investigating for the past five years? A ship would have set off the sensor array alarms, unless they'd set down outside of range. Possible, but a damned long walk. And from what she'd seen of the Shlovkur's injuries, if they'd had a ship, they'd either been cast away or they'd crashed. Either scenario could explain why they'd commandeered a vessel with no weapons.

Despite the muzzle bruising her right kidney, Ari stopped walking at the ship's hatch and turned her head. "Take me in via cargo, straight to decontamination," she said. "I've been mining specimens for the past two days."

"Your beam system didn't issue a decon alert," he countered, but he didn't shove her up the ramp.

Ah. The first useful tidbit of information about her mystery captor. No science background and no experience with science ship protocols. She shrugged. "I'm fine with gambling the lives of your remaining, injured crew if you are. A quarantine lockdown would strand your people in the cockpit. Medical is accessible from there, but I'm betting you don't have anyone trained in anything but combat first aid."

He swore and wrenched her off the ramp. She stumbled. He let her get her footing. She marched into the cargo bay still filled with half-finished experiments and crates of samples waiting to be sealed. Near the doors to the rest of the ship, her father and his crew sat, hands and feet bound, under armed guard. She glanced at them but didn't stop. Delaying decontamination could be fatal.

"Ari!" Jayleia, her father's xenobio tech cried, stark relief in her voice.

Ari met the young woman's gaze.

Jay flushed. "I'm sorry."

The young guard with red blond hair looked from one to the other, apparently feeling some deeper message passing between the two of them.

"It's okay," Ari said. Jayleia's people trained their women to be warriors, but Jay had chosen to reject the path laid out by her mother's family. She'd chosen a life of science. Ari gathered that her friend felt responsible for the hijackers' incursion.

Ari offered Jayleia a smile as she keyed open the decontamination unit and stepped inside. Maybe between the two of them, they could take back the ship after they'd cleaned up any stray pathogens.

"You're next in decontamination," she said to the captain.

He arched an eyebrow but lowered the rifle and nodded. Good. She wouldn't have to argue the point. He'd touched her. If she'd picked up a bug, so had he. As the decon door shut and the pulses of energy and antimicrobial-treated water saturated her, she sighed. The pirates had been tramping all over the ship, and their captain had proven he didn't understand decontamination protocols. Those men had made the ship a plague carrier. Without some drastic measures, they'd be shot out of the sky of any inhabited world or station they tried to approach.

The system cycled down. She stripped. At least she had access to sterile clothes just outside the door. A chime and the system cycled back on, the medicated water stinging in the cuts and scrapes she'd acquired. When the spray shut off, she wrung the water out of her hair and waited for the water recycle to suck the moisture from her body. She shoved every last scrap of clothing into the laundry bin and slapped open the door.

"Go," she said to the captain as she accessed the lockers.

"Don't let her catch you trying to get an eyeful," Pietre, her father's second in command said. "The Ice Princess doesn't like it."

Ari sighed. *Ice Princess*. Didn't Pietre realize she'd been forced to make the words true while the Chekydran held her? Ari shook off a sense of loss and glanced around at the surprised and riveted stares.

The captain swept his appreciative gaze up her body to meet her eye. A tingle followed the path of his stare as if he'd done far more than stroke her with a look. Swallowing a curse, Ari stepped into and fastened a pair of fatigue pants.

"Jilted lover?" the captain asked, nodding at Pietre.

She snorted and jerked a shirt over her head. "History? Yes. Lovers? Hell, no."

"Alexandria!" her father barked.

For a moment, she wilted, still a little girl desperately wanting Daddy's approval and never getting it. She clenched her teeth and, yanking the rest of her clothing into place, slammed the locker door on her reaction.

She turned on the pirate captain and snapped, "Decon."

He ignored her in favor of glaring at Pietre and her father.

"Put them off," the captain ordered.

One of the men heaved Pietre toward the open cargo door. Pietre stumbled and fell, cursing. "You're going to maroon us because of her? I always knew she was going to get us killed."

"No," Ari snapped, spinning on the captain, her hands balled into fists.

"Another word out of you and I'll maroon everything but your tongue." Palpable menace radiated from him as he stared down at Pietre.

Ari shivered at the deadly earnest tone of his voice and at the power he'd twined into the words. The force of it hadn't been turned upon her, but she could still feel the coercion rippling through her head. *Silence*, it urged.

The captain turned his gaze upon her.

Something in the depths of his golden eyes shot heat straight through her body, startling her. She stomped on the sensation. The man could manipulate her with that voice talent. He had already. She would not hand him yet another advantage over her.

"You give orders like you forget you're not in command," he observed, his tone a silken caress.

Anger burned the back of her throat when she had to suppress a sensual shudder. "I'm not in command, yet."

Humor flashed briefly in his eyes before his face darkened. "Are you challenging me?"

Hesitating, she raked him with a glance. He sounded eager. He outweighed her by half and every last bit of it was muscle. His reach exceeded hers, but she could get around that. Maybe. What would he demand of her if she couldn't? Unbidden, the image of those strong arms wrapped around her flooded her internal field of vision. A rush of weight and heat pooled in her abdomen. Ari backed away a step, disarmed by the sensation.

"Got a name?" she forced herself to ask. Her voice sounded rough to her ear.

"Cullin Seaghdh, at your service."

"Shaw?"

"Close enough. Your language doesn't use the same set of sounds."

"All right, Cullin Seaghdh," Ari said. "I'm not the one stealing someone else's ship and threatening to maroon her crew. You challenged me. So let's . . ."

"Choose your weapon," he commanded.

She blinked. He'd pounced on her use of the word "challenged." What trap had she walked into? "You can't be serious."

"Alex, I forbid . . . Oof!"

A glance assured her that her father had damaged nothing more than his pride by being shoved into a bulkhead by one of Seaghdh's goons. "No one gets left," she said.

"Not that long ago, you wanted the scientists secured off ship," he noted, his voice again threaded with power that brushed against her in lush promise.

She sucked in a slow breath as goose bumps rose on her arms. Damn, he was deliberately using his racial voice talent to distract her. It pissed her off no end to have to fight for concentration. More than that. He was using his talent to break her open, to pry apart her defenses and lay her bare. It was wrecking her control, and he had no idea how dangerous that made her.

"If they stay, I stay," she gritted.

"No."

"Then no one gets left."

"You seem to forget who has the ship and the guns."

"Threatening to hurt me won't get you anywhere," she said. "If you harm them or leave them behind, you lose your leverage."

"Oh, I don't think so," Seaghdh countered. "You don't seem to lack imagination, and you obviously understand persuasion. We both know these people aren't your sole weakness."

Ari did not want to discuss weaknesses while goose bumps still prickled her body. She commanded the sharpest Prowler crew in the . . . No. She used to command the best Prowler crew in the Armada. That had been taken from her. Now she was in limbo, nothing more than an adult child who disappointed her father at every turn. The thought laced pain through her chest.

She glanced down, expecting to see that Seaghdh had shot her. He hadn't. It wasn't much comfort. She blew out a shallow breath. She desperately needed options.

"Cycle through decontamination, Seaghdh," she said. "Then . . ."

"Losing your nerve?"

"You're on the run with an exhausted and injured crew. You need off this world. Just so happens we're done here and it suits me to lift anyway. I'll cooperate. We lift with everyone and I take you to the nearest neutral . . ."

"Choose. A. Weapon."

Thrice-damned, single-minded bastard wanted a fight? Fine. "I win, we lift with everyone?"

"Yes."

"Alive."

He grinned. "Yes."

"Energy blade."

Seaghdh scanned the cargo bay where she'd laid down a practice floor so many years ago when her father had first gotten the ship and made it clear he'd wanted her aboard. Seaghdh nodded. "Energy blade."

His grin widened, and Ari realized she'd gone still at the apprehension prickling through her. She hadn't expected such ready acceptance. Energy blades weren't exactly common. They were relics, really, and the skill required to use them relegated to little more than an unpopular sport. He could only have learned one place. The same place she had, at a military academy, where the Art of the Blade was valued for the discipline it instilled. Cursing, she strode to the equipment locker, opened it, and threw a shielded jacket at him. Why wouldn't he go through decontamination? Not that it mattered, considering the fact that the ship itself needed to be sterilized. Still. What did he have to gain by refusing?

"Federated Worlds Regs?" he drawled, confirming her fear that he knew more than which end of the weapon to hold.

"Sure." Three touches to the jacket or one solid hit to the tiny heart symbol on the left breast. She could do this. Couldn't she?

"Too late to pretend you don't know your way around a blade grid," he chided. "We both know you're no scientist. Military, maybe."

"You obviously don't know as much as you think you do," Jayleia shot. Her attempt at an iron tone wobbled. "Ari holds a master's in xenonanobiology. Those samples she tricked you into transporting aboard are her PhD thesis."

"Oversharing, Jay," Ari sang through a tight smile as she donned her jacket.

The younger woman flushed again, but anger and determination sparkled in her eyes. By the Twelve Gods, Ari hoped she wasn't inspiring her father's crew with this idiotic display of bravado.

Seaghdh plucked the weapon's locker key from her fingers, his eyes dancing with suppressed mirth. He handed the key to one of his men with a flourish. The man opened the locker, zeroed in on the best blade in the collection, and handed it to Seaghdh. He grabbed the most ragged, beat-up hilt and brought it to Ari.

Seaghdh tested the blade in his hand and glanced in appreciation at her father. "This is a fine weapon."

She swallowed a laugh. Bless her father's stony countenance. Ari trusted only she could see the confusion in his eyes. He couldn't work out why Seaghdh was complimenting him on the weight and balance of a competition-grade energy blade that belonged to her.

"That's . . ." Pietre began.

"Shut it," Ari commanded, not wanting Seaghdh tipped off to the fact that she had a competition ranking. If the man was any good at all, he'd figure it out the moment they crossed blades.

"I hope he skewers you," Pietre snarled.

"Pietre!" her father snapped.

The sound of a pistol being whipped from a holster drowned out anything else her father might have said. Ari saw the gun Seaghdh had taken from her pointed at Pietre's face. She raised an eyebrow at Seaghdh, silently urging him to pretend that neither of them noticed the stain of rage in her cheeks. He studied her as she sealed her jacket. What the Three Hells had she let him see in her to make him rise to her defense like this?

"Why don't I kill him for you?"

She glanced at Pietre and for a long, pleasurable moment contemplated agreeing. The thunderous expression on her father's face drained her.

"If you're in the trouble I think you are," she said, accepting the ratty but oh so comfortable hilt of her practice blade from Seaghdh's man, "you're going to need all the ammo in that pistol."

Seaghdh laughed and holstered the weapon. "You're a right thoughtful girl, Alexandria Rose Idylle. Ah. A-R-I. A ready-made nickname, courtesy of boot camp?"

"Congratulations." Damned pirate. Should have known he'd guess right.

"Clear the floor," Seaghdh commanded and gestured at her father's crew. "At the slightest sound from them, shoot her." He pointed at Jayleia.

CHAPTER

2

ARI caught in a breath, but didn't dare protest as the Shlovkur closed in beside the tech. She stared at Jayleia's suddenly pale face and tasted the first bitter edge of panic.

"Care to concede?" Seaghdh murmured at her shoulder.

Breathing too quickly, her heart beating too hard, she stumbled into the center of the cargo bay and took position on her end of the floor. Seaghdh sauntered into the grid, his sharp gaze taking in every thought plodding through her head and across her face.

"You know how to use that thing?" He nodded at the energy blade in her hand.

She swallowed outrage and awarded him a tight smile. "I am proficient."

He grinned. "Ever fight for your life?"

"No," she said, pleased her tone remained steady.

His smile deepened. "Then this isn't so different. We aren't fighting for your life, are we? We're fighting for theirs." He gestured at the knot of scientists.

Fear gripped her. She'd won matches. She had awards. She practiced religiously. Sure, she'd fought Chekydran with the might of an Armada Prowler at her disposal. But energy blade combat had always been a highly regulated sport, a dance with specific choreography designed to minimize injury. She'd never dueled for anything of more value than a bit of metal or a piece of paper to hang on her office wall. Swallowing hard, she eased into guard position.

Taking his time, he matched her stance. Ari did her best not to frown at the avid smiles on his men's faces or at the effortless way he sank into position and crossed his blade with hers.

Her mind raced. She had to find a way to keep everyone alive. No matter the cost.

Captain Cullin Seaghdh tapped her blade with his, bringing her attention back to her predicament and his damnably cocky grin.

"You're willing to trade your life for theirs?" he asked, his question pitched for her ears only, his smile gone and his gaze searching.

Troubled, she shook her head. "Are you intimating I have a choice?"

"Then fight." He lunged.

Ari scrambled back, her parries thrown off by the aggressive attack. He didn't press his advantage. That maddening grin flashed at her as he backed off. One step. Two.

Charity. She wanted to scream at him. She clamped her jaw shut and advanced the ground he'd offered.

"Out of practice?" He opened his defenses, daring her.

She accepted, ignoring the taunt. She had no intention of explaining that she'd had a hard time keeping up on weapons practice while a prisoner of war. Her attack wavered, but she pulled it together and forced him back a step to avoid her blade. He drew her in and then pushed her back, like a teacher hearing lessons. She ached to wipe that smile from his face.

"Point," he said, nodding at her chest.

She glanced down. The bastard had sliced clean through her jacket and the buttons of her shirt. A shiver ran through her. One millimeter more and she'd be bleeding, probably on the floor. A slice like that one took enough control and skill to scare her.

"Lesson one," he said. "Watch the man wielding the blade, but never lose sight of the business end."

Lessons? Or something more? From the shock of physical awareness twining through her blood, she suspected they were no longer discussing energy blades.

Snarling to cover the grudging admiration at Seaghdh's skill welling up within her, Ari charged him. He did not retreat. They locked, body to body, blade to blade. Feeling the leashed strength coiled in him, she knew instantly that she'd made a mistake, one that in any other circumstance would have been fatal. Scorched where their bodies strained against one another at chest and hip, she struggled to control the rush of yearning crashing her defenses. What was wrong with her?

She met his hooded gaze. Desire glittered in the golden depths of his eyes. Pleasure rocketed through her, almost painful in its intensity. She'd forgotten what it felt like to be appreciated as a woman and the want in his eyes, shadowed by surprise, took her breath away.

He smiled in pure masculine satisfaction.

Ari whispered a curse.

His gaze dropped to her mouth and the fire flared in his eyes. He whipped his off hand around, grabbed her by the hair, and fastened his mouth on hers. She tasted exotic spice and the faint trace of salt. Fire shot through every fiber to her core, urging her to melt into him. Before she could rouse the least bit of bracing rage, he released her and danced away. She wiped a sleeve across her mouth, as much to erase her mortifying lack of alacrity—she should have shoved her blade through his chest—as to obliterate the feel of his lips on hers.

His men guffawed.

"Lesson two," he said. "Never offer what you cannot afford to lose."

She'd lost everything that had mattered the day the Chekydran had captured her. She'd be damned before she'd let a too-handsome pirate destroy her self-respect. "One to zero," Ari countered, pressing her voice and her body under iron control before coming back to center.

Seaghdh's men stood relaxed, grinning, eyes dancing. The glimpses she caught of her father's crew showed green faces and averted eyes. Except for Pietre. He watched with spiteful vindication in his face. Her father wore a patently neutral expression, one she knew all too well. It masked a wealth of disapproval. Her heart froze. The damned pirate making her look like an imbecile must be having the time of his life. She glared at him.

Cullin Seaghdh returned to center to tap her blade with his. Ari met his gaze and paused. A grim light in his eyes belied his taunting smile. Was it possible he wasn't enjoying belittling her in front of his men and her family? Or was it possible she was getting to him? His gaze still centered on her mouth. Maybe she had another weapon in her arsenal after all.

Buoyed by the possibilities, she lunged.

He gave her the point. Her blade grazed the shoulder of his jacket and shirt as he turned aside. Practice jackets had notoriously weak shields at the seams. The blade had no trouble penetrating. She pulled up short as the fabric of his shirt split. More charity. She hadn't counted on it. Ari stumbled past him, struggling to keep the point of her weapon out of his flesh. It was a point as graceless as his had been elegant. He slapped the flat of his blade against her backside as she passed. She yelped at the sting and heard an instructor's voice say in her head, *Get mad, get dead.* The Art of the Blade had always taught, *control your anger or be controlled by it.*

They were wrong. Anger dumped a powerful cocktail of drugs into the human body. Eyesight sharpened. Hearing became more acute. Thoughts sped up. Heart rate increased delivering more oxygen to muscles, making them supple and fast. It was a dangerous, heady high; a bloody, razor-sharp, double-edged sword that a fighter learned to control or was disemboweled by.

Somewhere in the past fifteen years, she'd learned to dance that razor's edge. She craved it, thrived on it. And she'd had enough of playing games. It was time for Cullin Seaghdh to learn a few lessons of his own. At the tip of her blade.

"Lesson three . . ." he began.

Flush with ire, Ari launched a smooth, fluent attack that instantly wiped the smile from his face. Lesson three. Never, ever challenge someone to a fight until you ask how many first-place medals she has in the weapon. Seaghdh gave ground and kept giving. She drove him. She'd have been lying if she didn't say he made her work for it. He did, but savoring the play of muscle, the coordination, the flash of the blades, and the sweat beading on his upper lip, she relished every last millimeter. She felt the smile on her face. She'd taken his measure while he'd mistakenly thought he'd taken hers. He was good, very good. With lives at stake, Ari had to be better. Lucky for her. She was.

Her father's look hadn't changed one whit at the sudden reversal of fortunes, but Seaghdh's men stood tight-faced, fists clenched. Concentration lined Seaghdh's expression and a gleam of appreciation lit his eyes. Uneasiness flashed through her. How could he appreciate being beaten? Or was he still dueling with more than one weapon and willing to sacrifice victory in one for an advantage in the other? Blood and awareness rushed low. Ari faltered.

Seaghdh riposted, meaning to beat her blade out of his way and take his point. She made sure her weapon wasn't where he expected. Ari lunged, dropping to one knee, and swept her blade up. It hit and bent against the heart symbol on his jacket.

They froze. A flick of her wrist and the tip of her energy blade would slice through force field, muscle, and bone and embed itself in his heart for real. A click sounded at her ear.

"Back off," one of his men growled.

She eased the pressure on the blade and raised her eyes to Seaghdh's face as she rose. He stared at the hole in the heart on his jacket. His crewman plucked the weapon out of her hand. Anger drained from her, leaving behind a familiar, sticky residue. Even the drugs supplied by one's own body produced unpleasant side effects.

Cullin Seaghdh turned his gaze to her. At the glitter of intensity in his eyes, Ari backed up a step. He closed the distance in two strides. He had a blade. She was unarmed, but she refused to run. If he meant to kill her, she preferred to see it coming.

He clapped a hand to her shoulder and shook her once.

"You played me," he accused.

"Yes."

"Well done!" he rasped. "Few blade masters of your skill would have let me humble them before family and friends."

Surprise fluttered through her. She flushed at the unexpected praise and at the heat of his touch, cursing at the same time how badly she craved both.

"Well done," he repeated for her ears alone, squeezing her shoulder.

Ari studied his face, the thread of unease twining within her once more. The Art of the Blade was a game, one designed to make your opponent underestimate your skill. Could she ever know for certain that Cullin Seaghdh hadn't just played her?

Had that been what the delay in decon had been about? He'd been trying to manipulate her emotions? Didn't he know the Chekydran had beaten them out of her?

"Decontamination, Captain," she said. "And if you want off this moon without anyone noticing anything out of the ordinary, I need my father's crew free to stow their experiments and their gear."

Seaghdh backed away a few steps, lifted his blade before his face, and swept it away in salute.

The unexpected courtesy of one fighter acknowledging defeat by another warmed her, but the inkling of respect she saw in his gaze pierced through a tight place inside her. She held her breath at the sudden burn behind her eyes.

He lifted the hilt of the blade in his hand. "This is yours?"

She nodded.

"Blade rank?"

"Doesn't matter," she said, even though she suspected he'd already guessed she'd been highly placed military. Her competition ranking would only confirm his impression.

"Second in System," Raj, her father's medical officer, said.

Seaghdh's eyes widened. So did his cocky grin. "Ever fight the first-place holder?"

"No. Not likely to get that chance," Ari replied, stripping her sliced-up jacket and lobbing it into the recycler. Not now that she was in the process of being drummed out of the military. "Now. Captain. About getting off this muddy rock . . ."

"Aye. You want me in decon. That eager to have me out of my clothes, then?"

Her body whispered *yes*. Ari strangled the traitorous voice. "How can you imagine I'd notice?" she shot back. She stalked to the line of lockers outside decon and flung them open.

"Help yourself," she instructed, gesturing to the clothes and coveralls in the lockers. "Assure Jayleia that your men won't be shooting her today, would you? And order the crew cut loose so we can get this stuff stowed."

"Bossy, aren't you?" Seaghdh countered, smiling down at her. "I do like a woman who knows her mind."

"Turrel!" he barked. "Pull perimeter, assign guard duty, untie the crew, and get this gear cleared. Our girl, Ari, prefers to be our insurance policy. This lot tries something silly, shoot her, instead."

The Shlovkur took the energy blade from Seaghdh, scowling at his captain as he did so. "She's the only one with the command codes."

"She is, isn't she?" Seaghdh agreed.

She smiled so she wouldn't frown. He'd guaranteed that Pietre would try something stupid, regardless of the codes, just to see her shot. Seaghdh's beatific leer as the decon door closed in front of him told her he knew precisely what she was thinking.

"Lock these up." Turrel handed the energy blades to a man in bloodstained freighter coveralls. "Then free the prisoners. Don't care what Captain Seaghdh says. Any of them make a wrong move, shoot them. Then I'll shoot her." He pointed his gun at Ari.

She grinned. After a decade and a half in the military, she recognized bluster. These men did not want to shoot anyone. Orders? Or were they trying to appear to be something they weren't?

"I suppose me stowing my specimens is out of the question?" Ari asked.

"I can hit a moving target," he snapped. "I just won't waste the ammo it would take to put you down clean. Stop grinning at me like I ain't holding a gun to your face. Only the captain gets to do that."

Clearing her throat, she wiped the smile from her face and turned to her father. "Dad?"

Her father rubbed his wrists and shot a glare at her. "Damned shameful display of ego," he grumbled.

The censure jolted Ari. She pressed her lips tight to keep from swearing aloud. Ego? No. More like very potent seduction. Shaking off the remnants of sensual awareness, she curled her hands into fists. The man had manipulated her into believing that he identified her as an equal, if not quite a trusted ally, and he'd used her runaway hormones to do it.

She might not have a command, but she was still an Armada captain. She had a job to do. One that didn't afford her the luxury of feeling. If she didn't put her defenses in order, Seaghdh would destroy every person and principle she'd pledged to protect.

"That display is keeping you on your ship," she said in answer to her father. "You're untied and you're going to get to keep valuable specimens and experimental data. What more do you want from me? Or am I supposed to single-handedly murder every one of these armed men for your convenience?"

"That is enough, Alexandria," her father said.

She stared at him, hurt and anger a knot in the center of her chest, then she did what she'd always done. She swallowed the emotion, put on an impenetrable mask, and looked anywhere but at him.

"Would you be good enough to supervise the load, Dr. Idylle? I seem to be otherwise occupied as a hostage," she said.

"Alex." Her father sounded weary. "Don't 'Dr. Idylle' me. This is still my ship, despite your sabotaging my command codes. You're endangering a very important mission with your games."

"*I'm* endangering?" Ari echoed, waving a hand at the armed man beside her. "A group of pirates hijacking your ship plays absolutely no part? I'm flattered, Dad. Load the thrice-damned cargo. Or is this a diversionary tactic so Pietre can make a break for it and get me killed?"

Her father pressed his mouth tight. Pain lined his face. He spun on his heel and, oblivious to the armed guard shadowing him, stomped out of the cargo bay. He began issuing orders in a clipped, anger-tightened voice. "Captain Idylle!" he shouted back at her. "Your decon was compromised. Go again."

"Twelve Gods, Dad! Now that they have my name and my rank, would you like to give them my serial number, too?" Rubbing a hand across her suddenly aching forehead, she sighed.

Seaghdh emerged from decon wearing nothing more than that damned grin.

"Captain!" the Shlovkur beside her barked.

Reflexes jerked Ari to attention before she could remind her military conditioning that the man wasn't addressing her as captain.

"We got a problem," Turrel said. "She . . ."

"Aye," Seaghdh agreed, eyeing her. "I, too, am disappointed. This birthday suit has inspired lust in many a woman's heart. I had hoped for at least a swoon from you."

Cursing the heat rising in her face, she jerked her gaze away from that long, lean dancer's—or was that fencer's—body. She had a harder time reining her imagination away from what that body could do to hers. How long had it been . . . she strangled the rest of the question.

"Yes, yes. A fine specimen." Ari choked. "Stunning. Really. If you have anything I haven't seen before, I'll be certain to shoot it."

He laughed. The rich, melodic sound tempted her to smile.

Her lips actually twitched before she conquered the impulse. Maybe she wasted her stony façade on him. She got the distinct impression he knew how strong a lure she found the lines of muscle. It didn't help that while she stood iron-faced, she was also blushing like a little girl.

He yanked on a pair of pants, and glanced around the cargo bay, his face all business.

She'd let him distract her. Again. Ari swore. Her voice shook. She routed through decon a second time and dressed in a set of coveralls Jayleia and she had modified for desert conditions by slicing out the sleeves and lowering the neckline. Not what she wanted to wear in front of a band of pirates but all she had left in the cargo bay that fit.

Seaghdh eyed her. "I want off this world. How long is this load in going to take?"

Ari scanned the bay. "Left to the science team? A couple of hours. Give me two of your men. I'll have it done in an hour."

"Do it."

The way she saw it, she suddenly had a double crew complement. Mentally, she'd divided them into a command team, the guys with the guns, and a science team, her father and his people. Her? She was wedged firmly between this gamma-ray burst and that black hole. Regardless, whoever had driven Cullen Seaghdh and his crew to commandeer a helpless science ship was probably still out there looking for them. If the pirates were found on the *Sen Ekir*, she doubted she'd get to explain before they were blown out of the sky. Or out of the mud if they didn't haul jets off this rock. Whether her father liked it or not, she'd made it her job to get them home alive where she might or might not still have a command waiting for her.

Over increasingly angry protests from the science team, she got the gear and the experiments packed. With her father upbraiding her over her handling of his equipment, she ushered everyone aboard ship, closed the cargo bay door, and glanced at Seaghdh before initiating a seal.

"Is this your entire crew complement?" Ari asked. "Any salvage work or body recovery?"

For a second, agony stood out in the lines of his face. "We're done here."

She nodded, swallowing sympathy. He'd either buried his dead already, she assumed, or had been forced to leave them to a burning ship. If, in fact, he'd crash-landed as she suspected. She knew a thing or two about how it felt to bury the men and women under her command. It wasn't a pain that could be comforted. She sealed the outer doors. The air lock claxon sounded as the inner cargo doors began closing automatically. Silencing the alarm, she slapped open a com.

"Crew count and location?" she asked.

"Eight personnel in cargo," her father replied.

"Acknowledged." Using the smaller personnel door beside the cargo doors, she exited the air lock and sealed the door behind her. "Initiating lock."

"Permission granted," her father said, his tone sardonic.

She entered the command and sighed under the cover of air being pumped out from between the two hulls.

"Ms. Idylle," Seaghdh said.

"Captain, Captain," Turrel corrected.

Great. Seaghdh knew far too much about her while she knew far too little that she could use to regain control of the *Sen Ekir*.

Seaghdh exchanged a glance with Turrel. "The problem you mentioned?" he surmised.

Turrel nodded.

"Captain Idylle," Seaghdh said in an arch tone. "Your presence is required at the cockpit command console."

"This is my ship," her father said. "Don't imagine you're in charge here, Alexandria, regardless of command codes."

"March." Seaghdh closed a hand around her arm.

Electricity tingled through her body. She glanced at him when he looked at her. The widening smile on his face and the interest in his gaze told her he'd sensed her response to his touch. Ari bit back a curse and frowned as the pirate broke eye contact and propelled her up the corridor.

"I'm not in command of anything," she informed her father. Least of all herself.

CHAPTER

3

SEAGHDH ushered her to the pilot station, waving off the Shlov-kur following them. Turrel eyed her with dislike. Let him. These men were on the run. Until Ari got them off world, recovered control of the ship, and got them out of her hair, they endangered everyone.

"ETA for lift?" Seaghdh demanded.

She thumped open the intraship. "Dad? Status?"

"Secure in five."

"Prepare medical to receive the wounded," she answered.

"Why would I waste medical supplies . . ."

"Update radiation exposure boosters, and then cycle all personnel through decontamination," Ari ordered by way of reply.

"Alex," her father's voice sharpened. "Don't be rash!"

"This is a plague world, Dad." She cut him off as she keyed in the decode sequence for the command lockouts, aware that Seaghdh stood at her shoulder both watching and listening.

He tensed at the mention of plague.

"Captain Seaghdh and his crew were exposed the moment they

set down on this moon. They've been all over this ship. I'm comfortably certain I don't have much choice."

"Damn it, Alex." Her dad sounded frustrated and furious.

Seaghdh slapped off the connection and spun Ari's chair. Before she could blink, he straddled her, his hands pinning her upper arms. She recognized it as a tactical move designed to deny her the leverage for an attack, nothing more. Regardless, awareness thrilled through her. She leaned back and swallowed hard.

Then she remembered. He knew she reacted to him physically. Was this move calculated?

"Explain," he demanded, no give at all in the power-laced whip of the word. "Now."

Annoyed by the command and the compulsion, she fought his voice talent for a moment before the reply spilled forth. "There is a plague. We're immune. Dad chooses his crew based on previous exposure and proof of immunity."

"You're immune."

"Yes."

"But you bothered with decon."

"No world hosts just one pathogen," she replied. "We may be immune to one plague, but there's nothing to say there aren't other diseases out there waiting to kill us. We can't afford to take chances."

He stared at her, the tension running out of him. He released her arms and settled his hand on her shoulder, brushing his thumb along her exposed collarbone. Goosebumps rose on her skin.

She didn't think he realized what he was doing until he smoothed his hand down her arm. Her heart squeezed hard. Ari forced herself to stay very still. *It isn't real. He's manipulating me.*

"Your father expected you to leave us to die of a sickness that can't harm you," he said. "We wouldn't have known until too late. You could have had your ship back."

"Unless I finish the command decodes, Captain," she said, cutting off the assessing look he slanted her, "the only thing we have is a cramped, uncomfortable shelter sinking into the mud of this moon."

He tightened his hand on her arm, then rose and spun her back to her station. "Get us out of here. Take sensors," he ordered Turrel as he straightened.

Ari's fingers flew over the keys, but she still saw Turrel's face darken.

"Captain . . ."

"She's on our side for the moment, Kirthin," Seaghdh interrupted. "I need you on eyes."

"Aye."

"Awaken, sweet prince," she murmured to the control panel. The discordant rumble of the atmospheric engines vibrated under her feet. "Lift in two. Secure all personnel. As soon as we shed the g's, get your people to medical and then through decontamination."

"I need to see what's out there," Seaghdh countered.

"You're hijacking a science vessel, Seaghdh. We have not one single weapon and only one set of interstellar engines. If whoever's hunting you sees us lift, you won't have long to worry about that plague."

He muttered a word in a language she didn't recognize. Ari coaxed the engines into optimal harmonic. The vibration eased.

"Secure for liftoff," Seaghdh commanded, his voice echoing over ship-wide. "Sixty seconds." He switched off the com. "Can you single-hand this tin can, Captain?"

"Captain!" Kirthin Turrel protested.

"Stow it!" Seaghdh growled. "We're going back alive!"

Better and better. They needed her. She nudged the throttle and felt the ship strain against the pull of the mud underneath them. No point assuring them she wouldn't be alone on the bridge, since Seaghdh had already been through decontamination. Maybe she could still get the ship back without killing anyone. Divide and conquer. So much the better if they did the dividing for her.

"Lift in ten, nine, eight . . ."

"You could fly this thing blind . . ." Kirthin began. He didn't finish. Ari assumed some gesture from Seaghdh cut him off.

"He couldn't," she interjected, watching her panels. She'd booby-trapped more than command codes. "No one could."

"Just how deep does your distrust go?" Seaghdh said. "What the hell is between you and those scientists, anyway?"

She honestly could not answer. Some days, she couldn't even trust herself and had a set of randomly selected traps she had to defeat each morning to release her from her cabin. If she wasn't fit to pass those psych tests each day, she did not want to be let loose on her father's ship. She caught Kirthin Turrel staring at her. He shook his head.

"Not Ice Princess," he said. "She's the damned queen."

Ari thought she heard grudging approval in his tone. She couldn't help herself. She laughed until she had to wipe her eyes, and heard the bitter edge in the sound. She couldn't remember the last time that had happened.

She caught Seaghdh's examination and wondered at the hint of surprise in his face. Had he thought her incapable of laughter? She had.

"I appreciate the promotion," she said to Turrel. "Now let's get off this rock. Give your captain the gun and report to medical. Decontamination will sting like hell unless you get that cut sealed up first."

Seaghdh nodded at his crewman. He traded her pistol for Turrel's rifle. The Shlovkur quit the tiny bridge.

"He's wrong, you know," Seaghdh said from behind her the moment the door slid closed. "I felt the fire in that kiss I stole. Pietre has misjudged you. Your father has, too, hasn't he?"

She sucked in a shallow, damnably audible breath both at the observation and at the brush of Seaghdh's hand against the nape of her neck. Cursing her body's reaction, Ari snapped, "Strap down or I'll flatten you against a bulkhead."

His chuckle made it clear that he knew exactly how his touch affected her. Without a word he buckled into the nav seat beside her. She woke his panel and shunted data to his screens.

"I'll take us out of atmosphere on manual. We'll exit here," she said, struggling to tap the plotter as increasing g-forces pressed her into her seat. "I need a thirteen-second brush with Occaltus's sun."

"A radiation bath?" he surmised.

Nodding, she cast covert glances at the data readouts showing on her panel, the inputs and results of his calculations. The man handled ships for a living, no doubt about it. But what kind?

"Were you in a shuttle?" she asked.

"No."

"You put it down on the dark side, then."

"No. It put us down on the dark side," Seaghdh corrected. "Landing is too generous a word for our introduction to this moon."

No information about his ship, nothing to tell her what weapons he might have had or what sort of enemy or emergency had driven him to crash on Ioccal, Occaltus's eleventh moon. Still. If he'd had weapons systems on his ship, he didn't deem them worth salvaging.

She opened intraship. "Clear six thousand meters. All personnel cycle through decon and report to medical for radiation exposure boosters. Shift to star drive in ten minutes. Thirteen-second skip, two hours out."

Seaghdh glanced at her. "I'll take it while you report to medical."

"No need," she said. "Raj will bring the shots to us after he's been through decon."

"Raj?"

"Dad's medical officer and our local genius. The radiation sterilization was his baby. Saved us from having to fly into a star five years ago."

Seaghdh's brain stumbled and his fingers paused on his keys. Ari turned her silver eyes on him. He frowned and saw she wasn't just pushing his buttons.

She shrugged. "Can't fly an infected ship to an inhabited world."

"Ari?" Her medi-tech's voice sounded tinny coming over the intraship.

"Yes, Raj?"

"One dose of Ioccal IX, one full gamma dose, and one booster?"

"Affirmative. I don't have a final destination yet, but is there any medical reason to postpone sterilization?"

"Not unless our 'guests' are symptomatic."

Seaghdh cursed under his breath. How many more ways could a simple find and retrieve mission become such a group baxt'k?

Ari glanced at him. "How long were you on Ioccal before taking the ship?"

"Fewer than forty-eight hours."

Speculation lit her eyes and softened the haunted shadows of her face. She caught his perusal and bristled. "How'd you get past my sensor array?"

Grinning, Seaghdh tucked a caress of power into his voice and said, "Trade secret."

She crinkled her forehead and looked away, but not before he saw the telltale shiver run through her body and felt his own tighten in response. Gods, he should never have accepted this mission. From the moment he'd become aware of Alexandria Idylle climbing the Blade Ranks within TFC so many years ago, Seaghdh had harbored a secret crush. It hadn't mattered that they'd never met, much less crossed blades before today. He shook his head. She had no idea she had him at such a disadvantage.

The medi cleared his throat. "We're well within incubation limits. We'll dose them and toast them."

Derailed by the man's tone, Seaghdh stared at the com speaker. "He sounded gleeful."

Ari ducked her head but couldn't hide her smile. "Hasn't gotten to test his plague cure, yet."

"What?" Even better. Not only were he and his crew infected, they were captive test cases to a shipload of righteously pissed-off scientists.

The door opened. Without so much as a greeting, the medi, Raj, strode up and popped Ari full of medication. She rubbed her arm.

"Thanks," she said.

Seaghdh forestalled him when Raj turned to him. "My men . . ."

"We've been treated," Turrel said from the doorway. "No one's keeled over yet. Even if he poisons you, there're too many of us for your commando, there, to take." He gestured at Ari from his spot lounging against the doorframe.

"That's all right, then," Seaghdh said. He sat perfectly still while Raj administered both medications.

"Your man is quite right, of course," Raj said. "There is the minor matter of my oath, that and I value Ari too highly to endanger her. You'll test positive for Ioccal IX for a few days yet, but none of you should experience any symptoms."

"You are a miracle worker, Raj," she said.

"Always nice to have one's work appreciated," he replied. "Jayleia and I stowed your samples, Ari. Come see me when you're ready to get started. I have a few tricks up my sleeves."

Seaghdh frowned at the solicitude in the man's voice. It bordered on condescension. Or pity. His information indicated that Raj Faraheed knew Ari well enough that he should comprehend the mistake he was making with that tone.

Raj quit the bridge with a wave, calling, "Must return to mending a broken arm."

Turrel shadowed Raj down the companionway.

Ari turned back to the piloting console. Strapped in so close beside her, Seaghdh could hear her breath tighten. He shot her a covert glance. The lush, white curls of her hair were long enough to hide her eyes, but not the thin line she'd made of her lips.

Sympathy wrung through his gut, forcing him to turn his eyes front. He gathered she'd heard the same thing in Raj's voice that Seaghdh had.

He'd seen her file. She'd been held by the Chekydran for three months, been accused of spying, and then, unaccountably, released. Another three months in a TFC military hospital hadn't produced any evidence that she'd been turned or controlled by the aliens. Her people lauded the woefully thin woman as a hero while her commanders stripped her of everything but rank. Armada was hanging her out to dry.

From a tactical standpoint it made sense. She'd survived three months with the Chekydran, something that had never been done. Her commanders had to believe the enemy controlled her in some fashion—assuming she was still sane.

Rage and denial shoved hard against his insides, protesting the thought. Seaghdh let the instinct pass. He couldn't afford to let his personal interest in her interfere with duty. If he found that she couldn't be trusted, whether the Chekydran controlled her or not, he would kill her. Regardless of what it might cost him personally.

His cousin had warned him that the damage done to Ari extended far past the horrific physical damage he'd seen catalogued in the file he'd had his spies steal from her government. She'd been little more than skin holding together shattered bits of bone. He had only to look into her eyes to see the stain the Chekydran had left on her soul. It tore at some vital part of his gut. He'd felt sympathy for a subject before, not that he'd let it get in the way of doing his job. He'd never wanted to save anyone. Until now.

"Hey, Ari?" a woman's voice hailed via the intraship speaker.

"You stowed my stuff," Ari replied. "Thanks, Jayleia."

"You're welcome," Jayleia said. "You want any sequencing help, make them let me out of my cabin."

"Thank you," she said.

"I'm going to cut all of the communications lines and lock the bridge door," Seaghdh grumbled, noting the tension in her jaw. He eyed her. Intelligence data had indicated that Captain Idylle would respond if he used Raj Faraheed and Jayleia Durante as points of persuasion. Certainly, it had worked in cargo, but her inability to accept the concern in her friends' voices made him wonder. "I have your coordinates for the radiation bath, Captain Idylle."

When she signed off the com and glanced at him, he winked. The troubled light faded from her eyes and pressure he didn't realize he'd been carrying eased in his chest. *Irrational.* He had no reason to feel like he'd won a blade match simply because he'd made the woman smile.

"Running out of blue sky," she noted. "Bringing interstellar drives online. Watch the harmonic on the starboard atmospheric. We had trouble with it when we set down."

Seaghdh let out a breath that whistled between his teeth. "I've never seen an engine config like this. You do the custom work yourself?"

Ari shook her head as she brought the star drive online to warm up. "The atmospheric engines are unique to the *Sen Ekir.* Dad demanded close-in maneuverability, slow speed, even hovering capability and station keeping, but wasn't willing to sacrifice interstellar speed to get his samples back to his labs for it. He made enough noise, and consistently turns up such impressive results that Tagreth Federated Command had IntCom design and build this ship for him."

"TFC handed you a science ship built by Intelligence Command?" Seaghdh echoed, stunned. How had his team missed that detail? Who knew how many taps and wires IntCom had on board?

"Not me, Captain. They handed it to my father."

"You think the distinction matters?" he prodded.

She glanced at him, pushing a strand of hair out of those silver eyes, seemed to note his perusal, and looked away, flustered.

He watched her clasp her long, elegant fingers together. The precision and skill with which she'd handled the energy blade had him imagining her touch on his skin.

Cursing under his breath, he shifted, discomfited by the suddenly too tight fit of his trousers.

"What I think is immaterial," she said, dragging his attention back to the ship and the question of who actually controlled it. Calculation shifted behind her eyes and she scanned the cockpit as if seeing it for the first time. "The question is whether the distinction matters to IntCom."

Seaghdh nodded.

"And you're manipulating me," she said, her tone mild, "trying to make me question the integrity of my ship."

He froze at her summation. Where had she learned the espionage techniques she'd so accurately identified? Nothing in her files indicated that she'd received training from IntCom, and his spies inside the Armada hadn't been able to identify the manipulation when it had been turned upon them.

"Your attempt to undermine and switch my loyalties does not negate the validity of your observation. If IntCom has the *Sen Ekir* in its clutches, I can't trust the *Sen Ekir*," she finished and then slanted him a sly smile. "Point to you. One to zero."

She'd heard and accepted the invitation to play he'd issued with his last use of power on her. The two of them seemed uniquely susceptible to one another, though he prayed she didn't know about his weakness yet. Savoring the want dancing through his blood, he answered with a lazy grin. "What does my point get me?"

Every inch of her exposed, pale skin flushed in reaction to his innuendo.

The visible rush of her reaction drew him. He shifted, wanting closer to test the heat of her skin with his lips.

She opened her mouth, but a single, urgent beep from her panel snapped her attention away from him.

He mirrored her move, scanning his panel. Time to switch from atmospheric engines to interstellar drive.

"We're on," she said, her voice all business. Ari opened intraship and nudged the star drive output higher. "Secure for transition. Change over in five, four, three, two, one. Mark."

He focused on procedure and drew down power on the atmospherics.

"Atmospherics at eighty," Seaghdh said.

"Acknowledged. Cut by fives every ten seconds, mark."

"Seventy-five."

"Seventy."

The ship trembled.

"Damn it," she muttered. "Cut to fifty percent. That starboard atmospheric is coughing. I knew it wasn't tuning."

Alarm drove through him and he grimaced. She'd corrected their angle of ascent and balanced engine output without so much as blinking. He admired her gifted piloting, but cutting power like that was flat risky. Against his better judgment, he shook his head and did as she asked. "Atmospherics at fifty percent. Altitude gain decreasing."

"Aye. We've got a little arc. That'll give us enough momentum to make escape velocity," she said as she worked on starting the interstellar drive. "Come on, you radioactive hunk of tin. Wake up."

"You spoke so nicely to the atmospherics," he said.

She flushed. "You weren't supposed to hear that."

The rumble of the interstellar drive gave him a much-needed distraction from watching her every reaction to him. "There it goes."

The starboard engine gave up the ghost. They lurched sideways. The two of them swore in unison as she fought the controls.

"Restart?" he demanded.

"Negative. Cut the port engine. We've got enough thrust in the star drive to clear atmosphere."

She hadn't even glanced at the nav or engine equations.

"No margin for error," Seaghdh warned, scanning both panels and running a rapid set of mental calculations. She was flying the ship by feel. He shook his head and bit back a grin. Damn, she was good. Why the hell had her career been stalled piloting this piece of scientific space debris?

"I suspect we've got a fuel interrupt on the starboard side," she said. "It's not going to restart."

Seaghdh scowled and eased the port engine back. "A bleed?"

"Twelve Gods, I hope not," she replied, her attention pinned to velocity readouts, "or this will be one short trip."

He punched the intraship. "V'kyrri?"

"V'kyrri, here. Feels like a fuel supply issue in your starboard atmospheric, Captain. Arm's all healed up. Want me to go have a look?"

"You're a mind reader, V'k."

"Not on purpose, sir."

"Go practice your magic on the machinery, V'k. Turrel?"

"I heard," the Shlovkur answered. "We've secured the scientists in their quarters."

"Acknowledged. I need you and Sindrivik up here."

"Transition complete. Port atmospheric off-line in three, two, one, mark," Ari said.

"Affirmative," Seaghdh answered. "Laying in course for the radiation bath. Nicely done."

She reddened and made a show of studying the nav numbers as Turrel and Sindrivik hustled onto the bridge and strapped in at the life sciences and geo-scan stations.

She couldn't accept commendation. Was that a relic from her captivity? Or had her entire life been bereft of praise? He frowned.

"Clearing ionosphere in three, two, one, mark," she said, then scanned her panels while the rest of them stared at the view screen.

Seaghdh cursed. She was right. Instruments were far more sensitive than humanoid eyesight. He'd obviously been away from the pilot's chair too long if he'd fallen back into bad habit.

The sky darkened from indigo to black. Stars leaped into view. The arc of the gas giant warming the moon they'd left lit the lower quarter of the screen and silhouetted a sharp-edged moon where there shouldn't be a moon.

Ari swore as sensor alarms blared. She shut them off.

"Friends of yours?" she snapped.

Seaghdh uttered a single, vile oath and joined her in demanding identification from the computers.

She froze, her fingers still poised in mid-command.

He glanced at her. Recognition stood out in her wide-open eyes. Terror lined her lips in white. Seaghdh felt a tremor move her. It didn't look like she was breathing.

"Ari."

Nothing. Not even a muscle tic to indicate she'd heard. Turrel turned from glaring at the view screen, his face grim, and eyed her.

From her file, Seaghdh knew she suffered flashbacks, and when she did, she hurt people. Touching her could easily trigger an episode, but damn it, he couldn't abandon her to the nightmare of her memories. He didn't know that he could help; only that he had to try.

He unbuckled his restraints, turned, and put a hand on her shoulder. She jumped. He knew the moment she saw him and registered that he peered into her face, seeing the horrors of her memories in the hard shine in her eyes. Defenses slammed into place shuttering her expression and locking him out.

"Chekydran," she rasped. "You escaped a Chekydran cruiser?"

Seaghdh met her gaze, his own searching, seeking assurance that she could perform. "That's up to you, now, isn't it? Get us out of here."

She uttered a harsh laugh. "This boat has two speeds. Slow and slower. We will not outrun a Chekydran battle cruiser. They're on us."

Turrel spun back to his readouts. "Confirmed. They're changing course. Coming around to intercept."

Seaghdh saw her lips moving as she stared at the ship growing on the view panel. When he finally made out what she was saying, a chill of foreboding gripped him.

"Any other ship, any other ship."

He turned front. The iridescent yellow script that comprised the ship's name resolved. He recognized it. The Chekydran's premiere soldier-ship. It had found and fired on his ship as if laying in wait for his arrival. Fury swept him. He'd lost his ship and most of his crew in that fight. Because the Chekydran hadn't followed Seaghdh's disabled ship into Ioccal's atmosphere, he'd figured they'd assumed the ship had been destroyed. Yet here the Chekydran were again.

He shot a glance at her. Were they after him? Or her?

Beside him, Ari started to shake. Seaghdh shoved aside his questions and swore. He'd run afoul of the ship that had captured and imprisoned her. She'd have to face her demons because he'd led them to her. Twelve Gods.

"No," she whispered, clenching her fists.

"They're hailing," Turrel yelled.

She gulped in an audible breath and survival mode seemed to take her over. "Get off the bridge!" she ordered.

"We . . ." Turrel protested.

"If they know you're on this ship, they'll blow us out of the sky. And if they want you alive—" She stopped and swore, tossing Seaghdh an unsettled look.

Seaghdh forced his expression to neutral. *Another in a long line of tests, Captain Idylle. Prove to me that the Chekydran don't control you.*

"Damn it. I won't give anyone up to those bastards. I don't care what you've done," she said as if tasting something sour.

Triumph spread through him. Despite everything she'd been through and everything that had been taken from her, she still had a heart. The fact obviously bothered her, but she let herself be guided by it all the same. First, she'd refused to let the plague kill them. Now, she'd allied herself with him and with the men who'd hijacked her father's ship. She'd justified his decision to disobey the order to neutralize her, but more than that, Seaghdh realized, Alexandria Rose Idylle was salvageable, and it would be a crime to not try.

"Go!" Seaghdh snarled at his crew. He shoved Turrel and Sindrivik to the door and slammed it after them.

"If they see you or hear you, we're all dead!" she hissed at him.

He dashed across the tiny cockpit and hunkered down with his back against the view screen in the one position the bridge camera lens couldn't cover.

Ari gaped at him, questions and assessments running rapid-fire behind her eyes.

Seaghdh choked on the realization that he'd blown his cover.

CHAPTER
4

THE console beeped. Ari jerked her attention back to her controls. Second hail. Force a Chekydran cruiser to call a third time and it typically used a missile to get your attention. Hands shaking, Ari drew a deep breath and keyed open the com, hating that Cullin Seaghdh sat there watching her every move, her every fear. Even though she knew who hailed, even though she thought she'd prepared, she flinched when the Chekydran who'd tortured her for three months came on the screen. Thank the fates her father and his crew weren't here.

"Dear Captain Idylle," the creature droned, his translator rendering his words in a mechanical voice. "Do you have still your rank, I wonder. Hmmm. Why are you here, in this place, where I hunt spies, I wonder."

"Science expedition X9-57J3," Ari replied, trying not to let the buzz of his voice get on her nerves. She wanted to crawl out of her skin. "All notifications and communiqués regarding this ship's activities are on file."

"Hmm. With answer like this, you make no answer." He leaned

forward. The tentacle ridges on his hunched shoulders shifted. "Like old times." He uttered a series of sounds in his own language, something his translator didn't attempt to define.

She knew what they meant. "My plaything." An abyss of despair opened within her. In one turn of phrase, he'd assured her she was nothing more than a toy for his amusement and that he wasn't yet done with her. *Damn it, Ari, stick to the business of survival.*

It took a moment to find her voice. "We missed our scheduled lift by eight hours due to repairs on a faulty atmospheric."

"Bridge empty. Not standard, I wonder."

"You know damned well I can fly this thing solo," she replied. "We established that early on, didn't we? Course it's normal. Everyone else is running experiments."

"Poor youngest," the Chekydran crooned. "Too stupid. Fly alone."

"Baxt'k you, Hicci."

"Hmmm. Much suggested. Never try, I wonder. How lonely, desolate is my poor ship without you."

"Is that what this is about?" she demanded, her heart pounding so hard she thought it would burst through her ribs. She could barely breathe. "If you want me off this ship, say so."

The Chekydran captain eyed her. "You come? I say? Hmm."

"Swear on your swarm to let the *Sen Ekir* and its crew go, and I'll come across myself."

Seaghdh shifted, the movement barely audible. It took every effort of will not to glance at him.

"I say. You come. I hurt." He sucked in a breath that churred.

She fought back nausea and the shrill of terror growing in her head. Cold sweat trickled down the side of her face. "Swear."

"No shuttle."

"I'd walk out the airlock."

Silence.

"Extra-Vehicular Suit?"

Ari twisted her lips in a grim smile. "No. No space suit. I'd rather breathe vacuum than give you the satisfaction. Ever. Again."

"I blow you out of space."

"No, you won't," she retorted. "If you meant to do that, you would have already. You want something, Hicci. What is it?"

"Data."

She heard the pause before he answered. He hadn't killed her when he'd accused her of spying. She'd never understood why not. She'd been free for three months and she understood it even less now. He hesitated to bring weapons to bear on the *Sen Ekir*. Why? Because she was aboard? There could only be one reason for that. He needed her alive. It meant the Chekydran had done something to her that they believed would pay dividends at her expense. It made her blood run cold.

"You have free access to all of the scientific data gathered by this—"

He cut her off with a garbled hiss of sound. "Ship! Twelve men! You see!"

Ah. There. Seaghdh and his crew. Twelve? And only four survivors. Interesting. "No."

"You agree. I know lies."

She started to shake. Bastard. "Then you know I'm not lying. I have not seen any ship but this one."

"Transmit array data!"

"Complying," she said, sending the sensor array readings that Seaghdh and his men had circumvented, disabled, or altered.

Offscreen, another creature gabbled at the captain she'd called "Hicci." Human vocal apparatus couldn't approach the Chekydran language at all. "Hicci" was the best she'd been able to do with his name. That she could get even that much had always annoyed him.

"Hmm. Game you play, I wonder."

Wonder all you want, you sadistic freak. Wonder right up to the day I kill you. "Course change for Occaltus's star upcoming," Ari said aloud.

"Standard. Hmm. Afraid of bugs. Hmm." Hicci's tentacles shifted again. He smoothed them with one foreleg. "Destination."

"Not plotted yet, and Dad's not talking to me after I scrambled his command codes," she said. "TFC space, I assume. He's going to want his samples and his data in the university lab's containment system."

"Bugs." Hicci chortled.

Ari frowned. What so amused him about decontamination and containment procedures?

"Go."

"Course change initiated," she replied. "Can't say it's been nice, Hicci." Every nerve and muscle fiber screamed to cut the connection. She didn't. She'd learned the hard way. Let him get the last word.

"We play." He made the same set of sounds again and the screen went black. The cruiser turned and flashed out. The energy wash from their engines hit the *Sen Ekir*. The science ship rolled hard.

Ari stabbed a finger at the button to cut the com connection. Shaking so hard she could barely focus her eyes, she hit the wrong one. An alarm rasped across the bridge. She gulped for air. Her chest felt like it had been clamped in a vise. A hand appeared on her panel. The alarm died.

"Turrel!" Seaghdh shouted, rounding the panel and reaching for her. "Get the medi!"

"No," she gasped. The restraints across her torso released. She sank to the floor and squeezed her eyes shut. No one could see her like this. She didn't want to see herself like this. Still affected by what that bastard had done.

She flinched away from the touch on her arm, until she realized it was warm. Human and warm. Seaghdh lifted her and backed into the command chair. He drew her onto his lap, tucked her head beneath his chin, and wrapped his arms tight around her. The chill of terror loosened its grip.

"Come on back, Ari," he breathed into her ear. His voice coaxed her to respond. It promised safety. And damn it all, so did his arms. "I need your help. You're breathing too fast. Slow it down. That's it. Good."

She forced in a deep breath and held it. When she couldn't stop shaking, Ari cursed. It sounded weak. She loathed herself for indulging in a breakdown. She loathed him for witnessing it. She pushed herself upright.

"Feeling better?" Seaghdh inquired, brushing hair from her face.

The caress left a tingling trail on her skin and brought her forcefully back into her own body. She met his gaze and stilled, captured.

He didn't flinch when he looked her in the eye. She saw concern there, yes, but it was pure, with no trace of judgment or pity. She stared into the molten gold of his eyes and saw acceptance, wonder, and the veiled shimmer of attraction. It touched off a surge of longing she couldn't afford. She struggled out of his grasp. How could he be attracted to her when she couldn't stand what she'd become?

Seaghdh let go, his gaze watchful.

She stumbled, caught herself, and stood at parade rest, her hands clasped behind her back.

"My apologies, Captain," she said, damning the quaver in her voice and the shame heating her face. "I request that you belay the order for the medical officer. I would like to return to my post."

Seaghdh rubbed a hand down his chin as he studied her. "Return to your post," he finally said, "after I have a medical scan on you. No one needs to know what happened here. I'll tell them . . ."

The bridge door opened. Raj, Turrel, and the other two crewmen bolted onto the bridge. Turrel went instantly to the panel to watch the cruiser departing.

"Ari?" Raj asked. "What's going on?"

"Captain Idylle took a tumble when that damned Chekydran hit us with his wash," Seaghdh said.

Raj cast a probing glance at her. She sat down at piloting and scanned her screens.

"We're on course, Captain Idylle," Seaghdh said. "An hour out from the radiation bath. Let the doctor do his job. Then you can do yours. Until then, you're relieved. Sindrivik?"

The tall young man with red blond hair put a hand on the back of her chair. Ari nodded and stood. Every muscle in her body hurt and her head would feel much better if it would explode and get it over with.

"The ship is yours. Until the radiation bath is complete, any attempt to alter course will result in engine shutdown," she said.

Turrel swore. Seaghdh frowned, but his eyes danced.

"Captain?" Raj said. "If you will come with me?"

"Damn it. I'm fine."

"Now, now, Captain," Seaghdh countered, laughter in his tone. "That's his line."

Raj gestured Ari into his tiny medical bay and blinked at the empty hallway behind her. "No guard?"

"The Chekydran cruiser is still out there," she said. "They're a little more worried about it. So should we be."

"Good point. You know the drill," Raj replied and nodded at the exam table. "Hop up."

"I'd rather not."

Raj narrowed his eyes. "I would have happily let it go, until you said that. You know I'm a stubborn bastard when I think you're hiding something from me, Ari."

She got on his stupid table.

"You fell. Is that the story?"

"I fell."

"Want to explain the strap bruises, then, Captain?"

"No."

"Okay." Raj left her side. A click. "Dr. Idylle. Secure medical channel. I am not initiating quarantine. Repeat. I am not initiating quarantine."

Ari closed her eyes. She should have thought of this, of the secure com channel from medical that did not route through the bridge communications panel.

"Acknowledged, Dr. Faraheed. What is the nature of the emergency?" her father asked.

"I have Ari in medical. We are secure."

"What the hell is going on up there?" her dad demanded.

She opened her eyes, sat up, and faced the screen. Her father sat before his room screen, his hands clenched on the desk, his knuckles white and the muscles in his jaw rigid. Furious. She caught the pucker between his silver eyebrows. Correction. Furious and worried.

"We were intercepted by a Chekydran cruiser," she told him.

He blinked. "Those pirates are running from the—?" He broke off, looking discomfited.

"Apparently. Our sensor logs were empty, fortunately." She shrugged. "Seaghdh and his men crash-landed on Ioccal's dark side. They must have gotten a lock on the *Sen Ekir* during descent. Haven't had time to get anything more useful."

"Do you want to explain to me what you're doing?" her father asked.

"Right now, I'm obeying orders and getting checked out after . . ."

"You're siding with those damned pirates!" he accused.

She stared at him, openmouthed. "I am not siding with anyone!"

"Doesn't that strike you as a problem? Your duty is to this mission and to this ship! Another twenty-four hours and those men would be dying. We would have had this ship back in our control. We could have spaced the corpses and radiation bathed in Tagreth's sun."

Raj whistled. "Your cortisol levels are through the roof, Ari. You have got to be feeling like your head is going to explode."

She shot the doctor a dirty look. "My father is advocating murder and you sound surprised about my levels of stress hormone?"

"Grow up, Alexandria. Billions of lives depend on the data we've collected. We haven't had time—" Her father hesitated, and Ari could see him weighing the wisdom of something.

She shook off Raj's hold and slid to her feet. "What?"

Her father sighed and looked at her. The lines around his pale blue eyes deepened. "We sequenced a unique set of markers in Ioccal IX. The plague was seeded."

"Chekydran," Ari concluded, beating him to the punch. She crossed her arms. "When are you going to stop treating me like a brain-addled invalid? Yes, I was captured by them. Yes, I was held for three interminable months. Yes, I was tortured. Your silence about it isn't going to make it go away. I am not going to melt at the mention of them." No. She'd melted at being forced to face her tormentor and had been sent to medical because of it.

She caught a glimpse of her father's reddening face. He looked like a man struggling for something, anything, to say. A hint of anguish slipped into his expression. Ari froze. What the hell was going on?

"Stop it and drink," Raj said, handing her a cup. "You've been through something none of us can understand, Ari. We're trying to be considerate."

They couldn't understand what she'd been through. No one could. Not even she. Whose problem was that?

She swallowed the medication. Instantly, the throbbing in her head eased. She sighed. "Thanks, Raj. My head was going to blow. Am I fit to return to duty?"

"Nothing wrong a month's leave on Betalla wouldn't cure," Raj replied.

"Damn it, Alexandria. Tagreth Federated Command and your commanders at Armada are watching every move you make," her father said. "Don't screw this up, too."

Was it footsteps she heard? Or some sixth sense that alerted her? Ari leaped to cut the connection, leaving her to wonder what her father thought she'd already screwed up. The bay door opened. Turrel stood looking between her and Raj. She handed the cup back to the doctor.

"Thanks again."

"Time the bath very carefully, Ari," Raj answered, as if the radiation exposure had been the topic of conversation all along. "Go for longer, not shorter. We picked up indications of a new strain."

"Chekydran nanotech has never mutated on its own before," she protested. "It would need reengineering."

"I know."

"Could it compromise our immunity?"

Raj's grim expression spoke volumes. "Finding out is right at the top of our agenda."

Turrel pointed at her. "Bridge. I'll be snugging the doc up in his cabin, but don't try anything. I'll be at your back."

She wasted no time. She had a radiation bath to handle. From what Raj had said, too much rode on getting the ship sterile. It had also occurred to her that Seaghdh might have insisted on her jaunt to medical so he could alter the ship's codes and lock her out. It would take time, but it's what she'd have done in his place.

". . . Just a change of venue, gentlemen," Seaghdh was saying as the door opened. "Objectives . . . Captain Idylle."

He glanced at the screen on the command console. The expectant look on his face died when it became apparent Raj hadn't sent a medical report to the command chair. Maybe she wasn't the only military op on board.

"I've been judged fit for duty," she said. "Raj's assessment of my health ended in a prescription for a month on Betalla."

Seaghdh's eyebrows climbed and he grinned. "Betalla? Boy's got good taste."

"Betalla, where pleasure is an art," Sindrivik said, his voice wistful. His gray eyes dancing with mirth. Or nerves? "From the conversation in the cargo bay, it sounds like you could learn a few things . . ."

"Mr. Sindrivik!" Ari cut him off, pleased by the iron ring of command in her tone. At least she hadn't lost that. Apparently, during her incarceration and recovery, junior crewmen still hadn't learned to trade successful jests with their officers. "We are currently on a collision course with a star. I invite you to contemplate whether you prefer being burned to a crisp or crushed by gravity. Both are possibilities unless I unlock the engine. You are relieved."

The young man stared at her, his expression remote and chilly.

"You heard the captain," Seaghdh said, his tone silky and dangerous. "Navigation. And Mr. Sindrivik, mind your manners."

"Aye." Sindrivik sounded grudging, but he shifted seats.

She strapped into piloting, aware from the quiver running through the ship that the gravity of Occaltus's sun had them in its grip. They'd begun final approach. She checked her screens, unlocked the engines, and nudged the nose of the ship higher. "I need a line to Raj."

"I haven't started cutting cords, yet," Seaghdh replied.

"Terrific. You'll want to strap in. Solar storms in this system have one hell of a reach."

"Sage advice." He punched a button. "Secure all personnel. Doctor, your services are required on com."

"Faraheed, here."

"Initiating entry, Raj," Ari said. "Shunting external readings to your location. I'm not happy with those particle levels. What do you think?"

"Particle density is too low. Take us deeper."

"Acknowledged."

The *Sen Ekir* bucked. Sindrivik swore and worked his panels feverishly. "You can't do this. Your atmospherics aren't even online. No way we'll get out of the gravity well. Give me the ship," he said. "Give me the ship!"

"I did not come up here to die, Mr. Sindrivik," she replied.

"No! Just to kill us."

CHAPTER

5

ARI didn't bother answering. She saw what she wanted, an enormous storm system rearing up out of the solar furnace. The *Sen Ekir* shuddered, metal creaking. Then she glanced at the data Sindrivik was working on his panel, swiftly and adroitly patching relays around her station to lock her out of piloting. Swearing, she shut him down.

"What the . . . Captain!" he yelped. "I'm locked out!"

"Captain Seaghdh! Relieve your man. I need your steady hand at navigation," Ari commanded.

Seaghdh heaved his young crewman out of the nav chair and shoved him down at geo-scan, the station Jayleia usually used to survey and map research sites. He growled something in the man's ear. Busy with trying to keep the ship generally upright and fighting the high-level solar wind with all her strength, she couldn't hear a word. Seaghdh dropped into the nav seat, pulling the restraint straps over his chest.

"Slingshot?" he asked, his expression tight with concentration.

She unlocked his station. "That's the plan. I want to ride the rim of the cyclonic winds. Find them for me. Hull stress data, here. Shield loss calculations are critical."

He nodded. "Heat gain and hull friction. I've got it. You've done this before?"

The ship jounced, rattling her teeth. "In a Prowler."

"A *Prowler*?"

"Particle levels rising on the hull," Raj said. "Levels are adequate. Permission to cut radiation shields granted. Repeat, granted. Give me a count on your mark, Ari."

"Negative, negative," Seaghdh replied when solar wind shear grabbed the ship and flung it off course. The engine whined in protest. "Wait until we're riding the beast."

"Agreed," Ari said.

Seaghdh teased the nav numbers into order, shunting them to her panel before she could ask for them. Damn, he was good. When she got her command back, she'd recruit him.

"There's your course, Captain," he said. "Laid and locked."

"Acknowledged," Ari said. "Mr. Turrel, stand by to drop radiation shielding on my mark. Once it's down, give me a by-second count if you please."

"Standing by."

"Give me the stabilizers," Seaghdh said. "I'll keep us upright."

She did. "Going in."

"Particle level increasing, Ari!" Raj warned.

"I see it. Gods I hate not being able to steer by the engines."

"Let me bring your atmospherics online," one of the men interjected. "Just enough to give you some steerage!"

Ari glanced at him. Copper skin, bloody coveralls. He'd been the one with the broken arm. She didn't yet know his name. "I can't afford the hull stress."

The lights died. Out of the corner of her eye, she saw Sindrivik shift to a systems panel and begin working. The lights flickered back on.

"Yes, you can!" the other man hollered back over the racket of the engine and the creak of hull plates. "Reduce your star drive output when you drop into the groove."

Without her okay, Seaghdh began reworking his calculations with the new parameters. Ari scowled.

These men had hijacked the ship and imprisoned her family and friends. She didn't trust them. She couldn't. But this wasn't about trust. It was about survival. Theirs as well as hers.

"Do it," she said, reconfiguring her piloting plan.

Through the noise of protesting metal, and the howl of stressed engine feeds, she thought she heard Seaghdh mutter, "Good girl."

New formulas fed into her panel from Seaghdh's station and it struck her how much trust and familiarity—almost intimacy—existed between a good pilot and navigator team.

Seaghdh helped her wrestle the ungainly boat into the course he'd plotted. For a moment, they spun helplessly in the grip of the solar winds.

"Atmospherics at thirty! Give the port side a blow!" the man in bloody coveralls yelled.

Ari fired the port engine. Their spin slowed. Wobbling, the ship strained, then abruptly leaped forward, riding the solar wind current. She cut the thruster.

"Raj? Levels?"

"Acceptable, but go now!"

"Acknowledged. Mr. Turrel?"

"Still standing by," the big man rumbled.

"Cut power to radiation shielding on my mark. Three, two, one, mark!"

"Radiation shielding off-line," he replied and began counting off the seconds.

The men listened intently, counting with him. Seaghdh shot her a glance when Turrel reached twelve, then thirteen and she didn't order the shields back up.

"That's it!" Raj yelled. "Saturation!"

"Get those shields up!" Ari shouted.

"Shields online!" Turrel replied. "Power fluctuating . . . Shields optimal."

"We're clean," Ari said. "Nice work. Let's get the hell out of here."

They picked up another burst of speed. She nudged all three engines. For several seconds nothing happened. Then, engines whining and metal straining, the *Sen Ekir*'s nose lifted and they broke free. The devilish winds hadn't finished with them, though, and they bounced, skipping like a stone once, twice, before the star relinquished its grasp.

Ari banked down the atmospherics, locked in a course that would take them out of system, switched the view screen to watch Occaltus's sun diminish in their wake, and then glanced at the man sitting at engineering.

"I take it you're V'kyrri?"

Pale, sea green eyes looked back at her. His light brown hair contrasted with copper-colored skin. He nodded.

"Thank you," she said. Sure, he'd talked her through using the atmospherics so that she didn't get them all killed. Survival. She could respect that, but a good captain knew to recognize a valuable contribution.

The man nodded again. "Never seen atmospherics quite like the ones you have strapped to this tub, but I have seen fuel feed clogs like I cleared from your starboard intake all the damned time. The valve is all but shot. You're riding tolerance right now. Next venture into atmosphere may cause a fuel bleed. Your engineer needs a good swift kick."

"So I've long thought," Ari replied, then sighed. "He doesn't keep spares. We'll have to risk putting down at the supply depot on Kebgra."

"Captain Idylle."

V'kyrri glanced at the geo station. His expression tightened. Ari followed his gaze. The kid. Sindrivik.

"What can I do for you, Mr. Sindrivik?"

The young man stood at attention, his gaze focused above her head. Damn it. They were military. Recently enough to still be habituated to chain of command and protocol.

"I apologize for my comments earlier. They were inappropriate," he said, his tone neutral.

Had Seaghdh threatened him into the apology? The man's expression again turned to ice, until his gray eyes were the only color in his face. Ari detected the flicker of anger buried beneath the mask and admired the young man's control.

"I regret trying to take the ship from you," he went on. He hesitated and Ari could see the discomfort and the sincerity at last. "I endangered the ship and the crew."

"I appreciate the apology, Mr. Sindrivik," she said, glancing at her panel and tweaking a specific light filter on the view screen. "But jettison the regret over trying to take the ship. In any other circumstance, your instinct to get me off the controls would have been right on. It's a damned risky maneuver in the best of ships."

From the tightening of the muscles around his eyes, she gathered he would have preferred she'd yelled at him. Ari glanced at Seaghdh's patently neutral expression. What the hell was she doing treating four pirates like crew members?

It didn't matter. She was still the captain with the most practical experience with the *Sen Ekir*. Whether they liked her command methodology or not, they'd hijacked her ship and were letting her fly it. They'd all but volunteered as her crew, at least until they shot her or shoved her out an air lock.

Scanning the drained, tight expressions of the men around her, she nodded at the view screen. "Watch this." Ari tweaked a filter setting on the view-screen input sensors.

The brilliant, raging inferno of Occaltus's star dimmed. Luminous, intense color flooded the field behind the star.

Sindrivik took a step toward the screen, his expression scrunched in concentration. V'kyrri said something in a language Ari didn't recognize, though the wondering tone of his voice was clear. Turrel grunted.

"What is it?" Seaghdh asked as if awestruck.

Ari realized she'd leaned over her panel, her elbows propping her up as she delighted in the play of ancient light and color. She glanced at Seaghdh, grinning. Pleasure gleamed in his eyes. He wasn't looking at the view screen. Something sparked in the short distance between them, and Ari found it hard to draw a full breath.

"Our reward for a job well done," she said.

He answered her smile, his eyes on her mouth.

Ari forced herself to look away. She cleared her throat, but still it took a moment before she could answer his question.

"It's a supernova remnant."

"Several thousand light-years away?" Sindrivik asked.

"Around twenty. That cooling debris cloud is all that's left of the massive star that blew," she said. She worked a few more filters. "If I mess with the resolution a bit, you get . . ."

"Stellar nursery!" V'kyrri said, his tone enchanted as pinpricks of white light appeared in the darker gas clouds.

"Stunning," Seaghdh murmured next to her. At the relaxed enjoyment in his voice something warm and comforting blossomed within her.

"Is this important?" Turrel demanded.

"Not from a tactical standpoint," she said, studying his impatient expression, "but from a morale standpoint, it is. You've had a rough few days, I gather. Consider this a reminder that there are sights and experiences out here that are worth dying for."

The impatience crumbled for a moment, exposing the exhaustion and something much grimmer riding his tight features. He looked like a man who wished he'd died. Ari blinked and clenched her teeth. It had only taken a few days of Chekydran captivity for her to know the feeling. She couldn't do a thing for him there, but the exhaustion . . . "Mr. Turrel, when was the last time you slept?"

"Wh . . . I . . ." he fumbled, startled into meeting her eye. He looked so nonplussed she had to struggle not to smile.

"You're off duty," she said. "All of you."

Seaghdh chuckled but didn't sound the least amused. "Nice try. Turrel, six hours. V'k, twelve. Sindrivik, eight hours."

"Aye," three voices replied.

"We take turns manning the galley," Ari said. "You'll have to fix and clean up your own. Watch supplies. The ship's not stocked for a crew of nine. The commissary unit here in the cockpit only dispenses soup, water, and tea."

"Acknowledged," Seaghdh said before glancing at his crew. "We're off when you report for duty, Turrel."

"There are six cabins," she said. "Shift Jayleia in with Raj. They're cousins. They won't like it, but they can share. Then, if one of you takes my cabin . . ."

"Belay that," Seaghdh commanded, his tone sharp. "Don't even open that door."

Turrel scoffed. "After seeing her lockouts? Hell, no, I ain't going in that room."

V'kyrri and Sindrivik laughed. They tromped off the bridge as Ari watched with growing trepidation. She did not want to be left alone with Cullin Seaghdh. Or did she? Maybe now she could get some questions answered.

She glanced at him.

He'd studied her, speculation in his eye. "The reminder," he said, pointing at the infant stars on the view screen. "For us? Or for you?"

Ari found she had no answer. How did he manage to see so much she tried so hard to keep hidden? Nonplussed, she swiveled back to her station, scanned her panels, and then let her hands drop to her lap. She didn't even know where he was taking her.

"Destination?"

"Plotted and laid in," Seaghdh said, rising.

She looked at the coordinates as he accessed the tiny commissary unit. The savory smell of vegetable soup made her mouth water, but she shook her head.

"I strongly recommend a more scenic route, one that at least looks like it's headed for TFC space," she said.

He returned, two cups in hand. Settling into the nav chair, he put one in the holder beside his panel, then leaned across her to fit the other cup next to her.

Ari held her breath at the shock that went through her at the proximity. He hadn't even touched her. She felt his gaze prying into her head as he straightened and glanced at the course he'd given her.

"You think the Chekydran cruiser's still out there?"

"I guarantee it. I have some acquaintance with that particular captain," Ari replied, ironing her voice flat.

He picked up his cup, sipped, leaned back in his chair, and stared at the newborn stars in their gas-cloud crèche for several seconds. "Tell me about this acquaintance."

Her heart trembled in her chest and her hands knotted in her lap. She had to remind herself to breathe. "It's none of your business. The only thing I'm willing to say is this: don't provoke him. I said I wouldn't turn you over to them. I mean it. We do the expected. That means pointing the nose toward Tagreth Federated. They'll follow us to the border, but they won't cross in and face the Armada. Once we're out of their sensor range, we can route to Silver City."

The impression rose in her that he was watching her too closely as he put his cup back in the holder, gauging everything about her, measuring, assessing. She felt like one of her own specimens. Time to turn those tables, to start thinking. The coordinates he'd laid in would take them to a crowded, racy trade station in the border zone between TFC space and the independent, brutal commercial sector governed by the United Mining and Ore Processing Guild. It was an area she knew well. Prowler crews spent plenty of time chasing down drunken miners who'd deviated from their flight plans and strayed into TFC space. Or so they'd claim.

Cullin Seaghdh crossed his arms. "You surprise me, Captain Idylle."

Ari glanced at him. His prying stare, along with that frown, probably wrung confessions from stone. At least he hadn't used his voice talent on her. Yet.

"Why haven't you asked who we are? Or what we want?"

She locked down the navigational computer and then the interstellar drive at eighty percent. She stretched and sighed. "Because I
already know. You're Claugh nib Dovvyth military." It was a guess,
but a good one, she thought. TFC wasn't officially at war with the
Claugh nib Dovvyth, a tightly allied group of systems next to TFC,
but the narrow band of Mining Guild space seemed to be all that
kept the two governments from one another's throats. Rumor had it
that both militaries maintained active spying programs upon one
another.

"Interesting theory."

Ari nodded. The tension in his voice tipped her off. She'd put the
pieces together correctly and he didn't like that one bit.

"What makes you think I'm Claugh military?"

"Trade secret," she said, meeting his gaze, and deeply regretting
that she had no voice power of her own to turn upon him, save that
she had no notion what she'd compel him to do. Scratch that. She did
know. The muscles low in her abdomen clenched. Very bad idea.

He'd turned to face her, elbows on his knees, and chuckled. He
leaned so close, she could feel the warmth of his body caressing her
like a touch.

Reaction tingled through her blood. She pressed back in her seat.
It didn't help.

"And what am I after?" he prodded.

She forced herself to shrug. "You already told me I was your
objective."

"Did I?"

"When I called the ship, I'd assumed you wanted the command
codes. You declined in favor of capturing me. Getting shot down by
a Chekydran cruiser altered your priorities, but I assume your original mission parameter did not require my death."

"My," he drawled, that damnably cocky smile on his face. "If
I didn't already think so highly of you, I'd accuse you of doing it
for me."

Ari awarded him a withering glare.

He only chuckled again.

"You could have easily lifted without me," she snapped.

"You forget your creative use of lockouts."

"Cravuul dung. From what I've seen of your ability to handle the nav systems, I think we both know you could have bridged your way around my lockouts. You didn't. You weren't, in fact, even attempting those things. Not the actions of a man running for his and his crews' lives. Therefore, you have orders."

"You're a beautiful woman, Alexandria Rose Idylle," he said, running fingertips across her right cheekbone. Heat trailed in the wake of that touch, jolting her upright. "Beautiful and bright," he went on, his gaze too warm for her comfort. "Why would someone hire me to kill or capture you?"

Beautiful? She was too thin, too weak, still too broken from the past six months, yet Seaghdh's appraisal broke open a pit of hunger in her heart. She wanted to be beautiful in his eyes.

She gasped and slammed the door on feeling anything at all. The man was a master manipulator. She could admit that to herself. He'd subtly maneuvered her, levering open her shields with his charm, and then he'd brought the conversation back around to the Chekydran. Fine. She still had a few tricks up her sleeve.

"You want the United Mining and Ore Processing Guild's Silver City Station?" she said. "I'll get you there in one piece. Beyond that, I am none of your business."

"I'm making you my business."

"Why?"

"Why?" he echoed. "Ari, I've got your ship, yet you refuse to let an illness we've already contracted murder us. You refuse to turn us over to the Chekydran. How could you imagine I wouldn't be intrigued?"

Intrigued? Why did that word and his honestly perplexed tone cascade adrenaline into her system?

"You can run from me all you like," Seaghdh said, straightening, "but I was here for that conversation with the Chekydran. You can't pretend nothing happened, that you didn't volunteer to walk out an air lock rather than be a prisoner again."

She clenched her fists and struggled to draw a full breath around the pounding of her heart. "I'm already a prisoner again, Seaghdh. You've seen to that."

He flinched in the process of reaching for her, his expression troubled. "Ari . . ."

"You have no right to questions!" she yelled, bolting to her feet and across the cockpit. "No right to pry! No right to pretend you give a damn about me or what happens to me! You hijacked my ship!" Right after the Chekydran had hijacked her life.

He stood slowly, watching her every move, sympathy and disquiet in his handsome face. "Talk to me."

Not quite the same phrase the Chekydran captain had used during interrogation, but close enough. She felt her lip curl as defenses smashed into place. She stared at the man, saw the concern, the hope in his face, but she could not respond. She told herself that she'd had enough of being emotionally batted back and forth. Between her father, Seaghdh, and the Chekydran captain, she felt like a puck in a low-gravity Hazkyt game. The only things missing were the body slams and the blood.

"Talk to me," he'd said.

She wished she could laugh.

"No."

Ironic. She'd accused her father of trying to sidestep the past six months of her life. Now Cullin Seaghdh wanted to cut into it and into her. Hell of a time to find out her dad's instinct to keep silent had been right.

"I was a Chekydran prisoner. You don't need to know anything else. If I discuss my experience," she said, shifting her shoulders to break up the tension there, "it will be with my family, not with you."

"Why not?" he prodded, his gaze assessing.

"An operative from a rival military sent to kidnap me?" Ari snapped, cutting off his intake of breath. She strode back to piloting.

"This isn't over, Ari."

She dropped into her chair and glared at him. "I was debriefed, Captain. If you want an account of my imprisonment, hack into TFC's military data stores and steal the file. Assuming you haven't already."

CHAPTER

6

SEAGHDH watched her pretend to ignore him as she reconfigured the view-screen sensors to show the star field in front of them. Then she ran a systems check. To his eye, it came back clean.

"There," she said, pointing to the readout. "That's our Chekydran shadow. Unless we deviate from standard procedure, they should follow us to the border and break off. They aren't above attacking the occasional, one-off target, but they tolerate us because we give them access to our science data. They won't cross the border and risk running into the fleet. You know TFC military, always spoiling for a fight."

"I'm familiar with the behavior. You've learned to detect camouflaged Chekydran ships?" he marveled.

"Yes."

"They have no idea?"

"We'd be dead if they did."

Seaghdh leaned over her to peer at the data from a forward sensor that registered a miniscule spike in an ion particle and shook his head. "How in the Three Hells did you pick that reading out of the background radiation?"

He noted the tremor in her hand as she appended the data to the logs and had to resist the urge to touch her again.

"This is a science ship," she said. "It's our job to notice patterns and to put two and two together."

Something his team had failed to do, it seemed. How had they missed what he'd begun to suspect was the strategic importance of the *Sen Ekir* and its crew? He grunted and retreated to the command chair behind her. If he didn't get some distance, he'd completely lose his mind and have her in his arms again. "You make it sound so easy. You do know that ship is their best spy hunter?"

She raised an eyebrow at him. "I did. How do you?"

He stifled a grin. "Putting two and two together is your job, understanding who wants me dead is mine."

"Speaking of putting two and two together." She swung around to face him, speculation in the set of her features. "Systems are green and we're in the lane for TFC space. You'll want to brief my father and his crew. Scientists without information will do anything to get it. Give them information and they'll spend all their time trying to dissect it."

He studied her. "What do you suggest I tell them?"

"The truth."

"And that would be?" he prompted, frowning.

"You'll release the *Sen Ekir* and its crew once we reach Silver City."

Seaghdh sat back in his chair and considered the notion. He'd been ordered to retrieve Ari, not her family and friends or their IntCom-built ship. He had no reason to hold them, unless he could use them to pry apart her defenses. Though to be fair, he suspected her walls weren't as well constructed as she wanted to believe. "What makes you think . . ."

"You have no use for the *Sen Ekir* or a bunch of scientists."

"Don't I?"

Eyeing him, she lifted one shoulder. "Your government doesn't take political prisoners, Captain."

"What about you?"

"I do wonder how my kidnapping will be classified if I can't be called a political prisoner. I am not technically a part of this crew. Telling them you'll release them won't be a lie."

"You suggest I omit the fact that you won't be with them."

"It is a level of detail that will ensure my father works against you at every turn."

He grinned. "I am pleased I've succeeded in charming you into joining us willingly, Captain Idylle."

"I have few illusions, Seaghdh. I'm aware you found me before someone hired to kill me did."

"No doubt about it," he said. "The old charm is potent as ever." He savored the surprised smile that softened her features.

"Tell me you intend to release the *Sen Ekir* and its crew unharmed once we reach Silver City and I'll cooperate," she shot.

"At least until your father and his crew are safely away?"

"I see you harbor few illusions of your own," she said. "Good."

He suppressed a chuckle, certain from the gleam in her eye that she enjoyed the verbal parry and riposte as much as he. It spurred him to tuck a tendril of come-hither power into his words. "You'll play the game my way, Captain. I assure you."

Her eyes widened and turned smoky.

He relished the rush of desire that twisted in his gut. Gods. He rubbed a hand down his face to keep from reaching out to her. Did she know what she did to him? Had she read some hint of her power over his senses? Leaning back in the command chair, he marshaled enough will to meet her gaze. He still had a job to do.

"What's the likelihood that the scientists will cooperate?"

She shook her head. "You had a graphic demonstration of the likelihood when my father preferred to let you die."

He mulled her statement as she watched him. Seaghdh wondered if she could see his plans shifting with each new tidbit of information she fed him.

Speculation moved behind her pale eyes. "Do you intend to tell me what is so important that your people are willing to risk war for my capture?"

He flinched. Straight for the jugular, despite her offhand tone. She wanted to trade. Information for information. Any other time, he'd take her up on the invitation. He'd give as little as he could and would enjoy eliciting as much as possible from her.

Anticipation sizzled through him, settling low in his belly. Cursing the tightening in his groin, he shifted and pushed the feeling away. They didn't have time. Too many lives hinged on her part in whatever plan the Chekydran were executing. He had to stick to business, the business of extracting information, no matter the cost.

Hesitating, he realized she still watched him, her gaze probing. She'd shuttered her expression, and he couldn't read her. If he pressed her now, she could fracture, and he'd have to resort to interrogation. Or she wouldn't. She'd already surprised him with her strength, her intellect, and her dry wit. Why not give her the chance to do it again?

Aware he was pushing her past her comfort zone, he pinned her with a pointed stare. "I need your trust, Captain."

She gaped at him. "Given the day I've had? Of course you do. No problem. Anything else while you're daydreaming?"

He choked back disappointment. Neither of his scenarios had been correct. She hadn't shattered or risen to meet his challenge. Instead, she'd retreated behind her barricades. He couldn't let her stay there. Smoothing the frown from his face, he pressed, "Is the bridge secure?"

The troubled light in her eyes and crease in her forehead suggested she'd seen more in him than he'd wanted. She rose, crossed to communications, and spent a moment entering commands before locking down the station.

"The bridge is as secure as I can make it," she said. "Audio logging disabled. We're on video only."

He caught the unsettled look on her face as she returned to piloting.

"Thank you, Ari." He gave her no opportunity to respond. If he gave her time, she'd undoubtedly work out just how carefully he'd guided her into yet another risk. "The Claugh are willing to chance war because war is certain if we don't have your help."

She sat, fumbling for her chair, looking stunned. "You're IntCom."

"Murbaasch Tu, the Claugh equivalent," he acknowledged. "Yes."

"Go on."

Seaghdh sighed. "Your assessment is correct, Captain. My men and I were sent to find you. The people I represent have uncovered a high-level, very secret alliance between the Armada Admiralty and the Chekydran."

"An alliance?" She boggled. "The Chekydran don't even recognize us as life-forms, Seaghdh. Your information can't possibly—"

"There's an army," he interrupted. "An army of Armada personnel modified by the Chekydran."

Ari paled and memory flashed across her expression before being suppressed. "Modified how?"

"The Claugh hope you can answer that," he replied.

She shook her head. "This is ridiculous. You want me to believe the Claugh nib Dovvyth gives a damn whether or not I cooperate?"

"Yes," he said. "Do the people giving the orders care whether I have to kidnap you? No. But ultimately, I think they'll find they care very much about your cooperation if their suspicions are born out. It isn't as if they'll be able to force information from you when three months in a Chekydran prison couldn't break you."

If he hadn't been watching her so closely, he might have missed the tiny, short-lived twist in her lips.

"How do you know they didn't?" she countered.

"You wouldn't be alive."

Memory glinted in her eyes. He moved to the edge of his seat, leaned into her, and stroked her hair before he could blink.

She started and sucked in an audible breath. Her gaze locked into focus on his face.

No, he realized. On his mouth. He held his breath until the need to kiss an unbridled response from her no longer clawed his gut so mercilessly.

"Stay with me," Seaghdh urged, fighting the impulse to ask her to divulge her memories. She'd already demonstrated that she'd gamble with external trust—matters of the ship, her family, and her own physical safety—but she would not, or could not, confide in him. He hoped, for both their sakes, it wasn't a permanent condition.

Seaghdh pressed back the thought and drew away from the silk of her hair. This was business. She could easily represent a grave threat to the Empire and he was making a mistake in responding to her in this way. Frowning, he sat back and blew out a short breath. Stop it. Do the job.

"I'm—I need evidence to shore up what you say," she said, sounding breathless. She turned her gaze away from him and visibly struggled to regain her concentration. "What data supports your theory?"

"This isn't hypothetical, Ari. You're thinking like a scientist," he said, "not a tactician. I've seen your record. You have a tactical ability that borders on the arcane. Don't let loyalty muffle the instinct whispering to you that I'm right."

She swore, jumped up, and paced the bridge, head down, hands behind her back. "You tell me about this alliance to gain my cooperation."

"Partly, yes," Seaghdh answered. "You asked why my people were prepared to risk war for you. You deserve to understand the stakes."

Her smile looked grim. "If my cooperation is your objective, what prevents you from embellishing your intelligence report?"

"You know I am telling you the truth," he rumbled.

"I know you believe you are telling me the truth," she countered. Ari planted her feet and stared at him through hair the color of sunlight on clouds. "You accused me of thinking like a scientist, Seaghdh. Thank you for the reminder. Now that I am thinking like an officer of the Armada you forfeit the right to complain about it."

A grin flashed across his face before he conquered the expression and obscured his amused appreciation with a hard mask.

She raised an eyebrow at him, clearly enjoying the fact that she'd gotten a reaction from him before he'd shuttered his expression.

"Point to you," he said. "One all."

"Your people believe there is a threat to their security," she said, blushing. "I doubt I can help, but I'm willing to put that aside to ensure the safety of my family and friends."

"Once they're safe?" It hadn't escaped him that she'd lost a command, one she obviously wanted back very badly. Armada Command wouldn't be able to deny her a ship if she managed to hand them a Claugh nib Dovvyth officer and three of his crew. No doubt about it. They were both engaged in a dangerous game.

"I will have my command back."

Alarm leaped in him. She didn't realize someone had stacked the game against her. "What if TFC has issued a hit for you?"

"They had plenty of opportunity to kill me," she countered, "in the military hospital, before, during, and after my debriefing."

"Ari, you're unique in the history of humanoid interaction with the Chekydran," he said. "You survived."

"Plenty of people survive Chekydran captivity."

"Not a single one of whom had ever been accused of spying. You were. You know Chekydran policy. If they say you're a spy, they kill you. No questions asked."

She stopped short, processing the implications. "You're working up to tell me my government didn't immediately order my death because I was an object of curiosity."

"Yes."

Seaghdh propped his chin in one hand to hide an admiring smile. Ari had accepted his pronouncement without flinching, even though it added yet another worry to the collection of fears dragging at her. He hated having to add to her burden, hated that in following orders he had to pick at her barely healed wounds.

She stomped across the deck plating, her too-thin face alight as she sifted through implication and possibility, move and countermove.

Had her commanders not bothered to assess her? To find out whether or not she'd been compromised? Or had they simply decided she wasn't worth the risk? He shook his head. Her commanders were idiots. He didn't quite have her. Not yet. But he would.

He watched her pacing. She'd come so far. The Chekydran had made no attempt to rectify the damage they'd done to her before they'd released her. She'd been unrecognizable. Bald, both from abuse and from malnutrition, her body had been little more than skin binding broken bones together. Her blond hair, so pale it was almost white, had grown back in curls that would relax as it grew longer. It did nothing to soften her sharp cheekbones, one of which had been shattered by the Chekydran and rebuilt by TFC military medical.

He'd kept count of the numerous surgeries and reconstructions that had pieced Captain Ari Idylle's physical frame back together and had wondered if anyone had invented a surgery to repair a fractured spirit.

Seaghdh reached out, halting one of her passes with a hand on her arm. "Come with me. I'll see to it you get a command."

She stared, the first flicker of real emotion in her eyes. He detected the hollow ache of what she'd lost in the depths of her silver gaze. Hope flared, died down to despair and then anger. She opened her mouth, but nothing emerged.

Seaghdh blinked. He hadn't just offered an enemy officer a ship. Had he?

Ari managed a weak laugh. "Unless you have rank you've failed to disclose, Captain, you're not in a position to make that kind of promise."

For a moment, he forgot about masks, about cover stories. Something cold and razor-edged moved through him. He should tell her the truth.

He looked at her. She studied him, eyes narrowed, assessing, as if he were a blade whose balance and sharpness she tested.

Stop it, instinct whispered, *or she'll deduce too much too soon.*

She'd freeze and he'd never stand a chance at gaining her cooperation, her trust. Ease back, Seaghdh, he instructed himself. Focus on
the mission.

He forced himself to relax his features and to release her. "You're
right," he said. "I don't have the authority to make that offer."

Feeling her gaze trying to break into his head, he shifted, trying to
encourage her to stand down.

"Even if you had the authority, you'd have me fighting my own
people. I can't imagine the Claugh are interested in that sort of moral
conundrum in a ship's captain. Are you in the habit of recruiting
from within TFC ranks?"

Shaking his head, he grinned at her light, teasing tone. She'd felt
something. Even if she couldn't identify it, she'd felt his tension and
had offered him a way out. Another point to her. "If you want to exact
revenge on me for capturing you and yours, tell my CO about this
conversation."

Ari lifted an eyebrow. "Presumably that would mean facing the
legendary Auhrnok Riorchjan."

"Her Imperial Majesty's inestimable cousin?" he said. "Yes."

"Dangerous and deadly cousin," she corrected, lowering herself
into the piloting chair. "You know the Armada has its own name
for him?"

Seaghdh shifted but did not meet her gaze. "The Queen's Blade.
Judge, jury, and executioner." He stopped speaking, hearing the bitter
edge in his own voice.

She shrugged, eyeing him as if trying to fathom why the name
bothered him. "I understand IntCom can't get an operative within
sight of him. With no hard data, rumor is taken as fact. Suppositions
are made and stories invented."

"I've heard a few of those stories," he said. "Most are true."

"The man owns a planet?"

Seaghdh laughed, unable to exorcise the grim note from the sound.
"He says it owns him."

"You're his, aren't you?"

Seaghdh went dead still, startled into meeting her gaze as lethal, glittering awareness moved within him. Perception sharpened and he studied her to see how much she'd already guessed. He felt as much as saw her quiver.

From the apprehension in her face, she knew she'd hit a nerve. Though her expression remained studiously blank, he could see her considering. Hit the nerve again to see if he'd crack? Or offer enough slack to see where he'd go?

"His?" he echoed.

She smiled and relaxed, ratcheting the tension forcibly down.

Still on guard, he mirrored her, letting her lead. Even after everything she'd been through, she was good. She projected such an Isarrite-clad air of harmless curiosity that he wanted to cheer. Why had TFC wasted such obvious talent on the bridge of a Prowler?

"You're from his planet," she clarified. "Do you owe him allegiance? Or are you family?"

He had to stifle a laugh. Family. Twelve Gods, if he hadn't already known everything to be known about Captain Ari Idylle, her so-close-to-the-truth guess would have made him think she was part of Intelligence Command. It would have scared and thrilled the life out of him.

"Damn it, Ari." He sighed, and running a hand down his face, folded easygoing, good humor around his tone. "Stop doing that. I'm too tired to have you picking secrets out of my head."

She laughed and he had to cut off the urge to yank her into his arms. Fear drove into her face and cut off the infectious sound. She stared at him, eyes wide, clearly asking herself how they'd become so comfortable with their verbal parry and riposte.

Pain for her burned through him. He hoped he'd helped her remember what fun felt like, a few uncertain moments notwithstanding. Shaking off the feeling, he reminded himself that he had no business hoping anything. She was proving all too skilled at getting under his defenses. If she'd had any training as spy, he'd assume it was calculated. But his files on her were exhaustive and there was no indication that she'd ever been recruited or trained.

She spun back to her station and stared at the readouts.

Seaghdh clenched his fists to keep from reaching out to her in comfort. What was it about her that kept throwing him off target?

"You can't offer me a command, and I can't have you abducting my family," she said. "Stick to plan, Seaghdh. You've got me."

A console beeped. Communications. She rose and crossed in front of him. He stopped her again.

"Give us what we need, Ari, and I'll get you back to Tagreth, if that's what you want," he said.

He felt impatience sweep through her. She slipped out of his grasp and went to communications.

"Don't insult my intelligence," she snapped, punching commands. "Audio logging online in ten seconds. We both know the only way I'll 'get back' anywhere is in a body bag."

"That's your government," he shot. "Not mine."

"It's every government," Ari countered, "that's in the business of protecting its citizens. At least in TFC space, I'm one of those citizens. In Claugh nib Dovvyth space, I'm the enemy. My life won't be worth a damn."

Two beeps from the com panel. She turned to glare at him. He met her challenging stare.

"I disagree with your assessment, Captain," he said. "I have time and the weight of evidence on my side. Now, brief your family."

"Bad plan."

"Not at all," he countered. "We want their minds occupied, yes? You brief them. I remain silent."

She sucked in an audible breath and nodded. "They won't be able to evaluate your veracity directly. They will have to filter everything through whether or not they believe I can be lied to."

He offered her a handheld. Ari reached for it and then met his gaze when he did not release it.

"Do not tell them who we are."

She cocked her head. "Giving them something to work out for themselves?"

"If you like."

"They will, you know."

"Maybe."

He let go. She glanced at the little screen, scanning the shift schedules, every last one of which he'd made certain she worked with him. A hint of resignation in her eye, she nodded.

"Discourage any notions they may have of heroics and work out a meal schedule if you think it's safe," he said.

"Give them access to their experiments," she suggested. "Dad's priority is saving the galaxy from covert Chekydran plagues."

Seaghdh pressed his lips tight, tapped his fingers on the arm of the chair, and shook his head.

"Brief them," he said. "If we can secure the cargo bay, I'll consider limited work on the experiments."

"During active experimental work, the cargo bay is an isolated environment with containment fail-safes," she assured him. "Worst case, the entire contents of the bay is jettisoned via vacuum."

Seaghdh uttered a breathless laugh. "Thank the Twelve Gods I wasn't any good at science."

"It is a unique calling." Ari leaned in to punch up commands on his console.

So close, Seaghdh inhaled her scent. Citrus and a trace of the forests where he'd grown up. Awareness flared through him. The heat of her body warmed him, driving blood low into his body. He glanced into her face and saw the flush staining her cheeks.

She jerked upright. "You can monitor the galley from here," she explained, her words hurried and her voice uncharacteristically rough. "Video and audio. I'll make supper and stow some for everyone. Best if I brief them over food. SOP on this ship."

"Thank you," he said, easing a thread of power into his voice. *Turn to me.* His tone warmed and he saw the cajoling, caressing note shimmer through her.

Her flush deepened. Confused emotion toppled the brittle look of peace that had finally settled on her face. She fled.

Seaghdh swore.

What the hell was wrong with him? He had no business being disappointed because his subject had broken and run when the sexy little games they'd been playing had intensified. Certainly, he'd known what a beautiful woman she'd been before her capture, had thought he'd known something about who she was. But damn it. Nothing had prepared him for the wry humor in her. Or the depth of pain or the sheer force of will shining from her. She'd been pretty before, but now, her once-lush beauty, shattered by the Chekydran and pieced back together by medical technology, promised magnificence tempered by nightmare. It was the sheer magnetic force of intellect and personality that hadn't crumbled beneath Chekydran brutality that made her so engaging, so stunning.

She took his breath away. He hadn't been prepared for that or for her response to him. She obviously hadn't, either. That he impacted her, he could plainly see. It was damned flattering, but the fear her feelings caused her felt like a knife in his gut.

CHAPTER

7

ARI fled to the galley, propped her hands on the counter, let her head hang, and grappled for control of her body. Three months of brutal captivity. Three months of attempting to recover. How in the Three Hells could she respond to any man, let alone the one who'd made her a prisoner again and who'd endangered the most important people in her life? Was this sudden awaking of her most primal self part of the recovery process? Was it even normal?

She sagged. No way to know. It wasn't like anyone had the data to define normal parameters for surviving Chekydran victims. They were a rare breed.

And the man sitting in her father's command chair was watching her every move on the galley transmitters. She straightened, scrubbed her face with her hands, unable to escape what she'd seen in his eyes.

He liked what he saw when he looked at her.

Some deeply hidden feminine core stirred to life within her. She'd seen so many feigned reactions to her appearance that she knew his appraisal had been honest and that it had taken him by surprise.

Maybe that's what had reached her. Extracting a response from someone who did not want to respond made Ari feel richer somehow. Armed, maybe, with a weapon she'd never realized she'd had.

A thrill of erotic promise fired through her. She turned away from the camera, folded her arms around her body, closed her eyes, and allowed herself a moment to enjoy the sensation. It would be all she could afford.

How long had it been? Four years? Five? No. Six. At least. That was the trouble with chasing a command. Everything Ari had done, everyone she'd associated with figured into her command suitability in the eyes of the admirals. Plenty of command candidates chose celibacy to safeguard their careers. The single greatest attrition factor in the leadership program was love. The admirals said it was "the urge to merge" overpowering the drive to captain a piece of hardware.

Maybe it made her cold. Or hard. Or maybe she had always been Pietre's Ice Princess, but she'd never wanted anything as much as she'd wanted her own sleek, lethal Prowler and crew.

Until Cullin Seaghdh made her think and feel things that could rip away the last hope that she'd ever sit in the command chair on the bridge of a warship ever again. Her only option was to do what the Chekydran had forced her to learn so swiftly and so well: block out every trace of emotion. If she could do that and concentrate on her job, she might still convince Armada Command to put her back in the number one spot on a Prowler roster.

Resolute, Ari made supper. As she dished out the thick, aromatic stew, she had Seaghdh unlock cabin doors. She punched the com buttons for her father's, Raj's, and Pietre's rooms.

"Supper's ready," she said.

"Alex?" her father began.

"Come to the galley, Dad. I'll explain what I can." She straightened, folded her hands behind her back, and waited the few minutes it took them to traverse the corridors.

The door opened. Linnaeus Idylle and his crew filed into the room. She drew a deep breath. Her dad sat in the chair at the head of the table, pushed his bowl of stew away, and clasped his hands, anger in the set of his shoulders. Pietre stood at his right, arms crossed, contempt in his expression. Raj and Jayleia sat side by side at the table, turning their chairs to face her. Ari nearly smiled. None of them would put their backs to anyone else. And they called her distrustful.

"I cannot give you much more than a tactical briefing," she said, sitting opposite her father.

"I don't want a briefing from a colluder." Pietre dropped his hands to his sides, his fists clenched. "It's time we took back this ship."

Raj lifted an eyebrow. "Are we secure?"

"No," she said, dipping her spoon in her stew.

Her father scowled.

Pietre's face darkened.

"At no time, while these men are on board, should you consider any conversation secure," she said, turning to be certain the galley sensor couldn't see her face. She pinned Raj with a stare and slowly closed one eye.

He took a deep breath and sat back. "I understand."

Ari hoped he did understand that medical might still be secure, but it was the only place, and she didn't know how long that would last.

"We are on course for Tagreth Federated Command," she said.

Her father narrowed his blue eyes, as if trying to adjust his focus. "We're being shadowed by the Chekydran."

"Yes."

"After they've veered off?" he asked.

"Silver City."

Her father scowled. "Nothing more than pirates."

Ari shrugged, neither confirming nor denying the supposition. "Once we reach Silver City the *Sen Ekir* and its crew will be free to go."

"Says who?" Pietre demanded.

She met Pietre's angry brown eyes and took a deliberate bite of stew.

"That pirate out there?" he asked. "A man without a conscience? Or honor? How can you believe anything he says? Are you even thinking?"

Her throat closed on her protest and she struggled to swallow the morsel she'd so unwisely chosen. Dropping her spoon in her bowl, she rose. That did the trick. She could breathe and talk again.

"You're still alive," Ari countered. "That pirate out there, the one without any honor, wasted time letting us pack up and stow your experiments and your gear. Not the actions of a man bent on murder."

"You are so stupid!" Pietre growled, his face red.

"Am I?" she challenged. "So stupid that I tuned the atmospherics when the problem was a fuel line clog? A clog so bad the valve is now shot? I have to risk blowing all of us, including your precious ass, out of the space ways by setting down on Kebgra for a spare. You've endangered everyone, again, because you couldn't be bothered to do your damned job."

"Stop it!" her father ordered. "Pietre, sit down and be quiet. Alexandria, Kebgra? You said we were on course for Silver City."

She drew herself upright and huffed out a short breath as Pietre dropped into a chair. Damn it. Barely sixty seconds in their company and she'd reverted to the Armada Captain her father treated like a two-year-old. She had to overcome these old habits, fighting with Pietre and letting her father order her around.

"We're in the lane for TFC, Dad," she answered, rising and shoving her bowl of stew into cold storage.

"So as not to alert the Chekydran," Jayleia said.

"I have noticed that I can't get our passengers killed without taking us along," Ari replied. "I am doing what the Chekydran expect. Kebgra and the engine repair are first."

"We're riding tolerance on the valve?" her dad inquired.

"Beyond tolerance," she countered. "That jaunt through the outer solar atmosphere didn't do it any favors. We're twenty hours out."

"What are the odds of a bleed?" her father demanded.

She shrugged. "I can go in on one engine if I have to."

"Risky," Raj said when neither her father nor Pietre commented.

"No more so than a bleed," she said. "Kebgra's nice, but I'm not interested in permanent residency. Either because we burned off all our fuel or because we exploded on entry."

"Very well," her father said, nodding. "Pietre will . . ."

"Not likely be allowed to do the repair," Ari finished for him. If she had control of someone else's ship, she sure as hell wouldn't give the crew any chance to sabotage the drives.

Pietre leaped to his feet. "I'm engineer on this ship, not . . ."

The door opened. Ari glanced up.

"Captain Seaghdh," she said, ignoring the gun in his hand in favor of wiping down the counters.

Jayleia gasped. Ari's father and Raj sat back in their chairs. Pietre froze.

"V'kyrri will handle repairs," Seaghdh said.

Ari raised her eyebrows when Seaghdh's second followed him through the door. "Turrel. Who has the con?"

"Captain Idylle," Seaghdh acknowledged with a nod, his tone mild. "We're in the lane. Turrel has the con on handheld. You're off duty."

Without waiting for her reply, he swept the people at the table with a glance that would have made her shiver had it been turned on her. The gun focused on Pietre. "I asked Captain Idylle to brief you as a courtesy," he grated. "You do not control this ship. I do. Captain Idylle is making the best of a bad situation. I suggest you do the same."

Her father rose slowly, his hands flat on the table. "None of this is necessary, Mr. Seaghdh. If you and your men require transport, return control of my ship to me. Diverting to Silver City is a minor issue. I will forego charges if you surrender control."

"That's touching, Dr. Idylle," Seaghdh replied, "given you preferred murder a few hours ago. You'll have to forgive me if I can't bring myself to trust you any more than I trust the Chekydran."

Her dad stood rigid. "You'd have done the same thing in my place."

"That's where you're wrong." The dead flat tone of his voice drew Ari's attention to Seaghdh. His features might have been carved from a solid piece of Dirthanian Isarrite, the hardest substance yet found in the galaxy. The light had gone out of his eyes.

"No man of conscience, or of honor, leaves someone to die a slow, agonizing death," he said, his voice honed to a keen, lethal edge. "Not when he can prevent it."

Silence.

Ari nodded. Point definitely to Seaghdh but not against her.

Her father lowered himself to his chair.

Seaghdh waved Pietre to the table. "If we've cleared up the question of open revolt, have a seat. No point missing supper."

Pietre stared at him, then at Ari. Very slowly, he edged to the table and sat down.

"You didn't poison our friend's supper, did you, Captain?" Seaghdh inquired as he eased into the chair she'd vacated.

"Not yet," she replied, sliding bowls in front of him and Turrel.

"Thanks," Turrel said. "Pass the bread."

"My appreciation, Captain," Seaghdh said. "You haven't eaten. Join us."

With the tension running so high, she'd never be able to choke anything down, but Ari retrieved her stew and slid into the only empty seat between Turrel and Seaghdh. Without looking at her or asking, Seaghdh dumped a slab of bread into her bowl.

She peered sideways at him. He ate, his gaze going from scientist to scientist.

"He's right," Turrel growled. "You got over a lot. No one would know, 'cept you still look like a prisoner. Eat."

Desolation stabbed through her chest. Did she really? True, she'd

developed a distinct loathing for mirrors. During captivity, her skin
had turned sallow from malnutrition. The Chekydran had assured that
most of her hair had come out in clumps. She'd been a towhead all her
life with eyes so pale they were silver rather than blue. They'd taken
advantage of the fact that bright light caused significant pain in someone with her eye color.

She'd flattered herself that she'd made progress at the hospital.
She still had to wear specially designed lenses to protect her eyes in
sunlight, but she could go outside, something she'd been unable to do
when she'd first been freed. She'd shorn her remaining hair brutally
short. It was growing in curly, something she knew by feel. After a
month in the hospital, she'd been able to look at her hands and arms
and see familiar translucent, rosy skin that freckled. Her once lush
figure had been skeletal when she'd been let go, but she'd put on
weight. Still, she had to admit that even after three months' freedom,
she had trouble eating.

Maybe her initial avoidance of mirrors had become habit. She
hadn't assessed her own appearance since the time at the hospital
that she'd caught sight of the frightening scarecrow she'd become.
Breathing around the ache in her chest, Ari wondered if she had any
hope of approaching normal ever again.

"Thanks for saying so," she managed to choke out. She had to
take her arms from around her torso to pull the bread out of her stew
and pick up her spoon.

"Captain Idylle recommended allowing you to begin experiments,
Dr. Idylle," Seaghdh said. His voice wrapped around her, urging her
to hold together, to not break down in front of her family.

She stiffened her spine. He'd done it again. Used his voice talent.
To help, this time, rather than to control. It was more of an offer, like
a hand extended to help her up. She accepted it gratefully. It made
her feel strong before the fear that she'd never be able to stand up
to her family on her own took over. She glanced at him.

He peered back, looking like a man trying to decide why he felt
he could trust her after only a few hours' acquaintance when her

father and his hostile crew sat facing them. Ari knew the feeling. Some of the bleakness lifted from her shoulders.

Seaghdh looked down the table at her father. "The captain indicated that your cargo bay is an enclosed atmosphere."

"Yes." Her father bit the word out.

"Tell me about your experiments."

"I doubt I can explain it so you would understand," her dad shot.

Ari drew a sharp breath.

Seaghdh cut off her reprimand with a look. "Ari thought your work against Chekydran pathogens was important, Doctor. I am sorry to find your priorities have changed."

She raised her eyebrows at her father. He wanted to ignore the jibe. She could see it in the set of his jaw. He glanced at her. His shoulders drooped and he shook his head.

"With the limited facilities aboard ship," her dad said, sounding weary, "we do little more than catalogue specimens and prepare them for experiments in the labs at the university."

"It saves us important time and effort in the labs, Dr. Idylle," Jayleia protested. "We have a very efficient system. It takes advantage of each of our specialties."

"Estimated hours to complete the work?" Seaghdh demanded.

"Would we have Ari?" Raj asked.

She shook her head. "Pulling watch."

"More work than can be completed in one trip, then," Raj answered.

Turrel glanced down at her. "What's a ship's captain do with experiments?"

"Slide and specimen prep," Pietre sneered.

She nodded. "Menial labor. Too obtuse for anything more."

Jayleia snorted and grinned at her. "The big, important Prowler captain leaves out the fact that her career doesn't allow time to master the specific and delicate techniques we've developed."

"Too busy running a ship and crew," Raj added, joining in the teasing. "The lot of us would be menial labor on her Prowler."

"What's your command?" Turrel asked, scraping the bottom of his bowl.

Ari hesitated. In part, she hated remembering she wasn't captain of anything anymore. It was just a rank. Another part of her shrank from admitting which ship she'd commanded. They'd pulled their share of taking potshots at Claugh spies through the years. It was possible she'd been responsible for killing their friends.

"Though I never understood her drive to a life of violence," her father said, "Alex has done well in her chosen profession. She commanded the Prowler *Balykkal*."

"The *Balykkal*?" Turrel gaped at her.

She felt like she had two heads. Ari dropped her bread into her bowl, threw her napkin on the table, and shoved herself to her feet. "By the Twelve Gods, Dad!" she swore. "When I do not answer a question, could you please respect that there are things I might not want the entire sector to know?"

"Cease your blasphemy on my ship," her father commanded, pinning her with a glare.

She stared at him. He was taking a thirty-two-year-old woman to task for swearing. And she was letting him. They were stripping her bare, her family and friends, before an enemy who'd masqueraded for a short time as an ally. When she got her command back, it would still be her job to hunt down and eliminate men like Cullin Seaghdh. And maybe, if she got back on the bridge of her own Prowler, she could be certain that duty kept her as far from her family as she wanted to go. It was a bracing thought.

Ari turned and walked out of the room.

"YOU'RE not asleep."

She blinked. Seaghdh. Inside the door of her cabin. A door she'd locked. Fatigue made her slow to quash the thrill that shivered through her. *Stop that.* "What are you doing here?"

"You've been very cooperative, captain of the *Balykkal*, and I thank you. Did you really imagine I'd give you eight to ten hours alone to plot my capture?" He cocked his head and frowned. "What is that noise?"

She tabbed down the ambient sound and leaned back in her chair. "Mating songs of a tiny amphibian native to Gloquess. You'll notice I'm not captain of anything at the moment, and you're going to have a tough time sleeping in here."

His keen gaze tried to pry past her defenses. "Because you need a mundane, distinctly non-Chekydran sound playing while you sleep? Do you want the lights left on, too?"

"No," she said too quickly, jumping up from her chair as he sauntered in her direction. Funny. She equated darkness with safety. When the lights came on, the Chekydran came for her. She desperately did not want to have to explain.

He obligingly dropped the subject. "That is a much nicer outfit than the coveralls," he said, grinning.

Shorts and a T-shirt from the last energy blade competition she'd won. Both so worn as to barely qualify as articles of clothing. Had she thought things through after walking out on her family, she'd have realized Seaghdh couldn't sleep anywhere but right here. She'd have done the same thing had their positions been reversed. Cursing, she rubbed her aching forehead and flung a gesture at the bed. "Help yourself."

"I won't take your bed from you. Unless you'd be willing to share?"

"Sleep where you like, Seaghdh," she growled, "but don't touch me no matter what you hear."

The teasing grin winked out of existence. The calculating, half-indignant set of his shoulders suggested he'd heard more than her words. A flash of memory of the Chekydran waiting until she slept and then yanking her physically from her cell brought her hackles up. Adrenaline flooded her stomach.

Again, Seaghdh's golden gaze pierced the chinks in her armor, seeing far too much. Smoothing the goose bumps on her arms, she looked away.

"I value my hide. How do I wake you if there's need?" he asked.

Ari glanced at him. No sarcasm in his voice. No arrogance, at least, not in the question. He took her at her word and that made a tight place in her chest soften. "I don't know. I guess you could always use a glass of water . . ."

"I would not," he countered, his shoulders hunched in indignation. At least she knew he wouldn't risk touching her to wake her.

"Where will you sleep?" It wasn't a casual question. The easygoing, look-I'm-not-a-threat way he'd asked told her just how important the answer was.

"Doesn't matter."

"It does."

"The closet."

"You are not."

"Not now that I've told you, no," she said.

A light went on in his eyes and the stubborn lines etched around his mouth disappeared. He nodded. "Will it bother you if I get cleaned up before bed?"

"No."

"Turn out the lights and go to sleep," he suggested as he wandered into the head. He glanced back, that damned grin on his face. "If only to preserve your maidenly modesty, my dear. I didn't bring anything to sleep in."

Ari laughed and closed scratchy eyes as the door shut behind him. Memory offered a detailed portrait of Cullin Seaghdh's lean, muscular body emerging from decon in the cargo bay. Heat shimmered through her.

"Mmm. Point to you," she murmured at the closed bathroom door.

CHAPTER

8

As the shower came on in the head, Ari debated the wisdom of setting the psych lock on the door. She finally enabled it, reasoning that she'd never sleep anyway. She could cycle through the test and disable the lock before Seaghdh woke. If she couldn't pass the psych test, he deserved to have a woman driven mad by the Chekydran on his hands. Before coffee.

She wrapped a silky, down comforter around her, grabbed her pillows, killed the room light and sat on the floor, her back to the corner behind the desk. She'd positioned it for maximum cover just before this trip. With another person in the room, she felt like she needed it.

The comforter warmed her. Tension drained from her body. Luxury had taken on new meaning after three months as a Chekydran prisoner. Too much and she felt smothered, too little and she flashed back to the filthy, cramped cell. She tended to be a wholly unpleasant person during flashbacks. More than one medi had to be treated for a broken nose because of her. She'd apologized each time it had happened but couldn't help noticing that her nurses had gotten burlier the longer she'd stayed in the hospital.

The shower and then the dryer shut off. She fought the anxiety rising in her gut but couldn't stop the gasp when the door to the head opened and light from the bathroom stabbed through the dark cabin. She caught a brief glimpse of him silhouetted in the doorway.

"Sorry," Seaghdh murmured. He slapped the control panel and she stared into darkness once more.

He stumbled across the cabin and ran into the bed. He swore. The mattress sighed as he settled his weight on it and fumbled with blankets. He yawned so hard, his jaw popped. The clean spice and musk scent of his presence wrapped around her. His breathing deepened and slowed.

It made her smile. He'd given her a non-Chekydran sound to listen to in the dark. It eased her jagged nerves, warming, soothing. She let the tension drain from her body, allowed the ebb and flow of his breath to shelter her.

"One question," he said, his tone lazy and relaxed. "What the Three Hells is between you and Pietre?"

He surprised a mirthless laugh from her. She hugged her knees to her chest. With her voice bouncing off walls and furniture, she hoped he wouldn't be able to place her in the dark. "Long story."

"I'm not going anywhere."

"He and I have been coming to Occaltus with Dad for five years. I was on the first run as a young officer aboard the *Balykkal*."

"Never send a science ship into the unknown without escort?" Seaghdh surmised. "Makes sense, but five years? That's a long time."

"Ioccal was an old colony world," she said. "Hosted a population of nearly a billion."

"What?" Surprise sharpened his tone.

"Our first mission was fact-finding, based on some ancient records in an old aboveground building being torn down. Among other things, the archaeologists found a list of colony ships sent from Ta-greth. We had antique charts and a reasonable idea of where the ships went. Occaltus interested Tagreth Federated due to its proximity to Chekydran space. We'd hoped to find a thriving civilization and new allies. When we got there, the mission turned archaeological."

"No one? No native culture?"

"Not a soul and no indications of other intelligent life that we've found. Just as well. You know TFC. When something gets in our way, we don't wait around to come to understanding."

"Scorch first, ask questions later?" he asked, his tone droll.

"It's why we have so many colonies and the Claugh so few," she said. "But it is also why we lack the diversity of your people."

He shifted in the bedclothes. "I've never heard an officer of the Armada describe it as a 'lack' before."

"Personal assessment," she hedged. "Maybe tactical. We're a methodical people. Makes for great scientists and for a very capable military . . ."

"Makes for a military that's a true thorn in my side," he inter-rupted.

"We have more ships and more personnel," she said, "but your military is lighter, faster, more agile. It's adaptable."

He drew in an audible breath. "We focus on knowledge and understanding."

"TFC is concerned primarily with superior firepower and price tag," she finished. "That meant that when we discovered that Ioccal was a dead world with reasonable soil fertility and a moderate cli-mate, TFC marked it for colonization. The ionosphere was more than adequate to filter out radiation. We were just finishing up digs . . ."

"When you discovered the world was plagued."

"Yes."

Seaghdh blew out an audible breath. "What happened?"

"I watched my crewmates die in slow, bloody agony, that's what happened." Her voice broke. She bit her lip. That had been so long ago. She thought she'd gotten over it.

"It wasn't your fault," he rumbled. "No wonder they promoted you. You got the survivors out."

She shook her head and then realized he couldn't see it. "No. They promoted me because I got a Prowler Class ship back to Tagreth without being detected by the Chekydran. I was very clear on my duty in those days. If the survivors had listened to me, I wouldn't have lived for Tagreth Command to promote."

"You were going to destroy everything?"

"Rather than fly infected ships back to an inhabited world? Yes. We'd already determined that those of us who'd survived weren't carriers. The disease either killed or missed altogether. To this day, we don't know why we're immune."

"Your father, Pietre, Raj, Jayleia, and you," Seaghdh murmured, a frown in his voice.

"We were clean, but the ships had become carriers."

"The plague isn't destroyed in vacuum?"

"What's outside the ship, yes. We'd tracked it in on our clothes, our shoes. It was everywhere. By the time quarantine kicked in, our sick and dying had shed incredible volumes of the disease into the ventilation and sanitation systems. We couldn't guarantee that normal disinfection routines, the UV and shielded irradiation of the O_2 recycling and generating systems, could handle it. Watch one person die from it and you'd never gamble with several billion lives by putting down someplace without knowing for sure."

"So Raj came up with the radiation bath."

"Yes. We were bickering about our lack of options. I'd locked Pietre in my cabin aboard the *Balykkal*, but he'd managed to get into the communications channel . . ."

"You and Pietre were alone on that Prowler?"

"Yes."

Seaghdh laughed. "You wouldn't sleep with him."

"Not even on a bet and certainly not after I'd just buried my first commanding officer."

"Why lock him . . . ?"

"He was incensed that I was willing to fly us into the sun and tried to take command from me," she said. "He'd destroy a civilization if it meant he didn't have to sacrifice himself. He wanted to believe that medical facilities on a central world could find a cure before we'd wiped out seventy to eighty percent of the population. I clubbed him over the head, hauled his ass to the nearest cabin, and locked him down."

It sounded like Seaghdh sat up in the bed. "You single-handed a Prowler from Occaltus to Tagreth? Ari, that's one hundred hours."

"Yes, it is."

"No wonder you were ready to suicide."

She sighed. She'd been full of ambition. Duty had seemed very black-and-white. Snuggling down in the nest she'd made of her comforter and pillows, she said, "Raj came up with the radiation idea after Jayleia made some comment about wishing we could rig UV with enough reach to sanitize every nook and cranny. He did some research and brought back hull penetration tolerances versus human tissue tolerances. The three of them, Dad, Raj, and Jay, mixed up the pre-exposure cocktail to minimize tissue damage. It's remarkably effective, but we had no way of getting it to the *Balykkal*."

"It won't teleport?"

"No."

"Radioactive all on its own, is it?"

"Just enough."

"You took a full dose of radiation."

"And exposed Pietre to a full dose," she said. "We both spent a good long time in gene therapy afterward."

"Ari, a radiation dose like that," Seaghdh said. "That does things to a man."

"Women, too, Seaghdh, I assure you."

"Aye. But the female genome is encapsulated. It's harder to damage and easier to repair."

"Yes."

"You sterilized him."

"Yes, and I'd do it again. Dead is dead. Pietre's alive. Dad has a grad student working on a way to repair the damage to a single sperm cell. I understand they're making significant progress."

Seaghdh uttered a harsh laugh. "You have had to make some tough calls in your time, haven't you?"

"Part of the job description."

"I don't envy you. I'd have done the same thing, up to and including flying into the sun. Think of the songs they'd sing. You might have gotten your own holiday."

She laughed, but his approval warmed her. It had been one of the few times she and her father had agreed. Radiation could be recovered from, death couldn't. It hadn't made it any easier to break the news to Pietre. She'd demanded to be the one to do it. He'd been on her ship and under her command, such as it was. She had to take responsibility for telling Pietre that her decision had left him sterile.

Seaghdh flopped back down in the bed. "He's not just an orhait's ass."

"Nope," she said, struggling to stifle a yawn and the picture of Pietre's face affixed to the body of one of Tagreth's infamous six-legged, nasty-tempered pack animals. "His hatred is justified. I only poke him in the eye when he lets it get in the way of doing his job."

"You told him to check for a fuel clog in the starboard atmospheric, didn't you?" Seaghdh demanded. She could hear the mirth in his voice. "He tuned the engines instead just to spite you."

"Yes." She couldn't choke back her yawn that time.

"Rest," Seaghdh said, his voice deepening. "Sleep."

Ari wanted to tell him she rarely slept, that when she slept she dreamed. She wanted to tell him, but unable to resist the caress of power in the rich, melodic voice curling around her, her eyes drifted shut.

*   *   *

ARI propelled herself from the depths of sleep, automatically swallowing the scream that tried to escape her throat. She was upright and halfway across the room before she realized what had happened. Breathing hard, she set her hands on her desk and leaned, head hanging, trying to calm the shudders wracking her body. Humming. She heard it now. It jolted her heart into high gear. It didn't matter that it was just a harmonic in the interstellar drive. It never mattered.

The bedclothes rustled. Seaghdh sat up.

"Ari? Are you all right?" he asked. "Half light."

The lights switched on. She flinched.

"Sorry," he said, rising. He moved as if afraid she might shy away. "Do the lights bother you?"

"No," she rasped. Not now that they were on and she could plainly see she wasn't in a Chekydran cell, no, they didn't bother her.

"Trouble sleeping?"

"Engine harmonic," she said.

"I hear it. I don't think it's anything to be concerned about. V'kyrri would be on it already . . ."

She shook her head. "Nothing to be concerned about."

He paused at her side, peering into her face, looking unsettled. Finally, he laid a hand on her shoulder. "You're shaking and you're cold. Come on. Into bed. I'll take the floor."

"I cannot sleep in the bed."

"You obviously aren't sleeping on the floor, either," he replied. "Just warm up. You don't have to sleep."

He put an arm around her shoulder, drew her to the bed, and released her as she climbed in. She huddled under the blankets, her knees drawn up to her chest and her arms wrapped around her shins. Concern puckered the skin between his brows. He eased down to sit facing her as if afraid she might object.

She flushed, embarrassed that in his company she felt so vulnerable, so exposed. Why, when he looked at her, did Cullin Seaghdh see so much more than anyone else? Every time her father or Raj or

Jayleia looked at her, she saw walls go up in their eyes, as if they couldn't stand to see what she'd become. To know what had happened and was still happening to her. Seaghdh seemed to accept her. She sighed.

"The Chekydran hummed," she explained, her voice shaking.

Seaghdh closed his eyes and nodded, but not before she saw pain flare in his gaze. When he looked at her again, only a hint of it remained. For some reason, it reached a deeply hidden part of her. He hurt because of what she'd been through. He hurt for her.

Ari swallowed hard and forged on, wanting him to understand, hoping he wouldn't look at her with that damning mixture of pity and hopelessness she saw in her family's eyes.

"Everything vibrated. Skin, muscle, bone, teeth. This damned, barely audible buzz. It never stopped."

Warm, strong fingers covered hers and she realized she'd twisted the blankets into a hard knot with her white-knuckled hands.

"From watching them, I gathered that it functioned as a kind of neural network, a framework of communication and awareness," she said. "If we could develop some kind of sonic disruption, we might be able to . . ."

"You were a prisoner and you collected intelligence?" he asked. His laugh sounded brittle.

"I became what they accused me of being."

"And when the engine drops into a harmonic?"

"I'm right back in that cell with very little to do to stay sane but catalogue details."

He shifted. Without a word, he turned and sat beside her, nudging her over. Propping his back against the headboard, he tugged her into his grasp. His thighs cradled her backside. He drew her against his chest, his arms closing around her. She blinked, uncertain how to respond, afraid to let herself feel. Or want.

"Relax," he rumbled, his tone unsettled. "Pretend for me that this helps."

He needed it, she realized in a flash, needed to feel useful. Why?

Why did it matter to him? He had helped her. She could admit that. Could she do as he asked and pretend she was okay in his arms? She sighed, loosed the tension from her body, and rested her head against his shoulder. Maybe she could. Heat seeped through her. The rhythm of his breath rising and falling rocked her. It felt so good. So safe. It dismayed her to find just how badly she needed to be held. She closed her eyes on the shudder of fear that rippled through her.

"How did you manage to wake up without screaming?" he asked, his breath puffing against her hair.

"Officers don't scream."

He chuckled. "Armada boot camp suddenly scares the hell out of me."

"It isn't something one picks up in boot camp. Besides . . ." Ari broke off, fear spiking through her again.

He tightened his arms around her. "Besides?"

She fought the urge to deny him. No matter the cascade of adrenaline and cortisol in her blood, her survival no longer depended on silence. She *could* fight back.

"Besides," she forced herself to say. "If I scream, they win."

Seaghdh swore, the sound angry, desolate. "V'kyrri will take care of the harmonic."

She nodded.

He released her to tab off the light, then wrapped her in his embrace once more.

She stared into the darkness for several minutes while his breathing deepened and slowed, lulling her.

"Would you be okay lying down?" he murmured.

She started and forced herself upright. By all the Gods. She'd fallen asleep in his arms after a nightmare. She'd never slept after waking from . . .

"I can't do this. If I dream again . . ." She gasped and shook her head at the desire welling up within her to stay locked in his arms.

"You won't," he whispered into her hair as he eased them down in the bed. "You won't. Sleep. Only peaceful, pleasant dreams."

He'd put that indefinable something into his voice, using his talent to compel her again. No. He was offering his ability to her, to help her. Again.

Desperate, needy, starving for the emotional comfort Seaghdh offered, a part of her lunged for and clung to the lifeline he'd thrown. Her eyes burned as he turned to his side and tucked her back against his chest.

"Sleep."

Weariness closed over her head like deep, silent water.

ARI had finished running her fifth kilometer in the cargo bay and had started loading weights on the weight bar when Seaghdh sauntered in. Wiping sweat from her forehead, she nodded, mistrusting the sharp look in his eyes and the hard line around his mouth.

"Didn't wake you again, did I?" she asked.

"No." He took up position at the head of the weight bench as she lay down and placed her hands on the bar. He spotted her off the rack.

"Thanks."

He watched her for a few reps. "Want to tell me about that psych lock on your cabin door?"

Her muscles froze, trembling. He'd seen her wade through the psych test. Misery and shame closed sharp teeth on her heart.

Seaghdh grabbed the bar and pulled it back onto the rack.

Did she want to tell him about the psych lock? Bastard. She sat up, breathing hard. "No."

"Do it anyway," he ordered. "What are you afraid of, Ari?"

"Damn it, Seaghdh. You're kidnapping me, not treating me."

Intraship chimed. "Captain?" Sindrivik said.

"Seaghdh," he replied, turning to glance at the speaker. "Go ahead."

"On approach to Kebgra," Sindrivik said. "No response to hails."

Ari stood up frowning. "No response?"

"None."

"We'll be right there."

CHAPTER

9

ARI showered and dressed so fast her hair was still damp by the time she bounded onto the bridge. Sindrivik vacated the pilot's seat. Scrolling through the data, Ari glanced at Seaghdh. "Automatic beacons are online, just no verbal response from the depot."

"What are our choices?" he asked, leaning back in the command chair, eyeing her olive-drab fatigues.

Let him. She needed to be in uniform. She stared at her panel. They could make Silver City, but the slightest emergency and they'd be running on one atmospheric unless they replaced the part. Doable, but it made the *Sen Ekir* fly like a garbage scow.

Swearing, she shook her head. Unacceptable.

"Running on one engine is a risk I'm not willing to take," she said.

She saw V'kyrri look up at Seaghdh and nod once. Confirming her risk analysis? Maybe the uniform had been a mistake. It reminded her she had a job to do, but it had obviously prompted Seaghdh to recall he'd spent the night holding the enemy. Who'd slept ridiculously well and long because of his arms around her.

She scowled. "We stop at the depot."

Her father had used the Kebgra settlement as a supply stop for years. The settlers weren't big on formality. More than once, the crew of the *Sen Ekir* had put down in the middle of a festival or a street party that encompassed the entire population. They'd always gotten a hurried "yeah, put down anywhere!" from someone before, though.

"They are isolated. Could be a com failure. Land here." She pointed to the depot a kilometer or so outside of town. "I've never seen another ship there, but we'll scan before committing, just in case."

"Agreed."

They broke orbit and headed in on both engines. V'kyrri huddled over the engineering panel as if holding the starboard fuel feed valve together by willpower alone. The ship shuddered into the atmosphere. Turrel shook his head as they rounded into position for final descent.

"Nothing there," he said.

"Initiating landing sequence," Ari said.

"Acknowledged." Seaghdh glanced at her. "Will we need your father for clearance?"

"On Kebgra? Hell no. Their notion of customs and clearance is to invite you to supper and ask if you're married to more than three spouses."

Seaghdh grinned. "Sounds like my kind of world."

They set down with a thump. Still nothing from the locals.

"Ari, Turrel, with me," Seaghdh said.

She led the way to the hatch and cycled open the air lock. Seaghdh stepped past her and sauntered down the ramp. She followed. It wasn't until they'd set foot to the pale lavender dust at the bottom of the ramp that a breeze blew away the scent of metal hot from entry. She drew in an experimental breath and frowned.

"Do you smell that?" she murmured.

Seaghdh wrinkled his forehead in concentration and nodded. "Yeah. I do."

"Back!" Ari ordered, instinct screaming. It was death she smelled. "Seal the ship!"

They backed up the ramp, Seaghdh coming in last to cover their retreat. "Sindrivik? Get sensors online and moving!"

"Recalibrating to read biosigns," Sindrivik acknowledged.

"No farther than the outer lock!" Ari said. "If this is a pathogen, we're exposed."

"V'kyrri!" Seaghdh hollered into intraship. "Break open those weapons lockers. I need rifles."

"There's an equipment port, vacuum sealed," Ari said. "Right beside the air-lock door."

"Got it!" V'kyrri answered.

Turrel brought the rifles. Ari tried not to notice he hadn't brought one for her.

"V'kyrri, bring two more rifles and report to the air lock."

"Aye, Captain."

Seaghdh leaned close, setting off a flutter in her belly. "Ari. Advisability of consulting your father?"

"Without some notion as to what we're facing, I don't know," she confessed. "When I'm an officer of the Armada, I suspect incursion. Aboard the *Sen Ekir*, I think of disease first."

He flashed her a grin. "Feeling schizophrenic, Captain?"

"Not according to the psych tests I completed this morning."

He chuckled. "Point."

She flushed.

"Ready to exit," V'kyrri said from the air-lock com.

"Establish positive airflow, V'kyrri," Ari instructed. "The panel beside the crew door has a command series for ship air and for atmosphere. Switch it to ship air and pull pressure up until the indicators read yellow. It will keep external air from contaminating the ship and it will be safe to exit."

"Aye."

Turrel glanced between her and Seaghdh. "We switched to atmosphere when we landed."

"It's scrubbed," she said. "Until you open the air locks and cargo doors without positive air pressure on board, anything coming into the ship is automatically sterilized. It's also why the water tastes like crap."

"Let me install an oxygenator," V'kyrri said as he slipped out the door and struggled to seal it behind him. "I'll have your water tasting like a mountain stream."

"My father would explain that the mountain stream you favor tastes the way it does because of the animal excrement contaminating it."

"Charming."

"Captain, the sensors were meant to be used from orbit. Range is limited planetside," Sindrivik said via the com.

"By the curvature of the damned planet," Ari countered, sudden fear making her heart tremble.

"Yeah," Sindrivik said. She disliked his grim tone. "Nothing. Not a single humanoid life sign within range of these sensors."

She'd started shaking her head before he'd even started talking. "No. That can't be right. There're two major settlements . . ."

"Nothing, Captain," Sindrivik repeated, sympathy in his voice.

She sucked in a sharp breath, staggered, and stared at Seaghdh. "Can't be an outbreak," she wheezed.

He frowned and hefted the muzzle of his rifle higher. "No?"

"Every illness leaves survivors," she said, choking back a curse. In trying to minimize the risk to her father and his crew, she'd dropped them straight into a body count. She'd run out of options.

Seaghdh spun to stare out the open hatch. "Sindrivik! Get me ships!"

"Already on it, Captain," the man replied. "Nothing in range."

"Keep those eyes on and this line stays open."

"Mr. Sindrivik. Free the scientists," Ari said. "Put me on ship-wide."

"Captain Seaghdh?" Sindrivik prompted.

Seaghdh took one look at her grim face and said, "Do it."

"Aye," Sindrivik said.

Ari waited through a series of clicks and muted beeps as the young man in the cockpit patched her into ship-wide.

"You're on," Sindrivik said.

Ignoring the prickle behind her eyes, she faced the com so she wouldn't have to watch the betrayal dawn in Seaghdh's eyes and said, "Initiate Level Two Containment. Authorization, Captain Alexandria Idylle. Repeat. Initiate Level Two Containment."

A flurry of voices competed for the com line.

"Medical emergency override!" Raj bellowed. "Clear this channel! All personnel, report, by the numbers!"

"Dr. Linnaeus Idylle, cabin."

"Pietre Ivanovich, cabin."

"Dr. Raj Faraheed, medical," Raj said, a hint of annoyance in his voice. "Our doors are unlocked. Get out there and initiate containment!"

"Jayleia Durante, cargo."

Ari resisted the urge to glance at the men behind her and said, "Captain Ari Idylle, Captain Cullin Seaghdh, Kirthin Turrel, V'kyrri. External. Kebgra. You're next, Sindrivik."

"L—Damen Sindrivik, piloting," Sindrivik said, tripping over trying not to say his rank.

"Ari?" Raj commanded. "Report."

"We've put down on Kebgra," she replied. "No response to hails. Bioscans . . ."

"I see them," her father interjected. He swore. "No biosigns?"

"No, sir," Sindrivik replied on the open channel. "Scans are limited by the curvature of the planet."

"Not a single survivor," Dad mused.

"Not the hallmark of a plague, Ari," Raj said.

Her chest tightened. What was worse? Hoping the people of Kebgra had been attacked and killed? Or sickened and killed?

"We won't know until we finish recon," Ari answered. "I'll bring back samples if I can, but I want containment for them and for us until we're certain."

"Agreed," her father said.

"Very well." She sighed and rubbed a hand across her forehead. She felt Seaghdh's gaze and glanced at him.

He lifted an eyebrow.

Longing raked her insides to bloody ribbons. In a different place, in a different time, she would have enjoyed succumbing to the teasing duels they'd been fighting since stepping off the blade grid. Enough.

Tapping into a sterile, dead part of her psyche, Ari slammed the door on feeling and forced herself to turn back to the com. "*Sen Ekir*, Captain Alexandria Idylle. Activation code 004-AA679-Idylle-Prime."

"What the hell . . ." her father grated.

"*Sen Ekir*," an unfamiliar computerized voice droned. "Authorization, Captain Alexandria Idylle. 004-AA679-Iydlle-Prime, acknowledged. Course laid. Lockdown complete."

"Oh, my Gods, 004," Raj groaned. "That's—Ari, you're IntCom."

She dropped her chin to her chest. This was not a conversation she wanted to have under these circumstances. She'd hoped to never have it, even though she'd wondered why it had taken a bunch of brilliant scientists so long to figure out why a career Prowler captain went on every single one of their missions.

"What have you done?" her father demanded. "We disabled all of IntCom's . . ."

"No," she said. "You disabled the packages IntCom left for you to find. What they did not want you to find, you didn't."

"The *Sen Ekir* is locked to a command set preprogrammed by IntCom," she told her father. "If worse comes to worst and you are forced to lift without us, the ship will take you directly to Tagreth. You will go in broadcasting on all IntCom channels. If that happens, Dad, I ask that you see Sindrivik returned to his people as soon as possible."

"Alexandria," he growled, "damn it. Your duty . . ."

"The irony of being captured by the Chekydran and accused of spying," she said, her voice sounding curiously dead to her, "is that it was true. My duty is to IntCom."

"You're a captain of the Armada!"

"I was. You'll notice I've been relieved of that command. IntCom did not relieve me."

"You know that was an oversight, you psychopathic bitch!" Pietre interjected.

"Was it?" she asked.

"IntCom doesn't forget, Pietre," Jayleia snapped, her tone sharp. She would know. Her father held an IntCom post of some kind. According to her, not even she knew what he did.

"Mr. Sindrivik," Ari said. "If we encounter trouble of any sort, under no circumstances are you or the scientists to leave this ship."

"Further," Seaghdh said, pushing his way in beside her, his shoulder touching hers when the space in the air lock didn't strictly require it. "We miss two check-ins, you lift. Do not attempt to aid or assist in any way."

"Aye, Captains."

Captains. Coming from one of his men. She liked the sound of it. Loneliness melted away and the lid she'd closed on her emotions edged open. A tiny sliver of hope lodged in her heart. Seaghdh had chosen to stand shoulder to shoulder with her rather than fire a laser bolt into her back.

"Alex."

Ari paused in turning away from the com as Seaghdh started down the ramp. "Yes, Dad."

"What is your assignment?"

With a grim smile, she said, "You."

Her dad swore.

She turned back to find Seaghdh blocking her path.

He studied her, his eyes bright, and his head cocked to one side and stunned her by offering his Autolyte. "You'll want a weapon."

She closed a hand around the stock, unable to speak around the lump in her throat. He didn't release it. Meeting his eye, she waited. She couldn't tell him she wouldn't turn on him. Once she knew what was happening, she might. Duty required it. What she wanted had no bearing on the situation. Problem was, Seaghdh knew it. All of it. But she was a warrior, trained in combat, tactics, and recon. Only he could decide how far he was willing to trust her. And for how long.

To her surprise, he grinned when she met his gaze. "Ari, you're a spy!"

"Something that should stand me in great stead on your side of the zone," she noted. "I'm not. Not really. They wanted someone watching out for Dad."

"He didn't know."

"No," she said.

"Do the Chekydran know?" he asked.

She blinked. She couldn't see why it mattered. "About my babysitting job? I neglected to mention it."

A slow, contagious smile spread on his face, but the pride burning in him warmed her. Scorched her.

"I've been looking for a way to recruit you, Captain. You just handed me the justification. You're with me," he finally said, letting go of the gun. "What's out there?"

"Two settlements," Ari replied, ignoring the flutter of her heart at the mention of being recruited. "Farms and cropland in between. Limited cover once we leave this tree line. From here, S-One is south by southeast, a click or so away. S-Two is due east, maybe a click and a half. Major temple site and provincial capital."

"Roads? Trails?"

"No," she said. "They weren't fundamentalists. Hover and flight technology was acceptable to them." It hurt her to speak in past tense of the cheerful, happy-go-lucky people who had always waved them into town as if they were long-lost relations come to dinner. She had to clear her throat.

"We might find a hauler behind the depot," she said.

Seaghdh nodded, indicating that she should proceed down the ramp. Ari eased the safety off the rifle, scanned the trees, and jogged across the open space to the building. When she glanced back from beside the shack, she saw Seaghdh, Turrel, and V'kyrri covering her from the ship. Proper application of a gun in her back. Good. They'd trust her with the Autolyte, and she'd trust them with weapons at her back. It had occurred to her that this mystery would make a very convenient accident. Take the Armada officer out into an unknown situation, even arm her and then shoot her while everyone else is occupied.

Seaghdh raced across the barren landing pad while she scanned the tree line. Turrel and V'kyrri followed. She rounded the building and swore.

"Nothing?" Seaghdh surmised.

Ari shook her head and kicked open the door of the depot.

"What are you doing?" he demanded.

"We do still need a part for the starboard engine," she said, scanning the orderly interior. Nothing out of place, no bodies, no sign of what might have happened.

V'kyrri crowded past her and sorted hurriedly through a box of fuel-feed couplers.

"They're dead, V'k," she said. "Take the box."

"You don't know that," he countered. "They could be in hiding, underground, out of reach of sensors."

She sucked in a breath. Why the hell hadn't she thought of that? "I hope you're right."

"We don't have time for this," Seaghdh said, as V'k looked for a match.

V'kyrri straightened. "Got it."

"I'll take it," she said.

The men stared at her.

"No one's shot at us so far," she said, "but if we have to risk someone crossing the open landing pad again, you can most afford to risk me."

"Maybe those bugs did get to your brain, Captain," Turrel said, taking the part from V'kyrri's hands. "'Cause that is one piss-poor assessment. V'k works on the ship. You got something in your head our employers want and the captain is the brains of the operation. I'm the expendable one here and you know it. That's the problem with you Armada officers. You aren't willing to order someone to do something you wouldn't do yourselves. Cover me and try not to shoot me in the back."

"You don't trust me not to hijack my own ship out from under you," she said, bracing her shoulder against the building and bringing the rifle to bear on the silent landing pad.

"Looks to me like you already have," he said before sprinting across the field. He secured the part in the air lock and spent a moment syncing a handheld with shipboard computers, something she should have done.

Seaghdh nodded and took her place when she glanced at him. She flipped open her pad and linked up. For Seaghdh's benefit, she brought over all the data for Kebgra, topography, settlement layout, arcane bits of local chemistry, even notes about the poisonous plants in the region. She gave it to V'kyrri, took his handheld, and did the same thing while Turrel crossed back to their location.

"No life signs, no ships," he said.

She finished the link on the last pad and put it back on her belt. "From the smell, I'm guessing the settlers have been dead for a day or two. Enough time for a strike team to get in and get back out."

"Why?" Seaghdh asked. The tone of his question made it clear he wasn't asking her. It was the question they all wanted answered. He shook his head. "Turrel, V'k, take S-Two. Com link stays up at all times, no chatter. Check in at five minute marks. Two missed check-ins, retreat to the ship. Do not attempt recon. Get off world and authorize the project."

Ari snapped to attention, frowning. "What project?"

"Aye," the men said. Neither of them would look at her.

Damn it. The adaptable, flexible Claugh military always had a contingency plan. Seaghdh intended to authorize an invasion of Tagreth Federated. They'd have to launch through United Mining and Ore Processing Guild space, which was precisely where his rendezvous was located. Talk about clandestine alliances. Not even her IntCom lockdown of the *Sen Ekir* would slow them down.

CHAPTER

10

IT concerned Seaghdh that it took half an hour to find the first bodies. He'd pushed the pace, maybe unfairly, but Ari hadn't complained.
Apprehension lined her face as they searched the outlying homes and
farm buildings. Every single one looked like the occupants would be
returning at any moment. Two of the houses had lunch on the table,
untouched, except for insects.

As they jogged into Settlement-1, a village of wood and stone
buildings built around a central stone well, she jerked her chin at a
tiny clapboard building. "Chapel."

Seaghdh raised an eyebrow but didn't answer. He stopped at the
foot of the wooden steps leading up to the door, shouldered his rifle
and took a deep breath to slow his heartbeat. Uneasiness walked a
prickle down his spine. The smell of death was stronger. She stood
beside him, moisture on her forehead, the butt of the Autolyte tucked
against her waist. Disquiet stark in her frown, she nodded.

Seaghdh went noiselessly up the steps and opened the door. The
cloying, sickly sweet scent of rot rolled over him. The buzz of insects

droned loud in the interior. Ari, rifle hanging, one sleeve covering her nose and mouth, pushed past him. She made it halfway down the aisle before she stopped dead, the muscles of her back and shoulders rigid.

The corpses slumped in the pews and chairs. Several had tumbled to the floor. Seaghdh lowered his weapon and sighed.

Ari spun and barreled out the door, gagging. He watched her go, knowing she hadn't told him everything regarding her involvement with these people, knowing he couldn't offer any comfort. She stopped in the center of the village. Her head hanging, she braced her hands against the well and sucked in great gulps of air.

He ventured into the chapel to confirm what he already suspected. He didn't need to go far to see what had killed the colonists. Clutching his rifle so hard his fingers ached, he left the building.

"Cancel containment," she rasped as he leaned a hip on the well.

"Alexandria?" Dr. Idylle's voice on the open com was tight with dread.

"They were shot," Ari said. "Every last one."

The man swore, his tone bleak and ragged. "Canceling containment."

Seaghdh studied her as she wiped moisture from her face. "You okay?"

She straightened and crossed her arms, as if holding back the misery he could see raging through her.

"You knew they'd be in the chapel. How?" he asked.

"We didn't just stop here sometimes," she said, not meeting his eye.

"Every time?"

"And then some. TFC doesn't run supply shipments to worlds this far out. Colonies live or die on their own merits. At least, until they produce something TFC wants."

Seaghdh nodded. "So the Prowler captain ran the occasional supply shipment for her friends?"

Slanting him an unhappy glance, she shrugged. "Patrolling the buffer zone brought us out here pretty regularly."

"I see."

"No. You don't." Taking a deep breath, she unclipped her ship's badge and eased it into her back pocket.

Seaghdh folded his badge in his fist. Whatever she had to say, she didn't want it broadcast on the open channel. "Go on."

"I vacationed here, Seaghdh. They didn't just accept me, they liked me. They dangled their unwed men in front of me every single trip, trying to keep me." She scrubbed her face with her hands and swore, avoiding his eye.

"Were you ever tempted?" Seaghdh blinked. They were on a potentially hazardous recon, had found her friends murdered, and he asked that?

Her expression bleak when she finally looked at him, she said, "Once."

He had to look away, swallowing an unexpected lash of jealousy. "Is he in there?"

"I don't know," she replied, desolation ringing in her tone. "I couldn't . . . the family I stayed with. They're there. Third row. Their youngest daughter. They'd named her Rose."

Seaghdh ached at the catch in her voice. Before he could conquer the impulse, he cupped her cheek, smoothing his thumb over her skin. "I'm sorry."

A blush crept up her face as she stared at him, wide-eyed. He'd noticed how much darker blue her eyes were planetside and guessed that she wore photo-restrictive lenses. Damn it, he was on a mission. He had no business noticing anything about her. He drew away and released his badge.

Ari shifted, retrieved her badge and affixed it to her shirt pocket. "It's like they were murdered by machines. I've never seen that kind of precision or cold, calculated execution. No brutality. No cruelty."

"Men, women, children. Even the damned infants. Single shot each." Seaghdh swore, spun, and slapped a hand against the stone well. A pebble fell. It took several long seconds to hit water.

"No enemy bodies," she said. "I sure would like to know who—or *what*—the hell they were."

Seaghdh shook his head. "There's not a single scorch mark or broken window in the entire settlement."

"No strike team is this clean. It's not possible."

"A few months ago, I'd have agreed," he replied, staring into the dark well.

Ari didn't answer.

He glanced at her. She stood motionless, her head cocked, eyes closed. A tepid breeze, smelling of green growing things and sun-warmed soil caressed them. A thin, frightened wail echoed up from the well.

Her eyes snapped open.

"Survivors," he breathed.

"Incoming!" Sindrivik shouted over the com. "Repeat! Incoming! Six blips, entering atmosphere. Damn it! They're right on top of you! Approaching from west northwest!"

"On top of who?" Seaghdh demanded, adrenaline dumping a boulder into his chest.

"You!" Sindrivik replied.

Ari ran for the north wall of the chapel. Seaghdh followed on her heels, scanning the western horizon. She shifted her rifle to her shoulder. He saw them before he heard them. He'd never seen a configuration remotely like the small, fast, single-occupant ships.

Frowning, Ari stepped away from the chapel wall. "What the hell are those?"

Seaghdh grabbed her, yanked her against his chest, and wedged her between the unyielding wall and him. He tucked his face into her hair. Even after everything they'd been through, it smelled like exotic honey. The warmth of her body where it pressed against his roused every single nerve ending.

"That proof you wanted?" he rumbled next to her ear, trusting that their ship badges wouldn't pick up his words over the howl of fighter engines. "This is it. Three Claugh colonies have been hit in the past several months. All exactly like . . ."

The shriek of engines drowned him out. He felt her clench her fists. She undoubtedly intended to make someone pay for murdering the innocents of Kebgra.

The engine noise faded. Ari slipped out from under the dubious protection he'd offered. "Where'd they come from?" she demanded.

"Unidentified mother ship in orbit, Captain!" Sindrivik replied.

Seaghdh swore.

"Get back here!" Dr. Idylle ordered. "So we can get off this world!"

"Negative," Seaghdh replied. "We're too far out. And if we send you into orbit, you'll be a target for that mother ship. Sindrivik." Knowing he was risking Ari's trust, knowing he had no choice, Seaghdh switched to his own language. Sindrivik answered in kind.

Ari raised an eyebrow at him.

He covered his ship badge with one hand and waited for her to do the same. Looking like someone waiting for the other shoe to drop, she did.

"My ship," he whispered. "It's within hailing." He uncovered his badge.

She started, eyes wide, and let her hand drop to her side.

"You can't lift the lockdown from here, can you?" he surmised.

"While I'm in enemy hands being tortured to accomplish those ends?" she replied. "Of course not."

"Keyed to genetic imprint?"

She nodded. "Retinal and print scans."

"Sindrivik? Please tell me you have communications."

"A few seconds, Captain," Sindrivik replied.

Ari cursed. Seaghdh gathered that she hadn't realized that Sindrivik was the best systems wizard in the Claugh nib Dovvyth. The young man could have had his pick of careers and lived very comfortably. Seaghdh wiped the sweat from his face and wondered if Sindrivik thought joining the Murbaasch Tu was the adventure he'd hoped for.

"What about the *Sen Ekir*'s fuel valve?" Ari demanded. "They won't have power for lift without . . ."

"It's in," Pietre snapped.

She barked a single laugh. "You damned spiteful bastard. Good work."

"Captain!" Turrel hollered over the open com.

Seaghdh and Ari glanced at one another at the scream of fighter engines in the background. "Flyby! They're coming around. Headed your way!"

"Acknowledged."

"Communications online!" Sindrivik cried. "Response to our distress call! Claugh nib Dovvyth carrier on routine patrol! She's an hour out! Get back to the ship!"

"No time!" Ari replied. "Lift! Now! Put the planet between you and the mother ship!"

"Alex," her father grated, "we won't abandon you . . ."

"Yes, you will!" she countered. "The fighters are back, Dad. If we run, we'll lead them to you. Now get out of here! Close open channel! Going to planetside com badges only!"

Six ships swept low over the town. The noise of their engines changed pitch. Light shimmered next to the well.

"They're porting in!" Seaghdh yelled, lifting the rifle and peppering the teleport shimmer with fire.

"Porting? That makes no sense! Why not land?" Ari added her shots. A second, then a third teleport distortion appeared on either side of the first.

"Why ask me? Where are the other three?" Seaghdh demanded, glancing wildly around.

A humanoid form materialized in the center of Settlement-1. Ari swore. Seaghdh's attention snapped full front. He echoed her curse.

"Save some fun for us," Turrel rasped over the open com.

"Our weapons have no effect," Ari said.

"Wonderful news," V'k grumbled.

The second shimmer resolved, then the third. They had once been humanoid or from one of the related races, but their bodies had been distorted, mutated into grotesque parodies of the humanoid shape. Their eyes were dead, flat white. Even from several meters away, Seaghdh could see veins distended and pulsing. Bulges of tissue and muscle where tissue and muscle didn't belong strained against repulsive, ocher, bio-organic armor. It reminded him of the chitinous exoskeletons he knew from the corpse beetles of his home world.

Seaghdh grabbed Ari's arm. She didn't move. Glancing at her, he paused. The haunted, sick look in her face struck him. He should pursue it, find out what she knew or was remembering, after they were safe.

He sprinted for the tree line half a kilometer away. Ari jounced along in his wake until she found her stride.

"No good!" she gasped. "They're on us. Tracking."

And firing. When they broke from the cover of the buildings, laser fire sizzled into the dirt behind them. Seaghdh scowled. Evidence suggested they were better shots than that.

Weaving to avoid the bursts of energy, he began to notice a pattern. The rate of fire increased, singeing the plants and soil, when he swung toward the trees.

Ari jerked out of his grasp and kicked his legs out from under him. He landed hard. As she dove to the ground, he saw the shimmer of another teleport distortion. She rolled to one side.

"Incoming 'port!" she shouted. "We're being herded!"

"They're on a trap-and-capture order, Ari, or we'd already be dead," he snapped. "Get to the trees!"

Cursing, Ari came to one knee and brought the rifle up. The three soldiers had stopped firing. They strode through the field, their deliberate pace never wavering.

Seaghdh saw the rifle in her grasp tremble. What was she . . . He stared at the soldier she'd sighted on. Scorch marks in the armor. So they weren't impervious to weapon's fire.

She eased her finger to the trigger and squeezed. The shot went wide.

"What are you . . ." Seaghdh began.

Ari fired another shot. It missed the leader. The soldier behind his right shoulder, however, stopped dead as the burst of energy impacted the side of his face. His limbs twitched as if he couldn't control them. Static crackled in the air before him.

Seaghdh dropped to the soil beside Ari, took aim, and swiftly placed three bolts into the leader's head, then another series of bolts into the third soldier's face. Without waiting to gauge the effect, Seaghdh hauled Ari to her feet and urged her into the trees just as the other three soldiers materialized from teleport.

They turned on their heels as one and followed.

"Looks like the capture order has been rescinded," Ari gasped.

Seaghdh risked a look back. The soldiers trailed them easily, their pace much faster than the first three. They'd raised their weapons, but weren't firing. The four colony sites he'd seen flashed through his memory, nothing broken, no burn marks, all the victims dispatched with a single shot.

He swore and struggled to put more trees between the two of them and their followers. "Definitive search and destroy," he affirmed. "Turrel?"

"Hold them off for a few more minutes!" V'kyrri shouted.

"Head shots," Ari managed to get out before a tree limb swiped her in the face. Blood oozed from a cut across one cheek.

"Negative, Captain," V'kyrri answered, his voice tight with effort. "I can't get a lock on them. It's like they aren't there."

Seaghdh's heart squeezed hard. "Belay that!" he shouted. He hadn't told her what V'kyrri was capable of, and he desperately needed to explain before she worked it out.

Pain showed in the crinkles of confusion surrounding Ari's eyes. Seaghdh lurched to one side as his foot slid out from under him. Fighting for balance, he loosed his hold on Ari. She ran several meters, before she seemed to realize she'd lost him and turned, hesitating.

He cast a glance back at their pursuit as he found his footing again. The soldiers ignored him. They'd turned for Ari. His heart clenched hard and he swore.

She echoed him. "They're after me. Why?"

Seaghdh sprinted into the underbrush, keeping the soldiers in his line of sight, but swinging wide enough to stay out of range of their weapons. He hoped. Ignoring the sting of whipping branches and burn of weary muscles, he jumped a deadfall before angling the direction he'd last seen Ari.

She'd run but not far. Good.

He stopped, brought his rifle up, and cursed. Trees and brush obscured his shot. At least he'd gotten far enough ahead that he could afford the time to find the clearest line of fire.

"Ari," he said to the com badge, "this way. Bring them to me."

"Negative," V'kyrri countered, his voice tinny on the com channel. "I've got survivors, Captain! She's headed straight for them. They've been shielded underground. They know we're here."

Damn it! V'kyrri hadn't stopped reading. How much had Ari picked up? Had she . . .

One of the soldiers jerked to a halt, turned, and opened fire directly on his position. How the hell were those things tracking? He fired, using the flashes of energy to target in on the soldier's face. It took three shots before the creature twitched and stopped firing. A high-pitched shriek built as sparks coalesced before the soldier's face. Light and energy flared. Seaghdh shielded his eyes.

When he could look at the creature again, its face was gone, blown away by some force from within. Swallowing hard, Seaghdh forced himself to his feet and struggled into a jog after Ari.

Two soldiers advanced on her. In seconds, they'd be within weapons range. While he was close enough to fire on the soldiers, his angle was wrong. He couldn't help her.

"Turrel!" he shouted.

He spotted movement behind Ari. Then Seaghdh heard it, V'kyrri coaching Ari over the com channel, directing her. He shoved his aching body into a sprint, letting V'kyrri's words guide him.

The trees thinned. Huge, craggy fingers of rock stood, poking up through the forest floor, as if replacing the trees. Seaghdh wove and dodged, desperate for a glimpse of Ari and her pursuers. She couldn't have gotten far.

"Down!" a male voice bellowed.

Seaghdh flung himself behind a stone finger. Belatedly, he realized he recognized the voice. Flashes of weapons fire and another high-pitched shriek confirmed that Turrel had found them at last.

"Captain!" Turrel's dread-laden tone brought Seaghdh instantly around the rock, racing toward Ari and the last soldier.

The creature had cleared weapons range and trained its gun on Ari. Seaghdh's heart leaped into his throat.

Ari stood rigid, facing the last soldier as he stalked her. The look of horrified recognition in her face stabbed ice through Seaghdh's stomach.

"Lieutenant Heisen!" she commanded. "Stand down!"

CHAPTER

11

AS the remaining soldier drew closer, Ari felt as if her heart was being ripped a centimeter at a time from her chest. Once upon a time, that thing had been Tommy Heisen, a junior crewmember under her command. He'd piloted her shuttle when they'd been captured. She'd always hoped the unfailingly cheerful lieutenant had met a clean death. Looking at the misshapen hulk the Chekydran had turned him into, she wondered whether anything remained of the young man she'd known.

"Lieutenant Heisen! Stand down!" Ari repeated, desperate to reach through that obscene armor, past everything that had been done to him. He had to still be in there. Somewhere. He had to. Or she was dead.

"Tommy," she said, putting on her best "the captain is speaking" tone, hoping military conditioning could break through. She willed him to hear, to understand. "It's Captain Idylle. I need you to think, Lieutenant. We were captured. Do you remember? Fight them. Don't let the Chekydran win, Tommy."

He wavered. The barrel of his gun drooped.

"I need your help, Tommy," she pressed, latching hold of the crewman she imagined was trapped inside the monster's body. "I can't survive without you. Fight them. Don't make me tell your mother that the Chekydran won."

He stopped, struggle evident in the visible tremor in his limbs and in his tortured expression.

Ari heard movement behind her and saw Seaghdh maneuvering for a clear shot. She ignored both to focus on her lieutenant. Her breath coming in short gusts, she approached him, aware that programming could reclaim him at any moment.

"Good man, Lieutenant," she said, staring him in the eye, not knowing if he could even see. "You're doing it. Remember. I need you to remember who you are."

Ari knew the moment Tommy Heisen broke through the Chekydran programming. Something snapped and she *felt* him break free like a swimmer rising from deep water. She saw him suddenly appear behind those milky eyes. His terror and despair leaped out at her. Pain lodged in her chest, stealing her voice.

He screamed and collapsed to the ground, his arms covering his head.

Shaking, she dropped to her knees in the dirt and put a hand on his shoulder.

"Gone," he cried, quaking. "They're gone. Can't hold."

"You did it, Tommy. You beat them," she said. "Thank you."

He sucked in an audible breath and drew his arms away from his face to look at her. The fear slipped from his eyes. She could almost see him smile. It felt like a kick to her gut.

"Kill," he whispered.

A hard, bitter knot swelled in the center of her chest. "Yes."

"Here." He lifted his chin.

"Rest, Lieutenant," Ari said. "Rest."

He reclined into the leaf mold and soil, his expression serene, trusting.

She tucked the muzzle of the Autolyte under his chin, making certain the gun didn't actually touch him.

"Tell?" the man's voice cracked.

She squeezed her eyes shut, then forced them back open, despite the burn. "Tell who? Your family? Yes. I can do that. They will be proud of you, Tommy. I know I am."

A single tear escaped down his cheek. She choked on the tears she couldn't shed and pulled the trigger.

Ari shook at the rage and hatred coursing through her. Rational thought retreated. She ached to destroy Chekydran. Any Chekydran. Her vision hazed. She heard her breath coming in ragged rasps as she struggled to remember where she was, who she was.

"Ari?"

She knew that voice trying to reach her from so far away, but then one of them touched her. Growling in outrage, she struck center mass, hard. It fell away, crying out in pain when it fetched up hard against a solid surface. She sprang to her feet, crouching, waiting. Where there was one, there were more.

"Back away." Another voice. It, too, felt familiar.

"What is it?" the first voice wheezed. "What's happening to her?"

"A flashback. She is very dangerous."

"Want help, Captain?"

"No," a sharp retort. "Back off."

Chekydran talking strategy. Her lip curled. Did they care that she'd learned to understand them? Leaves rustled. She lashed out again to have her blow blocked and her wrist wrapped in a hard grip. Fury, sharpened by an edge of panic, took possession of her. She exploded, biting, kicking, hitting, and shrieking.

"Damn it, Ari! Stop it before I put you over my knee!"

Something, the desperation, the anguish in that voice, pierced the primitive flood of fight-or-flight chemicals fogging her brain and she knew him. Seaghdh. She slumped and uttered the filthiest single word she knew.

Gingerly, arms closed around her. She felt him nod.

"Yeah," he said.

"Sorry," she rasped.

"I'll live."

Her eyesight cleared and she found herself looking at Tommy Heisen's body. She shuddered. Seaghdh's grasp tightened. How could she have recovered so quickly? It couldn't be Cullin Seaghdh. She wouldn't let it be. If she became dependent on his presence, on him, she'd be as much a prisoner as she had been aboard the Chekydran cruiser.

"Ari," he rumbled, resting his forehead against her hair. "I'm sorry. If you'd given me a few seconds more, I would have spared you . . ."

Ari twisted out of his arms, shoved herself to her feet, and plastered a thoroughly regulation expression on her face. "Don't coddle me, Captain," she said. "He was my crewman and therefore my duty. No one else had the right."

Blotting blood from his mouth with the back of one hand, Seaghdh nodded.

She'd done that to him. Guilt raked her.

"At least you didn't break his nose, Alexandria," a familiar male voice said from behind her.

She turned, hardly daring to believe she'd heard right. "Augustus." A sore spot in her heart eased.

The man who'd once tempted her to stay on Kebgra grinned at her. The memory felt old, like it had happened a very long time ago.

"I am relieved to see you safe," he said. "You will want to bury your crewman, I take it? Shall I take the rest of your men below? Or do you wish to tend to your Chosen's injuries yourself?"

"He . . ." She stopped short and glanced at Seaghdh as he climbed to his feet, shooting a speculative look first at Augie, then at her. Was that jealousy in his eye?

Seaghdh. Her Chosen. Honest mistake. One she'd have to let stand while they were on Kebgra because Seaghdh wasn't going to let her out of his sight regardless of cultural mores.

"Thank you, Augie," she said. "I would like to bury Tommy, but shouldn't we get shielded? I can't risk exposing you or the other survivors."

"My people engaged the mother ship and are in pursuit," Seaghdh said. "They have other things to worry about than sending in more soldiers."

She nodded and slid a glance at Seaghdh. She owed the man an apology at the very least for injuring him. He couldn't help it that she responded to him. Or could he? Just how far could he imbed compulsion when he used his vocal talent on someone? Did she care? For the first time in six months, she felt as if she'd reclaimed a lost part of her. Damn if she wasn't starting to crave his brand of therapy.

Ari put a hand on Seaghdh's arm. "I'd like help burying him. Would you be willing? I'll patch you up when we're done."

His expression lit from within as he closed warm fingers over hers and she realized what she'd done. For the first time, she'd reached for him of her own volition. The golden fire in his eyes and the tantalizing caress of his thumb on the back of her hand drove fierce, pointed want straight through her core.

"He was a good man, Captain," he said. "Just show me where. Turrel?"

Surprise lit through her. Turrel? He and V'kyrri should still be en route. She realized the big man lounged against a tall, thin standing stone, watching with a neutral eye.

"The boy fought off the Chekydran when the chips were down," Turrel replied. "He deserves a proper send-off. Count me in."

She carried the oversized and outdated mobile teleport unit that would dig the hole for them. Seaghdh and Turrel dragged the corpse to the makeshift graveyard Augie and his handful of survivors had been using to inter the few settlers' bodies they'd been able to recover so far. Once she'd programmed and activated the noisy teleport console, Ari removed her ship's badge from her pocket and tucked it inside Tommy's armor.

Seaghdh raised an eyebrow.

"He's the most intact of the six," she said.

"You're going to dissect him?" Turrel boggled.

She sighed. "He can still help us. When your ship returns, we can transport him onboard. I can't leave him to the scavengers until that time. With a fully equipped research lab, we might be able to tell how he was modified. We'll then know something about methodology and purpose."

"I think the purpose is damned clear!"

"Why go to so much trouble for an army?" Ari pressed. "Think of the R and D time alone. The failures. It would be faster and cheaper to conscript, train, and equip a few hundred thousand soldiers or mercenaries."

"You think they have different intent for this technology," Seaghdh surmised.

"It might be useful to have a population of biddable slaves modified and enhanced for their tasks." She shrugged. "Sheer speculation. Without research, we'll never have anything more."

Seaghdh blew his breath out in a low whistle.

"Will your ship take the risk?"

"What risk?" Seaghdh demanded, his gaze sharp.

"I can't guarantee that death deactivates everything. There may be components in the body still broadcasting."

"We could be tracked," he said.

She nodded.

"I don't know," Seaghdh finally answered. "I can promise I will ask."

"Think our CO's pretty hot for everything she can get on these guys," Turrel said.

Seaghdh's look turned forbidding. "Let's get this done."

"Aye, Captain."

"One last transport," she announced. "Go ahead and get him in position."

They buried Tommy without much ceremony. What could she say? Any praise she might have for his dedication and heroism had played out before witnesses. Tommy's Pyrrhic victory over the Chekydran would be legend before she left this world.

Turrel gathered up the teleport unit. Seaghdh picked up the shovels and they trudged back the way they'd come.

Maybe she should have been consumed by self-pity, or some sense of loss, but as far as she was concerned, she'd lost Lieutenant Heisen six months ago, the day they'd been captured. If he'd endured three more months of Chekydran captivity than she had, at least in the end she'd helped him gain freedom. After three months in an alien prison, Ari was very clear that death did indeed represent liberation. It might have been less than compassionate, but her brain kept turning away from her dead lieutenant. Instead, it shoved snippets of conversation and flashes of impossible things into her awareness.

One of the impossible things walked beside her carrying a heavy teleport unit as if it were a toy. Turrel finally caught her watching him.

"What?" he demanded.

"Trying to work out your run speed, because that was a mighty quick trip from S-Two."

He nodded.

"So quick, V'kyrri should still be several minutes out," she said.

Turrel grinned without humor. "Now you know why someone would exterminate every last member of my race."

Ari straightened. "What? No! It was a plague . . . Wasn't it?"

He turned away without answering.

Shlovkora, Turrel's home world, had been administered by TFC, had, in fact, been a member of the governing council. She remembered the media-casts covering the unfolding disaster on Shlovkora—the illness, the swarm of doctors and researchers sent to help, the quarantine that went into place when most of them died, the staggering numbers of dead. She'd always wondered why TFC hadn't sent her father. He headed their very best research team. Now, Turrel's accusation of genocide, combined with her dad's exclusion from the research teams, made her wonder.

She tossed an uneasy glance at Seaghdh.

He lifted an eyebrow.

"The outbreak happened while we were on our third mission to Ioccal. We were too far away. Dad was so frustrated. He wanted so badly to help." She shook her head. "Do you know, even after it was over, no one would give him access to the samples or the data? Said there had been some kind of containment accident and all the samples and data were useless."

Turrel growled but said nothing.

"I've mounted run-of-the-mill offensives before," she groused. "I can't imagine the logistical nightmare and expense of genocide. It doesn't make sense."

"Since the Shlovkur opened their world to the rest of the galaxy a couple of generations ago," Seaghdh said, "there have been outcrosses with a few startling results."

Staring at him, she found herself shaking her head. "Meaning my government feared the natural development of some kind of super warrior race?" Only fear forced a government to overcome inertia and coordinate the kind of attack Turrel and Seaghdh wanted her to believe had been committed.

"Who the hell cares why they did it?" Turrel demanded, hefting the teleport unit to one shoulder.

"Trying to figure out how deep this goes, Turrel," she replied.

The big man grunted. Seaghdh looked vaguely like a man who had just dodged an energy bolt. Mentally, Ari checked off impossible thing number one and moved on to impossible thing number two on her list, Seaghdh's engineer, V'kyrri. While she'd been running for her life, she hadn't taken the time to analyze the bits of orders and explanations that had come across the com channel. She did now. V'kyrri had said he couldn't get a grip on the soldiers. He'd said that while he'd been kilometers away. A chill walked down her spine.

"Do you want to explain V'kyrri?" she asked. "Or did you want me to guess?"

Turrel laughed.

The relieved expression on Seaghdh's face evaporated. He shook his head. "He deserves the chance to explain it himself," he said. He activated his com. "V'kyrri?"

"Captain?" The engineer sounded breathless but cheerful.

"You blew your cover trying to get a grip on the soldiers, V'k."

"I warned you it wouldn't take long," V'kyrri replied. Good humor drained from his tone. He sounded almost resigned. "She's a smart gal."

"A smart gal." Ari sighed. The brightest thing she could think to say was, "Telepath, huh?"

"Aye, Captain," V'kyrri answered. She hardly recognized his voice, made tinny by the com and so serious.

"Would I know if you'd been rummaging around in my head?" she asked, looking straight at Seaghdh. Why else would you bring a telepath on a find and retrieve mission unless you intended to use him to read your retrieval subject?

Damn Seaghdh's hide, he didn't look the least discomfited by the question.

"I don't know," V'kyrri said. "Any training in your background?"

She blinked. "For what? Telepathy? No. TFC member races don't produce telepaths even as mutations. Interesting. Do you suppose that means the mutation on the genome renders the gamete nonviable?"

"No amount of telepathy on my part could possibly answer that question," V'kyrri said, his tone droll.

Heat flushed her face. "Sorry."

"I can give you a demo if you want," he offered. "In the meantime, I can swear that I haven't read you."

"Beyond knowing where I was in relation to Augie and the other survivors," she corrected.

"That's not reading, per se." V'kyrri sounded embarrassed and she spent a moment wondering what color his copper skin turned when the blood rushed to his face. "I can't turn that off, it's another sense, an awareness."

She nodded and wondered if she'd lost her mind. She believed him. "Okay. Thanks."

"My pleasure, Captain." The cheer, and a note of pleased surprise, returned to his voice.

"Do I need to come find you?" Turrel grumbled.

"Find yourself, slowpoke," V'kyrri said. "I'm in the caverns. And Captain Idylle? Thanks."

"What for?"

"You haven't developed a sudden case of fear and loathing for me," he said. Despite the habitual note of good spirits in his tone, she heard the hurt beneath it.

What kind of person would she be to suddenly dislike someone because of some aspect of his genetic profile? It would be like hating Seaghdh for his golden eyes. "I'm saving all that up for the Chekydran," she managed.

The men laughed.

She couldn't.

CHAPTER
12

SEAGHDH moved stiffly, walking like a man trying not to let on that he hurt. When he started opening and closing his left fist as if he'd lost feeling in the hand, fear flashed through Ari and she hurried to where Augie waited.

"Ari!" Augie waved them toward a rocky outcrop. "I apologize—"

"I'm sorry, Augie," she interrupted. "Welcome will have to wait."

"Good," he replied with a wry smile. "I was apologizing for having nothing to conduct the ceremony with."

"Please tell me you have Deaccolo tree antivenin."

"Not much more than that," he answered, eyeing the three of them.

"I need a medi-kit, the antivenin, and a place to treat this one." She jerked a thumb at Seaghdh, who awarded her a sour look. "Oh. Cullin Seaghdh, Kirthin Turrel, Augustus Ortechyn."

Seaghdh and Turrel nodded.

"Welcome, brothers," Augie said. "Alexandria is family among us. So will you be. Come. If you will permit me, Kirthin Turrel, I will take you to your friend. Our resources are limited, yet, but I can offer you food, drink, and a basic first-aid kit. When your man is well, Alexandria, we need to talk."

She nodded. "Agreed."

Turrel followed Augie into the labyrinth of caves.

Ari hesitated.

Seaghdh glanced at her, discomfort in the lines around his mouth. "Claustrophobic since your release?"

Ari squared her shoulders and looked away. He needed treatment. She didn't have time to indulge her legion of fears. "Let's go," she said.

When she caught up with Augie, he glanced back and a much older, much graver man than the boyish redhead she remembered met her gaze. "Treat your Chosen. Here. This room has been prepared for you."

The first-aid kit already sat on the pallet that served as a bed. She raised her eyebrows.

"Your Chosen took injury when you remembered too much," Augie said. "I anticipated the need."

Guilt closed its teeth on her rib cage. She broke other people's bones during flashbacks. Seaghdh had to be a skilled hand-to-hand fighter as well as resistant to protein-based poisons if he was just now symptomatic. How lucky was she that he hadn't broken one or two of her bones? It meant something that Seaghdh handled her far more carefully, more thoughtfully, than duty dictated.

Whatever it meant, she couldn't face it. Not yet. Augie left, pulling a thick hide curtain over the doorway as he exited. She turned to Seaghdh. She didn't know if she'd ever be able to look him in the eye and not flinch at what she'd started to believe she saw there.

Uncertainty made her terse. "Lose it." She nodded at Seaghdh's jacket and shirt.

"No need."

"I've seen everything there is to see, Seaghdh, and enjoyed it," she said. "Don't tell me you're wasting my time with macho cravuul dung."

"Did you?" he drawled, grinning, the desire flaring higher in his gaze. He drew a breath and flinched.

She crossed her arms, daring him to deny that he hurt.

He took off the jacket and shirt.

"Spawn of a . . ." She broke off and sighed at the sight of the ugly bruises on his torso. She laid a light finger against a lurid purple spot on his left flank. "Damn it, Seaghdh, I could have broken that rib. Why didn't you say something?"

"Wasn't your fault. Entirely," he replied, his voice pleasantly rough. "Unplanned arboreal introduction."

"Did this tree have thorns?" she asked.

"Definitely."

She'd hit him, thinking he was a Chekydran. Ari remembered his subsequent yelp of pain and swallowed a curse. Just her luck. She'd sucker punched him right into a venomous tree. She touched the skin below the bruise again, intrigued by the thrill that warmed her from the inside out.

An ache woke in the pit of her abdomen. She yanked her hand away. "Any numbness or tingling other than your left hand?"

He turned to her, a sly smile on his face. "Numbness? Left hand and arm. Tingling? Yes. It has nothing to do with that tree." He ran a fingertip across her cheek.

Her body tightened with need, and she knew exactly what he meant. She looked into his face, intending to call him to task by explaining the paralytic toxin exuded by the tree.

His gaze focused on her mouth, eyes glittering.

Sudden want flooded her body and every last rational thought drained from her head. Too close. Too unprotected. Too uncontrolled. She stepped back, her breath shallow and her heart thundering.

"Don't," he coaxed. "Don't pull away. I want to know the taste and feel of you, but I can wait."

She shuddered and wondered, despite the fear wracking her at being so vulnerable, whether she could wait. Clearing her tight throat, she gestured at the first-aid kit, desperate for distraction.

"Your arm and hand," she fumbled. "The thorns are poisoned. Let me . . ."

"Poisoned?" he echoed, frowning. "You aren't just trying to throw me off point, are you? Of all the unbelievable luck."

She knelt to draw a dose of antivenin and to examine the tools available in Augie's primitive first-aid kit. "I can't do much for the cuts and bruises, but I'd better dig that thorn out of your side before the paralytic reaches something vital. Make yourself comfortable."

The idiot grinned at her and waggled his eyebrows. "In your bed? I'll always be comfortable there, my Chosen."

A pang of—was it regret?—went through her. Why couldn't he have picked any other endearment than "Chosen"? The title could rightfully have been hers if she'd only made a different choice.

He knelt on the bed across from her. His hand closed over her wrist. "Ari, I'm sorry," he whispered.

She looked at him. Ari couldn't identify what she saw in his face. She only knew her pulse quickened and when his fingers slid from her arm and he lay down on his side, they were both smiling.

She injected the antivenin swiftly before going to work on his side.

"Damn it, Seaghdh," she said, examining the purple weal. "You might have told me about this before you dragged Tommy to the graveyard. The thorn burrowed deep."

"Then it's good the spot is mostly numb, isn't it?" he rumbled.

Mostly. Great. She swabbed his skin with antiseptic and cut into the straining, puckered flesh. Where was Raj when she needed him? She snorted. Of course. He was on the ship she'd programmed to abandon her on this world. And to this man.

She worked fast, searching for the broken tail of the thorn. Seaghdh's "mostly numb" would wear off when the antivenin kicked in. "Gotcha, you bastard," she murmured as she eased the thick splinter from Seaghdh's flesh.

His respiration sped up and turned shallow. The toxin had reached his diaphragm.

"Damn. Easy, Seaghdh. Nice, deep, even breaths. It'll get better in a minute."

She gave him another dose of antivenin and carefully cleaned the toxin from the gaping wound in his side. She knew the exact moment the antivenin conquered the poison.

Seaghdh groaned. Once his breathing normalized, she taped a tissue regeneration unit above the site and set it to seal and repair. At least with the unit working, his pain should diminish. He'd shut his eyes somewhere in the process, but she knew from the occasional tremor wracking him that he was awake.

"Can you roll to your back?" she asked. "Let me check the rest of your injuries."

He obeyed, turning gingerly. His right hand came to rest on her thigh.

Swearing at the rush of blood to her lower belly, she raised an eyebrow but wasted the gesture. He still had his eyes closed. The smile on his face, however, gave her to believe he thought he was getting away with something. Maybe two could play that game.

Admiring the lines of muscle delineating his chest and torso, she had to remind herself to assess his injuries. When she laid her hand beside a spongy-looking bruise on his stomach, the muscle twitched. She glanced at him. Eyes shut.

"That looks suspiciously like the right size for my elbow."

"It did get my attention," he mumbled in reply, sounding relaxed and half asleep.

Damn it. Why did he have to carbonate her blood? Just the sound of his voice dumped an intoxicating blend of hormones and adrenaline into her system. She felt things she had no business feeling. It was eroding her defenses.

She forced herself to switch on her handheld and look for internal bleeding. Shifting, she leaned closer. Seaghdh's hand moved to her hip. Fierce yearning sizzled down her spine.

No internal injuries, just one hell of a bruise. He'd risked death to find her and serious injury so that she wouldn't be alone in the midst of memory.

She squeezed her eyes shut and realized how badly she wanted to gamble on trusting Cullin Seaghdh. Opening her eyes, she smoothed a palm over the bruise. He shivered at her touch.

"I'm sorry," she said. "This could have been bad."

"I knew what I . . ."

Gently, she pressed her lips against the black-and-blue mark.

Seaghdh's hand curled into a trembling fist, and his breath hissed in between his teeth. It didn't sound at all like pain.

She drew back as her handheld beeped and reported an increase in heart rate, respiration, and blood pressure. In both of them. She turned it off and tucked it away.

Seaghdh's fist uncurled. He opened his eyes. "Unusual medical technique. I approve."

She rested both hands against his collarbones. No pain response. She ran her palms from shoulder to waist, pressing lightly, testing for soreness and cracked ribs. She found none. The texture of the fine, brown hair on his chest intrigued her. She allowed herself a moment to enjoy the sensation.

His eyes drifted shut again as if encouraging her.

Under different circumstances and with a door that locked, she'd be tempted to accept the invitation. Surprise rocked her at the thought. Armada captains didn't indulge in affairs and certainly not with the enemy. Sure, she owed him, but hadn't he made certain that she would?

Unsettled both by her train of thought and by the magnetic force Cullin Seaghdh exerted on her, she glanced around the tiny cave. It was nearly the same size as a Chekydran cell. What if she wasn't free? What if everything, her release, her "recovery," her father, Seaghdh, all of it, what if it was an elaborate hallucination incited by Chekydran mind-control drugs? What if she'd created the damnably attractive, compelling Cullin Seaghdh out of her own fantasies? Out of her wish for rescue from the Chekydran? If that was true, then she'd become her own worst nightmare.

She heard him shift.

"Ari?" Seaghdh. He'd obviously recovered enough to rise. He laid a finger along the line of her jaw.

Abruptly, she saw him instead of a Chekydran cell and realized her breath came in shallow, rapid gusts. She sucked in a deep breath and held it.

"Sit," he urged. "You're bleeding. Let me clean that cut. Sit still." His voice enfolded her. He dabbed her cheek.

Antiseptic entered the cut. She let her breath out in a rush. Her eyes watered, but her head cleared. She sighed and touched his face. "You had better be real."

He started and stared at her, horror in his expression as his imagination took her statement and ran with it. Struggling for something to say, he turned his head to plant a kiss in the palm of her hand. "I am going to murder every single one of those bastards," he said, his tone unaccountably pleasant.

"Get in line," she replied.

He crouched before her. He'd put his shirt on but hadn't buttoned it. Had he done it on purpose, knowing what effect the exquisite lines of his body had on her? The want consuming her flared.

Point to him.

"Close your eyes?" she asked, hating how her voice shook.

Looking mystified, he obeyed.

She needed to feel something other than fear, other than self-loathing. She kissed him. He leaned in, nearly fell. Wrapping an arm around her, he pulled her closer and deepened the kiss. Liquid fire surged through her blood, settling low in a rush. Something ignited between them. Passion. Far more than she'd bargained for. She pulled away, gasping.

For the first time in six months, she felt alive. Something fragile and trembling swelled inside her. It tasted like hope.

Seaghdh let go but brushed hair from her face. Sensation followed the path of his caress.

"I hate that I'm afraid of everything," she grumbled, looking away. "I hate being weak."

"Weak?" He grasped her chin and brought her back to face his disbelief. "Alexandria Rose Idylle, if you were weak, you'd be dead. Weak women don't survive three months of Chekydran questioning. Three Hells, no one survives it."

Before she could answer, someone cleared his throat in the hallway. "Sister Alex?"

Augie.

"May I enter?" he asked.

"A moment," she called before looking at Seaghdh. "How's that arm? Any residual numbness?"

He grinned and stood, closing his shirt. "No. Just tingling."

Ari choked on a laugh, rose, and held the curtain aside. "Come on in, Augie. If I haven't mentioned it yet, I can't tell you how glad I am to see you alive."

He cast an apologetic glance at Seaghdh and embraced her. "We thought you were dead, Alexandria."

"Me, too," she answered. "I know I wanted to be."

He released her and backed away, tucking his hands behind him. "Mr. Seaghdh, you are feeling better, I trust?"

"Captain," she corrected.

Augie's pleasant expression faltered as he looked between them. He nodded. "Of course. Someone who understands your first love."

She flinched.

Seaghdh crossed his arms, frowning.

"Forgive me, Alex, and Captain Seaghdh." Augie smiled, his eyes sad. "Perhaps Alexandria explained that I'd asked her to marry me. I could not entice her to leave the bridge of her ship. If I thought I could convince you both to stay, I'd offer again."

Her head reeled. "You'd offer for both of us?"

The truly disconcerted look on Seaghdh's face drew a pained laugh from her. Augie echoed it. She heard the loss beneath his chuckle.

"We expected you yesterday," he said to her.

"I know. Sorry. We were delayed by a . . ." She stopped short, dots of data connecting in her head in slow motion. Cold, oily horror spilled through her. "The attack on the Settlements was yesterday, wasn't it? They were after me. Why? The soldiers out there were trying to capture me, not kill me."

"We had it all planned," Augie said. "A great celebration to welcome you back. We were working on decorations while everyone else attended a service of thanksgiving that you'd been delivered from the Chekydran. The soldiers appeared in the middle of both towns, right outside the chapel and the temple. I don't know that they have souls left, but surely for committing murder on sanctified ground, they'll suffer for eternity."

Ari's legs gave way and she sank to the floor. So many dead. "This is my fault."

Kneeling before her, Augie stared into her face. "Would you have been able to save them if you'd been here, Alex?"

She blinked. Swallowing hard past the boulder lodged in her chest, she shook her head. "No," she admitted. "Not all of them."

"You would only have been captured again or killed," Augie said.

She didn't like it, but what he said made sense. Shoving guilt to one side, she forced herself to think, to evaluate. She had data here. Parsed properly, she could coax answers from it. Answers she didn't like.

Heart pounding, she snarled, "The Chekydran didn't do this. They couldn't have. It had to have been Armada." She turned and glared at Seaghdh. He lounged against one wall, his arms crossed, disquiet in his face. "Damn you! You knew this!"

He straightened, his features tight. "No, I didn't, Ari. You're jumping to conclusions . . ."

She shoved herself to her feet. "One: the only people who knew about the Kebgra stops were Armada and IntCom. Two: whoever sent these things thought they knew my schedule. IntCom is out. With all the sensors they have on board, they'd have known the *Sen Ekir* was delayed before we'd even admitted it to ourselves. Three: those damned soldiers were targeting me."

"The Chekydran—" Seaghdh began, anger flashing in his golden eyes.

"Didn't know about Kebgra!" she interrupted, her voice rising. "I have precious little to protect, Seaghdh, but what I have, I do. Not even you knew."

He stopped dead, pain replacing the irritation in his face. "You were questioned and tortured for three months and never told them— What did you tell them?"

Less than she'd told him. What did that mean?

He peered at her, his look thoughtful and calculating. "You're right. We didn't know about Kebgra. You may be a better spy than I am."

She closed her eyes and turned away. It was the only way to keep him from reading just how close she was to shattering. While she'd been a prisoner, she'd thought only of getting away, getting back to normal. She'd focused on returning to the life that had been interrupted at her capture. She'd wanted to lose herself in the flux and flow of mundane details, specimens to be gathered and analyzed for her dad, supplies of seed and cloth for the people of Kebgra, and routine patrols of the border interspersed with chasing down drunken miners violating TFC space.

Where in the past six months had it happened? At what point, exactly, had her life been choked off and twisted into this wrecked and limping parody that left so many people she cared about dead?

"I can't stay here," she said.

"I agree," Augie answered, anguish in his tone. "We cannot protect you."

She opened her eyes and choked back a laugh. "And I can't protect you."

"We never once asked you to," Augie replied. He shrugged and she realized she was gaping at him. "We've always wondered when the Tagreth Federated Council would tire of the media events we call protests."

"You're dissenters?" Seaghdh asked. He closed his eyes. "You're the Citizen's Rights Uprising, aren't you?"

"You've heard of us. Good." Augie smiled. "We are vociferous, but peaceful, in our disagreements with TFC."

"You think this strike was a matter of two orrkel with one rock, then," Seaghdh surmised.

"It is possible," Augie agreed.

Seaghdh laughed, as unhappy a sound as any Ari had ever heard. He glanced at her. "You've been running goods to the CRU?"

She could see in his face that he believed this to be the source of her troubles. If only it were that simple. Still, she should have seen that Augie and his people would suffer. She should have been able to figure it out on her own, but it was coming at her too fast, from all directions. She couldn't seem to shake off the damage the Chekydran had done. Her blood ran cold, and she shuddered. What if it was permanent? Or worse, a sign of brainwashing far subtler, far more insidious than had turned her lieutenant into a killing machine?

CHAPTER

13

ARI didn't know what Augie saw in her face, but he took her hand and squeezed before releasing her and saying, "I am sorry. I allowed myself to be distracted. I came because Captain Seaghdh's ship has returned and sent a shuttle to retrieve you."

Ari glanced at Seaghdh's frown.

"You didn't really expect them to be able to track the mother, did you? Much less catch it?" she prodded.

He shot her an annoyed glance.

"What's the matter, Seaghdh?" she said, grinning. "Not used to a woman with a grasp of e—tactics?" She'd almost said "enemy tactics."

Seaghdh's hand closing around her arm told her he'd heard. "Is that what you have a grasp of?" he countered, ushering her out of the cave. He and Augie laughed.

At the narrow mouth of the cavern system, Turrel waited beside a young woman. She'd braided her long brown hair since last Ari had seen her, but she recognized Larna, Augie's wife. He'd proposed to her after Ari had turned him down.

"V'k's at the shuttle," Turrel said by way of greeting. "That mother ship has jump technology we can't touch. Or trace."

Seaghdh closed his eyes and nodded.

"They're waiting for us," Turrel went on. He glanced at Augie and Larna. "Appreciate your hospitality, folks. If we can do anything for you, just say so."

Neither got the chance to respond. Kirthin Turrel marched into the open and angled out of sight.

"I need a moment," Ari told Seaghdh.

He opened his eyes and studied her. The corridor wasn't lit, but enough daylight filtered in through the opening that she could make out the uncertainty in his face. "Need privacy?"

What did he have to fear from these people? Or was it her he feared?

"No," she said. She left him standing in the cavern opening and went to offer one hand to Augie and one to Larna.

"Sister," Larna said, smiling. "You promised to wed here."

"This wasn't exactly planned," Ari replied.

"The Claugh nib Dovvyth are undisciplined people," Augie noted. "I'm surprised to find you in this man's company."

"Undisciplined?" Ari echoed.

"You come from an ancient race," he said. "One with nearly a millennium of tradition and belief. The Claugh—"

"Have a long-standing tradition of accepting others in a way that our people find unacceptable," she interrupted. "I didn't say this would be easy."

"They have raised deception to an art form, Alexandria. Be certain you are not his canvas." Augie's hand tightened on her hand and he darted a look over her shoulder at Seaghdh. "Have you given yourself to him?" he asked, his voice pitched low.

Ari blinked at the mental picture the question painted. "No." But Gods, she wanted to.

"You are not married, then," Augie said.

She shrugged, uneasy. "Not the way you mean. You know things aren't quite as cut-and-dried off Kebgra."

"Church Law does not change for your location or your convenience, Alexandria," Augie replied.

"Meaning that my capture and three months of torture were Judgment?" she demanded, ignoring the fact that she'd never converted to the Citizen's Church, even though most of Kebgra had always treated her as though it was inevitable.

Augie grabbed her by the arms.

Larna caught in an audible breath, unhappiness in her face.

"No! Alex, I cannot pretend to know," he rasped. "It is not—I only wanted to ask you to stay with us. We both want you. You have not yet committed. Please. Consider turning your back to your past. Build life anew. Build a future and a family."

"You were first," Larna said. "If you will only say yes, you will be again, regardless of wedding dates."

Ari closed her eyes. "That's not Church Law."

"It may be selfish of me. I don't care," Larna replied. "You're worth it."

With a sigh, Ari opened her eyes. For a moment, she felt the pull of living a simple, uncomplicated life surrounded by people who liked her.

Ari shook off the temptation. She wasn't in love with Augie or Larna. They deserved better. That they didn't understand her was clear. Turn her back on what had happened to her? On what she'd begun to suspect was happening in the Armada? She couldn't. And they'd never understand why she believed she could make a difference. How could she have missed that? Or was it why she'd said no to Augie in the first place seven months ago?

"If I thought you'd be safe, if I thought I'd be safe, I'd consider it. But a lot of people seem to want me and everyone around me dead. I've already brought more trouble upon you than I can bear. I will not be the cause of more."

Augie and Larna traded a bleak glance. He nodded. "We knew you would say these things." He released her and stepped back. "We need you, Alexandria. Resolve these dangers plaguing you. When you do, know you have a place in our hearts, in our home, waiting for you."

"Thank you." Ari kissed him, then Larna. No fire shimmered inside her skin, despite the fact that each of them leaned into the contact, obviously hoping to change her mind. From the farewell she tasted in Larna's lips, it was plain that the woman did not expect her to return.

"Now," Ari said. "What arrangements for evacuation and relocation may I offer?"

"We are not leaving."

"They could come back," she said.

"Yes, they could. And if they do not, the Chekydran may," Augie said. "This is our home. If they'd meant to destroy us, they'd have burned the crops, poisoned the soil, and bombed our towns and our homes."

Ari found herself nodding as Augie spoke. "So. Scare tactic?"

"Or a test run," Seaghdh offered.

She threw him a sharp glance. "Get me evidence of it. If I can then find out who issued the order, I'll feed him or her through the *Sen Ekir*'s fuel valves. A piece at a time."

Seaghdh, Augie, and Larna stared at her as if not certain of what they saw. Ari looked back, unwilling to alter the cold, hard expression she felt on her face.

"It concerns me," Seaghdh commented, his tone mild, "that you sound like you know precisely how efficiently humanoid flesh and bone burn in an atmospheric engine."

"It should," Augie answered for her. "Why do you think I asked her to marry me?"

Ari couldn't help but laugh. She nodded to Augie, squeezed Larna's hand, and turned away.

"Ready?" Seaghdh asked. He put a palm in the small of her back.

How could so simple a contact touch off a cascade of chemicals in her body?

She let him usher her to the shuttle, aware that she could no longer ignore the obvious. She was attracted to Cullin Seaghdh, but how often had she heard it said? Sex has nothing to do with love. And she couldn't love the man, could she? She was too traumatized to let anyone get that close. She had no idea whether she'd ever be able to love.

Still. Once this was over, once she'd provided the information his government wanted and she was cut loose, she'd miss him. She'd miss his challenges, the sparring, that damned, cocky grin, his voice reaching out to her in the dark. She'd miss the sense of safety, of acceptance she felt in his arms. She'd miss the way he made her laugh.

Baxt'k.

In the shuttle, Turrel and V'kyrri strapped in on either side of her, as if they'd appointed themselves to guard her. Were they guarding her against someone? Or everyone else against her?

Seaghdh took position at piloting. A young female officer shifted to the copilot's seat. They ran their checklist in their own language. Even though Ari didn't understand a word, she could follow based on Seaghdh's question, the girl's hand on a console activating the system, and her affirmative reply. The atmospherics hummed to life.

Her heart thumped hard in time with the word resounding in her head. *Prisoner*. Adrenaline flooded her middle, cold, sharp. Muscles trembled, urging action. In a flash, she gauged the distance to the hatch. Fewer than three seconds from her seat to the door. Memory handed her the lock code. Barring a fat-finger mistake on the command pad, four seconds to open the hatch and run for her life. Seven seconds from freedom.

She dropped her chin to her chest and sucked in a harsh breath. Get a grip, Ari. She was seven seconds from condemning Augie and everyone on Kebgra to death, even assuming she could outrun Turrel. Granted, she knew far more about Kebgra than Seaghdh and his men. She could conceivably hide from them. But she had some evidence that she couldn't hide from the mutated soldiers that had been sent after her.

Any question of playing hide-and-seek in the fields and forests of Kebgra evaporated as the engines ramped and lifted her from the ruins of her life. She closed her eyes on the thought that while she wasn't shackled and neuro-locked, she was as much at someone else's mercy as she had been the day the Chekydran had captured her.

A prisoner for three months, free for three months, and now, who knew? Was it better or worse that she'd walked into this captivity half willing?

They passed six thousand meters. She opened her eyes as Seaghdh's copilot began a melodic, if disjointed, conversation with the Stalker Class cruiser in orbit.

Seaghdh glanced over his shoulder at Ari. Whatever he saw in her face made him frown. He turned back when the copilot spoke to him.

Funny. She'd have thought she'd catch his name when the copilot addressed him. But then, maybe she'd simply said "Captain." The reference to his boss, the Queen's Blade, that Ari caught. How bad a sign was it that the Auhrnok Riorchjan was aboard the Stalker? She'd heard plenty regarding his interrogation techniques. She sincerely hoped she wouldn't get a firsthand demonstration.

Nodding at the information the copilot relayed, Seaghdh changed course. The Stalker looked knife-edge sharp hanging in space, sleek and deadly. They came in under the cover of her forward guns. Ari felt the shuttle hesitate as it passed through the outer shield layer. She sat up straighter and scanned the darkness visible through the viewports.

Nothing.

Yet the Claugh obviously expected something. From whom? Armada? They were inside the TFC border. They had to know the border sensors had alerted Command the moment they'd crossed out of the Buffer Zone. Or did they suspect Chekydran? This close to the Buffer Zone, they were a possibility.

A shimmy ran through the plating beneath her feet. Seaghdh and his copilot took their hands from the controls. Guidance beam. Interesting. Ship's weapons and shields hot, but taking the time for shuttle guidance. Ari was sure it meant something, she just couldn't work out what it might be. She supposed it meant that stealing a shuttle and making a break for it would be much harder with the little boats locked by guidance.

They set down in a shuttle bay, white and gray deck plates scorched by engine discharge. It looked like every other shuttle bay she'd ever seen. Just bigger. She waited until Seaghdh unhooked his harness and rose. Turrel and V'kyrri stood. All three men looked different, somehow. Worn, apprehensive. Like the worst was yet to come. They studiously avoided looking at her.

Seaghdh offered her a hand. She rose without it. The concern in his face deepened as he dropped his hand back to his side. Despite her challenging stare, he didn't say anything, didn't give any hint about what to expect.

He keyed open the hatch. Turrel and V'kyrri took position behind her. Showtime. Spine straight, chin high, she marched down the ramp before Seaghdh could order her escorted off the shuttle.

A woman in a stiff, khaki uniform, two conspicuously armed guards at either shoulder, stood at the bay door. Dark brown, curly hair, secured at her nape, gleamed like a criot pelt. She strode, fluid grace in every move, across the floor, smiled, and extended a hand. Ari could see the faint tracing of veins through her fair, freckled skin.

"Captain Idylle," she said. Her accent turned Ari's language into poetry. "I am so pleased you agreed to assist us. This cannot have been easy for you."

Ari took the elegant woman's hand and noted the grime embedded in her own skin. Her filthy, rumpled uniform reeked of death and fear. She'd killed one of her own crew today. Easy? Yeah. Thrice-damned hell of a day.

"I am Eilod Saoyrse."

Ari's breath stopped in her chest. The queen of the Claugh nib Dovvyth. By all that was holy, she was screwed.

"Captain Alexandria Idylle, madam," she forced herself to reply.

TFC didn't have royalty, didn't confer titles. She had no idea how to address the head of an enemy state. She'd never been trained as a politician. "I don't know how I can help. You are already in possession of my debriefing files. I doubt I can add to them."

"Someone believes you can, Captain," the queen replied, releasing her. "If you didn't represent a danger to someone important, you wouldn't have been attacked." Her gaze touched Turrel and V'kyrri, then moved farther left. Her smile deepened.

Ari felt Seaghdh beside her. Out of the corner of her eye, she saw him salute. He began speaking in his language, his words hurried and his tone urgent.

"Auhrnok Riorchjan," the queen interrupted.

Ari froze. She knew that title. Auhrnok was obscure, a title of nobility, akin to lord. She couldn't remember how she'd come to know its meaning. But every officer and grunt in the Armada knew Riorchjan, even if no one knew precisely what it meant. It belonged to Her Majesty's spymaster. The Queen's Blade. Judge, jury, executioner. The queen herself had just attached it to Cullin Seaghdh.

The blood drained from Ari's head. Feeling sputtered and died in her heart.

"You have a great deal of explaining to do, Auhrnok," Her Majesty snapped at Seaghdh. "You will not alienate our guest by speaking a language she does not understand."

As the woman berated him, the devil-may-care man Ari had known seemed to dissolve. Someone honed and dangerous stood in his place. She'd caught glimpses of this over the past few days, noted the dichotomy and dismissed it. How could she have so ignored the cues?

She could neither cry nor laugh at her stupidity. At least it cleared up one question. He was undoubtedly real. Not even Chekydran mind-control drugs could concoct so far-fetched a scenario as the damaged Armada captain falling for the infamously manipulative Queen's Blade.

Her heart clenched. Cravuul dung. Had she really?

Rage scorched the cobwebs from her brain. No. It had barely been three days during which she'd trusted Cullin Seaghdh because she'd had no choice. He'd done his job, using whatever means she'd offered him to pry her away from her family. He'd exploited her need for approval, her desire to be a part of something, her attraction to him. She gritted her teeth. It was all a lie, and she'd played right into his hands.

Fine. He'd played her. Just like she'd played him on the energy blade floor. Or had she? She cast a sidelong glance at that long, lean fencer's body and shivered. Had she ever dueled the top-ranked blade master? He'd asked her that. She'd said no, not realizing she just had. Evidence suggested, by virtue of the fact that she was a prisoner again and her captor had gotten her to walk into his trap willingly, that she'd been played from the moment Cullin Seaghdh had taken her father's ship.

Straightening, Ari focused on the woman watching her so keenly.

"Congratulations, Auhrnok Riorchjan," Ari said. The placid, even tone of her voice pleased her. "Match to you."

"Ari," he grated, warning in his tone.

"No, no," she said, glancing at him. She strangled the chagrin trying to rise within her at the pain in his face and turned her eyes front. "Masterfully won. I now understand the distinction between first and second rank. I concede. Your skill far outstrips mine."

He growled.

Her Majesty glanced between them, trouble flickering across her features for a moment. "Captain Idylle, quarters have been prepared—"

"You wanted my help," Ari interrupted. "A shower and a change of clothes are all I need." She would *not* ask what they intended to do with her. "We don't have time for anything else. Armada beacons registered your presence in TFC space two hours ago. If my commanders aren't lighting up your com panels, it's because my ship, with my former first officer commanding, is en route to begin knocking impolitely at your front door."

Eilod Saoyrse opened her mouth, then closed it, staring.

Ari reached for her handheld.

The guards twitched.

Glaring at them, Ari unclipped the device in slow motion. When she offered it to the queen, Seaghdh took it. Ari refused to look at him.

"You'll find a com badge code," she said. "Bring it aboard. It may require some overrides on your teleporters. 'Port directly to containment."

The woman blinked, looking momentarily flustered. Drawing herself up, she smiled again. "Thank you, Captain. What are we teleporting?"

"The corpse of Lt. Tommy Heisen."

"A compatriot?"

"Six months ago, yes. After time spent with the Chekydran, no. He was one of their soldiers."

Eilod sucked in a sharp breath and her green eyes lit. "One hour!" she commanded, pointing at Seaghdh. "Clean up. Report to medical. Captain Idylle, I insist that you submit to a full medical scan. This is for your protection as well as ours. When it is complete, I expect you both in Conference One."

"I recommend completing teleport before the *Balykkal* arrives."

"It's not that simple," Seaghdh rumbled. It sounded like he had his teeth clenched.

Ari looked at him. Muscles bunched up in his jaw, anger in the set of his lips. Good. Why, then, did her gut twist and demand she smooth away the lines in his forehead? Manipulative bastard. *Focus, Ari.* He'd said they couldn't teleport Tommy. She frowned.

"This is a Stalker Class cruiser," she said.

"Yes."

"With a sizeable science team."

"Yes."

Ari lifted her hands from her sides and dropped them again. "They'll understand containment."

Seaghdh scowled. "They should, yes . . ."

"Containment isn't independent of ship's systems?" she surmised, resisting the urge to smack her palm to her forehead. She should have known. TFC hadn't begun designing containment independent of ship's grid until after the Occaltus disaster. The Claugh hadn't yet been forced to learn from bad luck. "Fine. Call in the *Sen Ekir*."

"Not possible."

"We both know that between Dad, Pietre, and Sindrivik, the IntCom files have been disabled," she countered. "They have control of the ship."

Seaghdh glanced at the queen, then back at Ari. He cleared his throat. "That isn't the issue, Captain."

"They have the containment system you need, Seaghdh," she prodded, "and an exemplary team. Explain to my father. He won't believe you until he cuts into Tommy and finds all that Chekydran tech adapted to Armada specifications. When he does, he'll understand. He's worked privileged information before." Ari hesitated, examining him to see if she couldn't discern some hint of intent in his face.

"Unless those of us involved are slated to simply disappear," she said. "Then I do prefer you leave Dad out of it. You might even be able to trade me back to the Chekydran and let them finish the job they started if you don't wish to be personally guilty of my murder."

Eilod Saoyrse chuckled. The real amusement in the sound baffled Ari. "I'll thank the two of you to leave your personal baggage at the air lock door. We have a Chekydran-backed problem that seems to be growing in threat and complication by the moment. Captain Idylle, can you work with Captain Seaghdh?"

Could she? How about would she? Swallowing ire, she nodded. "If I can be forgiven the occasional cheap shot? Yes, ma'am. I'll work with whoever it takes to stop the Chekydran and their allies."

"Excellent." The queen turned on her heel and quit the bay.

"Ari," Seaghdh essayed, reaching for her. "Let me explain."

Without thinking, she sidestepped his grasp and pinned him with a hard glare. "No need. It's all perfectly clear."

Something chirped. He activated a com badge she'd missed seeing. She didn't catch a word of the conversation.

He closed his eyes and rubbed the heel of his hand against his forehead. "Damn it, Ari." He sighed, wiped the pain from his face, and straightened. "Turrel. Escort Captain Idylle to medical. I will relieve you."

"Aye, Captain."

"V'kyrri, with me."

"Yes, sir."

Seaghdh thrust the handheld back into her grasp and stalked out of the bay, anger in every line of his body. V'kyrri followed, but not before he tossed a disquieted glance at her and looked like he wanted to say something. He pressed his lips tight, nodded, and jogged after Seaghdh.

"Baxt'k."

"Yeah," Turrel rumbled. "Politics. What a group baxt'k."

She eyed the big man standing next to her with his arms crossed and the hint of a smirk on his face. "Rank?"

"Colonel."

"Ground forces," Ari said.

"Different military entirely. At least, I was."

Until someone in her government had ordered the slaughter of his people. Ari sighed. Staying pissed off at Seaghdh would have been a lot easier if he'd lied about everything.

CHAPTER

14

THE queen's bodyguards flanked the door emblazoned with the emerald, silver, and black standard of the royal house. Both men saluted as Seaghdh approached.

"Her Majesty awaits, Auhrnok Riorchjan," one man said as his companion opened and held the door.

Eilod Saoyrse turned from staring out the viewport, her green eyes flashing. "Auhrnok? What the hell happened out there?"

Seaghdh crossed the gold carpet and tried not to grin. Clever. She gave the court gossip mill grist by taking him to task in front of her bodyguard. He folded Her Majesty's right hand in both of his, knelt, and touched his forehead to their clasped hands.

"Gentlemen," Eilod said. "Secure these chambers."

"By your will, Your Majesty," the men replied in unison.

Seaghdh heard them leave the room, close the door, and lock it behind them. A few moments later, the subtle, low-level hum of a sonic shield rose.

"You can get up. They're gone," his cousin said, curling her fingers around his and lifting.

Suddenly aching and weary, Seaghdh accepted the assistance.

"Are you all right? Cullin, you look awful."

He rubbed a grimy hand over scratchy eyes and relaxed completely for the first time since accepting his mission to find one Captain Alexandria Rose Idylle. "I'll be fine, but I think the sonic shield blew the regen unit."

"Regen?" Eilod frowned, taking a seat at her desk. "You're injured? You should have gone to medical."

"I will," he promised. "This is important."

"What happened, Cullin, that eight of our best are dead and you come to me when you should be in treatment?"

"We hit a nerve." Seaghdh sighed and dropped into an armchair, resting his head against the padding. Leather creaked. He rolled his head to one side to look at Eilod, her hands folded, her face lined with concern.

"Go on," she said.

"The Chekydran were waiting for us. Great, big battleship. No hail. No warn off. They opened fire, punched a hole in our shields with three shots and finished us in six."

"Do we have a leak?"

"Not necessarily," Seaghdh said. "Ar—Captain Idylle's whereabouts weren't classified. We went in knowing we weren't the only ones looking for her. There's no reason to believe the Chekydran weren't expecting us."

"Or were they counting on us?" Eilod mused. She shook her head. "Enough. I'll review your report and we'll address it in debriefing. Tell me about Captain Idylle."

"She's IntCom."

"What?" Eilod sat bolt upright.

Seaghdh straightened, nodding. "She is either the best spy TFC has ever trained or the luckiest spacer since Ormynd Mbumbakii stumbled on supralight."

"She was captured and held by the Chekydran."

"I know. Not my definition of lucky, either." Seaghdh sighed. "On the other hand, I sense no duplicity in her. I'm beginning to believe it's because she doesn't say anything."

Eilod grinned, abruptly looking much younger. "On the contrary, my dear, I gather you and she have traded more than a few words."

Seaghdh drew breath to protest, then deflated. He should have known his sharp-eyed cousin would catch a hint of what he'd hoped burned between Ari and himself. "You know what I mean," he grumbled. "She does not trust. Not me. Not herself. Not anyone."

"So I gathered," she replied. "I'm sorry. We've done the bad Claugh/good Claugh so often, it never occurred to me that you had made yourself into the good one."

"I didn't. She saw through it."

"Did we recruit a mole, Cullin?"

"No."

She looked at him for a moment, then sat back in her chair. "The evidence that makes you so certain?"

"Gut," he admitted.

"Gut? Or something significantly lower? Auhrnok Captain Cullin Seaghdh nib Riorchjan," the queen said, her voice ringing. "You have ten seconds to explain before I have that woman confined to one cell and you to another."

"Her involvement with TFC Intelligence Command is off record."

Eilod frowned and relaxed. "Off record? Tagreth Federated doesn't do anything unless it's in triplicate. That is, in part, why you are valuable to me. You have an uncanny knack for wading through their landslide of data. Are you certain she's IntCom? Could it have been bravado? Meant to impress an attractive captor?"

Seaghdh laughed. "No. Bravado she has, I admit. But no. She'd kept her status secret her entire career, even from her family. She would have kept it to her grave, I think, had we not run into our soldier friends on Kebgra. In fact, Lieutenant Sindrivik is still aboard the *Sen Ekir*, trapped by IntCom's systems' lockdown."

Awareness dawned in Eilod's face. She chuckled. "She initiated a lockout of her father's ship? Perhaps I'll offer Captain Idylle asylum in exchange for her cooperation."

"She'll cooperate, regardless," Seaghdh said. "It's personal."

"Her crewman. Yes." Eilod sighed, drummed her fingers on the tabletop for a moment, then said, "Speak plainly to me, kinsman. What did I bring aboard this ship?"

Seaghdh should have known Eilod would invoke bloodbond. She didn't often remind him that he was as bound to the throne and its duties as she. Doubtless, she envied him the luxury of being able to forget that particular burden. Eilod Saoyrse never disregarded the yoke of her station.

"My assessment," he said, "is incomplete. Captain Idylle suffered considerable mental and emotional damage while a captive of the Chekydran, but her sanity and morality seem intact."

"I require more assurance than 'seem,' Seaghdh."

He shrugged. "I have yet to discern whether she is under Chekydran control, either via brainwashing, implants, or some other device. My initial impression is that she is not, though why she was released if she wasn't under their control, I can't say. The Chekydran do nothing that does not benefit them directly."

"Your initial impression is tempered by that fact," his cousin guessed.

"Yes."

"What do I do with her, Cullin?"

"I need time, Eilod," he said, fighting the urge to lean forward, to give away just how important this was to him. "I need her with me in close quarters where I have access to her fears, her memories."

A troubled light fired in Her Majesty's eyes. "For whose benefit?"

He hesitated. "I don't deny I will help her if I can. If she will let me. The safety of the Empire, however, comes first. If she is a threat, I will neutralize her."

Grim-faced, the woman behind the desk held his eye for several seconds, then inclined her head. "What are you not telling me?"

Damn it. Growing up as Eilod's foster brother made her far too familiar with what did and didn't show on his face. "I'm missing something."

She looked startled. "Missing? You?"

"You've seen her file."

"Very thorough," his cousin said, her tone cautious.

"One might say clinical," he mused.

"Cullin . . ."

Seaghdh leaned forward, propped his elbows on his knees, and peered hard at the queen. "Files are a starting place, a basis, if you will, for interaction with a subject. In this case, I believe Captain Idylle's file uses detail to hide the fact that her file is omitting something vital."

Eilod frowned. "What?"

"I don't know, yet. It's damned frustrating."

"You have a distinct talent for identifying information patterns, or you wouldn't be my Riorchjan."

"Review her brother's and sister's files. Compare them to hers."

His cousin shot him a sharp glance. "Tell me."

"Brother, Hieronomus, firstborn. Sister, Isolde, second-born. Hieronomus's file is typical firstborn data. Details of the pregnancy, journal entries, DNA scans, lock of hair, first steps, very detailed until the birth of the second child. Hieronomus's third through eighth years are sketchy. Isolde's file doesn't begin, save for date, time, place of birth, and her weight, until she's five years old. I gather Miss Isolde Idylle was a handful."

Eilod frowned. "Yet Captain Idylle's file is exactingly detailed, virtually from the moment of conception."

"Yes. And the tone is markedly different," he said.

Nodding, she murmured, "Detached."

"Captain Idylle's file reads like a report," Seaghdh said.

"She is significantly younger than her siblings, isn't she?"

"Yes. Her brother was at university when she was born."

"A midlife accident, then?"

"When everything else in the file is so deliberate?" Seaghdh mused. He shifted, listening to the faint breath of instinct. "We may have to bring in the *Sen Ekir*."

"That is a complication I would like to avoid, Cullin. Why?"

"I need Sindrivik to steal another file for me."

His cousin raised an eyebrow at him. "Her mother's?"

Seaghdh nodded. "I'd like to know what would cause a mother's love to change so radically between children."

"Didn't she die shortly after Captain Idylle's birth?"

"Two years."

"Could it have been illness?"

"I don't know, Eilod. Until I do know, there's too much I can't know about Captain Idylle. I don't think we want her out of my sight."

Her Majesty rose. "Report to medical. I'd like to relieve you of duty, but you've forced me to trust your instincts over the years. Your mission remains unchanged. Find out what that woman is."

"By your will." Seaghdh stood and flinched as newly healing flesh pulled in his side.

"I will alert Dr. Annantra to prepare for your arrival and your injury," she said.

"Eilod."

"Don't argue with your sovereign."

"Or what? You'll tell Aunt Kys?"

Her Majesty stuck her tongue out at him and lowered the sonic shield with the click of a button. "Or I'll relieve you of duty and assign V'kyrri to keep a close personal eye on Captain Idylle." She smiled sweetly and unlocked the door from the panel embedded in her desk.

Seaghdh ignored the spike of alarm that drove through his gut. Pasting a thoughtful expression to his face, he shrugged. "That might not be a bad idea."

"Get out of my sight, you intolerable faker," his cousin ordered, laughing.

*   *   *

ARI had always said the irony of a medical scan is that it bores you
to death. Claugh medi-tech was similar enough to hers that she could
follow the procedures even if she couldn't follow the language. The
doctor, a solid, older woman with salt-and-pepper hair, greeted her
in her own language and ushered her into a tiny private exam room
with pale green walls. She'd scowled when Turrel followed. He
crossed his arms and slouched against the wall.

Ari expected questions. She didn't get any. The doctor directed Ari
to the scan bed and after a flurry of instructions to a teenaged male
nurse, initiated the scan.

"My son," she confided when she saw Ari watching the boy.

Ari nodded.

A com buzzed nearby. The doctor answered.

Ari listened and was rewarded this time, catching Seaghdh's title,
Auhrnok, and her name. As she became accustomed to hearing the
language, she seemed to get better at distinguishing the words. It
wasn't just a jumble of sounds all run together. But she still didn't
understand it. She'd need to change that, without fanfare, if she could.
People who believe you don't speak their language are far more willing to speak freely in your company. She felt like she needed every
advantage she could garner.

"Stay still if you can," the doctor instructed. "Not long."

Long enough to wonder if she'd been nothing more than a conquest, no more than a game to Cullin Seaghdh. Ari closed her eyes
trying to sift Seaghdh's lies from the bits of truth he'd fed her.

"Captain Idylle. Captain Idylle, can you hear me?"

She flinched in surprise at hearing someone else's voice resounding in her head. Her eyes opened.

"Easy," the doctor said.

Ari blinked. Not the same voice and it hadn't come from inside
her skull. It dawned on her, then. The damned transponder embedded
in the skin behind her left ear.

"Captain Idylle, come in."

She tapped her tongue against the activation switch and recognized the voice. Admiral Jecaldo Angelou. His office had issued the decree requiring that transponders be implanted in all senior personnel. He'd done it right after she'd been taken by the Chekydran. He'd said, when she'd asked following her release, that he never again wanted to sit by while one of his officers rotted in a Chekydran prison. Then he'd ordered the device implanted in her head. She hadn't mentioned that she'd kill herself before willingly becoming a Chekydran prisoner again.

"Ari?" he asked. "Tap twice for yes, once for no."

She hit the switch twice.

"Are you alone?"

One tap.

"Understood. Are you all right?"

Suspicion fired through her and she damned Cullin Seaghdh for making her doubt the man who had spent the better part of his career nurturing hers. She tapped twice. Still. Why would he ask that question now? For that matter, why contact her this way? Had IntCom already advised him that the *Sen Ekir* had taken off without her?

She rolled from the scanner bed, eliciting a yelp of protest from the doctor. Turrel straightened. Ari grabbed her handheld, switched it to record, shoved it against her left ear, and collapsed back on the bed.

"Ari, if you're secure?"

Define "secure." Two taps.

"Captain, I know these are difficult times," he said. "You've been relieved of duty and sent in pursuit of something I know you don't want. Alex, believe me, this isn't my doing. You're a damned fine officer and I want you back out there on the bridge of a ship."

A part of her knew Seaghdh was there a moment before he walked in the door. Her heart rate picked up speed. He looked at her quizzically, then traded a confused glance with Turrel who shrugged.

"Ari?" Seaghdh reached for her, concern in his face.

Before Ari could put a finger to her lips, the doctor grabbed Seaghdh's arm and shook her head, her expression grim. She pointed at instrument readouts. Seaghdh's confused gaze flicked from Ari to the panel. His eyes widened.

"To that end, Captain," her CO went on. "I'm putting you on unofficial assignment."

Interesting. When he hadn't confirmed her status? Or her location? Was it possible he didn't know about the attack on Kebgra? She tapped twice.

Seaghdh shoved the doctor, her son, and Turrel out the door. He closed and locked it before turning back to watch with apprehension in his face.

"Boundary beacons indicate a Claugh nib Dovvyth Stalker has crossed into TFC space near Kebgra. I have a ship on intercept. Captain, this is vital. You must not allow yourself to fall into Claugh hands. I should have warned you before we sent you on this expedition with your father," he said, then sighed. "My fault, I suppose. Armada Command wanted to assign you to a desk where they could keep an eye on you. I argued against it, and in doing so, sent you out there into danger. Alex, we've had word that agents from the Claugh are after you."

Two taps.

"What I am about to tell you is highly classified, Captain."

Two more taps.

"After you disappeared, the Council initiated a mission of discovery based on rumors coming across the Zone. We don't have anything concrete, Captain, but we do have enough evidence to begin to make out a sinister pattern. The Claugh nib Dovvyth is working with the Chekydran. Over the years, they've taken hundreds of TFC personnel captive. We believed our people dead. We were wrong."

Ari sucked in a sharp breath.

"They've created an army of mutated soldiers. I have reason to believe, Captain, that the Claugh intend to do the same to you."

CHAPTER
15

"YOU be very careful out there, Captain," Ari's CO ordered before signing off.

Sage advice. Several days too late.

She lowered the handheld, tabbed it off, and stared at the ceiling.

Seaghdh shifted.

She glanced at him and tried to imagine him wanting to turn her into something like Tommy. She couldn't. He'd been genuinely horrified both by the efficient carnage on Kebgra and by the soldiers themselves. Further, he'd helped her destroy them. If she was slated to become one at Cullin Seaghdh's hand, why sacrifice six undoubtedly very expensive prototypes? He'd already had her firmly within his grasp.

"Clear?" he asked.

"No, Auhrnok," Ari said.

He flinched.

"But my CO signed off and I made damned sure the transponder is off. I take it the transmission showed up on instruments?"

Seaghdh unlocked the door. "Only because we were running a

medical diagnostic. You and I both know that transmission should have tripped unauthorized com alarms. It didn't. How the hell did TFC manage that?"

"They didn't, as far as I know," she replied. "This is Armada tech and applied only within the ranks."

He cocked his head and narrowed his eyes at her. All business. "When?"

"The command went out after I was captured," she replied. "Mine went in shortly after my release."

"Kept secret?"

Ari nodded. "Supposed to be only Armada Command that knows, but . . ."

"You suspected something and told your father." Grim satisfaction showed in his tight smile.

She opened her mouth to protest, then feeling resentful, closed it. He'd lied to her and used her. Why the hell was she answering him? How could one notoriously devious and manipulative man elicit information from her when three months of torture hadn't? Of course she had suspected something when Armada Command put the transponder in her head. She'd just been freed from a Chekydran prison. Distrust had kept her alive and maybe, just maybe, sane. She'd not only told her father about the transponder, she'd given him the code. Look where that had gotten her.

"Quick thinking, Ari," he said, his tone far too warm for her comfort, "recording what you could. Are you okay? I should bring Dr. Annantra back."

She nodded and wondered why he'd jettisoned everyone in the first place. Dr. Annantra had known she was receiving. What had Seaghdh feared? That she'd be teleported out? She doubted the *Balykkal* could get a lock through the Stalker's shields, even with her transponder code programmed into the computers. Unless the crew of the *Balykkal* had orders to retrieve her at any cost. She knew perfectly well that translated to dead and 'porting through shields, dead she'd be.

Seaghdh opened the door. "My apologies, Doctor. We are secure."

Secure? Was that what this was about? He suspected that Armada Command had built a destruct function into the transponder? Ari choked back a curse. It made sense. If Admiral Angelou decided she'd been irrevocably compromised, he could just blow her fool head off from the comfort of his padded leather chair. Maybe it was time for an extraction.

"Very good," the woman said, returning to Ari's side and tweaking instruments. "You took no tissue damage from that transmission, Captain. Mmm. I see a spike in stress hormone levels. I'd like to keep an eye on that. Have they run abnormally high since your release?"

"Some days are worse than others," Ari said.

The doctor peered hard at her and finally nodded. "I imagine."

Dr. Annantra turned to Seaghdh. "Auhrnok, Her Majesty advised me that you took injury planetside. Will you permit me?"

"I'm fine, thanks to Captain Idylle," he replied.

Ari risked pulling away from the scan bed. "Done with me?"

"Yes, Captain," the doctor replied. "I will require several minutes more to analyze and review the data. Would you care to shower?" She opened a door to a tiny closet. "Take your time. I will have clean clothes waiting."

Ari shrugged out of her filthy jacket and unstrapped her empty holster. Upon Turrel's advice, she'd left the Autolyte on the shuttle. Seaghdh still had her pistol. The only thing that made her feel better was that he, too, went unarmed aboard ship.

"Captain Seaghdh took a dose of poison on Kebgra," Ari said. "And had two shots of antivenin to counter it."

The doctor's genial expression died. "On the scan bed, if you will, Auhrnok. The nature of the toxin?"

Seaghdh grimaced at Ari and sauntered to take her place.

"You might as well take off your shirt and jacket, Auhrnok Riorchjan," she said, stressing the title. "I am going to tell her about the hole in your side."

"Damn it, Ari, is this your notion of revenge?"

"You have no idea," she countered before looking at the doctor. "Deaccolo tree venom, species unique to Kebgra. It's a paralytic neuro-toxin. Plant based but with an enzyme set that can induce time-delayed reactions."

She turned on her handheld, called up the Kebgra data, and handed it to the doctor.

The woman scanned the information and scowled. "How long ago?"

"Two, three hours?" Ari glanced at Seaghdh for confirmation.

He sat, bare-chested, watching the back and forth, a smirk on his handsome face. He nodded.

She flushed, remembering her lips pressed against the warm, taut skin of that torso, and the reaction that had blazed through him. Could he possibly be that good an actor?

"A neural scan, then," the doctor said.

Ari jerked her attention back to the doctor. "Permanent muscular damage is possible with this venom in advanced stages of poisoning, but I think we got to Captain Seaghdh long before that became a risk. He did have a brief episode of hypoxia before the antivenin took hold."

"Yes, I see," she said, studying readouts for a moment. "Minimal cellular destruction. Good."

The woman zeroed in on the regeneration unit Ari had applied to Seaghdh's side. The lights had died on the control panel. Doctor An-nantra eased the dead instrument from Seaghdh's skin. "Puncture wound. Very clean."

"Thorn," Seaghdh said.

"Some thorn." Annantra glanced at Ari. "You removed it?"

"Yes," Ari said, pulling her shirt off over her head.

"You did good work, Captain. Thank you."

Ari tried to smile at the doctor but ducked into the shower, still confused over what she felt toward Seaghdh. The attraction was intact, damn it all, but she couldn't ignore the fact that he'd lied to her. Was still lying to her, for all she knew. And then there was the admiral's accusation and the question of whether Ari should trust

Dr. Annantra enough to ask her to remove the transponder from her head. Was there anyone she could trust?

Angelou had said "unofficial" assignment, yet other than staying away from the Claugh, he hadn't laid out a mission or parameters. Reviewing the one-sided conversation, she paused. He hadn't given her any detail regarding the evidence he said had been gathered regarding a Claugh/Chekydran alliance. Had he done that on purpose? Trying to give her something to believe but nothing to follow up on?

Surely, he hadn't learned to so underestimate her in six short months. Granted, he did not seem to know she wasn't aboard the *Sen Ekir* with her father. An interesting development, since it meant Int-Com wasn't confiding in her commanding officer and that he did not want anyone to know about this "assignment." Why not?

Seaghdh had accused Armada Command of a treasonous Chekydran alliance. Question now was whether Seaghdh differentiated between Armada Command and IntCom as two distinct entities the way Ari did. If he didn't, she could have just made a fatal-for-her-father assumption. What if it wasn't Armada Command colluding with the Chekydran? What if, in fact, it was IntCom? It made twisted sense. Intelligence Command, operating in the vein of anything for information, resorted to all sorts of nonstandard methodologies. She could see rationalizing a marginal alliance as an infiltration bid. Except that every single previous attempt to breach Chekydran defenses had an extreme body count.

Ari shook her head and turned on the water in the little shower room. Funny. Miniscule though the alcove was, it didn't trigger a flashback. She smelled the water and the faint scent of antimicrobial cleaners, not the musty, dry odor that permeated the Chekydran ship. Regardless, she did not linger. She shut off the water, dried, and peeked around the door.

Doctor Annantra was still repairing the wound in Seaghdh's side. Ari had to smile. He didn't look like he appreciated the doctor's medical technique quite the way he had hers.

As if he'd heard the thought in her head, Seaghdh opened his eyes and met her gaze. Something searing reached across the exam room. Her pulse pounded in her ears and heat flooded her. She spotted a stack of neatly folded khakis. Snatching them, she retreated to dress.

One good thing came from the revelation that Seaghdh was the Queen's Blade. With rank came responsibility. He wouldn't have time to go on tormenting her. She'd be able to stay far away from him. At least until she'd managed to armor herself against feeling anything.

Ari put on the pale khaki uniform and choked back a humorless laugh. No one had stripped the knots and wings that marked rank among the Claugh. They'd given her a captain's uniform.

She slipped back into the exam room. Seaghdh was alone and up, buttoning his shirt. He eyed her, his look unreadable. Abruptly self-conscious, she fingered the too-loose waistband of her trousers and studied the instrument panel beside his right elbow. "You're all patched up?" she asked in a rush.

"Yes."

"Good."

"Ari."

"Be straight with me for a second," she commanded. "Why am I here? You didn't get shot down by Chekydran and lose eight crew just to hear me tell you what you've already read in my debriefing file. And a captain's uniform, S—Auhrnok? You do nothing you don't mean to do. Is this your way of telling me I'm never going home again?"

"Ari, stop and listen to me for a moment!"

The ripple of power in his voice silenced her. Anger rocketed through her. "Damn it, Seaghdh! If you want me to listen, stop manipulating me!"

He flushed. Rage or shame?

Somewhere in the last six months, she'd lost her ability to read faces. Was it simply because she had so little access to her own emotions?

He rounded the scan bed. A shiver of anticipation went up her spine.

"Ari." His voice rasped the raw edges of her suddenly sensually aware nerves. "Let me explain." The plea in his voice did not ask for the same thing the words did.

She stood transfixed, her skin flushing, and he hadn't even touched her. How she wanted him to. How she wanted to be able to let him draw her into his arms. Screwing her eyes shut, she cursed. How could she want something like that? He'd lied to her, manipulated her. Hell, with that voice talent of his, how could she be sure he wasn't pulling her strings even more subtly and adeptly than the Chekydran ever had? Wasn't he using desire against her even now?

Ari opened her eyes and stared straight into his pained expression.

"I want . . ." Power again. Battering her, wearing her down, urging her to step into his embrace, to take refuge in his lips on hers. He reached for her.

Heart pounding, she dodged and slapped her hands flat on the scan bed. Something beeped in protest. She shook with the effort it took to keep from crawling across the bed into his grasp.

"Stop it!" she shouted. The breath she drew sounded like a sob. "You asked for my trust. I gave it, when all this time there was so much you weren't telling me! With everything going on, a massacre on Kebgra, a secret army, some treasonous alliance, and me in the hands of the two most powerful people of an enemy state, all I want to know is whether you were playing a part."

"No," he said, his tone even, rational as if he could bring her back from the edge of reason where she teetered at the slightest breeze. "If you believe nothing else, believe that."

"You're the Auhrnok Riorchjan. The Queen's Blade," she accused. "Playing games with people is like breathing to you. Do you even know anymore how many games you're playing?"

"Ari. What do you want from me?"

"The truth!" she screeched. "What is it about me that made a queen send twelve operatives to ask me oh so nicely if I wouldn't come answer questions?"

In a blinding move, Seaghdh rounded the bed, grabbed, and pinned her against the bulkhead with his body. "You listen to me, and to that magnificent body of yours," he breathed into her ear. "I am not your enemy."

He was right. She seemed to be all the enemy she needed. She'd meant to hold herself rigid, straining away from him. Instead, she was leaning into him, her craving for his touch melting her bones. Desperation uncurled within her. She could not afford this kind of need.

"You are," she gasped. "I am TFC. You're not just Claugh, you're the Auhrnok Riorchjan. Of course you're my enemy. I had no idea when you let me win our blade duel just how outmatched I was or that we'd still be dueling after so long.

"I can't know anymore what your original mission parameter required," she said, ignoring the tremor in her voice. "But if you meant to destroy me, a crew of twelve was overkill. It took only you, after all."

He released her as if he'd been burned. "Those men and women sacrificed their lives to find you."

"They did not," she countered, clenching her hands and struggling for control of the impulse that would have her take him into her arms to soothe the creases from his forehead. "They did it to protect their loved ones, their way of life. They died because they believed in a cause. Put down the blade, Seaghdh. You win. I lose. You can't break me more than the Chekydran already have."

"I am not playing you!" he insisted.

She shrugged. "You use your voice-control talent on me and then go on pretending you give an orhait's ass. Wouldn't you believe you were being subtly and skillfully interrogated were our positions reversed, Auhrnok?"

Seaghdh swore in his own language, a long, musical string of words.

The desolation in his voice made her ache. She closed her eyes and rubbed her fingertips against her forehead. She heard the door open.

"Move out, Captain Idylle," he growled.

She opened her eyes.

He stood to one side of the door, his expression hard.

Nodding, her heart pounding, she picked up her handheld and followed him. Lovely. Accuse the man of devious interrogation in time to be led to the real thing.

Without a word or a look, he ushered her through a labyrinth of corridors to a set of double doors emblazoned with an emerald, black, and silver standard. Guards saluted and opened the doors at his approach. Voices within the room stilled. When she hesitated, Seaghdh grasped her elbow and steered her to an empty chair two removed from the head of the table where Eilod sat. He plunked her down, one hand on her shoulder warning her not to rise.

Faced with more than a half dozen interested pairs of eyes watching her every move, Ari swallowed a snarl. She folded her hands on the rich, golden bleached wood of the conference table and focused on her ragged nails. She absolutely did not want to see the expressions on the faces of the people around her as the queen introduced her personnel.

"I am Captain Alexandria Rose Idylle, formerly of the TFC ship *Balykkal*," she said when Eilod paused. "As the situation has been explained to me thus far, I understand you have questions regarding my imprisonment by the Chekydran. Where shall we start?"

Silence.

Ari glanced at Eilod.

Her Majesty studied her, then flicked an assessing look at Seaghdh. Her lips thinned. "May we offer you refreshment, Captain?"

Seaghdh rose.

"Thank you, no," Ari said. She watched Seaghdh from her peripheral vision until she could no longer see him without turning.

"Very well," Eilod said. "Given the unusual nature of our situation, I am instituting sonic shielding of this room. Please log any protests now."

Sonic shielding? Interesting. Who did they not want listening in?

"Begin, if you would," Her Majesty instructed after Ari felt the subtle vibration shimmer through the room, "with a summary of your captivity."

A hand landed on her shoulder, lighter this time, but she started all the same. Seaghdh had come up behind her, silent on the thick silver carpeting. Her blood warmed at the simple touch of his hand. Before she could jerk out from beneath the contact, he set a steaming mug of thick soup before her.

She stared at it like an idiot.

He returned to his seat.

Disconcerted, Ari outlined her imprisonment, tentative at first, concerned about triggering a flashback. To protect his queen, Seaghdh would have reason to forget about being careful with her this time. Somewhere in the midst of her recitation, Ari folded her hands around the warm mug.

"Captain Idylle," the queen said, leaning into the table to mimic her posture. Ari had raised her gaze to Eilod's shoulder before stopping herself and looking at the mug again. It was half empty and she felt—better. When had that happened?

"When the Chekydran questioned you so repeatedly, what did they want?"

"I don't know," Ari said. Several people shifted around the table. "At first the questions revolved around the expected. My ship, my mission, and my crew, but they abandoned that line within a week. From that point forward, they asked anything at all. Questions about my childhood, memories, favorite family recipes, stuff that made no sense. I never understood . . ."

"We have some evidence, Captain, that the Chekydran have telepathic talent," V'kyrri said.

Ari blinked and closed her gaping mouth. She sat up straight and met V'kyrri's serious gaze. He believed what he said. Bits and pieces clicked into place in her head.

"They were distracting me?"

He nodded. "It's possible they were attempting to guide you into a state that would allow them access to your thoughts, yes."

"I always had the impression—" She stopped short and pushed the cooling soup away. It sounded ridiculous.

"Go on," Eilod encouraged.

She let out a breath she hadn't realized she'd been holding. "I got the impression, over and over again, that they wanted me to be something, to do something I couldn't be or do. Once they started drugging the food, they tried even harder, and all I remember is a sensation like someone trying to take a dull knife to poke a hole in my skull."

"They drugged your food?" Seaghdh echoed, a ripple of some unknown feeling in his voice.

Ari shrugged. If it was power, it wasn't turned on her and she was grateful. "They were putting something in there. So I stopped eating. Nearly got them that time."

"I beg your pardon, Captain Idylle?" Eilod said.

Ari glanced at her and had to wipe a grim smile from her face when it appeared to startle and frighten the queen. "Sorry?"

Eilod drew composure around her like a cloak. "You said 'you nearly got them that time.' What does that mean?"

"Oh." She hadn't meant to say that aloud. "The Chekydran don't know much about what keeps humanoids alive. I'd lapsed into a coma before they realized I was starving to death and began force-feeding me."

CHAPTER
16

ARI glanced around the table. Shock, horror, one or two studiously blank expressions peered back. She was suddenly glad she'd looked up. She wanted to see these people realizing just how intrusive and painful their curiosity could be. They'd taken her from her family and from her life so they could ask questions they had no right to ask. Let them regret getting the answers. Let them realize they'd sent Cullin Seaghdh to do exactly what the Chekydran had done to her, despite the veneer of civility.

"The Chekydran kept trying to strip me bare, like a kid peeling the bark from a stick," Ari said. "Of course I resisted. At first. We all did."

"All? You were not the only prisoner?"

"No," she said.

"You said, 'you resisted at first,'" Eilod prodded.

"They wear you down," she answered. "All it takes is time. Sleep deprivation, physical pain, drugs. Until all you want is to make it stop. Even after I stopped actively resisting, they could not get what they wanted. To this day, I don't know what they had hoped to achieve. That they meant to modify me is plain, but their nanopaks never seemed to take."

"Nanopaks?" Eilod echoed, her tone mystified.

"The Chekydran favor nanotechnology that alters protein processing at the genetic level. A nanopak is a delivery mechanism based on viral infection models," a sharp-faced woman on Turrel's right said. "If the subj . . . If Captain Idylle has been exposed, we can be certain her body has been altered in some fashion to suit their purposes."

Every head in the room swiveled in Ari's direction as if looking for a sign that she'd turn into a slavering, mindless puppet for the sadistic aliens that had held her. Icy adrenaline dumped into her chest. She sat very still waiting for Seaghdh, Eilod, Turrel, or V'kyrri to pick up the sharp-faced woman's assurance that Ari had indeed been modified.

Seaghdh shifted, his face impassive. He'd looked at V'kyrri. "Is there any evidence to suggest Captain Idylle is a latent telepath? Or that the Chekydran were attempting to break her mind open to make her telepathic?"

V'kyrri shot a glance at Ari.

She met the engineer's gaze and raised an eyebrow at him.

He smiled. "All kinds of evidence of something, sir, from what I'm hearing. To find out, I need but a moment and your permission, Captain," he said to her.

"You want me to let you read me?" Ari asked.

"I would like to attempt to make contact," V'kyrri hedged. "It's not an invasion or a reading of your thoughts. Think of it as connection testing an uplink."

She smiled at the mental image of satellites and ground stations. Since there was absolutely no chance she was a telepath, V'k's connection test couldn't hurt. "What should I do?"

V'kyrri rose and took the seat next to hers. "Turn and face me. I will try this without touch, first, but if I cannot get through, may I put my hand on your arm?"

"I promise not to bite," she said.

"Aw, go on, Ari," Turrel urged. "He'd like it."

Laughter resounded through the room. V'kyrri grinned at her. She nodded.

"Relax," he said. "Close your eyes if you like. If it gets too uncomfortable, raise your right hand and I will stop immediately."

"Thanks," she said, trepidation marching up and down her spine.

Ari couldn't bring herself to close her eyes even though V'kyrri shut his. He drew a deep breath and sighed it out. She shifted her shoulders, remembering she was supposed to relax. Abruptly, pressure built in the center of her forehead. This knife trying to gain access to the inside of her skull had been sharpened. She gasped and pushed back in her chair. She could take this. She would not raise her right hand.

She started to shake. This wasn't the enemy . . . Ari wanted to laugh aloud, but couldn't control her trembling body. This wasn't the Chekydran, she corrected, but ultimately, as much as she wanted to think of V'kyrri, Turrel, and Seaghdh—especially Seaghdh—as friends, they were indeed the enemy. They were an enemy who thought her people were building a secret army to use against them and who would do or say anything in the name of preserving their people.

"Stop it, V'kyrri," she heard Seaghdh say.

Cold sweat trickled down her face. "No," she snapped. "I can do this." She was not broken beyond repair, damn it. She refused to be. "I will do this."

V'k set his fingers on her forearm. The pressure increased. Nausea surged within her. Ari swallowed weakly and leaned her throbbing head against the back of her chair.

And she retreated. The part of her that Ari reserved for herself fled down into darkness, into a watery, subterranean landscape where nothing else could reach. Her physical body still registered the pain of friendly fire trying to pry open her skull, could still feel V'k's fingers against her icy skin, but it was distant, as if she wasn't in residence any longer. She was safe.

Except she wasn't. Fear reached her in her hideaway, fear and anger, contained in Cullin Seaghdh's voice. It drew her back up the well, back into the body with the throbbing head and the—nothing on her arm. The ache behind her eyes eased. She blinked up at Seaghdh's face, no longer impassive. Fear for her stood out in the lines around his mouth and eyes. The pressure of his warm hands on her upper arms registered then.

"Are you all right?" he rasped.

She licked dry lips. "Sure could use a swig of painkiller."

"Ari, I'm sorry," V'kyrri said, his voice so contrite she tried to sit up to reassure him.

"Stay still," Seaghdh growled at her.

"It isn't supposed to hurt!" V'k protested.

"I bet you say that to all the girls."

Turrel barked a laugh before a glare from Seaghdh made him muffle it.

"Here, drink this." Dr. Annantra—when had they called her?—put a cup in Ari's hand. "A little something for nausea in there, too."

"Thank you," she said, then focused on Seaghdh, still distraught, still holding her down. "Help me?"

She knew damned well he wasn't simply going to let her go so she could drink. He lifted her head gently from the back of the seat. If he hadn't worn such a distressed look, she would have rolled her eyes, but his concern smote her conscience. He might be a liar and a manipulative spawn of a Myallki bitch, but it looked like he really was concerned for her welfare.

"Gods, that's great," she sighed as the medicine burned a path through her veins and stopped the headache short. She glanced at a perplexed-looking V'kyrri. "I'm surprised you don't have a headache after battering your head against my thick skull, V'k."

"You're feeling better, Captain Idylle?" Seaghdh asked, straightening as if he'd just realized he might be acting unprofessionally about his prisoner. He stabbed a quick glance around the table.

Ari sat up straighter. She'd forgotten that her every move was under observation and evaluation by a room full of strangers. "Yes, Captain," she said, reminding herself that she was still pissed off at him. "Thank you for your concern."

Regret and hurt stood out in his face for a moment, then he turned away and sat next to Eilod.

"Assessment," he demanded, pinning a glare on V'kyrri.

V'kyrri shook his head. "I've never run into anything like it before. Ari, I got nothing. Less than nothing. If you aren't a high-level telepath, I'll eat this conference table."

Ari started. "What?"

"If you . . ."

"I heard you! I thought you said you got nothing!" she protested. "I'm brain dead! Ask anyone who knows me. Hell! Ask my father!"

A troubled light grew in V'kyrri's eyes. "This isn't something your father could understand, Ari, much less measure. I don't know . . ."

"What?"

"I don't know who or what could have trained you to shut down a probe the way you did," he said.

"I don't understand."

"Me, either," V'k said. "But you're either the antithesis of a telepath, or a strong telepath who found a way down some kind of rabbit hole when another telepath comes knocking."

"A well," she corrected.

"What?"

"It's not a rabbit hole. It's a well that I go down," she said, suddenly interested that she'd had a means of defying the Chekydran all along and hadn't known it. Neither had they.

V'kyrri nodded. "Telepath. No one else would need so strong and instantaneous an image. It also means the talent predates Chekydran captivity. Damn, Ari. Is your educational system that broken? You should have been identified and trained!"

"We're not a telepathic people, V'k. No one knows what to look for. Leaving that aside, do we agree that this is the reason the Chekydran couldn't turn me to their purpose?"

"You believe they had a purpose?" Seaghdh pounced on her turn of phrase, leaning forward to pin her with that smoldering, golden gaze.

To snap back "I don't know" sat on the tip of her tongue. No matter her personal disagreement with him, they were both after the destruction of that army of mutated soldiers. Weren't they? She held her caustic retort and purposefully did something she'd avoided since her return home. She took a deep breath and tried to remember. Flashes, confused and terrifying, assailed her. She gripped the arms of her chair and struggled to breathe. She found herself nodding.

"Yes," she gasped. "Yes. They had a purpose." Abruptly, a vision of Hicci, mottled and restless with anger took over her sight. At the time, she hadn't understood his rage or her failure. Now, in hindsight, knowing she had an ability that thwarted the Chekydran captain, she could suddenly see the source of his distress.

"They had a purpose," she repeated. "But nothing they did would make me work right."

"Whatever you're doing," Seaghdh growled, "stop it. You're tearing up my ship."

None of his voice talent in his command this time, but his voice drew her firmly back into her body just the same. Ari blinked. Her fingernails had punctured the leather covering the padded arm of her chair. Peeling her aching, white-knuckled hands from the armrests, she met his gaze and nodded. He'd known. She swallowed a curse. Somehow, the bastard had conditioned her to respond, and he'd known he could pull her out of memory with just a word. It should probably have enraged her. Instead, relief trickled through her veins.

"Taking a walk down memory lane," she said. "Sorry."

"Give us something we can use, Captain, and I'll let you rend the entire conference room," Eilod said. "You mentioned that the Chekydran couldn't make you work right. Can you tell us anything about what their purpose might have been?"

She sighed and sat back in her chair, letting her arms hang. "I keep going back to the basic-training metaphor and the nanopaks. The methods were so similar, tear down, rebuild. I'm an Armada officer, not a fresh recruit. I just wasn't susceptible. So they changed tactics. The drugs, the psychological torture, physical torture, but time and time again, just as Hicci would tell me I was coming along nicely, he'd become so agitated, so angry. Yet no matter what I said or did, I could not make him kill me."

Silence. Nearly everyone stared at her without comprehension. Turrel's grim expression as he met her eye and nodded once told Ari he understood. The hint of torment in Seaghdh's expression caught and held her. He would not look at her. What was going on?

Eilod Saoyrse cleared her throat and leaned forward. "Perhaps we should take a break. I've ordered . . ."

"We don't have time," Ari said.

Tension reared up in the room.

The queen's assessing gaze felt like it could cut. "What makes you say that, Captain?"

"The *Balykkal* is en route," Ari said. "It wasn't stated as fact, but I gather she's on search and destroy."

Her Majesty sat up straighter and arched one glossy brown eyebrow. "Your ship won't fire on us with you aboard."

"They might if your spymaster's intel is any good."

Seaghdh outlined their run-in with the soldiers on Kebgra. To her relief, he left his injury and her first aid out of the explanation.

The sharp-faced woman sat forward, her black uniform gleaming. "Your weapons could not penetrate the soldiers' armor?" she asked.

"No," Seaghdh said.

"Because you were carrying a TFC-issue rifle," Ari interrupted, glancing at Seaghdh. "The Autolyte did some damage. It might have eventually punched through."

His gaze turned inward, Seaghdh nodded and muttered, "Three shots to your one."

"Auhrnok?" the sharp-faced woman prompted.

"Captain Idylle discovered the weakness in the soldier's defenses," he replied, focusing on the people at the table once more. "A single shot from a Claugh weapon to a soldier's head destroyed the soldier. My weapon, an Armada-made Rez-Whit 367, could not stop them with fewer than three shots to the exposed skin of the face."

Turrel shook his head. "Don't know why they'd go to so much trouble to create indestructible soldiers and then leave an exposure like that."

"It doesn't make sense," the woman in black said. "Why didn't they cover their faces?"

"Because when they grew armor over prisoners' faces," someone said, "they went mad."

The weighted silence drew Ari's attention. She glanced around the table. Turrel looked like a lifeless statue. He refused to meet her gaze. At the head of the table, Eilod's eyes were wide with revulsion. Seaghdh, his lips edged with white, met her eye.

"You witnessed this?" he asked, his gruff voice reluctant.

Only then did she realize she'd been the one who'd spoken.

She stared at him, panic hammering against the inside of her ribs. Icy sweat gathered on her forehead. She had no memory to explain the statement she'd made. She didn't want to have any memory of that kind of horror. She screwed her eyes shut and swallowed hard.

"Clear the room!" Seaghdh commanded.

She'd thought she'd heard him use his talent before now. The harsh, raw power in his order nearly threw her from her seat.

"Cullin," the queen protested.

"Get her out!" he shouted.

"He's right, ma'am," Turrel said. "When Captain Idylle has a flashback, she's deadly. I'd be surprised if the Chekydran didn't lose a few to her."

That was a bracing thought.

"I'm all right," Ari wheezed. Planting her head in her hands, she concentrated on drawing in slow, measured draughts of air.

"Ari?" Seaghdh. Crouched beside her from the sounds of it. "I'm going to put a hand on your arm, if that's okay."

She turned her head and glared at him. "Two things, Auhrnok.

One, that is a damned vulnerable position to take when you think I might be about to have a flashback. I am mad at you, but I'd rather not kill you. Don't make it so easy for me. Two, don't coddle me. I will never tell you I'm all right if I'm not."

Hand still hovering in midair, Seaghdh blinked. A slow, engaging smile spread and lit those golden eyes. He wrapped his fingers around her upper arm and said, "I might be a little tougher than I look."

She considered launching an attack to prove her point. Sighing, she straightened and slid her gaze from his. They were still in a room full of people watching their every move. He had tried to humiliate her in front of her family and friends when they'd engaged in that silly duel. Remembering how he'd let her turn the tables on him when he could have beaten her at any time, she refused to take the bait he'd dangled to let her return the favor.

"Do you have Zomnat tea?" she asked.

"Let me find out." He squeezed her arm gently and rose.

From his pause at her side, Ari assumed he gestured everyone back to the table. Feet shuffled over carpet. Chairs creaked. Seaghdh walked away.

"My apologies," she said.

"None necessary, Captain," Eilod said, her tone grave and sincere. "Are you able to proceed?"

"Yes."

"Thank you."

Ari shrugged. "Can we change the subject?"

"Ari, Turrel told me what happened with your crewman," V'kyrri said, hesitation in his words. "May I ask some questions?"

He hadn't witnessed a full-fledged flashback and she'd scared him already? Meeting V'kyrri's eye, she nodded. He relaxed.

"You talked him down?"

"I gave him a command," she said. "I trusted there was enough of my lieutenant left to respond."

"What kind of command? What happened?"

"I think I ordered him to stand down."

"What were you feeling?"

She peered at the engineer. He wasn't just asking questions. He was driving her toward something. "I don't know, V'k. Just tell me what you're after."

"Zomnat tea," Seaghdh said, placing the cup before her. A mug of the same soup he'd given her earlier appeared beside the tea.

"I suspect you influenced your crewman telepathically, Captain," V'kyrri said.

Ari reeled. "No. I couldn't have. I didn't even know—" She broke off, casting back through that memory. "I tried to reach past what had been done to him. When I found the young man I remembered, I talked to him. He broke free. I *felt* it. Did I do that?"

"It is possible," V'kyrri hedged, his tone telling her that he knew exactly what his answer might cost her.

She'd used a power she didn't know she'd had to influence someone. That made her no better than Seaghdh. Where had this ability come from? How could she have not known? What the hell was she?

Seaghdh took over. He paced the room, focusing attention on her assessment that Armada Command had sent the soldiers to kill or recover her. Save that they'd done so a day early.

Eilod blew out a sharp, frustrated breath. "They have made more progress than we were led to believe."

"It gets worse," Ari said. "I assume your Auhrnok told you I had an IntCom mission?"

She nodded.

"IntCom isn't talking to my CO."

Seaghdh's gaze darted to meet hers. Calculation ran rapid-fire behind his eyes. "Separate entities?"

"Yes. Intelligence Command and Armada Command each report directly to Council so that each may provide oversight on the other."

"And IntCom, for whatever reason, no longer trusts Armada Command," he mused.

"I don't know that," she corrected. "I only know that IntCom isn't talking to my commanding officer at Armada."

Eilod shifted. "You sound like you've been briefed, Captain."

"I have. In medical."

"What?" Her Majesty turned on Seaghdh.

"Medi-scan results incoming," he said, tapping a screen embedded in the table in front of him. "The transmission came in near the end of Captain Idylle's scan. Medical diagnostics picked up traces of the communication. Com alerts did not."

A murmur of voices and bodies shifting let Ari retrieve her handheld unnoticed. One young man rose and raced from the room.

"Why did you not bring this to my attention immediately?" Eilod demanded, glaring between Ari and her cousin.

Why hadn't he? He didn't know the content of the conversation, but he damn well knew she'd had it.

"Admiral Angelou . . ." Ari began.

"Your commanding officer?" Eilod clarified.

"And my mentor," she acknowledged. "Friend" she kept to herself. "He made some accusations. Ones I've heard leveled at Armada Command."

Seaghdh swore.

Ari activated the handheld and turned up the volume. Admiral Angelou's voice sounded oddly muted, punctuated by her taps of acknowledgment.

The transmission ended with a barely audible click.

"That c'ruhb rwotsh dung eater," the queen whispered.

Ari frowned. She had no idea what a c'ruhb rwotsh dung eater was. She could guess she didn't want to know.

Eilod's gaze flicked to Ari. "How do I disprove this claim?"

Ari studied her for several seconds while trying to remember what she knew about the young queen. Her empire was a constitutional monarchy. She answered to her Nobles Council and to her Peoples Voice Council. The history of the empire was checkered with monarchs of varying efficacy. The Councils had always bound things together. Until three generations ago, when a vibrant, charismatic king had galvanized the Councils and greatly expanded his empire, absorbing worlds and entire populations into the chaotic mix of races and species comprising the Empire. His son followed in his footsteps, heading the Councils and carving out a reputation of fairness and compassion. Rumor claimed he'd been assassinated. Official announcements stated that he'd died after a protracted illness. Walking through some of his media clips, Ari wondered if he hadn't spontaneously combusted. He blazed when he spoke. She'd felt scorched just watching him.

While Eilod had charisma in spades, she didn't have the fire-eaten look her father had worn. When had she come to the throne? And what connection did she have to Cullin Seaghdh? And he to her? They were cousins, that much was common knowledge. Despite the fact that TFC didn't recognize nobility, or maybe because of that very fact, many TFC citizens took an interest in the Claugh royal house. Ari could see the attraction. The queen was a beautiful woman. She had quite a following among both men and women. Speculation about her preferences in partners abounded. As far as Ari knew, she had neither husband nor consort.

Seaghdh was damnably attractive, but she'd never heard much about him. The Auhrnok Riorchjan had too formidable a reputation for ruthlessness. She had trouble reconciling the Cullin Seaghdh she thought she knew with the remote, rumor-ridden Queen's Blade. Reports claimed he'd do anything for Her Imperial Majesty. Speculation about why that might be focused on the bizarre and nasty. It didn't help that Eilod didn't seem to indulge in romantic liaisons.

She wasn't acting. Ari didn't know how she knew, but she did. Someone was lying, but it wasn't Eilod Saoyrse. That left her with only one lead. "Call in the *Sen Ekir*. Allow my father and his team to examine Tommy's body."

The queen glanced at Seaghdh.

He nodded. "With our options fast diminishing, I concur. Dr. Idylle's profile suggests his allegiance is to science, not to a political entity."

Ari raised an eyebrow. She wouldn't have given the same assessment of her father's loyalties. Entirely. However, if Seaghdh's read was correct, it explained why her dad had been left out of the Shlovkura disaster. Wow. There was a price attached to being too good at your job.

"Would he defect?" Her Majesty asked.

"No," Ari replied. "Family."

"Will you?"

Ari gaped at her. "Don't pull your punches, Your Majesty."

"You ought to defect because of your family," Turrel grumbled across from her.

Ari scowled at him.

"They'll make it worth your while," Turrel assured her. "I'd know."

So that's why they'd put her opposite him. Ari looked back at the head of the table but refused to meet anyone's eye. She couldn't risk seeing anything in Seaghdh's face. "I—don't know," she hedged. Impatience broke past caution and she kept talking when she'd meant to shut her mouth. "Hadn't I better live through whatever you and your spymaster have planned for me first?"

CHAPTER

17

"YES." The queen stretched the word to its limits as she stared at Ari. Abruptly, she looked away. "Clear the room. Captain Idylle, please stay."

That hadn't been a request. Baxt'k. Weariness swept her as Ari took a sip of tea and noticed how badly her hands shook.

"Your Majesty," Seaghdh began.

"Clear the room, Auhrnok," Eilod repeated without looking at him, her voice flat. "Await our pleasure. All other personnel, we require your reports within the hour. Dismissed."

Ari'd never heard royal-speak before. It made her smile. Everyone rose and bowed before filing out of the room. She felt the sonic shield drop as the door opened. Seaghdh left last, a tick in the muscles along his jaw letting her know he wasn't at all happy. He glanced at her as she took another swallow of tea. The tension in his expression eased.

The barely audible hum of the sonic shield engaged the moment the door shut behind him. Ari leaned into the table and examined Eilod Saoyrse. The queen wore an assessing, distrustful expression.

"Are we done being polite?" Ari asked.

Eilod smiled. It didn't reach her eyes. "I hadn't realized I was sending him to retrieve a beautiful woman. Has your hair always been that blond?"

Thrown off balance, Ari blinked and fingered a curl. She was nodding.

"What are you, Captain?"

"What," not "who." Interesting.

"Seven months ago, I could have answered that question," Ari said. "I can't anymore. I don't know. I do intend to find out."

"Why did the Chekydran let you go?"

"Grand-prize question, isn't it?" Ari pushed the tea away in favor of the soup mug and shook her head. "We all know they had a reason. Damned if I can work out what it was."

"Is that why you lock yourself into your cabin each night aboard your father's ship?"

Damn Seaghdh's hide. He'd probably reported on her unusual medical technique, too. She deeply regretted not putting her fist in his throat when he'd crouched beside her. Ari pinned an angry glare on his prying cousin.

"Ever lie awake nights because you know damned well someone is using you? You just don't know how or for what?"

Eilod pressed her lips thin and nodded.

"At least the ones using you are humanoid," Ari said. Mentally, she added, not to mention that you have someone like Seaghdh watching your back. How many of the people trying to use you end up dead or missing?

Looking stricken, Eilod frowned. "You cannot ascribe human motivation to the Chekydran. Is it possible they sent you to kill us?"

"Absolutely," Ari said. "Your cousin has tempted me a few times. More than once, I've regretted not following up on the impulse."

"What have you done to him?" the queen demanded. The sharp edge in her voice told Ari they'd reached part of her real point.

"What have I done?" Ari boggled. "You send him after me. He

hijacks my father's ship, endangering my family and my friends, and you have the gall to ask what I've done? Lady, with all due respect, you and your precious cousin can roast in the lowest levels of hell. I'm sorry I answered any of your questions."

Eilod grinned. The smile didn't just reach her eyes this time. Amusement took over her entire countenance. "No, you're not," she retorted. "I sent a man I know and trust on a mission to recover you at any cost. I admit that may have been shortsighted. Captain Idylle, the man who returned is not the one I sent out."

Ari's anger stopped short. "Not the same how?"

The queen hesitated as though sorting through how much to confide. Did she mean for Ari to see that?

"He seems to have lost his objectivity, Captain," she said.

The queen wasn't sure she could trust him. Because of her? How could—Ari gasped. "You think I've done something to him telepathically?"

Discomfort shot into the woman's expression, then disappeared. "Perhaps not consciously."

"Serve him right if I had."

"I beg your pardon?"

"Don't think he hasn't taken full advantage of that voice talent of his. If I did something to him telepathically, that's only fair, wouldn't you say?"

Eilod leaned forward, her eyes wide. "He's used Nwyth Okkar in his dealings with you?"

"In varying shapes and sizes from the command that all but tossed everyone out of the room earlier," Ari said, trusting "Nwyth Okkar" equaled "voice talent."

Eilod sat back hard, drumming her fingers on the table and glared at her. "He has evaluated hundreds of subjects before you. He is a brilliant, cunning strategist and is ruthless regarding the safety of our people. Yet when he looks at you, the rational, almost cold man I know and trust evaporates."

Stunned and gaping, Ari shook her head. "He's playing a part!

The part he's been playing since he took my father's ship! Why should he work at extracting information from me when he can charm it out of me?"

"Damn it, Captain! You aren't listening!" Eilod accused. "I can't trust you! Yet I have to ask you to put your life on the line for me and for my people! Something about you has my Auhrnok Riorchjan acting like a schoolboy! What am I supposed to think?"

"Whatever you please," Ari answered, clinging to the thought that it couldn't be true. He was a dueling master. He was using her. Wasn't he?

Staring witlessly at the queen like she was, Ari saw the flicker behind Eilod's eyes and straightened. She was considering having Ari killed. Not today, but eventually. Ari could see the thought running through her head. The notion clearly repulsed the young queen, but she forced herself to examine it, to be logical and unfeeling about Ari's eventual murder. It was something Ari could understand and even respect. Maybe their cultures weren't so far apart, after all. She'd have considered the same option in the queen's place. The fact that Eilod wanted Ari to risk her life on behalf of the Claugh Empire meant Ari could trust her. Briefly.

"I'm nothing more than a piece on a game board. It is increasingly clear that I have been for far longer than the six months of hell my life has been since my capture. If I'm going to find out why, I'll need your help," Ari told her.

That startled Eilod out of contemplating her death. "My help?"

"Get this transponder out of my head," Ari said, nodding. "Armada can't track me with it, but they can communicate through it and I can communicate with them. Using the unique ID associated with it, they can initiate a teleport. It hadn't occurred to me until that conversation with my CO, but it is possible there's functionality built into the unit that I'm not aware of."

"Such as?"

"Record and report. Not remotely, or they'd know where I am and it's clear they don't. Auto-destruct is also possible."

Eilod's breath hissed between her teeth.

"I don't know that it's true," Ari said, "but in my commander's place, I'd have wanted the option. They don't know why I was freed, either."

The queen's gaze sharpened. "They implanted this without your permission?"

"I'm a soldier. That was all the permission they needed."

Eilod eyed Ari for several seconds, her expression thoughtful. "Captain Alexandria Idylle, what do you want?"

"I want my life back," Ari blurted in response. "That doesn't seem likely, so I'll settle for my command. It's the only thing I've ever had that was really mine."

Folding her hands on the table, Eilod dropped her gaze. "Then perhaps cooperating with the Claugh nib Dovvyth is not in your best interest."

"On the contrary," Ari replied easily.

Eilod shot her a narrow-eyed look.

"Let's call this what it is," Ari suggested. "We're talking about an alliance, temporary though it may be. My oath when I joined the military was to serve and protect all the citizens of Tagreth Federated, nothing about loyalty to a political body or an organization."

"You believe that uncovering an alliance with the Chekydran will justify collaboration with the enemy?"

"We're not at war."

"You're not at war with the Chekydran, either."

Ari hesitated. It was a mistake.

The queen smiled and sat back. "I see."

"It is more a sense of inevitability within the ranks and command structure of the Armada than a secret war."

Eilod sighed. "More TFC doublespeak."

"Someone in Armada Command saying one thing and doing another," Ari said. "It's military. I'm used to it."

The queen laughed and rose.

Caught off guard, Ari struggled to her feet as Eilod touched a command screen and the sonic shield died.

"Captain Idylle," Eilod said, that I'm-speaking-as-the-queen tone in her voice. "On behalf of the citizens of the Claugh nib Dovvyth, we thank you for your dedicated efforts against Chekydran incursion. We are pleased we could assist the Tagreth Federated Council in fending off the attack on its Kebgra outpost.

"At present, Captain, it would seem your goals and those of my people coincide. I offer a temporary alliance, a truce, if you will, in the best interests of both our peoples against a common enemy."

Damn, she was good, not naming the enemy, even if she'd just pinned Ari between a black hole and a supernova. Ari grinned. "At present, I can't speak as a representative of the Armada, ma'am, much less as an official of TFC. Inasmuch as I am still bound by my oath to the Council, however, I agree. It is an efficient use of resources to protect the citizens of our respective territories. I am, for the moment, at your service."

"Splendid," Eilod said, an answering twinkle of amusement in her eye. It did not show in her voice. "Allow me to extend the hospitality of the Empire, Captain." She touched another button on her command console. "Auhrnok Riorchjan, enter."

The doors opened. Seaghdh entered, strode to where Eilod stood, knelt, took her hand in both of his, and touched his forehead to the back of her hand.

"Auhrnok Riorchjan, my trusted advisor, I ask you to take up the mantle of ambassador," Eilod intoned.

"By your will, Your Majesty," he replied.

"Rise, Auhrnok. Captain Idylle will be our guest until we can arrange with officials of Tagreth Federated for a mutually acceptable meeting place with her ship, the *Sen Ekir*," she went on as Seaghdh stood.

He shot a glance at Ari.

She raised an eyebrow.

"The results of your medical scan indicate a number of nutritional deficiencies, Captain," Eilod said. "Dr. Annantra would be pleased to offer treatment. Copies of all files will be forwarded to your ship upon transfer."

"Thank you," Ari said.

"Thank you, Captain," the queen replied. "Auhrnok, Captain, if you will pardon me? I am due in conference with the Councils."

"By your will, Your Majesty," Seaghdh said. He bowed.

Ari blinked, uncertain how to respond.

Eilod winked, but wiped the grin from her face by the time her cousin rose.

"Captain? If you will permit me," he said, his tone remote and his expression chilly. "I will escort you to medical if you wish or to quarters if you prefer to rest."

He didn't say whose quarters. Cravuul dung, on two fronts. It occurred to Ari that since the queen had lowered the sonic shield, news of her whereabouts would reach Admiral Angelou sooner rather than later. She did not want to find out the hard way just what functions her CO had built into the transponder.

"Medical, please, Auhrnok Riorchjan," she said as he ushered her out the door. "I understand you are the top-rated energy blade dueler in the Empire. I admit it is a hobby of mine. Perhaps after I'm in better physical condition, I could impose upon you for a few pointers?"

Her Majesty's Auhrnok Riorchjan stared down at her. The cool mask cracked and a gleam of humor crept into his eyes.

"You wouldn't be lulling me into a false sense of security, would you, Captain? Luring me onto the dueling floor in order to trounce me?"

"How could you think it of me?"

"How indeed."

CHAPTER

18

SOMETHING warm and comforting stroked Ari's bare arm. She couldn't order her eyes open. She couldn't move. She'd been drugged. Panic reared up within her. That gentle, persistent touch soothed her, assuring her frayed nerves that she had nothing to fear.

Consciousness returned piecemeal. A dull ache woke in her left cheekbone. Her head cleared and she remembered. The transponder. Not Chekydran. Seaghdh and the Claugh nib Dovvyth.

She'd asked for this. She groaned and opened her bleary eyes.

It was Seaghdh's hand on her arms.

"Is my head still attached?" she rasped.

"Yes."

"Stop petting me and fix that."

He smiled. "I can do better than that."

Something beeped. The ache faded.

Seaghdh resumed caressing his palm down her arms, first one, then the other.

"I am not a feral hiztap," she mumbled, referring to a memory from childhood. She'd found a family of hiztaps, little furbearing carnivores prized for their ability to eradicate vermin, living behind her father's labs. They'd been filching food from the university students. She'd found homes for the youngest hizzetts. The adult female, however, had been on her own too long. She would not warm to Ari or any other person.

The local animal practitioner had anesthetized the hiztap and sterilized her. He'd put Ari at her side and advised her to stroke the creature's plush fur as she woke. Ari had. For hours. The animal had growled and flashed her teeth when she fully woke, but she didn't actually bite. Ari didn't know what changed that day, but while the hiztap never became a loving companion, she and Ari did reach an accord. She'd lived with Ari, sharing her quarters and warning her of prank-minded interlopers until she died of old age just after Ari'd entered the Armada Academy. She hadn't thought of the hiztap in years. Why did Ari miss her so sharply and so suddenly?

"I could think of no other way for you to wake knowing you weren't in a Chekydran cell," he said.

"It worked," she replied. "I'm awake. Why are you still doing it?"

"I like touching you."

As the anesthetic cleared her system, the feel of his skin on hers strengthened her heart rate. Sensation seeped warm and tingling throughout her body. She sighed.

"It's against regulations," Ari murmured, "dueling a handicapped opponent."

He smiled. She heard it in his voice when he answered, "A blade master takes every advantage. It worked. You're not still mad at me."

"I am," she replied. "I just can't do anything about it right now."

"Now who's dueling?"

She felt his heat a moment before he touched his lips to her left cheekbone. Her breath hissed in between her teeth. It wasn't from pain.

He chuckled. "I take it you approve of my unusual medical technique?"

"I do," she breathed, savoring the thrill racing across her nerve endings. She stared up into his face, so close to hers and frowned. Tension stood out in the crinkles at the corners of his mouth. Without thinking, she smoothed shaky fingers over the creases.

"Auhrnok!" Dr. Annantra exclaimed.

They both jumped. Ari hadn't heard the door open. Apparently, neither had he. Seaghdh straightened. Her hand fell back to her side.

"You are disturbing my patient," the doctor warned.

"I hope so," he replied.

"You will desist," the woman said, her voice shimmering with amusement, "or I will expel you from my medical bay and delete your clearance. Captain Idylle needs rest. Not distraction."

Ari laughed and found the control to lift the head of the bed so she could sit up. She felt better. Far better than she should have after the kind of surgery she would have needed to remove that transponder. A chill moved through her. "Where is it?"

"Where is what?" Dr. Annantra asked, her smile bright.

"The transponder."

The doctor's grin disappeared.

Ari growled.

Seaghdh jerked his chin and the doctor fled. He secured the door before turning to meet Ari's glare.

"You changed the codes," she said. Of course they'd left the transponder in her head. They'd reprogrammed it so that it would no longer respond to Armada Command orders, but it certainly would respond to theirs.

"Yes."

She ground her teeth together until her jaw hurt. Without intending to do so, she'd just handed Eilod Saoyrse the means to kill her remotely. A few hours ago, she'd at least had the Armada code for her transponder. Now that was gone and she had nothing but an enemy that imagined they had the means to control her.

"Interesting," she managed before the lines of tension returned to his face. She caught a hint of distress behind his carefully neutral mask.

He pressed his lips tight. Trying not to say anything? Rage slipped into his expression.

It dawned on her. He wasn't furious with her. This was aimed elsewhere.

"Must have been a hell of a fight," she said, "you and your cousin. Sorry I missed it."

Seaghdh's mask crumbled. Rage, bitterness, and fear shone in the tight muscles of his shoulders and the line along his clenched jaw.

"She pulled rank," he grumbled. Shaking his head, he ventured toward her as if unsure of his reception at her bedside. "She's made a mistake."

"Yes. She has." Sharp pain filled her chest, as if something was swelling within and trying to break free. Ari gasped and tasted it again. Hope. Damn it. Her eyes burned. "I miscalculated," she admitted. "I ignored the fact that women define honor differently than most men. It didn't occur to me she'd lie so naturally."

"She didn't. That's my job."

"She said one thing and did another, Seaghdh," Ari countered. "There's a word for that."

He wouldn't meet her eye. "Removing the transponder would have required extensive recovery time. Time we don't have."

The queen had put him in a tough spot, probably on purpose, testing his loyalty, forcing him to choose between the two of them. Ari nodded. "That makes it all right then, doesn't it? Did you deactivate the destruct capability, Auhrnok?"

A moment of anguish clouded his features. His pain took the breath from her body. Of course they hadn't disabled the destruct feature.

She took his hand.

He looked at her, then, his gaze searching and uncertain.

Ari didn't hear or feel the hum of a sonic shield. She had to assume that meant anyone could be listening. How could she warn him that he was being tested? Or did he already know?

"Not telling me who you were," she said, "pissed me off, but I could justify it. Enemy territory and all. I'd have gotten over it. But this? Your government is holding me hostage, Auhrnok Riorchjan. Please tell your queen that believing she can motivate me by threatening my life presupposes I value my life in the least. And that is a mistake. You have proof of that."

She watched Seaghdh sift through her words, processing the fact that she hadn't accused him. She'd specified his cousin. She'd also reminded him that she'd already offered once to die on his account. At the time, it had been a bid to stay out of Chekydran custody, but if she had walked out the air lock and died sucking vacuum, Seaghdh and his men would have survived. She couldn't give him many more clues.

His com badge trilled. It wasn't the same pattern of sound Ari'd heard in the shuttle bay. That he didn't answer the call confirmed her suspicion. The Claugh coded their hails. Armada hails were all the same. You found out what someone wanted when you answered. She released his cold hand.

He went to the door. It opened. Seaghdh paused. "You can't make me want to kill you, Captain."

Message received and understood. Good. She met his penetrating stare. "I don't have to, Seaghdh. Your cousin has already made the decision to handle it."

Disbelief fired in his eyes, then alarm. Biting out a curse, he stomped away. As he went, Ari heard him acknowledge the com call in his own language.

Dr. Annantra stepped into the open doorway, her expression troubled. "May I come in, Captain?"

Ari blinked. It was Annantra's medical bay and Ari was just a prisoner, no matter how politely they wanted to play that game. "Why not."

"I am sorry, Captain Idylle. I could not risk extraction." The doctor activated instruments and watched readouts for a moment. "Are you in pain?"

A single humorless laugh escaped Ari. "I deserve it."

Startled, the woman stared, eyes wide. After a moment, Annantra cleared her throat, looked unseeing at her instruments, and nodded. "Whoever installed the transponder included a fail-safe."

"A trap," Ari surmised.

"Yes. One I could not circumvent. It will require a specialist."

"Neurosurgeon?"

Dr. Annantra's frown wrinkled her nose. "Possibly a bomb squad."

"Great." Armada and Claugh vying for control of one freed Chekydran prisoner. Ari had made some assumptions about why that might be. She was starting to question them. Simple curiosity about why she'd been released didn't justify the kind of machinations she'd been caught up in.

"Captain Seaghdh would not leave your side."

"Touching," she said, damning the warmth that flared within her. Was someone still listening now that Seaghdh had been called away? Ari couldn't risk it.

The doctor shot her a sharp glance.

"He worked hard to get me here," she told Dr Annantra. "Your government seems to think I might be helpful. He's invested a lot in that belief."

The woman turned to her, planted her hands on her hips, and awarded her a disapproving glare. "You are being deliberately obtuse."

Ari raised her eyebrows.

"It was not the Auhrnok Riorchjan at your side, Captain," Dr. Annantra snapped. "It was Cullin Seaghdh, a man I'd only met once before when his cousin was ill and confined to my bay. Yes. He is the

Auhrnok Riorchjan, and yes, he can seem heartless. But he isn't. He's simply spent his life protecting the ones he loves."

Which didn't include Ari or she wouldn't still have a bomb in her head. She sucked in a deep breath and ignored the heat behind her eyes. Even if he'd only deactivated the destruct sequence . . .

"The fear I saw in that man at your side suggests he has invested considerably more than you credit him for." The doctor shook her head and dropped her hands to her sides. Before turning back to her instrument panel, she said, "You have far more at stake than your life, my dear. In my professional opinion, he wants your heart. I believe I know Auhrnok Captain Cullin Seaghdh nib Riorchjan well enough to suggest he'll stop at nothing to win it."

Shock rippled through Ari. Her heart? Did she still have one? Was that the expanding pain in her chest? She drew her knees up, rested her forehead against them, and prayed Eilod Saoyrse hadn't just heard a word the doctor had said.

Dr. Annantra chuckled and patted Ari's shoulder. "When you erect your considerable defenses, be certain that you are indeed protecting yourself."

Ari frowned. What the hell was that supposed to mean? Throw down arms and shout "come get me"? There was a good idea. The instrument monitor beeped. Increased heart rate and respiration. Damn it.

"You are recovering well," Dr. Annantra said. "I will leave you to rest."

Ari lifted her head. "Wait. Is my handheld here?"

"Yes. With your clothes."

"I'd like to download a language program, if that's permitted."

Dr. Annantra brightened. "An excellent idea."

WHAT was wrong with him? Seaghdh slammed a fist into the lift wall. It had taken Ari's warning to nudge his brain into gear. He should have seen for himself that his cousin was testing him. Flexing his hand, he leaned back and closed his eyes. He'd been ready to face Ari's hatred and rage when she discovered they hadn't removed the transponder. Instead, she'd seen straight through him and offered understanding. *She'd trusted him.*

The lift stopped.

He opened his eyes.

The doors whisked into the bulkhead.

Eilod stood behind her desk, her features arrayed in what he recognized as her best politician's mask.

He squared his shoulders, strode into the queen's chambers, and saluted. "Your Majesty." He felt the sonic shield go up.

"Auhrnok Riorchjan, we thank you for your prompt attention," Eilod said. She touched a control on her panel and a holo-image flickered to life beside him. A man, olive complexion, black eyes, silver hair that had once been black, dressed in TFC navy blue, eyed him in return before glancing at the queen.

"Admiral Angelou, my Auhrnok Riorchjan," she said. "Please, gentlemen, be seated."

Ari's commanding officer. Seaghdh's gut tightened. He sat. Angelou pulled a chair into line with his holo-camera and lowered himself into it.

Eilod looked between them for a moment, then perched on the edge of her desk. "Admiral Angelou requests the return of his officer, Auhrnok."

"Arrangements for Captain Idylle's return are underway via diplomatic channels per the Baalkryt Accords signed by our respective governments nearly four decades ago," Seaghdh said.

Angelou's lips tightened.

"Something concerns you, Admiral?" Eilod prompted.

"Your Majesty," Jecaldo Angelou said, inclining his head to Eilod before meeting Seaghdh's eye. "Auhrnok. Thank you for meeting with me off record like this. This is . . ." He broke off and sighed, shaking his head. "Please understand. Captain Idylle was a promising young officer, one of our finest. Her record is exemplary. When she was captured, we gave her up for dead. We were elated when she was returned to us. Except . . ."

"The young woman returned to you was not the woman you knew," Eilod finished for him.

"Precisely." Angelou lifted his hands in a helpless gesture. "Physically, Captain Idylle has begun to recover. Mentally, however, and this is difficult to say, mentally, our doctors tell us she may never be who she once was."

"You believe your officer has gone rogue, Admiral?" Seaghdh demanded. Something icy spilled into his blood. It could make sense. Read a certain way, everything that had happened since he'd taken her father's ship could have been an elaborate setup to get Ari into proximity with Eilod. Or the Auhrnok Riorchjan.

Pain clouded the other man's features. "I don't know, Auhrnok. I don't know. She has been diagnosed with paranoia and delusions. Her psych eval stopped just short of schizophrenia. My doing, I'm afraid. I had hoped I could redeem her, keep her in the ranks. Now, I'm just not sure. She commandeered her father's science ship as if her own family were a danger to her."

Before or after he had, Seaghdh wondered, trying not to smile.

"I hesitate to say she's a danger," the admiral said. "She means a great deal to me, personally."

Seaghdh felt the ring of truth in the man's words at last. It gave him the key to unlocking the man's lies. A warning fired through him, one he made certain no one else saw.

"As an officer of the Armada, however, tasked with protecting those Accords you mentioned, Auhrnok," Angelou said, "I confess that Captain Idylle's mental state frightens me. I don't want her killed. Neither do I want a galactic incident. She has flashbacks. And when she does, people get hurt."

"Captain Idylle saved my life." From the swiftly stifled surprise in the man's face, Seaghdh gathered he'd not heard that story yet.

"Admiral, Auhrnok," Eilod said. "Gentlemen, let us return to point. Admiral, your Council has given this ship clearance to enter the Buffer Zone and to rendezvous with the science ship *Sen Ekir*. We are to transfer custody of your officer to the personnel aboard that ship. We are ten hours from that meet point."

Angelou hesitated, then shook his head. "If I could be certain of Captain Idylle's state of mind, Your Majesty, I would be satisfied. I cannot, in good conscience, however, leave her aboard your ship. If she has decided to take it upon herself to eliminate what she perceives as a threat to the Tagreth Federated Council, you could be in grave danger."

"You wish us to transfer her to the ship you have mirroring our movements at the edge of the Zone?" Eilod surmised.

Angelou smiled and steepled his fingers before him. "The *Balykkal* is merely a precaution, madam. They were ordered into place before it became clear you had entered TFC on a rescue mission."

His cousin glanced at him, her expression patently neutral. "Auhrnok? You came directly from medical. What is Captain Idylle's status?"

"Medical?" Angelou echoed.

Seaghdh nodded, catching Eilod's intent. "Dr. Annantra classifies her condition as critical. I regret that Captain Idylle's medical status precludes teleport at this time."

Angelou's polite expression fell, and for a second, Seaghdh caught a clear glimpse of the conniving, cold man under the façade. "What happened?"

"She took a dose of poison from a tree on Kebgra," Seaghdh lied. He caught the approving look Eilod tossed him. "Our doctor was not familiar with the toxin. Your officer seemed fine when first we brought her aboard, but she slipped into a coma just prior to my arrival in this office. We believe your captain will recover, but the paralytic affected respiration and heart rhythm. The doctor will not release her until Captain Idylle is out of danger."

"I've heard of these trees," Angelou murmured. "We have extensive experience handling . . ."

"Appearances, Admiral," Eilod interrupted with a smile.

Angelou frowned.

"We have in our custody an Armada officer your people laud as a hero," she said. "Imagine how it would play in your media if anything at all happened to harm her while she is in our care or being transferred from our care. Just as you feel you cannot risk leaving Captain Idylle with us, the Empire of the Claugh nib Dovvyth simply cannot risk the public relations disaster that would result if Captain Idylle suffered harm at our hands."

Seaghdh watched the plans and calculation running rapid-fire behind the admiral's eyes. His desire to recover Ari at any cost warred with his need to make his request appear reasonable, rational. Seaghdh congratulated himself on the fabrication of Ari's illness. If Angelou tried to contact Ari via the transponder now, he'd assume she hadn't recovered from the paralytic enough to respond.

"Given the information you have graciously shared with us, Admiral," Seaghdh continued, "I will require that Captain Idylle be sedated until after transfer. Her Majesty's safety is paramount, of course, but I respect and admire your desire to protect your officer's reputation. If a few hours' sedation can facilitate that . . ."

"It will." Some of the tension in the lines around Admiral Angelou's eyes dissipated at the mention of sedation. "Thank you, sir."

Seaghdh wondered what the man feared. Ari? Or what Ari might say?

"Thank you, Admiral, for your frank disclosure," Eilod replied smoothly. "Rest assured, we will hold Captain Idylle's questionable mental state in strictest confidence. I will have the meeting coordinates forwarded to you via this private channel should you wish to send your ship to protect the transfer point."

Eilod and the admiral exchanged empty pleasantries and then signed off. His cousin pursed her lips.

"Balls of solid Isarrite," Seaghdh grumbled, relaxing back into his chair.

"He's a politician. It's part of the breed description," she replied without a hint of humor. "Assessment?"

Even after a coded request that he report to her chambers via her private lift and a clandestine conference with Ari's commander, Seaghdh felt the stilted tension between his cousin and himself. Eilod hadn't forgotten that he'd disagreed with her regarding Ari's transponder. He hadn't forgotten, either. Thanks to Ari, he now suspected his cousin had planned to pin him in such an uncomfortable situation.

"He's desperate to recover Captain Idylle."

Eilod nodded, slid from her desk, and dropped into her chair. Weariness showed in the boneless way she collapsed into the depths of the leather.

Seaghdh frowned. "You're exhausted."

"So are you. Stay on task, Auhrnok. His accusations against Captain Idylle do make sense."

Biting back a curse, Seaghdh straightened slowly, anger wiping away fatigue. "You know as well as I that he was lying."

"On some points."

"On most points," Seaghdh corrected.

"Rather like you."

He stared at his cousin, his breathing tight. "Eilod, what makes you believe I've lied to you?"

"I saw your face, Cullin. For a moment, when you said it, you believed that Captain Idylle might have gone rogue. That means you'd thought of it before this and not mentioned it. I was right to order that transponder reprogrammed."

Ice drove through his middle. "If you've lost faith in me, Eilod, tell me so."

"If she has your heart, how far behind is your loyalty?" his cousin shot. She caught in an audible breath, as if she could call back the words.

"I can't believe this," he countered. "You're jealous? Are you asking me to choose between you and Captain Idylle?"

Outrage and the slightest hint of guilt creased her brows. "That's . . ."

"You think I'm compromised." He flopped back in his seat and shook his head at the ceiling, stunned by his cousin's assumption.

"I don't know! Do you?"

He bit back a harsh reply and listened to the instinct whispering in his chest that something had gone horribly wrong with his objectivity on this mission. "I have wondered."

She sighed.

Seaghdh glanced at her troubled face. "She believes you mean to kill her."

"I did toy with the notion. To protect you."

He chuckled. It sounded strained to him. "And by extension, yourself. I'm flattered, but I have proven adept over the years at taking care of myself."

"Yes, you have," she replied, propping her chin in her hand as she watched him.

"But?"

"I've never seen you so invested in a subject, Cullin. You expected her to hate you for leaving the transponder in her head, didn't you?"

"Yes," he murmured, unfamiliar feeling stirring in his chest. Ari had trusted him.

"I saw that stunned, ghur-in-the-sensor-eye look on your face when she didn't blame you," Eilod said. "You're wearing it now."

Seaghdh took control of his expression and forced himself to pay attention. "If you had given me smart, tough women as interrogation subjects, I might have been tempted to set aside objectivity before now."

"What do we do?"

At the lost look in her eye, Seaghdh rose and went to crouch beside her chair.

She faced him.

He took her hands in his. "You have a choice to make, Eilod. The same one Captain Idylle faces."

She scowled.

"Only you can decide whether or not you can still trust me. Nothing I say will make that easier for you."

She smiled.

The sadness in the expression took his breath.

"We've been through so much," she said.

"Yes, we have. Undoubtedly, there'll be more. I'm not going anywhere, Eilod. Family is forever."

"It just doesn't always stay the same," she finished for him. "Isn't that what Mother used to tell you?"

Seaghdh nodded, a knot in his throat at the memory of the first time his Aunt Kystran had said those words to him at his parents' funeral.

Eilod's smile turned sympathetic. She drew her hands out of his. "Finish this, Cullin. One way or another. Here. A token of my esteem. And my trust."

She offered him a handheld.

He raised an eyebrow at her.

"The codes for Captain Idylle's transponder," she said. "All of them. The people of TFC border on xenophobia when it comes to races with extraordinary abilities. When her admiral discovers that Captain Idylle is a telepath, and I do not doubt he will, he will use the fact to turn public opinion against her. It distresses me that you now become as much of a target as she is."

Seaghdh's heart lifted. He took the handheld. "Story of my life and far preferable to you being the target. You know it's my job to draw fire away from you."

"Not for the next eight hours. I'm ordering you off duty, Cullin."

"I'll return the favor," he replied.

"You seem confused about the chain of command," she said, grinning at him.

"Off duty," Seaghdh ordered, pinning her with a glare as he rose. "Or I'll tell Aunt Kys about that third-year cadet you seduced just after graduation."

"You wouldn't! How did you know . . . ?"

Grinning at her, he waved and stepped into the lift. "Sleep tight."

CHAPTER

19

ARI finally closed Seaghdh's computer console. She'd gone fishing in his files, looking for information to add to her growing intel files on the Chekydran, Kebgra, and the Armada. She'd been parsing data for the past hour and still couldn't wring any sense from it. Guilt prodded her into saving a copy of her reports and calculations to Seaghdh's files. He'd need it and she owed it to him since she hadn't exactly asked permission to muck around in his computer system. Leaning back in her chair, she tabbed on her handheld, bringing up another language lesson. She'd shed the uniform jacket and draped it behind her. The Claugh insignia dug into her back as she stretched and yawned.

Ordered off duty, Seaghdh had said when he'd fetched her from medical. He'd leaned against the doorframe, arms crossed, that cocky grin lighting his face.

"You're learning Claughwyth," he'd said. "Quick study, aren't you?"

"What? Not really," she'd replied. She hadn't wanted anyone knowing about the language lessons. Or how swiftly she absorbed languages. Especially since the Chekydran had done something to enhance her ability. She'd been so busy hiding her handheld that it had taken several seconds for his chuckle to make her realize he'd spoken in his language and that she'd answered him in kind.

He'd been elated.

Sighing, Ari closed her eyes and drew a deep breath. His scent, his presence, surrounded her in his cabin.

She heard him stir in his bed. The rustle of bedclothes from the other room and the shush of his bare feet on carpet told her he'd come to look in on her.

"Ari?"

"Quarter light," she said in Claughwyth and opened her eyes. He stood in the doorway between his office and his bedroom. She had to smile. He wore a ragged pair of workout shorts. Add a threadbare T-shirt from his last energy blade competition and he'd match what she'd worn for bed aboard the *Sen Ekir*.

"Nice outfit," she said in her own language. She was too tired to rake her memory for vocabulary.

He rubbed a hand over one bare shoulder and frowned as if that would keep her from seeing him flush.

"Sorry I woke you," she said.

"I'd sleep better if you'd get some rest," he replied.

She looked away.

"What is it, hwe vaugh?"

"Hwe vaugh." She waited for the words to resolve to something she could understand. They didn't. So much for being a quick language study.

She shrugged. "I'll never have my command back, will I?"

She'd spent the past hour forcing herself to think, to face what she'd blinded herself to until now. She'd been compromised by three months in Chekydran captivity. Armada Command couldn't promise her a ship. They couldn't know what kind of security breach she represented. She'd be lucky to ride a desk. Damn it, she didn't want to be a scientist working in her father's labs for the rest of her life. A PhD was no substitute for a command.

"Not that one," Seaghdh murmured. He rounded the desk, caught the chair, and spun her to face him. He knelt before her, his hands warm on her arms.

She nodded and felt something dark and poisonous crack open inside her chest. Yet another wound she couldn't grieve. She'd gotten used to that. But it was another tick on the side of "nothing left to live for."

"Ari," he growled, warning in his tone.

She cursed. Of course he'd seen every desolate thought playing across her face. The unhappiness in his expression as he stared at her made her breath catch.

"I'm still a prisoner," she said, shaking her head. "I'm not on that damned ship anymore, but they destroyed so much, I might as well have stayed and died."

"No," he ground out.

"What does it mean to have survived if the life I knew, the life that kept me resisting, kept me from giving up, is ripped out of my grasp?"

"You build a new one!" he insisted. "You find something worth fighting for and you go after it every day."

Her laugh sounded cynical, bereft. "When I'm being shoved around like a pawn on a chessboard? I am all out of fight."

Seaghdh rose and extended a hand. "No. You're not. I'll prove it to you."

She blinked and put a hand in his.

He lifted her to her feet and led her through his bedroom to another door, one she had taken for a second closet. It wasn't.

"You have a dedicated practice floor? On board a ship?" Ari marveled, padding in bare feet to the center of the dueling grid.

"Privilege of rank," he said. "Now. About that rematch."

A glimmer of life woke in her body. She tried to smile and found she could. Nodding, she stripped down to uniform trousers and undershirt.

Seaghdh put a dueling jacket on her, smoothing the seam closed with exaggerated care over her chest.

She laughed at the flood of desire turning her knees to jelly. "I'm on to you and you will not distract me this time. It isn't just your language I'm learning."

He flashed a devastatingly sexy smile at her and shrugged into a jacket of his own. When she sidled close to seal his jacket, he planted a kiss on the tip of her nose. He backed hastily away, however, when her fingers slid between the edges of fabric to caress his bare chest.

He returned with practice blades.

"We'll start at the beginning," he rumbled. He circled her, stepped in, pressing his chest to her back. Tucking a hilt into her right hand, he put his mouth next to her ear. "Hold it like you would a lover. Firm. Confident but not too tight, otherwise, you'll choke off . . ."

She darted out from under him, gasping with laughter, her body clenching with want. "You had better guard, Seaghdh. I am very clear that lesson one reads, 'All's fair in love and war.'"

Golden eyes dancing with mirth, he met her in the center of the grid, his look avid. They crossed blades.

Excitement sped her heartbeat.

"Nice and easy?" he suggested. "Warm up?"

She snorted. "Oh, hell no."

Ari attacked.

It was an utterly different contest than their first match. More dance than duel, they tested defenses, probed for weaknesses in technique, in finesse. They both knew they had no reason to hold back, to pretend they were any less skilled than they were.

Since she'd taken and held the TFC blade title, Ari had known she'd have trouble finding willing dueling partners. For the first time in years, she had an honest challenge. The rapid-fire clash and fizzle of energy blade contacting energy blade was exhilarating.

She felt the pressure of his blade tip on her ribs before he said it. "Point."

They broke apart, breathing hard, wiping sweat from their faces.

"Nice," she said, meaning the compliment. "Never saw it."

Pleasure glowed behind the thoughtful expression on his face. He jerked his chin at her sword arm. "Old injury?"

She nodded. "Shoulder blade shattered four and a half months ago. Good as new after surgery and bone regen, but I still have three more months of physical therapy."

He counted back four and a half months. Chekydran. His expression darkened, but he left it. "You drop your blade tip defending outside right once the muscles get tired."

"Damn." She shook her head. "You'll have to become part of my physical therapy routine."

"I intend to, I assure you," he said, leering at her.

"Ah, ah," she warned, wagging a finger, savoring the sudden thunder of her heart. "He who is easily distracted is easily skewered."

His grin widened.

She groaned at her choice of words and choked on a ripple of panic. Damn it. Not now. Not while she was actively having fun, actively enjoying Cullin Seaghdh's company.

Maybe that was the trigger. He was the Auhrnok Riorchjan. She was still a prisoner and his assignment. Why shouldn't his charm, his warmth all be an act?

He either saw or sensed the change in her. Frowning, he closed his free hand around her left arm. "Breathe, Ari," he urged.

Fear for her in his voice. One part of her felt it coursing through his body. Maybe he wasn't acting. Unless he enjoyed using his position to take advantage of women, to humiliate them in the process of pumping them for information. She stumbled over the mental turn of phrase, then shook it off. Couldn't be true. The look in his eyes when they'd dueled aboard the *Sen Ekir* had plainly said he hadn't enjoyed belittling her—unless *that* had been the act. Ari's head spun.

Thrice-damned Chekydran. She couldn't go on second-guessing herself into paralysis her entire life. She didn't want to go on living in the wasteland of never knowing, of never having tried to recover some small bit of herself. So what if Cullin Seaghdh was pretending?

One thing she knew for certain. After the Chekydran, she could survive damn near anything. She wanted the man. So what if her heart was entangled? She'd live even if Seaghdh all but dumped her out an air lock the minute he was done toying with her.

Only she could decide if what she felt in his company was worth the risk of heartache. She drew in a deep breath and focused on Seaghdh's concerned face.

"Guard, Blade Master," Ari whispered. "Or the next time a woman falters in the middle of a duel, you may end up dead."

He scowled. "You weren't acting."

"No. I wasn't."

His gaze searched her face and he relaxed. "Which is why you didn't take a point from me."

"You have two seconds before I do," she countered. "I haven't forgotten your advice in the medi-bay."

His grin back in place, he nodded and danced away. "A blade master takes every advantage?"

That was the one. She intended to take every last advantage he'd afford her. Anticipation shot a heated, heady mix of craving into her blood.

They met in the middle, touched blades. She looked him in the eye. She didn't know what he saw in her face, but his humor died. Desire smoldered in its place. Fire stabbed through her, speeding her pulse and robbing her of breath.

"Fight," he whispered. A ripple of power in his voice wrapped around her, suggesting a very different contest than this one.

Ari sucked in a slow breath and delighted in the rush of need lighting up every nerve ending. "Cheater."

He laughed and attacked.

She couldn't take much more. She ended it quickly, charging him, locking body to body, blade to blade. Once more, she felt leashed strength coil in him. She trusted she hadn't made a mistake, one that would shred the tiny sliver of hope blossoming in her heart. A thrill rippled through her. He stared, his expression unreadable.

"Lesson two," he said.

"Never offer what I can't afford to lose," she finished for him. "I am lost already, Cullin Seaghdh. Help me find me."

Growling, he took the blade from her hand and threw both weapons against the wall, then pulled her tight against him. His mouth covered hers and he kissed her as if he'd been dying of hunger for her. She returned the favor. The feel of his skin under her hands and the taste of his lips drove startling urgency through her. She wanted more. Much more.

He gave it.

She tried to remove his jacket. With delicate kisses to each of her palms, he stopped her. She tried to take off her jacket. He pulled her hands behind her back.

"What is the First Point?" he whispered against her lips.

Her overheated brain worked in slow motion. He wanted her to recite the lesson points of the Art of the Blade? "What?"

"First." He brushed his lips against hers. "Point."

Gasping as he nibbled his way down her throat, she stuttered, "P-patience."

He tucked her fingers into the waistband of her trousers at the small of her back. "Patience." He tripped the seal on her jacket and, easing the fabric open, explored what little skin was exposed.

She strained against him, biting back a groan. Her body ached for his touch. "Stop coddling me," she managed.

His mouth on hers cut her off. When he broke the kiss, he looked at her with so much fire in his eyes that her will melted. "That is the last thing I'm doing." His hands eased the jacket from her shoulders before caressing a path to her breasts. He traced the outlines through the thin fabric of her undershirt.

She had to force her legs to go on holding her. "You are."

"I'm not." He dipped his head, his mouth taking over where his hands had been.

Breathing hard, barely able to choke out the words, she said, "You're not what?" It had finally occurred to her that he was talking her in circles and enjoying doing so.

"Going to stop."

Raw hunger burst through her body and shorted out the rest of her brain as he dropped to his knees. He tugged her undershirt out of her trousers.

Ari tensed. Three scars wrapped her torso, mementos from her stay in a Chekydran prison. She did not want to remember which of them had been self-inflicted and which hadn't. They were the few physical reminders that surgery hadn't been able to erase.

Seaghdh brushed his lips over the fine, white lines. Wrapping his arms around her hips, he rested his cheek on her abdomen, on the reminders of her past and hugged her hard against him. Her heart thundered so loudly she could barely hear him when he said, "You deserve to be coddled, Ari. To be treasured. Let me."

She groaned and, ignoring his implied order to keep her hands locked behind her, threaded her fingers through his hair. "Hurry. Your dallying is killing me."

Laughing, he surged to his feet, hooked a hand in the loose waistband of her pants, and drew her into his bedroom.

"What is the Sixth Point?" he said.

"Seaghdh," she growled from between clenched teeth and reached for him.

He dodged her grasp, swung behind her and pulled the dueling jacket down her arms where it tangled, imprisoning her. He used the coat to pull her back against his chest. "Sixth Point," he murmured, puffing breath into her ear.

Sensation sizzled across her skin, shaking her to the core. She caught in a sharp gulp of air and struggled for possession of her hands.

His chuckle sounded wicked and he closed his teeth softly on her earlobe.

Excitement, augmented by far too many hormones, thrilled through her body. "S-sixth Point. By the Gods, how do you expect me to think?"

"The blade master . . ." he began as he nuzzled the sensitive skin below her ear.

Choking on a moan, she said in a breathless rush, "The blade master conquers his opponent by first conquering himself . . . you wouldn't."

"Hwe vaugh, I already have."

"Hwe vaugh." Her brain picked that moment to translate his words. "My heart." Ari's breath stopped and her own heart clenched hard.

Seaghdh folded his arms around her, brushing a hand up under her shirt to caress one breast. The friction of his palm against over-sensitized skin dissolved every thought in her brain. She dropped her head back against his shoulder.

He murmured approval against her collarbone as he eased her trousers open and began exploring her body's secrets.

She cried out.

He took his time, too damned much of it. Every fiber quivered, waiting for the next sensation. It was a little like torture where nerves coiled, taut, anticipating each new hurt. It was utterly unlike it, in that now, she luxuriated in the pleasure Seaghdh lavished on her body. She felt stretched tight, nerve endings rising against her skin, silently begging for more while she gasped at the exquisitely gentle way Seaghdh soothed and massaged and drove her to the brink of sanity.

He explored every inch, removing clothes as he went, finally freeing her to revel in her desperate desire to touch him.

She shook with the force of the want he'd built in her, but she took her time easing his jacket from his shoulders. Indulging her need to trace each line of his muscle with her lips, she tested his control, halting her caresses at the waistband of his shorts. Sixth Point indeed. Did he really believe he couldn't be mastered just as she had been?

He groaned, swept off his shorts with trembling hands and urged her to her feet before she could do more than admire the rest of his magnificent body. When at long, achingly last, he pushed her onto the bed, he shifted against her. His eyes closed and he paused. Savoring? Or tormenting?

She thought her heart would burst. "Now," she demanded in a strangled voice. "I need you now."

"The blade master never forces a point," he rasped, his breath trembling, and pressed home in one long, deliriously slow stroke.

She arched, imploring him to hold nothing back. His body heard and responded with abandon, until the white-hot fire he'd built between them went abruptly and shockingly supernova.

CHAPTER

20

WHEN her heart rate slowed, Ari choked out, "Match. Who won?"

Seaghdh cracked open one eye and laughed. Gathering her into his arms, he pulled her tight against him. "Draw."

"Nothing for it then," she mumbled as her eyes drifted shut. "Rematch."

"You're trying to kill me."

She smiled, opening her eyes. "Didn't I tell you? It's all clear now, my programming."

For a moment, he tensed. Then he pinched her backside.

She yelped.

He turned her around, tucking her back against his chest and wrapped his arms around her waist. "Rematch," he breathed into her ear. "What is the Third Point?"

He drove into her, quick, fierce, hot.

She gasped. "E-endurance! Gods, don't stop."

He bit her at the junction of neck and shoulder, rumbling low in his throat as he moved. One hand played over her breasts. With the other at the joining of their bodies, he took her swiftly to the edge, then deliberately paused, waiting for her quivering muscles to unclench.

"Will you forfeit, Blade Master?" he panted, his voice raspy with the effort of denying them both.

Smoothing a hand over his tight backside, then his hip, she reached between them and cupped him in her palm.

He trembled, swore, and with a groan rocked hard into her over and over until she pleaded for release.

"Now," he ground out. "Now."

The ripple of power in his voice shot through her like lightning. She thought she screamed. He shouted and once again, the passion they'd ignited detonated.

They collapsed, boneless. She turned. He tucked her head against his shoulder and sighed, sounding pleased. If she'd been any more pleased, she'd have been dead. Her body still thrummed.

Seaghdh flipped the covers up over them. He smoothed hair out of her face.

Her eyes closed.

"Sleep, hwe vaugh," he said to the top of her head.

Ari's eyes snapped open and she tensed.

"What is it?"

She pulled out of his grasp and sat up, rubbing her hands hard against her face to wake herself. "Jettison that, Seaghdh," she warned. "Don't make it harder. You know I have to go back."

"What happened?" he pressed. "You're running away. What frightened you?"

She gaped at him as he watched half-formed thoughts plod across her face.

Sympathy darkened his expression. "You aren't with the Chekydran. It is safe to feel again."

A reflexive stab of panic shook her. She waited it out and forced herself to smile at him. "I halfway think you planned this brilliant and amazing seduction to get me to volunteer to destroy my own government."

He blinked and sat up slowly, looking alternately smug and like a man who'd just taken a sucker punch. "Want to explain that?"

"I have to get into TFC military databases if we're going to proceed. We need positive IDs on everyone involved with the Chekydran and proof of both the IDs and the alliance. I can't bring the traitors down without it."

"No," he corrected. "Explain the brilliant and amazing seduction part."

Scowling at him, Ari saw the uncertainty behind the carefully neutral mask he wore. Damn it. He was right. She was running away from feeling anything for him. Stricken, she crawled into his lap, took his face in her hands, and kissed him. She'd entrusted her emotional well-being to the man and look at her trampling all over his feelings. How many kinds of idiot could she be?

He folded her in his embrace. "You cannot save the galaxy tonight while you're exhausted."

"And hungry."

He chuckled. "Sleep first or food?"

"Sleep. If I can stay here. With you?"

"Right where I want you," he said.

"Will you do that voice thing? So I don't have nightmares? Or flashbacks?"

He nodded slowly. "Not ready to kill me just yet?"

"Sex is specified as the weapon of choice."

He chuckled. "Remind me to thank whoever programmed in that particular condition. Rest. Peaceful. Pleasant. Dreamless."

His voice and the power it contained twined around her, drawing her into sleep as surely as Seaghdh shifted her into bed beside him. Still. It wasn't his ability that made her sigh as a sense of safety enveloped her. All that required was his arm around her and Seaghdh, warm and solid at her back. Three Hells. What would he do if she said "hwe vaugh" to him?

*　*　*

WHEN Ari woke, Seaghdh sat on the edge of the bed, already in a uniform so dark green it was nearly black, caressing her face with a touch that made her shiver. Baxt'k. She'd succumbed to the dangerous, remote Auhrnok Riorchjan.

"Duty calls," he said.

She stretched and sat up, nodding. "The completion of my programmed mission to destroy you in bed? I'm game, but I really need breakfast first."

The intimidating Queen's Blade sitting beside her smiled, his eyes half lidded. "I do look forward to your next assassination attempt. Sadly, we have no time right now."

His formal phrasing brought Ari fully awake and into "Captain, enemy ship approaching" mode. She stiffened her spine, swung her legs to the floor, and stood. "Report."

"The *Balykkal* is on approach."

She rocked back on her heels.

Seaghdh rose swiftly and grabbed her elbow to steady her.

"Do I have time for a shower?"

"Yes. They're ten minutes from visual. You will speak to them?"

"I'd better. I need my uniform," she said, wishing she had something more impressive than her combat gear.

"Yes."

That's when she noticed he'd already placed her olive-drab fatigues, clean and folded, on the foot of the bed. She showered and dressed quickly. When she strode into his office, Seaghdh rose from his desk and brought her a tray. She tried to take it.

He wouldn't release it.

She glanced at him and finally saw the light dancing in his golden eyes, the only sign of the man she knew in the formidable officer before her. "There is a price to be paid for everything," he said, his voice lazy and tinged with humor. Leaning across the tray, he claimed a lingering kiss that ramped her pulse.

Her stomach grumbled.

He released her and the tray but followed her to the couch. It was just as well. He'd given her far too much food. She ate the few bites she could stomach, grabbed the cup of tea, and started to rise.

"Relax," he ordered, hand on her arm. "Even if they are within range, there are protocols. You have time." He took the tea from her and put it back on the tray. He held a morsel of Grebnol fruit to her lips.

She shook her head. "I can't . . ."

The Myallki spawn popped the sweet fruit into her mouth where it promptly dissolved. Twelve Gods, it was good.

"If I eat too much at one sitting," Ari warned, "I'll be sick."

"You haven't yet eaten anything at this sitting." He offered another piece, his gaze on hers, coaxing. When she just looked at him, he said, "What is the Second Point?"

"Strength."

He forced the fruit on her again and nodded. "As in, I intend that you'll need every last bit of yours."

Her blood went hot. She cursed.

He laughed, low and heartless, and fed her another piece.

Something on his desk chirped.

He straightened, the cool mask claiming his expression once more. Wiping his fingers on her napkin, he rose, dropped the cloth on the tray, and strode to his desk.

Ari admired the play of tight muscle outlined by the seat of his pants.

A click. "Riorchjan," he said.

"Auhrnok, Her Majesty requests your attendance and that of your guest to com channel two," a young man's voice said. "Will you comply?"

She grabbed a hurried sip of tea and rose.

"By Her Majesty's will," Seaghdh said. He glanced at her and held up a hand.

Message received and understood. Ari waited.

"Engaging visuals," the voice said.

Did Seaghdh have any idea that she now understood nearly everything he and his crew said? Would it matter?

"Acknowledged. Visual engaged," Seaghdh replied. "Awaiting Her Majesty's pleasure."

"Auhrnok Riorchjan," the communications officer said, "Her Majesty, the queen."

"Good morning, Your Majesty." Seaghdh snapped to attention.

"Fair morning to you, Auhrnok Riorchjan," Eilod replied.

Ari stood behind the screen, unable to see her, but her lilting voice was unmistakable.

"Auhrnok, the *Balykkal* requests speech with Captain Idylle," Eilod said. "I believe they wish to assure themselves that she is recovering well from the brief coma brought on by that tree venom."

Ari blinked. Coma?

They'd spoken to Armada personnel at least once already without mentioning the fact to her. Should she be concerned or encouraged that they'd lied to her people on her behalf? Why had they done it at all?

Ari smiled, not at all amused. Her commanders had tried to reach her via her transponder after the codes had been changed, or more likely, Armada had activated the destruct code on her transponder. When that had failed, they'd dispatched the *Balykkal* with orders to retrieve her. By any means possible.

"I stand ready, Your Majesty," Seaghdh said.

"Our appreciation, Auhrnok. Yeoman Onnyth?"

The screen apparently blanked. Seaghdh tossed Ari a troubled look. When the yeoman announced the patch through complete, he'd switched to her language.

"Captain Idylle," Seaghdh said, firmly back in his guise of official representative of the Empire. "The captain of the *Balykkal* requests your presence on com."

She flinched at "captain of the *Balykkal*." That was her title. Hearing it applied to someone other than she felt like a knife in her solar plexus.

She discovered her vanity was still intact when she found herself looking down at her uniform and straightening her bars. The irony of the move made her scowl. She strode to Seaghdh's side.

"Thank you, Auhrnok Riorchjan," Ari said after making certain the com link was video enabled. She offered a hand to Seaghdh.

Expression set in the hard lines required of his station, he shook her hand and nodded.

"I appreciate your assistance, sir," she said.

A glint of amusement lit his eye. He squeezed her hand, released her, and stepped back.

She turned to face the screen. "Captain Xiao. Good to see you," she said to the man sitting in her command chair. "I don't believe I had the opportunity to congratulate you on your promotion, Zhong. It was long past time you had your own ship. You wear the bars well."

Her former first officer hesitated. His eyes slid sideways. Checking his screens for data, to see if the Claugh were using her as a distraction while they powered up weapons. Good boy.

"Captain Idylle," Xiao said. "Are you all right?"

Raising her eyebrows, she nodded. "Of course, Captain. Perhaps you've not been briefed. Our outpost on Kebgra suffered an attack. The *Sen Ekir* issued a distress call. The Claugh nib Dovvyth Stalker, the *Dagger*, was on patrol at the edge of the Zone. They were kind enough to respond."

Xiao blinked. "Kebgra? I had heard . . ." He broke off, his gaze turning inward as he considered. "Survivors?"

"Unknown," she lied.

Xiao frowned, propped an elbow on an armrest, and leaned forward.

Ari recognized the gesture and had to suppress a smile. Apparently, she'd trained her first better than she'd intended.

"Death toll?"

"Also unknown," she replied. "I didn't have time to count before the creatures attacked again."

Xiao's eyes lit and the bridge crew spun to run scans without being told. "Chekydran?"

"No," she said. "I've prepared a report for Armada Command. I will trans it into isolation at a location of your choosing."

"Lieutenant Whyt," Xiao ordered.

"Aye, Captain," Celene Whyt, Ari's former computer security officer, said. "Isolated block path on your screen."

"Acknowledged. Prepare to receive data, Captain Idylle."

Seaghdh stepped up beside her, touched a command code, froze the path information, then opened an access port for her handheld. "With your permission, Captain?" He took the unit from the desktop where she'd left it and plugged it in, then entered another command set. A familiar control panel, in her language, materialized in the tabletop before her. "Use this panel for your transmission."

Ari glanced at him. "You understand, Auhrnok Riorchjan, I must report your replication of our technology to my superior officers."

He looked at her from beneath his brow, enjoyment obvious in the crease at the corners of his eyes. The rest of his expression reflected only ominous disapproval.

"You will, of course, do as you see fit."

She sent her report to keep from laughing at his clipped tone.

"Transmission received, Captain Idylle," Whyt said.

"Thank you, Lieutenant."

The woman grinned. At least someone was happy to see her. Ari had expected conflicting emotions in Xiao. It couldn't be comfortable facing the captain whose command you'd taken when she'd been presumed dead. She wasn't dead and was still called "Captain." Xiao had to wonder what that made him. They were even. One ship couldn't have two captains. What did that make her?

"Security sweep on the file complete, Captain Xiao," Whyt said. "Copied to your screen."

Xiao didn't answer in favor of scanning the first few lines of the report. He knew she got straight to the point. Frowning, he looked up at her. "Source of the attacking soldiers?"

"Mother ship in orbit," Ari said. "Ran when the *Dagger* came to our aid. There's more, Zhong."

Xiao sat back, bracing himself, conditioned to know by the tone of her voice that she had bad news.

"It isn't in my report," she said, "and it occurs to me that it's no longer my job to notify next of kin. It's yours."

His eyes widened and he nodded.

"Tommy Heisen was one of them."

"Baxt'k."

"This is the Claugh royal flagship," she told him. "You'll want to mind your p's and q's, Xiao."

Seaghdh suppressed a chuckle. He knew a code phrase when he heard one. He watched the surprise on the man's face followed by a real smile. Xiao rubbed a hand over his scalp. Though he would have a head of thick, glossy black hair to complement his dark complexion and black eyes, he seemed to favor painfully close buzz cuts.

"Understood," Xiao said, looking like a man who'd never expected to hear a code phrase again, but who thoroughly enjoyed having to respond to it. "We owe you a debt of gratitude, sir," Xiao said to Seaghdh. "Captain Idylle is a valued member of the Armada. We are relieved to find her safe."

Seaghdh inclined his head.

Xiao's gaze darted to Whyt's station, then back to Ari. "P's and q's, Captain. Logging disabled. We have only a few minutes."

She grinned.

Seaghdh's blood quickened and he cursed under his breath.

"It is damn good to see you, Xiao," she said. "It's good to see all of you."

"Thank you, Captain. All due respect, you've lost too much weight."

"Chekydran prisons are a hell of a diet plan," she agreed.

Xiao grimaced. "We lost six crew attempting to recover you. We spent three months in dry dock, patching up the ship."

Ari dropped her chin to her chest.

Seaghdh's heart constricted in sympathy. He knew too well what it felt like to lose crew.

"I never doubted that you disobeyed my direct orders to not engage the Chekydran," she said, her voice muted.

Xiao's smile looked sad.

She straightened. "You owe me a beer. I told you you'd get the next command."

They grinned.

Misgiving prickled through Seaghdh and he peered hard at Ari. Just what had their relationship been? Was she merely facing down the man who'd taken her command? Or a former lover?

Xiao looked troubled. "I do owe you a beer, Captain. I wish to all the Gods I didn't. The last ship I wanted was yours. You are still senior, you know."

She shook her head. "I was relieved of command, Zhong, and from all indications, it's going to be permanent even if it isn't fatal. I've prepared a recorded statement for Tommy's family. Would you review it? You're in the best position to decide whether it will help."

"Understood. Transmit to the same secured block."

"Acknowledged." She keyed in rapid-fire commands and in an offhand way said, "You might relieve your transport officer. You won't get a lock on me through the shields without my transponder code."

Seaghdh allowed himself a tiny, admiring smile. She'd broadsided Xiao with her guess about the purpose of Xiao's com call. The man's discomfited look gave Seaghdh a clear glimpse of his motives. He was trying to decide if she deserved to be murdered by trans-shield teleport.

The pained look in Xiao's black eyes said he had indeed been ordered to teleport Ari out, at any cost, and that he hadn't had the heart to make the grab. Encouraging.

Ari seemed to see the same thing. She pressed harder. "Get your transponder removed. The implant is armed with remote destruct capability."

Xiao froze. Horror clouded his features, followed swiftly by denial and disbelief.

"Think," she ordered. "It makes sense."

Shaking his head, Xiao said, "If it's true, why not use it rather than order me to kill you with a trans-shield port?"

"It may have been tried, Captain," Seaghdh said. "When Captain Idylle's medical scan revealed the transponder, I programmed our shields to disrupt command streams coming into the unit. I cannot ignore the fact that Captain Idylle's distress call coincided with the brief time this specific ship was within range of Kebgra. It hasn't escaped me that Captain Idylle might have been sent as an unwitting assassin."

"Assassin?"

"Her Majesty, Queen Eilod Saoyrse, is aboard this vessel," Ari said.

CHAPTER
21

SEAGHDH could see Ari's former first officer working through the implications of her on board a Claugh ship in the company of the two highest-ranking officials of the Claugh nib Dovvyth.

"You're an Armada man, Xiao," she said. "Yet you just disobeyed a direct order to teleport me out. Why?"

"Two hours ago I received a coded, off-channel message from IntCom," he replied, his look assessing, "claiming you as an undercover operative. It ordered me to retrieve you unharmed."

Surprise showed in the faces of the few bridge personnel Seaghdh could see over Xiao's shoulder. A stab of alarm drove through him. Had she neglected to disclose her exact mission? Scientist-sitter or master operative?

Ari uttered a sharp laugh.

"Is it true?" Xiao asked.

"Yes."

Seaghdh glanced at her. Captain Alexandria Idylle stood at his side on full alert, her expression unreadable. He couldn't tell if he'd just heard more truth than she'd wanted him to hear or if she didn't want to burden Captain Xiao with the details of her undercover baby-sitting job.

"Twelve Gods," Xiao breathed. "What in the Three Hells is going on, Captain? The rumors—"

"Unknown, attempting to compensate, Captain," Lieutenant Whyt interrupted.

Movement caught Seaghdh's eye. Ari. Touching thumb to forefinger. First time mark? He could guess that Lieutenant Whyt was disabling com logging. How much longer?

"Evidence suggests an Admiralty alliance with the Chekydran. Purpose: development of a biomech, wholly mind-controlled soldier. Prototypes were humanoids mutated by Chekydran nanotech processes combined with biotech implants."

Xiao shook his head. "The Citizen's Uprising broke that story to the media. Armada accuses you."

"What a surprise. Citizen's . . . You knew there were survivors," Ari said.

"So did you," Xiao replied.

"Sorry. I couldn't risk tipping off anyone in Armada who might be listening. I don't yet know the scope of the situation."

Xiao looked shaken. "Understood."

"Captains," Seaghdh interjected, determined to make Xiao pick a side. "The *Dagger* is due to meet the *Sen Ekir* within the next three hours for Captain Idylle's transfer."

"I have the coordinates," Xiao answered. "And orders to be certain Captain Idylle ceases to be the grave breach of security she currently represents."

Ari snorted.

"You do not have the coordinates," Seaghdh countered. "You have the false data I fed your commanding officer."

Xiao sucked in an audible breath and sat back in the command chair. "The admiral?"

Ari slanted a wary glance at Seaghdh. "You talked to Angelou? That can't have gone well."

"I did give him false coordinates, Captain," he replied.

She grinned, her pale eyes sparkling. "You are a scholar and a gentleman, Auhrnok."

Desire sizzled through him. "I hope not," he muttered under his breath as she turned back to the screen.

"Whoever is pulling the strings ordered the murder of every man, woman, and child on Kebgra," she said to Xiao. "I'm after proof I can take to Council. I mean to get it."

"Your IntCom mission," Xiao murmured.

Seaghdh glanced at Ari when she let his assumption go and had to fight back the sense that he stood beside a stranger. A stranger whose sharp mind and strong, lithe body made his blood run hot.

As each moment passed, he could almost see the mantle of responsibility, the weight of command decisions, settling around her shoulders. How could her undernourished, abused frame take strength from the burden? Not alone, he swore, something unfamiliar swelling in his chest. Never again.

"Do you intend to obey Armada's orders or IntCom's, Captain Xiao?" Seaghdh demanded.

"I almost have it, Captain," Lieutenant Whyt said, still busy at her panel.

Ari's thumb jumped to her pinky. Seaghdh gathered they had only a few seconds more. He didn't envy Xiao the pressure for a snap decision that might alter the course of his career, but Seaghdh had to know, and Ari deserved to know, just how much Xiao would risk for her.

"Old habits," Xiao said and sighed. "I trust Captain Idylle despite the smear campaign. Do you know they accuse you of paranoia as if three months in a Chekydran prison didn't justify it? Besides. Every soldiering instinct I have says something is going on. We follow the IntCom model."

"How many officers have implants?" Ari asked as if she'd known all along what decision Xiao would make.

"Three."

"Get them out, or change the codes, but do it now," she ordered. "Respond to no more Armada hails. Communicate only with Int-Com." She turned to Seaghdh. "Would Her Majesty permit your CMO to transmit data to the *Balykkal*'s medi-officer?"

Seaghdh glanced at his instrument panel. A light flashed twice. "I believe that can be arranged." He suppressed a smile at the sour look Ari tossed him. She hadn't expected Eilod to listen in? The captain had a great deal to learn about Claugh politics. He looked forward to teaching her. Another, more urgent rush of want startled him. He cleared his throat and directed his attention away from her.

"Here's the problem, Captain," Lieutenant Whyt said. "The hull plate protecting our broadcasting array came loose again. The equipment took a charge. I bled it off and we're neutral again, but it means another EV walk to lock that thrice-damned plate."

Ari's fist clenched and she frowned.

Seaghdh got the message. They were out of time to speak freely.

"Acknowledged," Xiao and Ari said in unison. Both grinned. A spurt of jealousy fired through Seaghdh at the camaraderie they shared. Was Xiao the real reason Ari wanted her ship back?

"Prepare to receive medical data," Seaghdh said, working the panel on his desk, aware that Armada would be listening in again. Back to playing a part. "The Claugh nib Dovvyth appreciates your diligence, Captain Xiao. Given this medical report, I am sure you understand why we cannot in good conscience permit the teleport of your captain at this time."

Xiao put on a pissed-but-trying-hard-to-be-professional face. "Understand? Auhrnok Riorchjan, you're holding an officer of the Armada and refuse to release her to her own people. You understand me. I will take this incident straight to the TFC Council. We may meet under far different circumstances. The ones you say you are so eager to avoid."

Seaghdh nodded slowly, marshalling his expression into some-thing appropriately deadly. "Do so, Captain," he purred. "By the time your politicians finish blustering over your report, I will have your precious captain returned to the agreed-upon location and personnel."

Xiao severed the connection.

Ari remained standing, her hands clasped in the small of her back, as if the screen might flicker back to life. The link indicator winked out. Only then did Ari relax, without his having to tell her she could, Seaghdh noted. Just how much of his language had she absorbed and learned to read overnight?

She rounded his desk and stomped back and forth, biting out a string of filthy words. He raised his eyebrows and lost count of the number of languages she could swear in.

Anger burned in Ari's blood. She was mad as Port Poison's horned sharks swarming for a kill. She actually felt it and could identify it. Score one for the prisoner.

"Twelve Gods damn it to all Three Hells," she growled.

Seaghdh sat behind his desk. His chin propped in one hand and amusement in his eyes. "Ari."

She stopped short, threw her arms wide, and said, "I am baxt'kal useless!"

"What an interesting evaluation," Eilod said, her tone droll.

Ari started. The queen had entered the office via a door camou-flaged by the royal seal adorning the wall behind Seaghdh. Damned open com. She'd forgotten. Again. She glared between Seaghdh and his cousin.

"Were you listening last night, too?" she demanded of Eilod.

"Should I have been?"

Alarm shot into Seaghdh's face.

"I learned a lot," Ari said.

Eilod smirked. "Congratulations."

"Stow it, Your Majesty," she countered.

Seaghdh dropped his head into his hands.

"I'm clear that I'm simply another mission."

That got his attention. "Ari," he grumbled.

"You, too," she ordered. "Any action is justified if it furthers the betterment of the people."

"You're quoting TFC regs," he said. "That's not us."

Ari stopped and stared at him. Damn it. She'd grown up living the philosophy, training, and studying in order to offer herself on the altar of TFC's collective best interests. She could rationalize being used in the name of furthering the interests of her people. Seaghdh acted as if the notion repulsed him.

"Maybe," she allowed. "The point is Armada just neutralized me. I can no longer go back into TFC space. My access to military records is being vaporized as we speak. Even if I could slip Armada personnel and report to IntCom, I prematurely exposed my cover when I locked down Dad's ship. They'll debrief me and show me the air lock. Gods, how could I be so stupid?"

"Save for that last bit," Seaghdh replied, "I agree."

"As do I," Eilod said.

"Oh, good. Give me the key to your blade locker and I'll go cut my own throat."

"Not until we've finished that duel," Seaghdh said, his tone silky. "You know Federated Worlds Regs don't recognize draws."

Heat flashed through Ari and pooled heavy in her belly.

"You *dueled*?" Eilod squeaked. "By the Gods, you two are hopeless."

"She's the second-ranked blade master in the known systems, Eilod," Seaghdh said.

"How well I know," his cousin replied, rolling her eyes. "You plagued me for years to negotiate a goodwill match."

Surprise unfolded within Ari. She peered at him. "You've been trying to meet me on the dueling floor? For years?"

Eilod snorted. "My cousin is your greatest fan, Captain. He's followed your blade rank from the moment you won your first sanctioned duel. He's always said you had the talent to be his match."

"That is enough," Seaghdh said.

"You don't want me to tell her about the media file you keep of every match she's ever fought?"

"Eilod."

"Or that you've spent hours analyzing technique? Telling me what kind of person she was likely to be based on her dueling style? Or how beau . . ."

"Your secret is safe," he growled, rising, palms flat on his desk. "Stop."

Grinning, Eilod subsided.

Beautiful. He'd told Eilod she was beautiful? Ari's head spun. That was so long ago. He knew everything about her. Everything. She'd won her first match before she'd graduated from the Armada Academy. Had he thought, when he'd accepted the mission to find her, that he'd be collecting that naïve, ambitious twentysomething? How disappointing had it been for him to find the scarred remains of the woman he'd watched climb the blade ranks?

"You really fought to a draw?" Eilod pushed, looking between them.

"Until we collapsed in exhaustion," Seaghdh replied, smiling in a predatory way that sent desire glittering through Ari's veins despite her mounting confusion.

"Oh, dear," Eilod said, her tone laden with false sympathy. "Is your title in danger, Queen's Blade?"

Seaghdh eyed Ari, looking like the hiztap who caught the tezwoul. "I expect it will take years of rematches to find out."

Her knees went weak.

"Splendid," Eilod said.

The bright delight in her voice told Ari she'd seen through Seaghdh's thinly veiled innuendo. Great.

"The empire requires your continued assistance, Captain Idylle," Her Majesty said. "Perhaps not in the form . . ."

They were conspiring to keep her. How would they justify it? Would she be a prisoner? A recruit? Or some kind of pet, a glorified mascot?

Ari dropped into a chair, closed her eyes, and felt doors slamming shut all around her, cutting away her options, severing her from the last mortally wounded remnants of her old life. She couldn't go home. She couldn't have a command. She didn't want a PhD and the prison of a lab. Ari gasped in pain. Not torture. Not Chekydran. Her. She was causing her own pain.

Seaghdh and Eilod wanted to put her in a box. Their box. Her father wanted her in his. Someone at Armada Command, possibly several someones, wanted her in a coffin. What did she want?

The rustle of fabric and the heat of his body told her Seaghdh knelt at her side. "Ari . . ."

A trill cut him off. Eilod answered in her own language.

"Your Majesty. System failure, engineering. I've traced the unauthorized access to your present location."

Seaghdh straightened.

The young queen swore and acknowledged. "Cullin. This is the third system failure in seven hours. Your station was accessed thirty minutes after you logged off duty last night."

The brittle tone warned Ari that Eilod blamed her for the system failures. Her stomach clenched and she opened her eyes. Had she been dumb enough to waltz right into the baited trap?

Seaghdh apparently heard the same thing in his cousin's voice. He strode to her side.

Had Ari found out what form Seaghdh and Eilod's box would take? An accusation of spying, a swift trial, and a prison sentence would assure that Seaghdh had his very own practice dummy for a long time to come.

"Baxt'k," Seaghdh said. His tone rang like Isarrite shattering at absolute zero. He stood, hands braced on his desk, his head hanging. He looked like a man defeated.

Ari's heart wrung hard, and she couldn't get her breath.

Eilod punched up a set of commands. Orders for a firing squad? She put a hand on his arm, her eyes shiny with unshed tears.

Seaghdh straightened. A hard, bitter stranger looked at her from out of his eyes.

She shuddered. This didn't feel like a repeat of the manipulative games Eilod and Seaghdh had played to get her aboard the *Dagger*. They weren't trumping up charges as a way of keeping her. Why?

Ari sucked in a sharp breath, hearing Xiao say it, "IntCom claiming you as an undercover operative." She hadn't burdened her former first officer with the details of her covert babysitting job. Eilod and Seaghdh obviously believed she'd lied to them rather than to her own personnel. She'd given them evidence of it by accessing Seaghdh's computer without permission. She'd even left data packets for them. What had she done?

He crossed the room, took her arm, and hauled her to her feet. Wordless, he dragged her out of the cabin and into the corridors.

She refused to ask where they were going. The Chekydran had never answered. Why should Seaghdh?

They followed Eilod to the conference room. The door closed behind them. Seaghdh released her like he couldn't stand to touch her. Her heart rose to her throat.

She glanced wildly around the room. Eilod vanished through a door hidden behind the royal seal on the far wall. Turrel, grim-faced, arms crossed, stood in front of the door they'd come through. He wore a sidearm. V'kyrri sat at the conference table, watching her. Ari met his gaze and felt him pressing against her awareness.

So that's how it was. She'd been foolish enough to believe Seaghdh's act—that he trusted her, cared for her—and now the people she'd thought of as her allies treated her like she meant them harm. Worse. She'd thought, if only briefly, that they'd understood her. She wished she could cry. Instead, she glanced at the other person in the room and started.

Sindrivik, logging into the computer systems.

"It is time you told me everything," Seaghdh said, the power in his voice a lash.

She reeled and bit her tongue to keep from babbling in response. He could have asked, but he preferred to duel. If it was a fight he wanted, she'd accommodate him.

Pinning her gaze on the serious young man sitting beside V'kyrri, Ari forced herself to ignore the compulsion rumbling around in her brain. Instead of spilling a confession no one would believe, she said, "Good to see you, Lieutenant Sindrivik. I gather my father is in range. Did he take his temper out on you since I wasn't there to castigate?"

Sindrivik blinked, a wry smile on his face, until he caught a glimpse of Seaghdh's expression. Humor died. He returned to task at a panel. Teasing apart her data? Analyzing the extent of her invasion into their computers? Scanning all systems for whatever damage she might have done? Their systems were extensive and since she hadn't done anything, looking for malicious code would take a while.

Ari took a deep breath. She hadn't heard a shield go up, which meant Eilod was listening, likely watching, and probably recording. It finally occurred to her that she was little more than a tool. They could use her as a means to declare war upon her government if the Claugh managed to wring a confession from her.

Her heart hurt and her throat felt tight. "Auhrnok Riorchjan," Ari said, refusing to look at him, "I formally request that you ask Mr. V'kyrri to stand down. Your little drama won't play well if I suffer a flashback."

"Answer me, Captain."

Again, the whip in his tone, demanding compliance. Heat rushed low into her abdomen and she flushed. Her body obviously remembered that he'd used his power to very pleasurable effect last night. She clasped her hands behind her back.

He pounded his fists against the table. "By the Gods, don't you dare stand there blushing like an innocent! Your admiral calls with a story of dread and fear designed to make us trust you. You admit you're an IntCom operative, but you neglect to disclose how much of one! What did I interrupt when I rose to check on you last night?

Theft of state secrets? An attack? Just whose brilliant and amazing seduction scene was that?" he yelled, fury and hurt raw in his face.

She gasped as if he'd struck her. The bastard was accusing Ari of what he'd done to her? Rage uncurled behind her solar plexus.

"Answer the damned question," he snarled.

"No," she snapped.

Silence. Deadly, sly silence that waited, circling, to close in for the kill. "No, you will not answer?" Seaghdh asked, his tone silky and dangerous. "Do you believe you understand my notion of interrogation?"

She struggled to contain the pain ripping her open from the inside out. What further proof did she need? He'd used her. She'd been right. He did get a charge out of humiliating his victims by seducing them. She'd just been wrong about the venue. He needed to make his conquest public. Damn it to the Three Hells, she couldn't deal with this, but she could stick to business. She could understand that, at least, before they threw her in prison. Or out an air lock.

"No," Ari repeated. "I am answering the question you don't have the courage to ask. The one at the heart of this set of faulty assumptions you and your precious cousin have made. No. I am not some super spy sent here to deceive you. Believe me. Don't believe me. I don't care."

The pressure against her increased. Movement beside her. She looked. V'kyrri. He'd alerted Seaghdh to her lie. "I don't care." The man was reading her, like the Chekydran had tried to do. Only he'd succeeded. That, along with the sharp-edged pain that had been her heart, infuriated her.

"Get off," she growled at him. Mentally, Ari flung him from her as hard and as violently as she'd always wanted to fling the Chekydran.

V'kyrri jolted back in his seat. The chair went over.

Shock and icy fear obliterated anger. Ari rushed to his side, righted the chair, and offered him a hand but pulled it back before he could refuse it.

"I'm sorry," she gasped. "V'kyrri, I'm sorry. I didn't . . ."

He levered himself back into his chair, his nose streaming purple blood.

She blanched. "I didn't mean . . . I didn't do that, did I? Please, tell me I didn't do that."

She got a wan smile from underneath his hand as V'k pinched his nose closed and tipped his head back.

"We need to get you some training," he said.

Awful awareness washed over her. She'd hurt him. V'kyrri had trespassed. Yes. The worst he'd done was to tell Seaghdh she cared when she swore she didn't. He hadn't harmed her, didn't want to harm her. And she'd injured him. With a thought. Horror pressed hard against the inside of her ribs. Ari bolted for the bathroom and lost not just her breakfast but what felt like every breakfast since time began.

CHAPTER

22

AFTER an eternity, a cool, sure hand applied a transdermal medication patch to the back of Ari's neck. Several seconds later, the dry heaves subsided and she curled, shaking and miserable, into a ball on the floor.

"You'll feel better in a minute," Dr. Annantra said.

"No," Ari rasped through a raw, swollen throat. "I'll have just stopped throwing up."

The doctor looked up at someone. Seaghdh. Ari could feel him there in the doorway, watching. Listening. Impatient.

"Hey," V'kyrri said. He brushed past Seaghdh, knelt, and put a hand on her ankle. "It's okay. I'm all right. Nice throw, by the way."

Is that what she'd done? She glanced at him. No blood. They'd cleaned him up before treating her. Good.

"What am I?" she pleaded.

He withdrew his hand as his troubled gaze met hers. "Besides frightened and feeling more alone than you did even in Chekydran captivity?"

Ari closed her eyes and pressed her lips tight against the surge of grief his words touched off.

"I don't know," he finished.

"V'k, don't," she croaked.

"I'm not reading, Ari," he said. "I don't have to. I can see it in your face."

Damn. She opened her eyes.

"Have her drink this," Dr. Annantra said. She handed V'kyrri a cup.

Gingerly, Ari slid around and propped her back against the wall. Hell of a start to the day. She was getting tired of ending up on the floor. Marshalling the fortitude to rise, she shook her head when V'kyrri offered her the cup.

She paused in the doorway beside Seaghdh. "You want an interrogation? Do it. See how it works for you. But I have to say. Aside from hurting V'kyrri, which was a masterful stroke if you planned that, your mind baxt'k doesn't hold a candle to what I've already been through."

A barren, bereft-sounding laugh escaped her. Ari desperately wanted to stop talking. She couldn't. "Problem is you had me believing you gave a damn. Worse, I fell for you. Hard. Or hadn't you noticed I would have answered you anything if you'd only asked?"

He looked staggered. "Ari." His voice cracked.

Heat rushed behind her eyes. She had to walk away before she fell weeping into his arms. It would have felt good if she'd been capable of it. Easing into a chair, she noticed that Turrel had left his post at the door, favoring a seat at the end of the table.

"Assassins don't barf at the sight of blood. You ain't here to hurt anybody," he grumbled when she raised an eyebrow at him. "Except maybe yourself. And him." He frowned at Seaghdh. "I'm wondering if he doesn't deserve it."

"I'm not entirely innocent," Ari admitted. "And it wasn't the sight of blood."

"Captain," Sindrivik interrupted. "I'd like to take your excellent advice and simply ask. What did you do to the computer systems?"

"Nothing. I accessed data regarding the alleged alliance between Armada and Chekydran," she replied, "merged it with my observations and data taken from the *Sen Ekir* and from Kebgra. I loaded the aggregated data to my handheld and backed up a copy in the Auhrnok Riorchjan's file share, being, as I was, under the impression that the Empire might value the data."

"Nothing else?" Sindrivik pressed.

"Not that I'm aware of." She glanced at V'kyrri. "Read. If you put a hand on my arm, it'll help keep me from flashing back on you again. I want to know if the Chekydran are controlling me without my knowledge."

"No," Seaghdh commanded.

Her hands knotted into fists. "I am not here to murder your personnel, you orhait's ass."

"I am attempting to recreate the sequence of events that led to the security breach, Captain Idylle," Sindrivik went on as if he hadn't heard a word. The flush in his face told Ari he'd heard just fine.

"You know how I accessed the file systems. Your boss all but handed me the control panel. If the Claugh nib Dovvyth intends to file charges so you can use me to declare war on TFC, do so. I am bound by an oath to protect the citizens of Tagreth Federated. I have served that oath and will continue to do so to the best of my ability per the verbal truce your queen and I agreed upon not twenty-four hours ago. For the record, I was left alone, unbound and unguarded in the Auhrnok Riorchjan's office for over an hour. He knew I was studying the language. Yet he did nothing to secure his workstation even after I'd watched him sign in."

Sindrivik started and Seaghdh took a step closer to the table.

"You recorded his sign in?" Sindrivik clarified.

"No," Seaghdh replied, eyeing her with an assessing light in his face. "I had the handheld."

He'd been uploading new language files for her.

"That's a sixteen-character code set," Sindrivik said.

Seaghdh spun on his heel and strode away from the table, obviously deep in thought. When his pacing took him past V'kyrri's seat, he returned with the cup of tea she hadn't drunk. He plunked it on the table in front of her.

She ignored it.

Sindrivik cleared his throat. In a rush and with an apologetic sideways glance at her, he switched to Claughwyth. "Your pardon, Auhrnok. Her father says that since her imprisonment, she will accept nothing, not even water, from another person's hand."

Seaghdh stopped short.

So did she.

He stared at her.

Ari could see him thinking it. She'd taken food and tea from him. What in the Three Hells did that mean? That she'd trusted him with her life long before she'd trusted him with her heart or her body? Twelve Gods.

Something warm and human thawed the icy mask he wore. He removed the tea, leaning closer to her shoulder than was necessary. "I do need you to tell me everything," he said, his tone carefully nonchalant and notably powered down.

The nonthreatening tone didn't fool her. She still had the spymaster on her hands, but a spymaster who knew he held every advantage since she'd admitted she'd fallen for him.

"Everything," Ari echoed. Her voice sounded dead. "What everything would that be?"

"You began learning Claughwyth twenty-four hours ago."

"I had a few lessons in the Academy," she said. When she'd dreamed of someday meeting the first-ranked blade master and taking his title. She'd wanted to thank him for the match in his own language. She squeezed her eyes shut and shook her head. "I began brushing up seventy-two hours ago. Give or take."

"We're speaking it now," he said. "Did you know?"

Cravuul dung. She was so busy guarding against the ache in her chest, she'd forgotten. She opened her eyes. Might as well. She'd already lost this round.

"You understand every word," he said.

"Not every word."

"That's quite a memory." Seaghdh placed a cup of soup before her. "Especially if you memorized a sixteen-character series having seen it only once and in a language you didn't know."

Ari blinked. He'd hit on something no one else had worked out. The Chekydran had amplified her memory. She'd only noticed once she'd been released and discovered by accident that she remembered every code and every name associated with each medi who'd walked through her secured door in the hospital. Seaghdh couldn't have worked out how her memory had gotten so good. Could he?

"What is my code?" He touched a button on the table. A panel lit in front of her. "Enter it. Please."

Wrapping suddenly chilled fingers around the mug, Ari wracked her brain for a way out. She sensed a trap, could almost feel the bite of the jaws, but she couldn't see it. She did not want him asking how she could remember so much. She didn't want to face the fact that the Chekydran had succeeded in modifying her.

He sat in the chair next to her. Too close. She smelled his spice and musk scent with every breath, felt his heat, desperately craved his touch. As if he'd heard the plea, he put his hand on her wrist. The contact shattered the ire she'd so carefully nursed as a defense.

"It's important."

Taking a drink of soup, she sighed as the warm liquid soothed the shredded feeling in her throat. She stared at the panel a moment, recalling the pattern of Seaghdh's code and then entered it. She shrugged when she looked up to find him staring at her.

"Spawn of a Myallki bitch," Turrel muttered. "Recruit that woman or I will."

"Ari," Seaghdh said. "I think you speak Chekydran."

The entire room held its breath. She let hers go. He hadn't asked why or how she could remember so much.

Cold sweat gathered on her skin. She shook her head. "No one speaks Chekydran." She was being deliberately obtuse, but she didn't like being herded into Cullin Seaghdh's snare.

"Three months, Ari. Three months to lie in a filthy, cramped, cold hole and hear them, to tear apart grammar, to codify structure and intonation. You understand their spoken language without need of a translator."

"You do know that not every language is comprehensible by our species base," she countered. "We simply don't have the same sensory range as other life types."

That gave him pause. He frowned, decided she was distracting him, and that he'd better stick to point.

Ari smiled, amazed that she'd become such an authority on the Auhrnok Riorchjan's impenetrable expression.

Her smile seemed to fluster him, but he insisted. "You understand the Chekydran."

"Sometimes," she allowed and swallowed hard.

"Sometimes?"

She rubbed sweaty palms against her fatigues. The line of conversation made it difficult to think straight. "Not via com," she said. "Only in person."

Seaghdh swore.

"Why?" Sindrivik asked.

"Their language encompasses more than you hear."

"Explain," Seaghdh ordered.

She glanced at the hard lines of his face and saw the concern in his eyes. "There's hum and vibration as well as the clicks and whistles you hear. The language is felt as much as heard. Humanoid com technology is calibrated to filter extraneous, nonauditory noise."

"Like vibration and low-level hums," Seaghdh finished. "Baxt'k. Can we recalibrate com systems to accommodate a fuller range?"

Sindrivik nodded.

"Ask whether you should," Ari prompted.

They looked at her without comprehension in their faces.

She shivered. "It's been nearly four months since I lay in a cell, captive audience to everything they said and did. Just saying that . . ." She broke off and forced a slow, measured breath out through pursed lips. "Brings it too close."

"With your permission, Captain," Seaghdh said slowly, his voice telling her he was reluctant to continue, "with Nwyth Okkar, I could implant a block triggered by a word or a gesture, something we agree upon. You need never suffer another flashback."

"You could do that?"

He met her gaze with trouble behind his eyes. "I could."

"Thank you," she said, touched by the offer. "No."

He frowned.

"I'll find my own way out."

Lights flickered and the *Dagger* shimmied. Ari stared at Seaghdh. Weapons fire? Who would be stupid enough to take a potshot at the *Dagger*? No one. The *Dagger* bristled with weapons and fighters. But the *Sen Ekir*? It had to be in range. She swore and spun to the control panels. She'd logged into the computer systems with Seaghdh's access code. Convenient. She punched up a communications panel.

"Ari."

"I read the language, Seaghdh," she said, keying in her father's com codes. "It took me a day to remember that I did, okay? Should I have said so? Sure. Just like you should have told me from the outset who you were. Where's my father?"

"Get that ship inside the shields! Now!" Eilod commanded, marching into the room. "And get that woman off of my ship and out of my computers before she finds my middle name."

"Incoming com, Your Majesty," Sindrivik said.

"On-screen," Seaghdh commanded, nudging Ari to one side.

She gave him her seat.

"On your screen, Auhrnok."

The screen flashed. Ari raised her eyebrows. Scales and teeth. Ykktyryk mercenaries. Nice.

"Give us the girl," the Ykktyryk hissed. "We split two million FedCreds and let little ship live."

She whistled through her teeth. "With a million Federated Credits I could buy my own ship. Do you provide Wrate Leaf on that tub?"

It sounded like Seaghdh sighed.

The Ykktyryk eyed her. "Who are you?"

"Me?" Ari shrugged. "The one you're offering to buy. You do know that FedCreds have no value in the Claugh monetary system, right?"

Turrel chuckled. "Recruit her."

Ari grinned. This was not how she'd imagined an interrogation by the Auhrnok Riorchjan ending.

"As you were, Colonel," Eilod growled. She strode across the room. "Confine the spy to the brig, Auhrnok, before I order her gagged or rendered unconscious. Weapons control?"

"Weapons standing by, Your Majesty," a voice responded via com. "Targeting Ykktyryk mercenary. Requesting permission to fire."

The Ykktyryk hissed and began barking out urgent stand-down commands.

Ari had to suppress the urge to cheer.

Seaghdh took her arm. "Captain Alexandria Idylle, you are under arrest for crimes against the Claugh nib Dovvyth Empire."

"No Wrate Leaf. Again," she said, noting the distinct lack of anger in his tone. They were playing. To what purpose?

He marched her out of the conference room, his lips twitching. He stopped and tapped his badge.

"Prep the *Lughfai*. Intraship teleport. Two at this signal to the *Lughfai* cockpit," Seaghdh ordered.

Confusion rocked her. "Wait," she protested.

"Acknowledged, Auhrnok. Two for teleport. Stand by. On your mark, sir."

"What the . . ." Ari squawked.

"Mark."

Teleport distortion always made Seaghdh dizzy. He shook it off the moment the shuttle cockpit solidified around them. Before she could pull away, he swept Ari tight into his arms and pinned her against the bulkhead so she couldn't slug him. He wouldn't blame her if she tried.

"I'm sorry," he whispered into her hair. "I am sorry. Three system failures and so many bits of partial information aligned . . ."

She nodded. Her arms crept around his waist. "I know. I'm sorry, too. I should have asked first."

A tightly bound-up place within him unknotted. Need rushed in to fill the void. He kissed her, ruthlessly launching an assault on her senses. Her body arched against his. He broke the kiss. She murmured a protest.

"Tell me again," he commanded, desperate to hear the words. "Please."

Fear shot into her eyes. It didn't carry the edge of senseless terror that glazed her eyes during a flashback. It was simple, comprehensible fear that drove a jagged stake into his heart. Her uncertainty stung.

This is what the Chekydran had robbed her of; her ability to trust herself, to anyone or anything. Yet she'd accepted food from him when she'd refused it from anyone else. And then the transponder. He closed his eyes. She'd trusted him. With her life. With her body. With her nascent emotions. Then, when it mattered most, he'd failed to return the favor. He swallowed a bitter knot of regret and prayed he hadn't destroyed her trust.

"I—" she essayed.

"Get that shuttle off this ship!" Eilod's voice ordered from the com panel.

They leaped guiltily apart and bolted for the helm.

"What the Three Hells is going on?" Ari demanded.

"The arrest was for show," he said as he buckled into the pilot's seat and woke panels.

She fastened in next to him. "I gathered. Mercenaries must be on the run, too, or I doubt you'd let me off the *Dagger*."

"Damned right," he answered. "You've got too much vital information in your head, and I have specific interest in keeping you alive for our next rematch."

She flushed and spent a moment scanning her console, before keying the instruments to standby. "Awaiting authorization codes."

Seaghdh smiled. A thrill rippled through him whenever she spoke his language. Time to begin rebuilding whatever trust he'd broken. "Authorization, yellow-kawlth—no, here." He made sure she was watching and punched in the code. "It describes a sound sequence. Yellow-kawlth-885."

"Authorization code, yellow-kawlth-885, acknowledged and accepted. We're green across the board."

"Green across the board, aye," he said, powering the engines hard and fast. "No time for a checklist. We want your father's ship inside the protection of the shields and you working on that lieutenant of yours."

"Dad's got Tommy? Good."

"Unless he's broadcasting in some fashion we can't detect," he said, throttling up. "If he is, then we have to work faster than the Chekydran."

She grabbed a headset and requested bay door clearance. The bulkhead rumbled open and the shuttle shot out into the darkness.

"Ever piloted a Claugh fighter shuttle?"

She glanced at him, a wary look in her eye. "No, but the specs look similar to TFC's midrange interceptor."

He nodded. "You have plenty of hours on that ship. Good. Take over. I want to make sure the Ykktyryk five man keeps a respectful distance."

Ari's head jerked up, and she shot a look at sensors, then at the view screen as she covered his controls, waiting for him to turn them over. Her accomplished hands took the helm.

Blood rushed straight for Seaghdh's lower body, recalling her skilled touch from the night before.

"They're still here?" she asked, yanking his attention back to the view screen. "A five man? They can't hurt us. Are we sure this isn't a lure? Something designed to get us out from under the *Dagger*'s shields and guns?"

"Damn it." He bolted for weapons.

Ari swore. "I need to tweak sensors. You okay with it?"

"Advise the *Dagger* to scramble her fighters and you can do anything you want," he countered.

The anticipation in the sly grin she tossed him shorted out his brain. He blew out a shallow breath and forced his attention back to weapons. Grabbing a headset, he patched in to Eilod on the bridge of the *Dagger*. "Full scan!" he said. "All sensors at maximum. That five man . . ." He spun. "Ari! Missiles incoming!"

"Acknowledged." She slammed the shuttle's engines to maximum and wrenched the controls. The ship dove hard. Gravity generators whined in protest, then failed. An alarm warbled, then fell silent when Ari slapped it off.

Seaghdh grabbed his harness and fastened himself to his chair. His lasers read hot, and the targeting system chirped as it homed in on the missile.

"Save your ammo," she said. "The *Dagger*'s shields took the steam out of it. It won't catch us, which means they're trying to drive us." She flipped the throttle hard to starboard.

Seaghdh felt as if his stomach had torn free of his body and hit the bulkhead behind him. She pulled out of the dive and the *Sen Ekir* hung before them, shields flaring as a missile impacted.

"Clearing the *Dagger*'s shields in three, two . . . Right on cue," she grumbled. "Incoming. We've got an Erillian Aggressor on intercept. Cravuul dung. They were hiding behind Dad. Their weapons and shields read hot. They're firing! I thought they wanted me alive! Get our shields online!"

"Returning fire," Seaghdh said, then cursed as the shuttle jounced. Sparks blew forward from a panel on the aft bulkhead. An alarm shrieked. "Fighters are scrambled!" he hollered above the din.

"Damn it!" Ari shouted and silenced the alarm. "Direct hit to the shield generator."

Something cold uncurled in his stomach. They'd been had by someone who knew the *Dagger*'s sensors couldn't read through the *Sen Ekir*'s energy exhaust and who knew the precise layout of the *Lughfai*'s systems. "Firing missiles."

The *Lughfai* took another two hits. Cabin lights died. Emergency lighting winked on. Seaghdh lobbed a barrage of laser fire at the mercenaries.

"Gods damn it!" she snapped as a missile hit them dead center.

Laser fire and another missile jolted the ship. The panel in front of Ari exploded. She ducked and cursed. Several alarms wailed at once.

"Sen Ekir! Sen Ekir!" Seaghdh bellowed. "Clear the shields! Clear the *Dagger*'s shields! The fighters will close on the attackers."

"Captain Seaghdh," Ari's father answered. "Our sensors indicate that you've lost life support. We are lowering our shields. Prepare for teleport."

"Negative!" Ari shouted. Blood ran down her face from a cut in her forehead. "It's a trap, Dad! It's exactly what they want!"

"Ari," Seaghdh said.

Something in his voice jerked her around to face him.

"The aggressor is powering their tractor beam."

She glanced at the panels and shook her head. "We won't make it. We're hemorrhaging air. It'll be a body recovery."

Teleport distortion broke the rage exploding through Seaghdh's chest but not before he heard Ari's "Damn it to all Three Hells, Dad."

CHAPTER

23

ARI materialized with Seaghdh beside her and recognized the medical bay aboard the *Sen Ekir*.

She leaped for Raj's desk and flipped the com switch. "Get this ship inside that damned shield! Now!"

"Do not use that tone of voice with me, Alexandria," her father snapped. "I have plenty of people yelling at me. I don't need to add you to the list."

Frustration choked her for a moment. Ari clenched her fists and managed to say, "On my way."

The *Sen Ekir* lurched. She relaxed. The *Dagger* had them on guidance.

"What do you think you're doing?" her father demanded. "Release this ship immediately."

"Belay that!" she shouted. "Dad! I think I'm a payday to those mercenaries. Dead or alive. I'm guessing they prefer dead. They obviously don't care about collateral damage. With the *Sen Ekir* on guidance, the

Dagger can keep us close enough to protect us with their shields and their mass. They're helping."

Her father snorted in derision. "After ordering me to Kebgra for a body retrieval? What in the Three Hells is going on, Alexandria? The only reason I've done anything they've ordered me to do was the possibility that I'd have you back."

Ari blinked, speechless. Her dad wanted her back? Again? Something warm unfolded inside her chest.

"Dr. Idylle," Seaghdh said, wrapping an arm around her waist. "Please power down, sir. Ari and I are in your medical bay."

Raj chimed in. "I'm finishing an autopsy sequence on the body we brought in. Once I've cycled through decon, I'll be right there."

"No need," Ari replied, grabbing a steri-pad and wiping the blood from her face. "Superficial head wound. Looks impressive, amounts to nothing. You got Tommy?"

"Who?" her father queried.

"The body. A former crewman. He was taken when my shuttle was snatched," she said.

Seaghdh held up a hand and shook his head.

She raised an eyebrow at him but closed her mouth. Did he not want her to air their suspicions until after her father had finished his examination of the corpse?

"The Chekydran did that to him?" Her father sounded shaken. "You know what happened to that boy? How could you do this to me, Alex, forcing me to look at what those bastards did to one of our own? At what they tried to do to you?"

"Sir," Seaghdh interrupted when Ari opened her mouth to answer. "Let us get cleaned up. Then we'll answer as many questions as we can. May I speak with my ship for a moment?"

Her father must have acquiesced. Pietre said, "Patching you through on channel two."

Ari opened the line and turned away to finish scrubbing the dried blood from her face and hair.

Seaghdh confirmed, in Tagrethian, presumably so her father could understand, the destruction of the *Lughfai* and subsequently of the mercenary ships.

"Please convey our sincere appreciation to Dr. Idylle and his crew for their swift rescue of Captain Idylle and of you, Auhrnok Riorchjan," Eilod said. "Captain Idylle. My cousin warned me that your grasp of tactics rivaled his own. He misspoke. You surpassed him by spotting that trap before it could crush us in its jaws. Thank you."

Turning back to the panel, Ari raised her eyebrows and flinched. Wrinkling her forehead hurt. "Flattery will get you whatever you like, Your Majesty," she quipped, smiling. "We'll get to work untangling this mess."

Eilod chuckled. "I can still charge you with spying, you ingrate," she said in Claughwyth.

"Why, thank you, Your Majesty," Ari countered in Tagrethian. "It is kind of you to say so."

Seaghdh, eyes dancing, covered his mouth with his hand.

She grinned at him.

"With Dr. Idylle's permission, I request that you check in on the hour, Auhrnok," Eilod said. "*Dagger* out."

Ari closed the line.

"You're the Auhrnok baxt'kal Riorchjan?" Pietre demanded over intraship.

"Guilty," Seaghdh replied.

She noticed that her dad didn't take Pietre to task for his language. Shaking her head, she clicked off the com.

"On the table with you," Seaghdh ordered. "I'll clean that cut."

"Raj will be here shortly," she said, hopping up.

He peered at her, remembered distress intense in his expression. "We missed being vaporized by seconds, Ari. Let me touch you."

Gentle heat expanded within her, pressing against her insides, growing too big to be contained by skin and bones. She wanted to smile at him. She couldn't. Ari took a deep breath and gambled.

"In the shuttle," she said. "You asked me . . ."

He laid a finger on her lips. "Enough fear. Sit still."

She subsided, discontent roiling her insides. She was sick to death of being afraid.

He dabbed antiseptic on her forehead, sprayed wound sealant, then activated Raj's regen beam.

"Did you mean to make me fall in love with you?" she asked, her heart trembling.

He froze. Elation and desire flared in his eyes before he closed them and drew in a long, slow breath.

She heard the regen click off and his arms went around her. He pulled her hard against him. "Gods know it's what I prayed for," he murmured, "but no. I didn't dare hope. Say it again. Please?"

She breathed a shaky laugh and wrapped her legs and arms around him, feeling suddenly more powerful than she'd ever felt in her life. "I fell in love with you."

Seaghdh leaned back and grinned, his roguish smile heightened by the suggestive glitter in his eyes.

She ran a hand up his chest.

He kissed the scratch on her forehead.

Alarms erupted. She leaped out of his grasp, pushed off the table, and stared in horror as the bulkhead doors slammed shut.

"No."

"What is it?" he demanded. "Ari? What?"

"Quarantine! By the Twelve Gods! Quarantine!"

The alarms died.

"All personnel report! By the numbers!" Raj's voice commanded via intraship.

"Dr. Linnaeus Idylle, cargo bay," her father said, concern thick in his voice.

Ari stomped across the bay, swearing, as Pietre, Raj, then Jayleia reported in with their locations. Grabbing up bits of medical equipment, she strode back to Seaghdh's side and flipped the com switch. "Captains Ari Idylle and Cullin Seaghdh. In baxt'kal quarantine."

"Alex!" her father barked. Only her dad could get so much reproach and worry into one word. "Symptoms?"

"None." She shot a look at Seaghdh.

He shook his head.

"For either of us. Damn it. Sampling blood now. Link me up. You know this isn't my forte."

"Initiating double backup of all files. Shutting down non-critical ship's systems. Routing power to processing. Direct computer links in ten," Pietre said.

"Link from cargo, Pietre!" her father ordered. "Raj? Get back down here! Clear containment! Secondary diagnostic refit!"

"Agreed. On my way," Raj shot.

She heard him scrambling around before he cut the link. It made Ari smile despite the adrenaline flooding her body, making her hands shake.

Seaghdh's fingers closed over hers as she set Raj's leech atop a blue vein showing through the skin of her arm. She glanced at him.

"Deep breath," he said. "We're not dead yet. You've got the best people in the galaxy right here to help."

She nodded.

"Dr. Idylle," Seaghdh raised his voice for intraship. "Contact the *Dagger* and advise them of our situation. If you'll permit, sir, Turrel can link you to the Royal University of Medicine. You will have the full cooperation of the best minds in the Claugh nib Dovvyth."

A moment's hesitation and then she heard her father move closer to his com speaker. "I will have Pietre patch you through from medical, Captain. I will afford your people access to our files, but I ask that you speak with them directly. I am a scientist. My diplomatic skills are . . . lacking."

Seaghdh winked at her wan smile. "Understood."

She thumbed the switch on Raj's leech and closed her eyes. Sampling blood didn't hurt, but in the past six or seven months, she'd developed a strong preference for having her blood on the inside of her body. The device beeped twice. Sample complete. Opening her eyes, she snapped the vial out, tagged it, and set it in the analyzer.

She snapped another vial into the leech and nodded at Seaghdh. "Need an arm."

"Just an arm?"

Ari pursed her lips to keep from smiling at his teasing tone. "I have a distinct appreciation for every bit of your anatomy, Seaghdh. Blood can be sampled from any visible blood vessel regardless of location."

Someone choked back a laugh via intraship. Seaghdh looked horrified. He'd forgotten the connections were open ship-wide. Or was he horrified by the thought of blood being taken from someplace other than his arm?

"Forearm sufficient?" he inquired, sounding sheepish.

"Yes. That vein will do nicely."

"I'll disable intraship and we can discuss your appreciation of my anatomy without your family eavesdropping," he whispered into her ear as she took a sample from him.

She glared at him.

He leered back.

Her heart flip-flopped in her chest.

The leech beeped.

"All done," she said. She tagged his sample and spent several moments entering information into the computer, creating a new medical file for him in the *Sen Ekir*'s system.

"Sampling complete and in the analyzer, Raj," she said.

"All right. I'll want a full scan," Raj replied, "but no sequencing. You're going to have to set this up, Ari. I don't have a link yet. I'll talk you through it."

"We don't have a sequence on file for Seaghdh."

"I know."

"Dr. Annantra can provide that," Seaghdh said.

Ari nodded. "That'll save time and processing power."

"Agreed," Raj said.

"Computer links are first priority," Pietre called from wherever he was working. "Unless anyone wants to override that."

"Nope," she said. "I'm going to need every last one of you."

"Almost there," Pietre replied, a hint of surprise in his voice.

"Have a seat, Ari," Raj said. "We'll get analysis underway. It's a simple, multi-command process."

Raj walked her through several screens' worth of test commands. The analyzer closed and cycled into action.

"Direct link initiated," Pietre announced. "Raj can read your screens, Ari, but you'll still have to issue keyboard commands."

"Thank you, Pietre," she and her father said simultaneously.

"Hailing the *Dagger*," Pietre replied. "Patching into com channel four."

"Acknowledged and my appreciation, Mr. Ivanovich," Seaghdh answered. He glanced at Ari for confirmation that his finger hovered over the correct button.

She nodded.

He hailed his ship in his own language, asking for Turrel and a secure channel.

"Turrel. Quarters secure. Sonic shield enabled. Narrow com beam, encoded," Turrel said by way of greeting.

"Kirthin," Seaghdh said. "We've got an outbreak."

Turrel swore.

"Have Dr. Annantra transfer a complete copy of my medical file to Dr. Idylle. I'll also need a link to the head of the Royal University's director of . . ."

The screen in front of Ari lit up with results. "Spawn of a Myallki bitch."

"What is it?"

"You want the director of virology, preferably someone with a specialty in Chekydran pathology," she said.

"Alex?" her father prompted via intraship.

"Now we know why the thrice-damned bastards didn't kill me," she said. "The Chekydran seeded a disease in me. It just went hot. They sent me back as a time bomb. Baxt'k! Turrel, listen to me. Lock down that ship. Teleporters, shuttles, fighters. Nothing leaves the *Dagger* except data."

"By the Gods, Ari," Turrel snapped. "I didn't dodge genocide to die in a Chekydran plague. Baxt'kal Three Hells. You were with the queen."

"Everyone," Ari retorted. "You. Sindrivik. V'kyrri."

"The Auhrnok," he breathed.

She dropped her head to rest on her forearm. "Twelve Gods. I am an assassin."

CHAPTER

24

TURREL took Ari at her word. He locked down the *Dagger* hard and fast. Eilod, angry and frightened, demanded that Seaghdh transport back. He refused.

"With luck, Eilod," he said, "only Ari and I were exposed. Let's keep it that way."

An hour later, Dr. Annantra called. She had three feverish crew members in isolation.

Ari traded a look with Seaghdh. He shook his head. He felt fine. Her heart lifted a little.

Raj traded notes with Annantra. Dad managed to confirm that the strains infecting Ari were related to previous Chekydran diseases, but he'd found indications that someone had spliced in something new, something their shipboard systems couldn't recognize without a sequence and structure readout. Sequencing the illness in the detail they'd need would take days. Ari doubted they had that kind of time.

Four hours later, Seaghdh had a fever and V'kyrri had reported to the *Dagger* medi-bay. Eilod relayed the news, her expression defeated. She slumped in her chair, her face flushed. She looked ill.

Ari's heart ached. It was a clean sweep. She'd destroyed the Claugh nib Dovvyth's royal family because she'd desperately wanted to belong, to matter. To trust. She closed the com line and cursed. What she wanted no longer mattered. It was time to think and to act. She started with her DNA. If something had been seeded, nestled dormant, into the cells of her body, she should be able to see indications of it. Dad and Raj were attacking the bug head-on, sequencing it and hoping they could formulate a cure. She'd come through the back door, tracing how it had slumbered undetected all this time.

The first victim died when her lungs filled with bloody mucous. Annantra declared the delicate Mannuvian dead at hour ten. Ari closed the channel and rested painfully, scratchy, dry eyes against her forearms. A slow count to fifty and she shook off sorrow and self-pity. They didn't have the time.

Seated at Raj's tiny desk in the *Sen Ekir*'s medi-bay, she pulled a blue gray blanket tighter around her shoulders and glanced at Seaghdh. He slept on the single diagnostic bed, not three feet away. The silent display of vital sign readouts assured her he lived still. Rubbing her tired eyes, she felt the weight of futility dragging at her as she scanned the endless lines of DNA on the screen in front of her.

That's when she saw it.

She leaned forward, froze the screen, and flogged her memory for the source of the discrepancy she saw in her own genome. She pulled up her dad's file, scrolled to the identical markers, and overlaid the codes. No match. So little match that her heart faltered. Was her dad not really her father? Swiftly, she retrieved the copy of her mother's file. The overlay flashed "no match." She stared, uncomprehending.

No genetic overlay, unless it was a self overlay, ever matched completely. Comparing her code to her parents', she should statistically see more matches on the genome than if she had compared her DNA to a complete stranger's. The matches on the genome between her parents' files and hers were significantly low, as if she and her parents were, in fact, unrelated.

Something made Ari pull up Hieronomus's and Isolde's medical files. She ran an overlay of her sister's file with their dad's. Match. As expected. Isolde had his pale blue eyes and their mother's light brown hair. An overlay with their mom's file brought another match, though one lower than their dad's. No surprise. Isolde was exactly like their father and just as hard to get along with.

Hieronomus's file matched both parents almost evenly. It startled her. Her older brother was a prig. She'd have bet money he matched their father. An unfair assumption on her part, perhaps, given that their mother had died when Ari had been two. The few memories she had of her mother didn't include a stick up her backside like Hieronomus had.

Ari was guiltily relieved when neither her sister's nor her brother's files matched hers.

Because she couldn't think of anything else to do, and because she knew she'd never sleep despite the weariness plaguing her, she combined all four files and ran the aggregate against her file. This time the system hesitated, then flashed "inconclusive."

Interesting.

Ari wasn't sure what she was looking for. She only knew that her DNA had a story to tell about who she was and about what had happened to her. She had to decrypt the message if she wanted to defeat whatever the Chekydran had done. She tiled the screen and brought up the single family file next to her own. And saw immediately why the computer had returned an inconclusive result.

Most of the code in her file *nearly* matched her family's. When parents mingled DNA to create a child, recombination took place, producing a few brand-new expressions of old codes. It produced the odd dark-haired child in a family full of blonds. Even with recombination accounted for, the genetic files of child and parent should make it plain each parent provided half of the child's genetic material.

Comparing the code representing her and her family, she could see indications of that relation. Her parents really were her parents, but something had altered her DNA, modifying this bit here and flipping that protein switch there. So many changes. Suspicion knocked at the back of her brain. How could she have forgotten that her mom had been an ambitious and driven geneticist?

Ari hadn't been a late-life accident. She'd been planned for. Exactingly. Huddling in her blanket, she shivered. She wasn't a difficult daughter. She was an experiment. The question was whose? How much of what she saw before her had her mother done? How much represented what the Chekydran had altered? Did her father carry the records of her DNA sequence at birth?

Before she knew what she'd done, Ari keyed her father's com code.

"Alex?" her dad's sleep-roughened voice asked after a few seconds. "Are you all right?"

"What am I?" she rasped.

Seaghdh stirred at the sound of her voice.

"I don't understand," her father said.

"Me, either," she answered. "Whose idea was it to engineer a human experiment?"

Her father sucked in an audible breath. The com switched off.

"Ari?" Seaghdh rose and stumbled to her side. He put a hand on her shoulder. He had a fever. "What is it?"

Her heart faltered as she glanced at him. Despair clutched at her throat. She was killing him. "You shouldn't be up," Ari said.

"We both know it won't make a bit of difference," he replied. "Talk to me."

"I wish I could. I don't have any answers," she said.

"And I have far too few," her father said from the doorway. The shimmer of the containment field blurred his face. "You are a creative thinker, Alexandria. I should have realized you would begin comparing your DNA to mine and to your mother's."

She scooted her chair closer to the doorway.

263

Seaghdh trailed as if drawn.

"You knew," she said.

"Not until after you'd been born," her father replied. "Your mother didn't tell me what she'd done until you were kicking and screaming in my arms. I suspect she feared that you wouldn't be viable."

Something about hearing those words spoken in relation to her clamped down on her ability to breathe freely.

"What?" Seaghdh growled. His fingers closed on her shoulders, massaging, warming.

"I was genetically engineered and implanted," Ari said.

Seaghdh stilled.

Her father nodded. "You were."

"I assume that's as illegal on your side of the zone as on mine?" Seaghdh said.

"After a few brushes with extinction due to lack of diversity? Absolutely," her dad replied. He sighed, retreated, found a chair, and hauled it back to the doorway. He settled into it as if he hurt.

Ari forced the pain welling up in her chest to one side. The fog cleared from her brain a little and she nudged the fuzzy gray matter into action. "From everything I've read and heard about her, Mom didn't tinker," she said. "She had something specific in mind when she designed me. What?"

"Immunity, a resilient, adaptive immune system designed specifically to tag and combat engineered infections," her father said. "When she began working on you, your mother was already ill. She told no one. Not even me. She kept so many secrets those final three years. I didn't know the woman who died in our bed. She'd become a stranger to me."

The knot of anger roiling in her middle eased. "She wanted to design someone who could keep you company," she guessed.

Her father looked at her, furrows in his brow and the shine of hard memory in his eyes. "Possibly," he whispered. Clearing his throat, he sat up straighter. "I could not countenance what had been done to you. After your mother's death, I determined that you would be allowed to choose your own way, to become whatever you wished."

Her mother had bequeathed her a destiny. Her father had countered it with freedom. "Did Mom's notes say anything about side effects?"

Her father raised his eyebrows. "What side effects?"

"Telepathy."

Her father blinked, then stared at her as if waiting for the word to penetrate his brain and make some kind of sense.

"Perhaps you are aware, Dr. Idylle," Seaghdh said, "that the Claugh nib Dovvyth includes one or two naturally occurring telepathic races."

Her father nodded.

"My engineer, V'kyrri, is a telepath."

"Engineer?" her father echoed, a knowing smirk on his face.

"As your wife may have proved, Doctor," Seaghdh replied, "there are all kinds of engineers. Among Ari's reports, V'kyrri noted several telltale signs of latent telepathic ability. He tested her."

The older man leaned forward, propping his elbows on his knees. "And?"

Ari disliked his intrigued tone. It sounded too much like the one he used when a pathology sample turned up unexpected results.

"He confirmed it," she said, leaving off "high level." She hoped Seaghdh would do the same.

Her father looked at her.

She saw the speculation in his eyes and dropped her gaze.

"Now, that is interesting," he murmured. "I wonder if it's heritable."

Ari bridled.

"You can hate me, Alexandria, for being what I am," he said, "a man of science. But I did not do this to you. I cannot change what was done. In honesty, I do not know that I would. You are all that any parent can hope a child will become, competent, accomplished, talented. It's my fondest wish that you might one day be happy. Until then, I can only do what I have always done. Protect the secret of your origin. I destroyed most of your mother's records, to make certain no one knew."

"Someone did know, Dad!" Ari countered. "Why else would I have been sacrificed to the Chekydran?"

"Your capture was an accident," he said.

"Not according to an encoded file my people intercepted seven months ago," Seaghdh rumbled. "It contained the *Balykkal*'s coordinates and a flight plan that would be followed by one Captain Alexandria Idylle. It was delivered to the Chekydran along with an order for capture."

She stared at him. "You knew? You knew I'd been set up by one of my own and you did nothing to warn me? Or to stop it?"

Agony stood out in the haggard lines of Seaghdh's face. "We knew and every single effort we made to reach you failed or was intercepted."

She slumped. "You went through Armada."

"What would have happened if we hadn't?"

"You'd have destroyed my career a few months early," she said and sighed. And she would have hated him for it. She could see the awareness in his eyes. They both knew she wouldn't have believed the queen's spymaster even if he'd come to her with proof in hand.

Had the Chekydran planned all along to use her as a political assassin? How could they have known she'd end up with the Claugh leadership?

She blinked. They hadn't. No. What they could know was that she'd end up in a hospital, then once released, that she'd follow protocol—she'd ship out aboard the *Sen Ekir*, collect samples, go back to Tagreth, prep her PhD, and then report to her mentor and CO, Admiral Angelou. Was he the target? Or simply acceptable collateral damage in pursuit of their real target? How could they know he wouldn't be immune to their plague? Did this mean that whatever alliance had been hammered out between the Admiralty and the Chekydran was in trouble? More important, could she use it?

"I assume you're tracing the file?" Ari asked.

"We're working on it," Seaghdh replied. The ominous tone underlying his words boded ill for whoever had given her up.

She smiled. It felt grim.

"Why would someone do that to you? To anyone?" The tremor of horror in her father's voice brought Ari upright.

Rage in his clenched fists. Pain in the hard glitter of his eyes and in his tight lips. Grief in the shadowed lines around his mouth. Very suddenly, her father looked startlingly old and Ari realized in a flash that for three months, she'd resisted seeing what her capture and imprisonment had cost him. She remembered some of the horrible things that had passed between them in the three months since she'd come home. Her heart clenched hard and she shuddered.

"Is it possible someone found out about Ari? Could someone have done what she has?" Seaghdh asked, gesturing at the lines still visible on the computer screen.

"We aren't the only people capable of teasing apart genetic data," she said, "but anyone not in our family would simply assume I'd been adopted."

Her father shook his head. "Anyone with a rudimentary understanding of species differentiation would know exactly what they were looking at if they'd run the sort of comparison scan you just ran," he said. "I can't believe I didn't think of it before now, though not carrying sequence files for you would have raised undue suspicion, too."

Species differentiation. By the Twelve Gods and all Three Hells. She wasn't even human. Did that mean she could never go home again? Being the sole member of a species, could she claim she'd ever had a home? Rubbing her forehead, she opened dry eyes and wondered why the knife-sharp pain under her breast bone didn't burst her rib cage. "Our working hypothesis is that I was marked for capture because I'm a genetic experiment. Do we assume the Chekydran were supposed to have killed me? They didn't and instead turned me into a weapon?"

"I'd say that someone in the Armada Admiralty is learning the hard way that the Chekydran can only be trusted to stab him in the back," Seaghdh said. He froze, staring at her. "Where were you supposed to be?"

Her father looked between them, understanding dawning in his face.

She nodded. "I'd thought of it. If the mission had gone to spec, Dad would have cleared quarantine yesterday, docked, and unloaded the ship. I might have prepped my samples and then locked them up. Today, I would have reported to my CO."

"Angelou," he said.

Her father frowned. "You cannot seriously believe . . ."

"I don't know, Dad," she said. "I don't have hard proof of anything, yet. Just casings."

Dr. Idylle nodded. "Chekydran plagues, when they die or are destroyed by an immune system cell, leave behind fragments of the molecular sheathes that protected the plague's genetic material," he said, Ari assumed for Seaghdh's benefit. "We can't tell much about the plague from its sheath, other than it had been present."

"What amounts to circumstantial evidence?" Seaghdh surmised.

"Evidence that often leads to an inoculation," Ari said slowly looking at her dad. "Hell of a difference in parsing molecular markers and a lot of coincidental information leading back to Angelou's office, Dad."

He nodded. "I know. Why do you think I prefer pathogens to politics?"

"We have to cure whatever this is," she said. "We'd always believed that the Chekydran worked for decades to create a plague that would wipe out humanoids entirely, but what if they were just poisoning vermin? Trying to keep humanoids from spilling over into their territory?"

Seaghdh straightened. "What?"

"No. You've seen the data," her father said.

"We've been assigning human motivation to a non-humanoid species, Dad."

Her father narrowed his eyes. "Explain."

"What do we know about the Chekydran? What is their societal structure? We describe them as bugs and assume they're a hive society. Based on what I observed, that seems to hold. My captor has a queen, but I'm not clear if there's only one or if every male has a queen or if 'queen' means to them what it means to us. We're limited by the fact that I'm evaluating my observations based on my only frame of reference."

"Which is defined by tiny insect and insectoid, hive-based creatures with a single queen, few drones, and an almost exclusively female population," her father mused.

"If the comparison holds," Ari said, "we could posit that the Chekydran hive had grown too large and that they were swarming in search of new territory to support the population."

"Something we cannot know for fact," her dad countered.

"If we can't know that," Ari pressed, "how do we define what's behind the slow but persistent escalation in Chekydran aggression?"

"Is that impression?" her father demanded. "Or do you have data?"

"We have data," Seaghdh answered in her stead. "Analysis is incomplete."

Ari blinked. Sindrivik worked fast if he'd already parsed through the data she'd dumped in Seaghdh's file share.

"The emerging data pattern suggests it's not just impression," Seaghdh said.

Her father nodded, disquiet in the lines around his eyes. "Yet we can't say for certain what drives them."

"We can't even say why they capture the ships and people they capture," Ari said.

"We can in some instances," Seaghdh countered. "They are damned single-minded about spies. They are quick to accuse and quicker to kill once they've accused. Can't we deduce from that behavior that they're territorial?"

"Yes," Ari allowed. She shook her head, frowning. "Or does it go beyond territorial? When a humanoid government is so defensive of its secrets, it's usually because there's a secret worth preserving."

Seaghdh and her father stared at her, no comprehension in their faces.

"Are you suggesting," her father essayed, "that the Chekydran are protecting a secret that could destroy them?"

"I have no idea how to find out."

Her father sighed and paced in front of the medi-bay door. He stopped short in the middle of his third pass and blinked at her. "Do you know, we don't even have a single genetic profile on the species?"

"No one has ever recovered a Chekydran body?" Ari marveled.

"Let me check some files," Seaghdh said. He opened a channel to Sindrivik and began issuing rapid-fire instructions.

"We've assumed," her father said, drawing her attention away from Seaghdh, "given the structure of plagues and delivery mechanisms, that the Chekydran must have a DNA structure similar to our own. It is another assumption based on no hard evidence."

"Then how does a non-humanoid species know so much about the DNA structures of humanoids?" Ari finished for him. A fleeting suspicion made her turn to Seaghdh. "Do you have records of known instances of the Chekydran taking prisoners?"

"I'll find out."

"What are you thinking?" her father demanded.

Ari turned back to meet his gaze. "What if the research we're doing, tracing back through layers of plague, represents the Chekydran's learning curve?"

"They didn't know our DNA but over the centuries learned it?" Her father surmised. "You think Ioccal is a Chekydran petri dish?"

Ari shrugged. "It is close to the border. We have direct evidence of generation after generation of disease, all related. It's almost like the plagues were timed and their results observed. Just like an experiment. How else do we account for the older illnesses that had such limited impact on the citizens of Ioccal?"

"Your PhD samples?" Seaghdh said, returning to her side and

glancing between them. "You had them in containment. If they weren't harmful . . ."

Her father cut him off. "You don't gamble with engineered plagues. We have no way of knowing how many generations occupied Ioccal, nor what had changed in the germ line."

"In the what?"

"Changes to the base genetic coding of the species," Ari clarified. "Planets force humanoids to adapt. When enough adaptations occur we talk about species differentiation. Because we had no surviving examples of the Ioccal citizens, we can't say whether their resistance to the samples I brought aboard was related to specific adaptations inspired by the planet."

"You never recovered DNA from the remains?"

"Of course we did," her dad said, "from only a few individuals, however. Certainly not enough for a statistically significant sampling."

"Can we use any of these samples to find out what the Chekydran did to Ari?" Seaghdh asked.

Dad shook his head. "We're working on that. It takes time."

Ari blew out a breath. Not good news. "That's going to cost lives."

"Yes, it is," Dad said, his voice muted.

The medi-bay com pinged. Seaghdh opened the channel.

"No first-contact record, Auhrnok. And no genetic files on this first pass," Sindrivik said. "However, I pulled and compiled all known captures of humanoids by Chekydran. It validates the impression that Chekydran activity has been increasing."

"Details," Seaghdh said.

"Several centuries ago, the fledgling mining guilds began sending prospectors into Chekydran space," he said. "No one knew it was anyone's space at the time, obviously, but significant numbers of those ships never returned. I'm counting them as Chekydran kills."

"Go on."

"Capture numbers remain steady for centuries, though I had to factor in aggression by the various humanoid factions. If TFC colonization or military activity increased near the border, so did the capture rates. Same pattern among the Claugh and the UMOPG."

Ari frowned. "That doesn't . . ."

"Until forty years ago," Sindrivik said. "There is a sharp uptick in the number of captures, regardless of colony or military actions."

"Define sharp," her father instructed.

"Twenty-seven percent, Dr. Idylle."

"Give me an analysis on . . ."

Sensor alarms erupted both in the background of the open com channel and aboard the *Sen Ekir*.

"Captain Seaghdh!" Peitre's voice rang over ship-wide. "The *Dagger* is taking fire from a pair of Chekydran cruisers!"

Ari gasped. "Chekydran?"

"Where the Three Hells are we?" Seaghdh demanded.

"Claugh space," Pietre replied.

"You're sure?" Dad barked.

"Gods damn it, Linnaeus!" Pietre said. "We left the border six hours ago! It never occurred to me to scan for Chekydran particle trails here!"

"Of course not," Ari said. "Their being here is a declaration of war! None of our intelligence suggests they would initiate this kind of aggression. They've preferred indirect methods up to now . . ." She trailed off, shuffled data in her head, and swore. "If we're guessing correctly and they're swarming, we have to treat this as an all-out power grab. Get us video to the *Dagger*, Pietre! Intraship stays open."

"All personnel, report to duty stations," her father commanded.

Hicci was out there. Ari's blood ran cold. She swore under her breath, trying to control her suddenly racing heart rate.

Video lit up the desktop behind her. She and Seaghdh spun. Ari had never seen the bridge of the *Dagger*. Eilod, flushed, ill, harried, and pissed as all Three Hells, sat strapped into the command chair. Turrel manned a station on her right. Ari flipped the channel open.

"You're on," she said to Seaghdh.

He demanded status in Claughwyth. A curl of blue electrical smoke rose from a panel behind Eilod's head.

Ari waited, braced against the desk for the jolt that would accompany another shot hitting the *Dagger*. It didn't come.

"They aren't firing," she said, frowning. "They want something." She swallowed hard, fear turning her innards to water.

Seaghdh straightened. He met her gaze with a grim eye. "You."

CHAPTER
25

ARI sat staring at her handheld, her mind spurred into overdrive, by the tactical data Turrel shunted to the unit.

Two Chekydran cruisers. Fully staffed, the *Dagger* would have given them a serious run for their money. But the list of the sick and dying aboard the Claugh nib Dovvyth royal flagship left half of the great ship's stations unmanned.

Eilod brought Ari's father and his crew into her conference room via holograph emitters. Ari knew the queen didn't like it, but she'd left Seaghdh and Ari on video, since Raj's tiny medi-bay couldn't support holographic projections. It was bad enough, Ari discovered, because Seaghdh, feverish and coughing, needed to pace.

Ari had to find a way to turn this group baxt'k to their advantage.

"They have declared war upon the empire of the Claugh nib Dovvyth," Eilod said. "Let us declare war upon them. I want proof of a Chekydran-Armada alliance. Captain Idylle. Can I put a strike team aboard one of those ships?"

Ari stared at Eilod's angry face. A strike team? Comprised of coughing, dying soldiers? Sitting upright, she grabbed fiercely at the thought dashing through her head. Strike teams ran risks, dying among them. If they could strike a solid blow before death came calling, so much the better.

"You need a diversion," she said. "Something that will let your team board and move about the ship without being murdered instantly." If most of them didn't drop dead from the plague on the way in.

Ari sucked in a short breath and bit her lip. She couldn't believe she was going to say the words. "You need me on board that ship."

Eilod frowned. "I don't believe that would be in anyone's best interests."

"Especially not mine," she agreed. "However, the Chekydran use a low-level aural hum as a sort of neural network."

Seaghdh nodded. "You once mentioned creating a sonic disrupter."

"Exactly. If it's going to have a chance at working, I have to be there."

"I don't see why," he argued.

"We need their computers," Eilod said, cutting off Seaghdh's willingness to quarrel. "Intact."

"They aren't computers," Ari replied.

Every face in the *Dagger*'s conference room, including the holograms of Ari's father and his crew, swiveled to look at her. In that moment, she realized how much information she had about the Chekydran that no one else knew. No wonder her life had been worth so much on the open market.

"They are a stunted larval form of the Chekydran soldiers you are familiar with," she said. "They are kept in the most protected portion of the ship in a climate- and nutrient-controlled crèche. Pull one out of its bed and it dies."

"They're alive?"

"Yes. Aware and part of the neural net of the ship. The hum that deep is mind and body numbing."

Seaghdh exchanged a calculating glance with his cousin.

Turrel, looking faintly distressed, rubbed his chin.

V'kyrri scowled, staring at a spot on the table. Sweat beaded on his upper lip and he frequently shook his head as if to clear his eyesight.

Sindrivik leaned forward, hands folded, gaze and curiosity intense. He and Turrel remained symptom free.

Her father and Raj watched her, concern lining their faces.

"We tried to capture a ship once," Turrel said. "Got some good shots in. Disabled propulsion and knocked out a communications array so they couldn't call for help."

"And it self-destructed before you could lock a tow on it," Ari surmised.

He nodded as if he'd known she'd be able to finish the story for him.

She offered him a lopsided smile. "From what I managed to overhear, there's a double feedback mechanism. Kill enough Chekydran soldiers and the aural net changes to such an extent that the brain array initiates an auto-destruct. Disable the brain array and that kicks off auto-destruct."

"Then a sonic disrupter will just blow the ship," Raj protested.

"Not necessarily," Sindrivik replied. He turned to her. "I take it the hum you describe is variable? Pitches, tones, volumes, and amplitudes all change, thereby differentiating meanings?"

"Yes."

"What happened to the hum when the ship entered a down cycle?"

Ari turned inward, searching for the memory, shoving aside the remembered pain and fear. "Pitch lowered. Tone . . . I can't describe it. Amplitude lengthened, I think. If that makes any sense."

"If we can override the natural hum with something of our own, use the entire ship's hull as a resonator," Sindrivik said, his voice rising in excitement, "we might disable the crew and the brain array."

"It isn't a sure thing," she cautioned. "I can't be certain there's not a fail-safe for that as well, but I think the key is making our hum so pervasive that it disrupts the entire network. It's the only shot. Leave even one soldier or one larva functional and all you'll have is space debris."

Sindrivik cast a sidelong look at her. "It can't be an approximation."

"I know."

"What?" Seaghdh growled.

"We have to record the real thing, bring it back here, modify it to spec, then find a way to embed a playback device in just the right location on the hull of the target ship," Ari said. "And the only way to do that is to put me on board that ship, tie into my transponder, and record everything around me."

"They'll kill you!" her father protested.

"I don't think so. They want something or I'd be dead already. The mercenaries must have been Armada sent. My commanders seem to think I'm a security risk. The Chekydran have the firepower to destroy both the *Dagger* and the *Sen Ekir*, yet they haven't. It follows, then, that they need something. Thing is, if they don't kill me, I may have to."

Silence.

Seaghdh slanted her a searching glance.

"They made you into a carrier," Raj finally surmised. "You're asymptomatic. The illness won't kill you, but it will infect everyone you come in contact with."

"Want to find out the hard way whether or not you're part of the immune thirty percent?" she asked.

The holographic projection of her father pounded the table in his office with a fist. "There has to be a way!"

"Ari," Seaghdh rumbled, "you can't . . ."

"There is a way," she replied. "Trade me for the structure and delivery mechanism of the plague."

Seaghdh dropped a tight grip on her shoulder.

A light fired in her father's eye, then he shook his head. "No. This is unacceptable."

Seaghdh spun Ari's chair to face him. He stared, disbelief and anguish stark in his face. "Don't make me give you to them."

Her heartbeat faltered. Hard. She gasped for air.

"Cullin. Dr. Idylle, I sympathize," Eilod said. She sounded weary, beaten down. "I do not, cannot, countenance the sacrifice of a woman's life for a sequence of code our own medical staff could uncover, given time. The loss of life might be significant before that happened, but it would be limited to these two ships. The Empire would endure without me if it comes to that. However. Other concerns take precedence."

"The soldiers, like Tommy," Ari's father murmured.

"Yes. And the alliance we believe has been made between the Chekydran and someone in your government," Eilod said. "We are duty bound to uncover the identities of those involved. If we don't . . ."

"The entirety of Tagreth Federated Command could fall to the Chekydran," Linnaeus finished.

"Yes, sir."

He sighed.

The resignation in the sound made Ari's heart hurt.

"No," Seaghdh ground out. "We make our own family, Eilod, you said that. I can't do this again."

Ari blinked. Again? She took his overly warm hands in hers and half turned so she could address everyone. "I'm sworn to protect the citizens of TFC. This is my job," she said with a calm she didn't at all feel inside. She hoped none of the turmoil showed in her face. It might be her job. Everyone knew she didn't have to like it.

Seaghdh stared as if he didn't recognize her. It drove a jagged blade of sorrow beneath her sternum. She might die. It was beginning to look like a necessity, but at least now, she'd die for a reason. She'd die protecting millions of lives from the Chekydran. From her.

Gods damn the advances that had been made in holographic and video-display interfaces. She saw tears gather in her father's blue eyes. His lips trembled, but he pressed them tight and sat up straight, outrage replacing fear.

Ari turned to Seaghdh. "Make the trade."

He pulled his hands from her grip, leaned across her, and cut all com connections. "No," he said, his voice cold, hard, and immovable.

She stared at him. Sure, she'd seen him become Her Majesty's spymaster, the dangerous, impassive statesman so feared by Armada and IntCom personnel alike, but never before had she glimpsed the sharp edge of rage, or was it pain, barely contained by his shuttered expression. Ari discovered she couldn't read the fever-flushed, Isarrite mask he'd hidden behind.

Uncertain, she retreated. She couldn't be counted on to sort out her own feelings. How could she hope to pry open the lid to whatever had shut him down so hard? Especially when she had no idea what had triggered him. She needed something to go on, some clue. Her thoughts stopped her. Triggered? Was he, in his own way, having a flashback? She peered harder at him, trying to catch a glimpse what might be going on inside the defenses he'd slammed up.

Her eyesight dimmed and a cutting, ripping sensation grew behind her solar plexus. Loss. She sucked in a breath and realized what she was doing. Cheating, by reading him. Twelve Gods. How long had she been taking advantage of an ability she didn't even know she'd had?

Stark, echoingly empty pain lay at the center of Seaghdh's shutdown. She hesitated. It would be kindest to walk away from it rather than probe the wound. She shook off the feelings and waited until her eyesight cleared. She hadn't the faintest idea how to help him, but his life and the lives of his family and crew depended on nudging him into action.

That's when she remembered. He'd said to his cousin, "I can't do this again."

"What can't you do again?" Ari asked, the words out of her mouth before she could debate the wisdom of uttering them.

Agony flared within him, a sensation so overwhelming, she sat back hard in her chair. He started to turn away.

Hurt all her own flared in her heart. She leaped to her feet and reached out but didn't quite dare touch. "Don't. Please, don't pull away."

They both twitched, hearing the words he'd used on her turned back at him.

He drew a shuddering breath and cast a look over his shoulder at her. The depth of torment in those gold eyes ripped at her gut.

"They massacred my family," he said.

"Your family?" Ari echoed. "But I thought . . ." Dawning awareness halted the words. Horror exploded through her. "Chekydran."

"They captured my parents and my sister. Accused them of spying," he said. "I survived because I wasn't there."

She closed her eyes, biting back a groan. She couldn't begin to comfort that kind of torment. Three Hells. She couldn't comfort her own. "I'm sorry."

He didn't respond.

She opened her eyes, bereft of an appropriate response. How ironic. Now that she gave a damn about someone outside herself and wanted to help, she had no idea of how to go about it. Needing to do something, anything, she set a tentative palm against the rigid muscles of his back.

He didn't flinch or pull away.

Emboldened, she moved closer and folded her arms around his waist, pressing tight against him and resting her cheek against his shoulder. "I am sorry, Cullin. How old were you?"

"Fourteen."

She bit her lip, saddened for the boy on the threshold of manhood. He'd had his innocence and his loved ones ripped from him just when he'd most needed them.

"From the accumulation of damage in their bodies, our specialist told me it had taken them two weeks to die," he went on.

Her heart stumbled in her chest.

"I couldn't even recognize them when the bodies were recovered."

Ari choked on a curse.

"My mother's sister took me in, gave me the best of everything," he said. "She arranged state funerals for my parents and a service of the innocent for my sister."

It hurt her physically to hear the suppressed ache in his level tone, but she could not stop him. As much as she needed to forget what had happened to her, he needed to talk, to air the wound she suspected he'd left too long unexamined. Pain had become a close, personal friend. She could bear its company a little while longer.

"I still have the medals awarded to my parents for acts of valor."

"Medals?"

"The irony is that they were spying," he said.

She caught in a breath and tensed. "Your sister was part of their cover?"

"She was seventeen," he said, "and already invested in reclaiming the Aubbary System. She was a recruit."

"Twelve Gods," she breathed. "You must have been furious."

He froze. Concerned, Ari straightened and drew away to peer over his shoulder at him.

He rounded on her. White lines stood out around his mouth as he stared, rage and disbelief warring for space on his face. "Furious? They were my family. I loved them. Especially Anwen."

"Your sister?"

He awarded her a curt nod and then shifted his gaze from her. The muscles in his jaw worked. She rested fingertips against the ridge of tension. He looked at her, anger stark in his eyes.

"Do you imagine I don't love my father?" she asked.

He blinked.

"He makes me so mad." She shook her head. "And I love him with all my heart. Despite the fact that he disapproves of what I do and he seems to resent the fact that I'm not as smart as the rest of the family. He must love me, too, or he'd have disowned me long ago.

"My point is that your parents took your sister into a dangerous situation and left you behind. Of course you were angry and hurt and betrayed by the people who were supposed to be there for you. None of that changes the fact that you loved them and that you love them still."

"You're in no position to act as psychologist," he countered.

Ari shrugged. "Why not? After weeks of passing psych tests to unlock my cabin door, maybe I have a new career option open to me."

He dropped his chin to his chest and sighed. "I was pissed as hell."

He spoke so quietly she had to lean in to hear him.

"I still am."

It hit her then. "Is that why you've encouraged me to talk about what happened to me?" she asked, not sure what she should feel. "You wanted some confirmation that they were better off dying, even if it took so long? You hope that by hearing what I went through for three months it will make their deaths bearable somehow?"

Hurt burst through confusion. She pulled away from him.

"I'd thought you'd asked because you cared about me." The words came out before she could stop them.

He struggled for something to say, bewilderment conflicting with guilt in his face.

She'd wanted so badly to matter to someone that she'd misled herself. Of course he couldn't care about her. It was too soon. His insistence on knowing the details of her imprisonment was purely selfish. Granted, he'd lost loved ones and he had a right to know . . . Ari halted the thought. Did he? Did he have a right to know what his family might have suffered before they'd died? Did it matter? It wouldn't change anything. Except him. It could only feed the rage and his thirst for revenge. Like it did for her.

Her father had said she'd changed. Well, small wonder. But maybe he wasn't talking about what the Chekydran had done. Maybe he was talking about the fire of vengeance she'd fed every moment of every day since she'd been released.

"Ari . . ." he essayed, his voice sounding raw.

"No," she said, backing away. "They died. I lived. I have no reason for that, no comfort to offer. The Chekydran robbed me of almost everything that made me me, but I survived. I'm broken, maybe beyond all hope of repair, but I survived. I can still fight with my father. He can still be disappointed by me. They may have taken everything else, but they didn't take that. Your family died, Seaghdh, murdered by creatures that do not recognize us as living, thinking, feeling entities. I can't make that all right for you."

Ari spun away, her heart a cold, shivering lump in her chest, and gasped.

Her father stood at the containment shield, misery in the lines of his face.

CHAPTER

26

"TWELVE Gods," Ari rasped. How long had he been there? How much had he heard?

"Dad."

"Alexandria," he said at the same time. He shook his head. "Disappointed? Is that what you think I am?"

She slumped.

"Of course, you would," he murmured. He squared his shoulders and looked at her. "Rest assured, nothing could be further from the truth, but that's not why I'm here. Alex, give me a few hours. Raj and I will have the key if not to the plague, then to the nanotech delivery structure."

"No, you won't," she said, amazed that he could say such a thing. "We both know it will take days to crack the full code, much less begin attempting to formulate a response. How long did the Chekydran give Eilod to make a decision about handing me over, anyway? We've run out of time."

"You have done enough!" he said, his fists clenched. "I don't understand why you have to be the one—"

"I don't expect you to understand," she interrupted. "You've never approved of my career."

He drew up short and cocked his head. "What gave you that idea?"

"You've made it very clear over the years how much you hated my involvement with the military."

"Yes!" He nodded. "I hated it. Because it frightened me."

"Frightened you?" she echoed, taken aback. Her father hadn't been afraid of anything in his life.

Her father sighed and stared into the distance. "You have no idea? Every morning, I got up and acknowledged that this could be the day the honor guard knocked on my door, your ship's flag in hand and the words I couldn't bear to hear on their tongues. 'We regret to inform you.' Do you know how I cringed every time I saw an officer in a thrice-damned dress uniform?"

The wobble in his voice renewed the burn behind her eyes.

"Then six months ago, Admiral Angelou knocked on my office door. Captured, he'd said. Prisoner of war. Accused of spying." Her father shrugged. "That was it. You were dead. I knew it. We all did. Your brother and sister took turns, sitting with me while I waited; waited for the honor guard, waited for it to finally be over. Day after day. And they never came. I wanted you dead." He buried his face in his hands. "The Twelve Gods help me, I wanted you dead because every day you lived, I knew those monsters were hurting you. And I couldn't stop them."

A fist seemed to close around her throat. "Oh, Dad."

"I wanted you safe. I hated your career, yes, and maybe I hated how good you were at it." He sighed and rubbed his hands down his face, smearing moisture from his cheeks. "My reasons were entirely selfish."

Gasping for breath, Ari smiled. "You wanted me safe beside you in a lab working with deadly pathogens?"

He barked a laugh. "Rational to the last, aren't I? I know I haven't been good at showing it, much less at saying . . ." He broke off, struggling for words. "I've always been proud of you, Alex. Always. Annoyed, confused, scared, all of those things, but always proud."

She let the words sink past the defenses she'd always erected against her father and shifted. "Even when it felt like I was rejecting you, your way of life, and everything you stood for by running off to join the Armada?"

Her father's gaze turned inward and he frowned. "Perhaps not at that exact moment, no." He looked at her again. "But then something happened to you. You didn't just survive the academy and your training. You thrived. You grew in ways I couldn't begin to comprehend."

"And even that was frightening?"

"No parent is perfect, Alex," he said. "I wish I could have been more, for your sake. It was galling to discover that I could not give you what you needed. It took a set of heartless strangers turning you into an automaton to do that."

"They hardly turned me into an automaton."

"I know that. Now," he said. "From the day Admiral Angelou showed up at my door, I thought about all the things I'd never told you. When notice came that you'd be released alive, I vowed I wouldn't waste the opportunity to tell you how much you mean to me."

She pressed the heels of her hands against her dry, aching eyes. "And then someone handed you a broken shell and said, 'Here's your daughter, Dr. Idylle.' "

"I barely recognized you."

"I barely recognized me," she assured him, letting her hands fall back to her sides. "I . . . couldn't respond. I am sorry."

"No. Don't be sorry. It wasn't something you could change. I vacillated between hope and despair. We all did. I'd never experienced such rage in my life as when I saw what those bastards had tried to do to you. Even though you'd been brought back alive, I wasn't sure I would ever have you back. To this day, I don't know how you survived."

"I survived because of you," Ari replied.

He blinked, a stunned look in his eye.

"When they tried to rake my mind, I recited the table of elements, or some other bit of arcane science trivia you'd made me memorize. I mentally practiced energy blade work in the *Sen Ekir*'s cargo hold on the floor you'd encouraged me to set up. I reminded myself that if I gave up and died, you'd have to find another pilot with immunity. I reminded myself that you'd insisted on the extra cabin for me when the *Sen Ekir* was built. I remembered how you emptied those two lockers for my energy blade gear in cargo. It was the one time you'd sided with me against Pietre. And I focused on the fact that when you were finally awarded the TFC Founder's Prize in Science, I wanted to be there right beside Hieronomus and Isolde cheering."

Her father's gaze turned inward, a tiny smile lightening his features. "And no one knew you're a telepath with the power to make those distractions work."

"Not even I knew," she replied.

Her dad nodded, then eyed her and Seaghdh, the two of them still standing as if preparing to take up arms against one another. "Captain Seaghdh," he said. "I believe it is long past time I inquired. What are your intentions toward my daughter, sir?"

Ari boggled, the fear that Seaghdh no longer wanted or needed her burning a hole in her composure.

"I warn you. If you hurt her," he went on, his eyes sparkling with fierce light, "so help me, I will make you my vaccination test case. I assure you there will be side effects."

"Dad!"

"If your test vaccines can cure this so I make good my intentions, Doctor," Seaghdh replied, "bring it on."

Ari choked on an involuntary laugh.

Her father's eyes narrowed, but he nodded slowly before smiling. "Very well. Alexandria? I presume you have a plan."

"Yes, sir." She opened a broad-beam channel, trusting that Hicci would be monitoring everything he could reach. "You can't get something for nothing, Hicci. Transfer the plague genetic sequence to this channel," she said. "I'll come out in a shuttle and hold station at the shields. You'll transfer the code. Upon verification from my people, I will complete transport."

Ari closed the com and turned to her father. "Teleport me to the *Dagger*. I'd rather not compromise containment on this ship."

"I understand."

"I'm going with you," Seaghdh said.

She looked at him. Anger glittered in the hard shine of his eyes. Hurt and confusion showed in the creases around his mouth. They hadn't worked anything out. It looked like they wouldn't have the time. Regardless. It was his right. She nodded.

"That is acceptable," her father said. "Dr. Annantra can administer . . ."

"Come now," Hicci's voice, made tinny by the translator, rasped over the com.

Ari clicked open the channel. Terror spilled, cold and greasy, into her gut. He hadn't made any counterdemands. What in the Three Hells did he need from her?

"No shuttle on this ship," she countered. "Teleporting to the *Dagger*. Transport in ten."

Hicci hesitated. "Game you play, I wonder. Come, my plaything, you talk much."

Icy sweat beaded on her forehead. Bastard. She'd talk? She had something he needed. What? She wracked her memory for a hint of what it might be. If she could work it out, her ability to stall for time would be that much stronger. "Acknowledged."

Her father activated the intraship com. "Pietre, advise the *Dagger* and prepare to teleport Captains Seaghdh and Idylle."

"Damn it," Pietre growled. "Can't we send you in with a weapon, Ari?"

Ari blinked at the discomfort in Pietre's voice. Twelve Gods. It sounded like it bothered him that she was going back.

"I'll be stripped when I arrive," she said.

Her father blanched. When she looked away from the horror in his face, she stared into Seaghdh's rage-reddened expression.

"I'll have to be weapon enough," Ari said, "until the strike team gets what they need."

"Baxt'k," Pietre and Seaghdh grumbled in unison.

"*Dagger* acknowledges, Doctor," Jayleia said. "They are standing by for teleport."

"On your mark, Doctor Idylle," Pietre said. "Kick their asses if they have them, Ari."

EILOD teleported them directly to the shuttle bay. She and Turrel met them at the door. The young queen slumped against a wall, her eyes red and her face wan.

"Captain Idylle," she rasped and flinched.

Ari grimaced. Brilliant. She'd infected the queen. After Eilod's plotting to kill Ari at some point, did it mean anything that the two of them had managed to kill one another without meaning to?

"We've prepped the *Lughfai*'s sister shuttle, the *Lamfeida*, for your use. We are at eight minutes and counting. Auhrnok Riorchjan, I put you in command of the strike team. You are needed in tactical. Get me an extraction plan for Captain Idylle."

"Five minutes, Eilod," Seaghdh countered.

She looked between them, her expression twisted by unhappiness. "Five minutes," she acknowledged. Her gaze rested on Ari for several seconds. She looked like she wanted to say something but didn't know what. Finally, she pressed her lips tight, turned on her heel, and walked away.

"Seven minutes," Turrel said.

Seaghdh swung on Ari, desperation behind his hard expression. "I never asked you to die for me."

"I'm not interested in dying for anyone," she replied, the emotional strain of his hurt wringing her dry. "This is my best and only chance to save your life."

"Damn it to all Three Hells, Ari!" Seaghdh swore. "It's not worth it!"

She stared at him, uncomprehending. "You brought me back to myself. You reminded me that feeling something didn't have to be bad. I think you saved my life." Warmth and sympathy twisted through her as she registered what he was really saying. "Hwe vaugh. You are more than worth it."

He caught in an audible breath. Unresolved grief and a bottomless pit of suffering echoed in the sound.

She cupped his cheek, trying not to notice how her hand shook.

His gaze found hers. Something broke behind his eyes and Ari caught a glimpse of the wounded man who'd crouched beneath his rank and ruthlessness for so long. Moisture gathered in his eyes. He blinked rapidly and swallowed hard.

Choking down the sudden prickle behind her eyes, Ari stepped back, into the shuttle.

"At least let us sedate you," he said in a trembling rush.

The quiver of panic in her middle spiked. She shook her head. "No."

Turrel, grim-faced, nodded. "Going to take a few of 'em out?"

She saw unhappiness in the hard, professional veneer he'd pasted on his face, but no hope. It looked like Turrel's expectations were as realistic and as pessimistic as hers. "That's the plan."

Seaghdh swore.

The door slid shut. Her heart fluttered and she stood, fists and teeth clenched to keep from pounding on that door and shrieking for release.

"Getting yourself killed renders our strike team useless," Turrel noted via com. "Factor that into your mission parameters, Captain."

She had to force herself to walk to piloting to switch open the line. "They can't kill me until they get whatever it is they need," she said as she strapped in.

"You think," Turrel bit out, his tone severe. "Fact is, Captain, you got nothing but assumptions. For all you know, they need you in pieces."

"Colonel."

"Yes, Captain?"

"Stop helping."

Silence. Or at least the occasional pop of static that passed for silence on a closed com channel.

"Ari," he began.

"You don't have to distract me, Kirthin Turrel," she said. "I appreciate the effort, but I'm okay." It surprised her to find she didn't have to lie to him. "Initiating launch."

She'd have a few peaceful moments, at least. Seaghdh would sprint to tactical where he'd be too busy to hound her. Ari sent a mental thank-you to Eilod for putting him in command of the strike team. Both women knew he needed diversion. Ari just hadn't known how to provide it.

The young flight officer sounded tense when she gave Ari clearance.

Ari lifted as the bay doors opened. No point delaying. She nudged the shuttle into space.

"Captain Idylle, you are clear hangar doors and the *Dagger*," the flight officer said. "Clear skies, Captain."

The channel closed.

Ari blew out a shaky breath. Five minutes to shields. It wasn't long enough. Nothing would be.

The com panel chirped a melodic series of tones. Frowning, she leaned over to peer at an indicator flashing. Two amber, one green. The sequence repeated. She activated the control.

"Ari, listen. Do not respond." Seaghdh.

Her chest tightened. She closed her eyes and spent a moment longing for his arms around her. Forcing her eyes open, she sat upright and paid strict attention to piloting.

"I am sending on a closed channel, tight beam, scrambled," he said.

She raised her eyebrows. He didn't want anyone to know what he was going to say, not even his cousin. That she'd know about the communication Ari didn't doubt. But it would at least take her a few minutes to decode it.

"Prepare to receive and record data. Use your handheld."

She did. Looking at what he sent, Ari swore. Her heart rate picked up speed.

"The codes for your transponder," he said.

She nodded. One was missing.

"You've undoubtedly noted the omission of the destruct sequence," he said. "You don't need it. I deactivated that some time ago."

She sat bolt upright. He had? When? And why not say so?

"We will conduct a transponder test while you are within the shields," he went on. "Once the test is complete, the transponder will be on and will remain on. Please do not, under any circumstances, shut it down. We'll get you out of there, Ari. Stay alive so we can."

The connection died. Ari swore. She'd stay alive, all right, just so she could kick him in the backside for dropping this bomb when he knew she couldn't answer or ask questions.

"Captain Idylle, Captain Idylle. This is a test of your transponder frequency," Sindrivik's voice resounded in her head.

She keyed on the transponder. "Cut transmission volume."

"Acknowledged. Level test, level test. How's that?"

"Another notch, Lieutenant," she said. "I want to be the only one hearing you."

"Roger that," Sindrivik said. His voice no longer rang in her skull. "Level test. Any better?"

"Much. Are you the only one with ears on?"

"Negative, Captain. We've got you on speaker in the situation room."

"Shut it down. I can't afford more than one person's head clouded by what you might hear. More to the point, the situation room personnel will need to talk. If I hear that, the Chekydran will know. Your ears only and pin your mouth shut if you have to, Sindrivik, or anything you say will get us all killed. Cravuul dung. I'm there. Going to com." She switched open the intership communications array.

"Approaching shields," Ari said. "All parties, stand by. Cutting engines. Thrusters at station keeping." She brought the shuttle right up to the shimmer of energy protecting the *Dagger* and the *Sen Ekir*. "Awaiting Chekydran transmission."

"Sending," a voice rendered by the computer translator replied.

"Awaiting confirmation of transmission and data."

"We are receiving," her father said. "Stand by."

"Acknowledged."

"Transmission complete."

"Confirmed," her dad replied.

"Complete transport," Hicci ordered.

Ari recognized his voice. A rush of adrenaline ripped her insides. "Awaiting file validation."

He stepped away from the computer translator and clicked/ hissed/hummed a swift, violent string of sounds directly over com.

She squeezed her eyes shut and refused to confirm for anyone that she'd understood what he'd said. She wished she could fool herself into believing she hadn't understood the series of promises to make her pay for frustrating him.

"Captain Idylle." Raj's voice pulled Ari out of a pit of nausea and dread.

She opened her eyes. "Go ahead, Dr. Faraheed."

"File integrity confirmed," he said. "Repeat. File integrity confirmed."

Damn. Her last chance to turn back going down in flames. At least Raj and her dad had a better shot at curing the illness infecting the *Dagger*. It's what she'd come for.

CHAPTER

27

"ENGAGING engines," Ari said. Her voice barely shook. "Clearing shields."

The shuttle slid sideways and shuddered, responding to a Chekydran tractor beam. So did Ari. Despite the assurances she'd given herself that things were different this time, that she was in control, that she felt nothing, she froze and blanked. She sat unable to move, unable to turn her gaze from the Chekydran cruiser dominating her screen. Awareness retreated. She didn't know where she went or what she accomplished by fleeing, but when the shuttle bumped to a halt in a dimly lit bay, Ari started, slammed into consciousness.

Their hum penetrated the shuttle, setting it to resonate in harmony. The deck vibrated beneath her boots.

Cold purple-blue light turned the bay hollow and endless. How could she forget that Chekydran vision only functioned in a narrow band of the spectrum? They lived in perpetual twilight and used bright light to condition and hurt her. A spurt of adrenaline threatened to short-circuit her tenuous grasp on her brain. She locked the memory away by forcing herself through shutdown procedures.

She tried to stand. It took several seconds for her body to accept the command. Ari's breath came in short bursts and her pulse thundered in her ears, but outwardly, she remained in control. She opened the door, deployed the ramp, and walked down under her own power.

A detachment of soldiers flanked her, their oddly jointed legs letting them creep silently on the chitin plating of their ship.

She did fine until the ring of her boots on the metal ramp touched the surface of the Chekydran ship. The dead-sounding thud started a quiver deep inside. The hum intensified, vibrating bone and teeth. She struggled for breath.

Not now. She'd staved off a flashback this long. She had to stay on top of this. Wanted to. Falling apart gave the Chekydran the advantage.

One of the soldiers shifted his—or her?—weapon. She didn't know the technology, but she understood the effect. Their weapons disrupted neural signals. A short burst would knock her on her butt and hurt like hell. Her muscles would twitch for hours afterward. A longer burst meant unconsciousness and days of tremors. They killed, too, something she'd seen once. The mercenary had died, convulsing, his nerve signals so interrupted he couldn't even shriek in agony.

If she forced them to shoot her now, who knew what it would do to the transponder? Besides, she wanted to walk up to Hicci under her own power before she went off. Did they know what kind of bomb they'd made her with flashbacks? She intended to show them, up close and personal. She took a step. Then another.

Hicci saved her the trouble. He stalked into the bay, humming and clicking his rage. Her brain shrilled. Terror shoved jagged icicles through her body. She'd never get out of here. Hicci knew how to keep her alive. Not even death could rescue her.

Ari lost her grip on her slippery self-control and attacked.

Hicci laughed and ordered the soldiers away as he reached for her.

She hissed at him, a poor approximation of an unforgivable slur against his queen.

He drew back the tentacle he'd extended, striking out.

Ari fended it off, diving close to his body, and landed a solid blow to his throat pouch.

He wheezed and fell silent. The hum of the ship faltered for a heartbeat, confused by his abrupt absence from the aural net.

She blocked two more strikes, landing little more than glancing blows, until Hicci swept her feet out from under her.

She went down screaming obscenities in every language she knew and several she didn't.

He wrapped a tentacle around her neck and dragged her out of the bay, her fingernails digging at his tentacle and her boots struggling for a purchase that would let her ease the pressure on her windpipe.

By the time he'd dragged Ari to the interrogation room she thought of as his office, she was only semiconscious. He released her, leaving her gasping for air. He'd recovered from her attack and his hum rattled her skull, driving her into awareness.

She heard a clink and glanced up.

A container of pinkish liquid sat in front of her.

"Drink," Hicci ordered via his translator.

Did this mean he didn't know she understood everything he said? Could she use that? She sat up slowly, eyeing the liquid. "What is it?"

"Game you play no," he said.

Before she could blink, he had her by the throat, toes dangling inches above the floor.

"I say," he snarled. "You do." He threw Ari against the far wall.

She heard the snap of breaking bone and landed in a heap. Pain hit. She blacked out.

ARI came to gagging on something bitter being poured down her throat. It was all so familiar. She felt as if she'd finally woken for real and that the past few months of freedom had been a short-lived dream. Her heart thumped hard. She choked and kicked, a shriek rising against the horrible, oily liquid burning her esophagus. Hurt sliced up her left arm while some more aware part of her brain took inventory. Left arm, broken at the elbow. Hicci's tentacle wrapped around her neck, lifting her, letting her head fall back while he poured the unspeakably vile stuff down her throat. Her uniform jacket and shirt sodden with something that smelled like bile. Uniform. That was different. She hadn't been stripped.

Hicci dropped her, his pallid yellow-and-white-striped throat pouch rippling as he clicked happily, and scuttled across the room.

She rolled to her right side, sharp stabs radiating from her left arm as she wheezed and coughed. The burn spread from her throat to her stomach. She groaned. Despite the pain in her broken arm, she curled into a ball. It didn't help. Acid tipped into her blood. It raced to her head where it seared the inside of her skull. Her rising moan turned shrill and Ari clawed at her scalp with her one good hand. Panting as the fire in her head built, she hazed, aware of but unable to affect the convulsions wracking her body. When they finally eased, her breath sounded like sobs.

Something wet and warm trickled down her cheeks. She brushed at the moisture with trembling fingers. Blood. Her heart constricted hard. A swift check confirmed her fear. A trickle of blood wept from her eyes and ears. A steady stream oozed from her nose. Maybe it was dangerous. She was past caring. At least she no longer felt the need to rip open the top of her skull.

With booted feet and one good hand, Ari slid backward an inch at a time until she found the wall. Slowly, painfully, she levered herself to sitting and avoided looking at the smear of blood she'd left in her wake.

"Remember now," Hicci said.

Remember? She stared at him. He'd screwed with her head for three months, ensuring she wouldn't forget anything ever again. Why be so concerned about his handiwork, now?

Hicci shut down the translator, stretched his neck, exposing more throat pouch, and hummed/chittered into the aural net of the ship. "Prepare swarm."

Ari shivered, cursing at the pain shooting up her arm. He was sending the Chekydran fleet to war. They were still in Claugh nib Dovvyth space. Weren't they? Hadn't she already killed everyone aboard the *Dagger*? Why did he need the swarm?

"Code," he demanded.

Ari hadn't noticed that he'd turned the translator back on. Her brain understood his order before the computer rendered it in Tagrethian. Numbers and patterns blossomed in her brain, jostling for space.

"Specify," she grated, alarmed to find she had to clamp down on her right hand when her fingers began tapping out a pattern on the floor. It hit her in a rush what the Chekydran wanted. Seaghdh's access code. She prayed Sindrivik still had active ears on the transponder and could read between the lines enough to change the *Dagger*'s computer codes.

Hicci spun.

Ari recognized the move and his posture. Terror spilled cold and paralyzing into her gut. She'd made a mistake questioning him.

He pounced.

"Which one? Which one?" she babbled, trying desperately to scrabble out of his reach.

He raised his two front legs from the floor, supporting his trunk with his other six, and rained punches down on her. His tentacles landed like whips, first shredding her fatigues, and then her skin. She dragged herself across the floor, trying to escape, even using her broken arm at one point.

He broke an ankle, then her ribs.

"Twelve Gods," Sindrivik muttered in her head.

Despair seeped through her. He was still listening. Did that mean he couldn't get a good recording of the Chekydran hum, or he couldn't create a file to do what they needed? Had the strike team not moved to her rescue yet? She couldn't survive much more abuse, and at this rate, she'd be forced to give up codes of some kind long before she died.

"You are brutal and I am suitably impressed that you are in control of the situation. She cannot give us their shield codes if she's dead," someone said. The words echoed around the chamber, but Ari recognized that voice.

Angelou.

Hicci hissed something Ari didn't understand. The translator offered nothing.

She couldn't move, could barely breathe. At least two ribs had been broken. Sipping in shallow gasps of air, she prayed the ribs wouldn't puncture a lung. What irony. After spending three months with Hicci, hoping to die, she now desperately wanted to live. She tried to laugh. Agony searing across her chest cut that short.

"Code," Hicci repeated, the growl beneath his hum a warning. He towered over her, his tentacles weaving an excited pattern just above her body.

She held her breath and remained silent. Her answer didn't matter. They both knew what came next. Nothing Ari could say or do would dissuade the monster swaying on his eight feet. He'd be careful. Much more injury and she'd be incapable of responding. Hicci must have had nothing to lose or he'd have reigned in his temper and left himself more room to persuade her to cooperate.

"Allow me," Angelou directed.

She heard the creak of leather and automatically glanced up as Hicci brushed a tentacle through her blood. The admiral sounded so close. But of course he wasn't. Chekydran audio tech brought Ari every nuance of Angelou's tone and of each move he made, despite the long-distance com channel.

Hicci tapped his bloody tentacle against the same spot on his foreleg repeatedly. The cadence of his hum hitched.

"Captain, you do understand, don't you, that physical violence is engrained in the Chekydran culture? The strongest, most physically fit soldier is eventually chosen to be the queen's consort. Please believe the beating you took is a sign of respect among the Chekydran. I am sorry you're in pain. I will do my utmost to make it transitory. We need you. You've never shown any tendency toward xenophobia. Don't start now."

Ari shuddered in revulsion.

Hicci trailed both tentacles over her broken skin, scraping his tacky, almost sticky, segmented skin on hers. From fondling her wounds, he caressed his tentacles alternately over his eye ridges and against the underside of his body.

The notion that Angelou, ensconced safely in his office, believed he comprehended any aspect of this alien society while Hicci jerked off with her blood made her sneer.

The background hum and vibration of all of the Chekydran aboard the ship quieted and shifted into listening mode as Hicci's hum and chortle intensified.

Ari pressed her eyes shut, wishing she could close her ears as well. She could only cling to Angelou's voice in an attempt to ignore the fact that Hicci took great sexual pleasure from her blood and misery. He'd done this for three interminable months, beat her to a pulp and been excited by it. She'd never told anyone.

"What do you want?" Ari whispered, desperate to hear anything other than the creature above her.

"The completion of your mission, Captain," Angelou replied.

She frowned. Even that hurt. What mission?

"Ari, you and I have always had an understanding surpassing commanding and junior officer," Angelou said in a rush, as if pleading for her comprehension. "You are one of my best and brightest. I don't need to detail the threats facing Tagreth Federated. You've demonstrated a tactical grasp of our situation. I couldn't tell you before now, but I head a few off-the-books projects designed to neutralize the most egregious of those threats."

Hicci's hums and clicks of arousal had risen so high, they registered only as squeaks in her ears. The aural net hummed encouragement.

Good. He'd finish soon.

She fought back nausea.

Concentrate, Ari. Admiral Angelou and his off-the-books projects.

He could be telling the truth. He undoubtedly believed he was. The Council had, in the past, authorized secret projects for the security of Tagreth Federated. The faintest note of superiority in the admiral's tone, as if only he knew and could appropriately assess a threat, raised her doubts that he operated within the purview of the Council.

"You and I both know the Claugh nib Dovvyth presents the most pressing menace to TFC security in this sector. Intelligence Command is dancing to its own tune, dangerously so. I'll be frank. The Admiralty for some time has been suspicious of Intelligence Command. I had no choice but to put my own agents in the field. IntCom denies the rumors citing a massive military buildup within the Claugh Empire, but my people in the field have seen it with their own eyes. Via someone within the Auhrnok Riorchjan's organization, we have indications of alliances forged between the Claugh and the most powerful of the mining consortiums."

A traitor inside Seaghdh's team? Did Angelou know about the strike team? Or that Seaghdh had authorized an attack against TFC?

As he approached climax, Hicci wrapped his tentacles around her, as if he wanted to lift her body and use it in some grotesque fashion.

She forced her awareness away, pictured Angelou's office as she remembered it. He had a window, one of very few in the Admiralty building. It looked out on the capital, the streets lined with trees and people. If you leaned just a little, you could even catch a glimpse of the silver-domed Council Building. The office sported white walls, black leather, and utilitarian lines as if Angelou had never quite given up the notion of commanding a battleship. He'd never settled into riding a desk, never gotten comfortable, not even behind the real ebony-wood monster that dominated his office.

Hicci shuddered and released her.

"I needed someone I could trust without question. I needed someone strong, determined, and committed, someone who could survive Chekydran brutality and biological manipulation," Angelou said. "You were the right choice, but I made the mistake of ignoring your considerable intellect. I hope you can forgive me. In retrospect, I should have brought you in with full disclosure."

Hicci peaked with a high-frequency shrill that made her head feel like it had split in two. Rage and hatred flamed through her.

"Full disclosure," she gasped. Her head spun as the implications sank in. "You planned this? You handed me over to these bastards?" She wanted to scream. The band of stabbing fire constricting her chest wouldn't allow it.

"No." Angelou shifted in his chair, the leather creaking again. "In the strictest, most shortsighted reading of events, I suppose I did. This is part of a much larger plan, one in which you have played a key role. Help me finish this."

By the Twelve Gods, all she wanted was to finish the entirety of the Chekydran species.

"Help you how?" she wheezed.

"Your memory has been augmented."

"Yes."

"We need it."

"A code." Ari tried not to move. Her head felt too full. Nausea surged and receded, surged again. It felt familiar.

"Not just any code. You've spent time aboard the Claugh nib Dovvyth command ship. You've seen people log into the ship's systems."

"You want the Auhrnok Riorchjan's code."

"You got close enough to get it?" Angelou marveled. He laughed. "Well done!"

She opened her eyes.

Angelou went on. "It isn't his code I require. Interestingly enough, our information indicates that the Auhrnok Riorchjan's security codes are not tied to command codes. Maybe his own people don't feel they can trust him. No. There's a young computer specialist."

Sindrivik?

"Give me his code."

"I didn't see . . ." She halted as memory unfolded, clear as if she stood in the doorway of Eilod's conference room. Sindrivik. Logging into the computers to fix the system failures. Panic rose and she quashed the vision, forcing her eyes to focus on right here, right now.

That's when she realized Hicci was reading her. He stood on eight legs, rocking back and forth; her blood crusting on his skin, his three rows of vestigial eyes all swiveled in her direction. His tentacles lay quiescent below his vibrating throat pouch. How long had she let him sift through her head?

It had been easy to close the Chekydran out before V'kyrri had told her she was a telepath. She'd had long years of belief that such mind talents were impossible in her people. Except she now knew there were no people she could identify as hers. Thanks, Mom.

The pressure in her skull increased unbearably and the first dry, desiccated alien tendril drilled into her thoughts. Ari's confidence broke. She retreated, diving down the well that had always been her safe haven.

Someone had beaten her to it. Soul chilling fear surrounded her, permeated her. She huddled, quaking, and recognized it. Seaghdh. He struggled against terror. He didn't fear for himself. It was for her. She could feel it.

She cursed. She should have known better. Seaghdh had offered safety. She'd clung to the illusion that another humanoid could keep her safe. This was the result. She'd made Cullin Seaghdh integral to her sense of security, maybe to her sense of self.

Hicci shifted. It was a tiny move and nearly silent, but it alerted a more aware part of her brain. For the first time since she'd been captured, he was picking up her thoughts.

Icy fear drove through her. She couldn't lock him out. Every bolt hole she'd ever used to escape him mentally had just slammed shut. Her heart raced, beating against shattered ribs. Seaghdh's anguish clawed at her. It was much worse than her own fear. No matter what had happened, she loved him.

The thought stopped her cold and Ari stared at it. She wanted to reject it, to throw it as far and as fast as she could. Loving Auhrnok Captain Cullin Seaghdh nib Riorchjan would only bring her, and possibly him, pain. All right. Acknowledged. But she'd survived pain. So far.

She loved him. Knowing in a way that no one else could, feeling in a way no one else could, the despair he suffered on her behalf shattered her self-control. She ached to fix it for him.

Hicci's hum deepened, vibrating hurt through every broken bone in her body. She suddenly felt his tentacles grasping her face. Thrice-damned bastard. He was sifting her emotions, her fears, her thoughts. It felt exactly like the touch of his skin, sticky, raspy.

Ari wanted to help Seaghdh, but she didn't dare try. She had to get out. Now. Before Hicci realized she'd managed to connect to Cullin on a rudimentary level. Even assuming she could deepen the telepathic contact with Seaghdh, she didn't know how to do it without hurting one or both of them.

She couldn't risk that Hicci might be able to read Seaghdh through her. And if Hicci finally got around to killing her, she couldn't risk being in Seaghdh's head. From what tiny bit she understood about telepathy, if she died while in contact with him, Seaghdh could all too easily die, as well.

Hicci crept through her head like a dark, unspeakable stain, spreading, blotting out. This was worse than having her blood and pain used for his sexual gratification. Yes, that horrified and sickened her, but this invasion ripped bits of her away, scattering the pieces into the dark. Ari gasped, desperate for respite. Retreating from his presence, she threw feeble blocks in his way to keep him from following her. Nothing held.

"Relax, Ari," Angelou coaxed. "Let your mind drift. Listen to my voice. Think back to the times you saw someone sign into the computers. That's all you need do. The Chekydran will take it from there. They're telepaths, Captain. Let your memories flow. We will take the code from you, disable the *Dagger*'s shields, and take the first steps to assuring the security of our people. I will have the Chekydran place you in a medical crèche while we bring the Claugh nib Dovvyth Empire to its knees."

Bring the Claugh nib Dovvyth to its knees? Why did they need her? Or the codes? Awful suspicion rolled in her brain. Hadn't they already decimated the ranks aboard the *Dagger* with the disease she'd unknowingly brought onboard?

Twelve Gods and all Three Hells. She'd sacrificed herself for a disease that wasn't fatal.

CHAPTER
28

HICCI chortled and shoved his way deeper into Ari's brain.

She writhed, unable to cry out or pound the floor with her bloody fists. Too late, she could plainly see that Angelou and the Chekydran hadn't needed to kill anyone; they'd only needed to convince her to return to Hicci's ship so they could access her memory the way they hoped to access the *Dagger*'s command codes. She was as much a prototype as Tommy had been.

She'd fled so far before Hicci's onslaught that she doubted she'd ever find her way back. Part of her recognized the incipient disintegration of personality, of sanity. Ari didn't care. Maybe if Hicci drove her into madness while in contact with her, he'd get sucked over, too.

She had to protect Seaghdh and his people, even if it meant throwing away her life to do so.

Clarity burst across her beleaguered mind like a supernova overwhelming view-screen filters and she knew what she had to do.

She had to die.

And she had to take Hicci with her when she went. He was

already deep into her head. If she could lure him just a little farther, maybe she could telepathically access her transponder and trip the self-destruct sequence. It was a long shot. She had to try.

She called up the memory of her last duel with Seaghdh, reviewing the blade and foot work move by move, uneasily experiencing the surge of remembered arousal that went with it. Ari shrank from allowing Hicci access to those feelings. She treasured them. He'd know that, though, and the memories with the accompanying emotions would be irresistible to him. Closing her eyes, she built the sensory detail.

Concentrating so hard on handing Hicci a memory of her choosing, she didn't quite catch the shift in the Chekydran aural net. She only noticed when Hicci wrenched free of her mind.

Ari cried out.

Hicci rushed from the room as the shipboard hum amped up in frequency and volume.

Her head reeled at the sudden emptiness. She lay dazed, unable to focus her eyes or control her shivering body.

"Captain?"

She whimpered.

"Something has happened. What is it?"

She tried to form a response and couldn't. Words and language seemed to have been misplaced. Or maybe it was motor skills that had been lost. She moaned.

Ari heard Angelou shove himself out of his chair, swear, and begin pacing. She could almost see him. He'd done the exact same thing when she'd reported for duty a month ago and he'd sent her on sabbatical. He folded his hands behind him, crossed back and forth in front of his prized window, head down, brows drawn together, and a scowl tightening his features. Despite the distance separating them, she felt like she was in his office with him.

"It's the drug," he said.

In her mental image, he didn't even stop pacing. He simply tossed the words out for her to catch as she could.

"Aphasia is a common side effect."

Terrific, but what was the drug supposed to do?

"It's designed to open certain pathways," Angelou answered her mental question as if he'd heard it. "In test cases, it allowed a telepathic species, the Chekydran, more reliable access to the thoughts and feelings of non-telepathic species."

Startled, Ari tried to frown. It felt like she still could. Had Angelou really heard her? Did he not realize she wasn't physically speaking? If the drug did what he said it could do, maybe he had heard her and simply assumed she spoke via com. The drug. It had to be new or the Chekydran would have tried using it while she'd been a prisoner.

"You weren't a prisoner," Angelou countered.

Ari froze, not even breathing. Twelve Gods. He could hear her. Mentally. How? They were sectors apart. How could she be both places at once? She consciously focused on listening to the Chekydran aural net, hoping it would mask the thoughts and questions racing through her head. If she'd managed to reach him telepathically, could she put herself in his office? Influence him and his actions?

"And yes. The compound is something we've had in development concurrent with your modification. The Chekydran wanted to introduce it into your program much earlier, but it wasn't safe and we couldn't afford to risk you."

Filling her mind with the vision of Angelou and his office, Ari concentrated on being there, on moving closer to Angelou, on not just imagining him, but on *seeing* him, being in the same place with him. He still paced, though more slowly, impatience lining his face. Closer. She remembered how she'd hurt V'kyrri. He'd been open, reading her, trying to make contact. That had been frighteningly easy, but she didn't want to hurt Angelou. Not yet. She didn't know if what she wanted was even possible.

The bastard had handed her over to the Chekydran. She'd damned well make it possible.

She reached for him mentally.

And *felt* him flinch.

"Stop," Ari commanded, picturing him standing still.

It took a moment to register with her physical ears, so far away, but the sounds of his boots on military-issue black-and-white tile stilled.

Grim satisfaction spread over her like a warm blanket. She had him. For the moment.

"Desk. Sit," she ordered.

He returned to his desk and sat. His movements sounded jerky and awkward, judging by the scraping and thumps she heard over the com. The sight of him in her mind's eye showed his face looking pinched and curiously blank. She wondered briefly if he was in pain, then decided she didn't care. A single drop of blood trickled from his nose.

Ari issued commands, controlling his moves and listening to the shrill of protest and distress rising in his head. Through Angelou, she found and bundled up his files and sent them to IntCom. He had no defense against her intrusion, no weapon to combat her presence. It was so easy. It scared her. Something flashed through his thoughts. She caught only a glimpse. It was enough.

Horror rocked her and she nearly lost her grip on him. How could she have overlooked something so obvious? Hicci knew about her transponder. Angelou had told him.

Ari gasped and had to still her shaking. The strike team. Seaghdh. They were flying straight into a trap.

Snarling, she wrapped a mental hand around her admiral's neck and watched his face turn purple. "This is what you get when you drug open a telepath."

She rummaged around his memories, hurriedly looking for the name of the traitor in Seaghdh's ranks. Angelou didn't know his name. He knew only that the agent supplying his information was a telepath close to Seaghdh.

V'kyrri.

Misery clenched a fist around her heart.

V'k. How could you?

She flung Angelou against the far wall.

He flew out of his chair, hit, and slid to the floor in a heap, bleeding and unconscious. Ari scrambled his door codes so he couldn't get out without some work.

It would have to be enough. Weariness dogged her as she fought her way back into her own head, her own aching body. Her heart bumped against the confines of her chest. She had to warn Seaghdh.

"Sindrivik!" she attempted to say. It came out as a croak. She tried again. If she could control a man two sectors away, surely she could control her own body.

She sounded like a mortally wounded animal. Maybe that's what she was. Shrieking in frustration, she hazed momentarily. Fear yanked her back. She wasn't getting enough oxygen. The broken ribs had punctured a lung. Damn. She refused to die while Seaghdh and his team were in danger. She'd have to risk telepathic contact with Seaghdh.

Ari heard the door open.

Hicci.

She recognized the hum and something more than that. Was she getting a sense of Hicci's mental presence?

He threw something into the room and chortled. "Rescue," he said, barely able to get the word through his amusement.

She blinked trying to make out both what Hicci was talking about and what he'd dropped. Never before had Ari picked up such a strong sense of emotion from him. Up to this moment, she would have sworn the Chekydran and humanoid feeling systems had no analogue. Could she use her newfound awareness to distract him while she warned the *Dagger*? She sensed something that made her plodding thoughts hiccup.

Ari focused on the jumble of cloth and leather Hicci had tossed into the room. Recognition jolted her.

Seaghdh.

He'd been unconscious when Hicci had dumped him in her line of sight. As he came to, she felt him in the room, in her head, in her heart. Her wide-open telepathic brain lit up and warmed with relieved recognition, even as despair flooded her. She wanted to wail. She'd been too slow, too late to warn him. To save him. The strike team, her only hope of rescue, had been captured.

They'd lost.

He stirred, sorted himself into familiar shape, and rolled toward her. He stared, pain, rage, and horror in his face, but no recognition as he looked at her.

Ari caught a flash from his surface thoughts of twisted, bloody, broken bodies. His strike team. She groaned and realized in a flash that Hicci must have picked up her memories after all. He'd recognized Seaghdh and dragged him here, knowing he could use her feelings for Seaghdh to torture her further. She closed her eyes and thought, "I am so sorry, hwe vaugh."

She felt his dread for her spike. Ari opened her eyes.

"Twelve Gods. Ari," he breathed. In an instant, he'd gained his feet and closed the distance between them, crouching before her.

"Don't touch me!" she cried inside her own head, praying he could hear as he reached for her.

In her haste, she failed to moderate her mental voice. She knocked him on his butt. And tipped off Hicci.

The alien swiveled to peer at her, waving tentacles and spurting short, inquisitive bursts of sound. He plunged into her wide-open mind. The invasion wrung a weak mewl from her hoarse throat.

"Telepath!" Hicci hummed, sounding delighted. He clicked in anticipation and stroked a tentacle lightly over her body, knowing it would cause pain, knowing she'd begged Seaghdh not to hurt her. Knowing it would infuriate Seaghdh.

Hicci ripped through her brain, glee plain in his unguarded mental presence. Ari shrank before the onslaught. Loathing rippled through her along with the fiery torment of freshly disturbed wounds.

"Leave her alone!" Seaghdh growled, wiping blood from his nose. The raw, unmitigated power in his voice took her breath.

It couldn't work, could it? How could his power translate via a computer program? Or did Nwyth Okkar transcend words?

For two heartbeats, everything froze. A tendril of hope lifted within her. Seaghdh drew a noisy breath.

Then Hicci lashed out.

Seaghdh tried to dodge.

She heard the sickening thud of tentacles connecting with flesh and then Seaghdh hit the floor with a grunt. From the wheeze that followed, Ari gathered the impact had knocked the breath from him.

Hicci, chortling and radiating excited anticipation, closed in and slapped Seaghdh hard enough to split his lip.

That it wasn't her body absorbing Hicci's punishment made her heart tremble. She was captive audience to Seaghdh's death by torture. Ari could feel it in Hicci's surface thoughts, hear it in the gurgling chur his hum had become.

Helpless and empty, she could only lay on the floor, hardly breathing, eyes achingly dry, heart shrinking and quaking in her chest. Somehow, she'd done something to Angelou, two sectors away. She wasn't sure what or how, but she did know she was perilously near the end of her strength.

Awareness arrowed into her fuzzy brain as Hicci urged Seaghdh to stand up and fight. Hicci loved that in destroying Seaghdh, he shredded her newborn sense of safety and the first hope she'd known since her capture. He relished knowing that she knew.

Ari choked on a sob. Nothing she could do would save them. But maybe she could afford them both a cleaner death than the one Hicci offered Seaghdh. He wouldn't kill her. Hicci would keep her, torture her, until he finally realized something had happened to Angelou. And then, without an alliance to keep him in check, if ever it had, she might finally die by his—tentacle.

Assuming IntCom had been paying attention and she'd really exposed Angelou's data. Please, Twelve Gods, let IntCom be awake at the switch. Something had to go right. She'd done everything she could to neutralize a traitor within the ranks. If IntCom let this slip through the cracks, Seaghdh's death and hers would be for nothing.

She closed her eyes, her ears, and her heart to the beating Seaghdh tried to fend off. At the first cry of pain ripped from his throat, Ari bit her tongue to keep from shrieking in unison. Pushing past hurt and weariness, she focused on Hicci, the feel of him in the room, his presence in her awareness. She wanted a link so deep he couldn't possibly escape when she triggered her transponder to blow. She had to get in.

She *would* get in if she edged past that outer shell and turned the corner into his core . . . alien thought patterns erupted around her. Images, emotions, belief structures, and arcs of logic for which she had no analogue clawed at her defenseless mind. Too late, Ari realized that not only did humanoids lack the physical structures to imitate Chekydran speech, they lacked the experiential framework to remotely comprehend what went on inside the heads of a species that had evolved light-years from the cradles of humanoid life.

All sense of her physical self vanished as if a vital cord had been cut. Perception of up, down, depth, breadth, and width morphed into something that bent her sanity. She felt a scream rising in her head and struggled to wrest free. She fought, ripping and tearing the foreign thoughts from her as she fled.

Her awareness slammed back into her body with a shock that drove agony through her like an energy blade. Her physical form lacked the lung capacity to do anything more than whine. Gasping shallow puffs of air into abused lungs, she forced her eyes open.

Seaghdh had given up standing. And defending himself.

Fear and anguish ripped Ari's gut. A hollow cry broke from her throat.

He twisted away from Hicci, dodging a blow to meet her gaze.

The grim, hopeless light in his bloody, swollen face brought a rush of heat to her eyes. As she stared, helpless, Ari felt tears on her lashes finally spill over. Baxt'k. It took the murder of the man she loved to teach her to cry again.

"I'm sorry," he wheezed.

She heard a pop.

Seaghdh groaned and his expression blanked.

Hicci had broken something.

Ari felt an answering burst inside of her. She'd had enough. That bastard would die if she had to rip him apart with her one good hand. She couldn't get into the monster's mind, but she could get into Seaghdh's.

She shut her eyes tight and concentrated, beating back panic. Nothing happened. Cursing under her breath, she shifted focus. Seaghdh's entire conscious mind fixated on the blows Hicci inflicted. Ari couldn't break through that. Praying her gamble would pay off, she retreated down into the watery center of herself, to the place no one else knew existed. Save for Cullin Seaghdh, who had become a permanent part of her.

He was still there.

"Listen, hwe vaugh," she whispered to his presence inside her. She felt the jolt of recognition go through him. "I have a plan."

Rather than explain, Ari took a deep mental breath and ignoring fear, opened her psyche and merged with him. She knew his astonishment as if it was her own. He tried to form a thought, to communicate something vitally important to him, but her panic screamed that they didn't have time for anything but action. He agreed.

Fatigue slowed her assent out of the well. Opening her eyes, she stared at Hicci and visualized prying him open, but not so much that she got lost in his thoughts again. Her perverse imagination gave her an energy blade and turned the effort into a duel. This she could both wrap her mind around and win.

Hicci slammed a tentacle into Seaghdh. Then, as Seaghdh slid across the floor to hit the far wall, Hicci lowered himself to all eight legs and looked at Ari.

"Guard, you cravuul's ass," she thought at him and mentally lunged, running her figment of her imagination directly through one row of eyes, straight into his alien brain.

He chortled.

"Now," she thought at Seaghdh.

For a long moment, nothing happened and Ari thought he'd been too badly injured to speak. Then she heard breath drawn slowly, whistling as if pulled through clenched teeth.

"You are paralyzed," Seaghdh commanded, his voice and power ringing through the room.

Ari picked up the compulsion and shoved it down the line she had opened to Hicci's brain. The monster squeaked and fell silent. The aural net of the ship hesitated, and then resumed, searching, questioning.

"Ari," Seaghdh said. He dragged himself across the floor with his hands.

Her vision went fuzzy and she may have lapsed into unconsciousness. She had to open her eyes when awareness returned. Seaghdh lay before her, his face inches away.

"Not much time," he breathed.

Ari caught in a breath and choked back despair.

"Can you get a mental lock on your transponder?" he asked.

Despite her injuries, she could still nod.

He echoed the motion. "Good. I won't abandon you to that sick baxt'k. I hope . . ." He fell silent and his lips trembled. "I hope my parents died together."

She closed her eyes as tears began slipping silently down her face again.

Hicci groaned. The aural net redoubled its efforts to prod him into answering. She heard him shift. He was throwing off Seaghdh's compulsion.

They'd run out of time. She didn't have to look for the transponder. It had felt like a sinister, immovable marble imbedded in the flesh behind her left ear. Sorting through to find the destruct command took seconds. No one in TFC thought to shield devices from tele-pathic intrusion.

Ari opened her eyes and fought for control of her voice. "G-got it," she mumbled. The words were garbled, but she'd said them.

Seaghdh cast a hateful glance at Hicci, before nodding and return-ing his overly bright gaze to her. "Finish this."

CHAPTER

29

IF they had to die, Ari wanted the last thing she saw to be Seaghdh looking at her exactly the way he was right now. Holding his gaze, she mentally turned to the transponder. She didn't need a code. A simple nudge in the right place . . .

A hum, loud enough to wring a cry of agonized protest from her, vibrated through the ship. It wasn't the hum that had tried so desperately to get Hicci to answer.

Confused, Ari frowned and saw the expression reflected on Seaghdh's face.

The hum sounded like . . . she glanced at Hicci.

He swayed, tapping his forelegs and rubbing tentacles over his eye ridges and under his body.

Elation tipped into her blood. Someone had placed a sonic disrupter. Sindrivik had recorded and adapted the sexual hum Hicci had uttered over her. Twelve Gods bless his circuit-minded little heart. She felt a grim smile on her face and glanced at Seaghdh. Did he realize what was happening? Hicci and his entire ship would die because

ENEMY WITHIN 317

Sindrivik had thought to turn sex into a weapon. Sindrivik had heard Seaghdh's capture and sent a second strike team.

"A second strike team?" Seaghdh whispered, drawing Ari's attention back to him, his question reminding her that he had unprecedented access to her thoughts. "There was no second strike team."

Ari shut down speculation and ushered Seaghdh out of her head. She couldn't let him know from her memory what had happened in this room. She hadn't been able to protect herself, but she could protect him. She'd pulled away and eased the mental door shut when he snapped his gaze back to her face. He'd felt her withdrawal.

"Stay with me, Ari. Hang on. That's an order," he commanded, effort in his tone as he pushed himself up on his hands and got one leg under him. He grimaced, but hobbled close to Hicci.

Seaghdh, a dire set to his features, mouthed invectives in what looked like two different languages. He swung hard at Hicci's front leg. He connected in precisely the spot Hicci had been tapping with one excited tentacle.

Ari didn't understand Chekydran biology, but that Seaghdh had landed a brutal shot to a highly sensitive bit of anatomy was apparent.

Hicci's throat pouch stretched tight in a scream she couldn't hear. It knocked Hicci out of whatever sonically induced trance he'd been in.

He struck with a lightning fast, vicious slap that sent Seaghdh spinning.

She drew a slow, deliberate breath, pushing aside fatigue and pain. Mentally, she picked up her imaginary energy blade and closed her eyes. She might not be able to attack the monster physically, but she could try to put the hurt on him mentally. Whether the attempt drove her mad didn't matter. Ari could help the man she loved.

Seaghdh was here. She loved him. Three Hells, she could do anything.

Marshalling her remaining strength, she lashed Hicci repeatedly in her mind's eye, driving him against the wall farthest from her body. Ari jammed her thoughts into his head, shoving deep.

His rage and fear ripped at her. She felt the hum from inside his head and body. It coerced a sexual response from him and from Ari. Sickened, she snarled into Hicci's brain.

"It would serve you right to be experimented on for the rest of your life," she snapped, "but I don't wish that on anyone or anything. Not even you. Don't feel bad. I still hate you enough to kill you."

With the mental strength born of six months of delayed vengeance, she hurled him across the room. Hard.

The floor at her feet shuddered from impact. Something broke inside his head and darkness began spreading.

Anticipation thrilled through Ari's physical body. She retreated slowly, watching and savoring the insidious, creeping stain. It blotted out pieces of him one hideous bit at a time. Torment spiraled through his dimming awareness. Vindication heated her blood like a potent aphrodisiac.

Ari opened her eyes and felt the ripples of pleasure running through her abused body.

Hicci lay in a heap at her feet, his throat pouch gashed and torn. The carapace along his back had fractured. Yellow-green blood oozed from his wounds. One tentacle flailed on the floor like a dying fish.

"Don't die so soon," she murmured inside Hicci's head. "You owe me months' worth of misery, you baxt'kal bastard."

"Ari," Seaghdh gasped, uncertainty—or was that fear—in his voice. "Twelve Gods." He stumbled toward her. Gunfire outside the door stopped him.

The door burst open. Literally. The explosion knocked Seaghdh to the floor. Pieces of chitin peppered her.

The hum vibrating the entire ship and every fiber of Ari's body never paused. It fed the delight streaming through her as she waited for the final light that was Hicci to wink out of existence. A noxious keen shrilled in her head, a last burbling plea for mercy, something that had never once been granted her. Ari wished she had the physical resources to laugh in his dying face.

Claugh soldiers in gray battle fatigues rushed through the door, training their weapons instantly on Hicci, whose form shuddered once and then stilled. His presence faded from her mind with one last hateful wheeze.

She gasped at the shudder of pleasure that rocked her body and began weeping like a lost child.

Ari tried to blink back the tears, terror chilling her. The mixed emotions confounded her. Realization broke over her and she choked on panic. She'd relished destroying her tormentor and not just mentally. Physically. To the point of physical climax. Nausea pressed against the back of her throat. By all the Gods. She'd let Hicci win.

She'd become the monster she'd so resisted. Choking back revulsion, she looked away from the shock in Seaghdh's face.

Turrel strode into the room, Raj on his heels. Raj? Ari's tired brain struggled with his presence until something clicked into place. The *Sen Ekir* was the second strike team. If she survived this, she'd kill her father.

"Captain!" Turrel shouted.

Ari barely heard him above the hum stimulating an unwilling response from her body.

Seaghdh waved Turrel off and pointed at her.

The big man turned. His eyes widened and he blanched.

Raj rushed to her side and dropped to both knees.

She squeezed her eyes shut, aware that it would hurt like nothing she'd ever felt when he touched her. He didn't. Gingerly, he lifted a shred of her uniform and clipped a Claugh insignia to it.

"Emergency medical teleport," she heard him bellow. "Prep stasis!"

"No!" Ari croaked. No one heard. The chill of teleport displacement pierced her wounds like needles of ice. She'd never been clear on the physics of teleportation. She'd heard you couldn't scream during teleport. She could. She just couldn't hear it. Hopefully, no one else could, either.

Ari materialized in a tiny, green-walled room and knew two things. First, she was sobbing over and over again, "No stasis. No stasis." Second, her father was in the room.

"By all the Gods," he breathed.

"Pain management onboard, now!" a female voice ordered.

Ari's brain sorted through files slowly and finally presented her with recognition. Dr. Annantra.

Face pale and eyes red-rimmed, the doctor strode into Ari's line of sight. Worry creased the woman's forehead and Ari thought she'd added a few lines around her mouth since last they'd spoken.

"Dr. Idylle, do you know how to establish a nutrient line?" Dr. Annantra asked.

"Yes."

"Be my guest."

"No stasis," Ari pleaded. She wouldn't survive the nightmares. They'd be new ones filled with speculation about how much of her humanity had been ripped from her when she'd been modified. And about how much of a monster she'd willingly become by exulting in another creature's pain and death.

"Alexandria," her father said, his tone gentle. "No, no. Stay still. You are gravely injured. It's a medically induced coma. You know that. You need this to heal. You will wake up. One of us will be here beside you every second you're asleep. I promise."

Anxiety gnawed on her insides. Without thinking, her exhausted, confused brain reached for Seaghdh. His answering presence in her mind felt like a warm hand wrapped around hers. Relief flooded her. He was on his way back. He was safe.

Something happened and pain fell away. She'd become so accustomed to it that its absence frightened her. Ari's eyes flew open even as her body relaxed and she dropped into darkness.

HER heart pounding hard, fear and the ghost of remembered pain pulled Ari up. She propelled herself up out of the floating, drifting sensation enfolding her.

"She's waking, again," a concerned female voice said.

Even in sleep, Ari had the impression she should know it.

"I shouldn't have sedated her until she'd seen everyone safe," the woman continued. "I'm bringing her up. Alert Her Majesty. Private channel. Tight beam. Scrambled."

Despite the grip of powerful sedatives, military conditioning held and Ari's brain shifted to full tactical alert. They were notifying the queen. Not Seaghdh. Not her father.

"Understood, Doctor," a young man answered.

Someone, presumably the doctor, moved beside her. "Captain Idylle, can you hear me?"

Dr. Annantra. Good. Ari tried to pry her cottony, thick tongue from the roof of her mouth. Warm spray moistened her lips and suddenly she could.

"Yes," Ari breathed.

"Do you know where you are?"

"*Dagger.*"

"Good. You're safe," Dr. Annantra said. "You've made remarkable progress healing but you will be my guest for several days yet. Are you in pain?"

"No." Unless you counted not being able to control your body as pain. Just to see if she could, Ari tried to open her eyes. It took several moments for her eyelids to obey the command. It took longer to realize she couldn't see because the room was dim.

"What—" she began but couldn't seem to complete the question.

"What happened?" Dr. Annantra guessed.

The sound of a door opening and a flash of light bleeding into the room cut off her answer.

"Secure the bay," another woman's voice said, her tone hushed. Eilod.

"Your Majesty," Dr. Annantra said.

"Doctor," Eilod replied.

The door shut and a very subtle vibration ran through the bed. Sonic shielding. No Seaghdh. Good sign? Or bad?

"Would you excuse us?" Eilod asked.

Bad.

"By your will, Your Majesty," Dr. Annantra answered and left the room.

"Half-light," Ari muttered in Claughwyth. The lights responded grudgingly, the glow coming up as if she might change her mind.

"Good," Eilod said. The relief in her voice confused Ari.

Via a monumental effort of will, Ari forced her fingers to search out and press the bed controls to raise her head. Ari studied Eilod. The skin of the queen's face looked too tight. Dark circles marred her eyes and lines of stress and unhappiness ringed her mouth.

Sympathy wrung through Ari. What the Three Hells had come apart while she'd slept? For all Ari knew, Eilod had come to tell her the Claugh, TFC, and Chekydran were busy fighting a three-way war.

"Empire safe?" Ari asked.

The tense set of the queen's shoulders broke and she slumped.

"After everything that's happened," she replied shaking her head, "that's the first question you think to ask me?"

Ari blinked.

Eilod sighed and slouched against the wall, a smile touching her features. "I don't want to like you, Captain," she said, "but you aren't leaving me much choice."

Ari's grin felt weak. "Sorry."

"Given that we both knew I'd contemplated having you assassinated, you'll forgive me if I doubt it."

Past tense. How nice.

"I'll brief you," Eilod said, the formal note vanishing from her voice. "We don't have much time. It won't surprise you that not even I can keep secrets from my spymaster and there are things the Councils are not prepared to apprise him of just yet."

The queen shifted. "The strike team failed."

"Yes. I'm sorry."

Eilod's shrug said she'd accepted the loss of crew and subjects, but that she obviously still felt it. "The sonic disruptor wasn't planted correctly. Our ship couldn't hold station well enough to allow precision placement."

"Didn't matter," Ari said. "They knew. Angelou was working with the Chekydran. They knew about my transponder and had anticipated us."

Eilod nodded as if Ari had confirmed what she'd already suspected. "We were reeling when your father's second in command insisted we try again."

"Pietre?"

"He and Sindrivik bicker like an old married couple, but they are a formidable pair. They used the *Sen Ekir*."

Of course. The *Sen Ekir* had been designed for precision station keeping. Granted, it had originally been for aerial surveys of research sites. It had never occurred to Ari that her father's science ship might one day save her life.

"Colonel Turrel took in a recovery team," she said. "He reported the Chekydran commander dead. You and Seaghdh?"

No. Some foreign and unwelcome part of her that had delighted in Hicci's pain. Ari swallowed hard and croaked, "Yes."

"Very thorough work," she replied. "All mission objects were achieved, but we hadn't gotten our people out when the second Chekydran cruiser brought weapons to bear on the ship we'd conquered."

Ari grimaced. She should have known the aural net connected ships as well as individuals. Damn.

"The *Dagger* engaged, but with barely one quarter of the ship's crew complement manning stations, we were ineffective." She shook her head in remembered frustration. "Then your friends arrived to save the day."

"My friends?"

"The *Balykkal*."

That surprised a smile from Ari. "Xiao."

"You've been in regen for several days," Eilod warned. "I gather some drastic changes have taken place within the government structure of Tagreth Federated."

The glance Ari shot the queen felt sharp, even to her. Before she could demand detail, Eilod's gaze turned inward and she frowned.

"Acknowledged," she said.

That's when Ari noticed the tiny headset she wore. Eilod's focus shifted back and she straightened and changed the subject.

"Information regarding your unique status has been brought to our attention, Captain," she said.

Twelve Gods, she was back to queen-speak. "Unique status?" Ari scowled.

"The Empire of the Claugh nib Dovvyth wishes to extend a formal offer of sanctuary. As we are a collection of varied races and misfits, we are best qualified to offer both the protection of the Empire and . . ."

And what? Asylum in the form of another prison? Given what Ari was, what she'd done, wasn't that the safest place for her? For everyone else, she meant. Plague carrier, mental assassin, experiment. She was a genetically engineered species of her mother's making, but it was Hicci who'd forced Ari to destroy her last claim to humanity.

Eilod broke off and turned her head slightly to the side where she wore the headset. Listening. "Send him in."

Ari's heart jumped in anticipation, then crashed when the door opened.

V'kyrri, good humor notably absent from his expression, stared at her as he edged in the door. Everything Ari had picked from Angelou's mind about the double agent played in her head.

"You're still alive." Surprise pulled the words from her before she could stuff them back down her throat. Dread pounded through Ari. Damn it all. She liked him. She'd trusted him.

He paled. "I'd prefer that not sound like a problem."

Ari closed her eyes and rubbed her forehead, grateful to find she could. "Twelve Gods, V'k."

"You dreamed," he said in a rush. "Damned horrific nightmares. I had to ask them to move you to a shielded bay. Point is I think I starred in a few of those dreams."

Opening her eyes, Ari stared at him. He'd read her while she'd been in a medically induced coma and stuck in regen? Given what she knew, why was she still alive? Shielded bay. Meaning that if she tried mentally to reach Seaghdh for help, he wouldn't hear. Ari glanced at Eilod, who watched the byplay with an assessing gaze.

She'd stationed her bodyguards outside the door. If Ari told her that V'kyrri had supplied Angelou with inside information, what would keep V'k from harming the queen? Unless Ari could reach and stop him while they were both inside a shielded bay.

"You know my CO was colluding with the Chekydran?" she asked.

V'kyrri's expression lightened the tiniest bit. "He's been captured. His court-martial is scheduled for next month, but there's some argument coming out of TFC about his fitness to stand trial. Go on, please."

"He was captured because I got inside his head and made him send his entire data store to Intelligence Command."

Looking staggered, V'kyrri shot a glance at Eilod. "Inside his head? While . . . ?"

"While I laid on the floor of a Chekydran interrogation chamber bleeding? Yes. I learned a great deal while in his head, V'kyrri. Do I have to say it? Or . . ."

Eilod and V'kyrri traded so discomfited a look, Ari shut her mouth and forced herself to reparse her information. She had to factor in the roar building outside her door. Seaghdh. Eilod's Auhrnok Riorchjan. Shielded room or no, Ari felt him. Her pulse thumped and her breath came faster.

The door snapped open and Cullin Seaghdh, thinner, a new scar lining one cheek, barreled into the room. "Twelve Gods!" he swore, his voice trembling as he stared at her, raw anguish and need stark in his gaze.

"You Carozziel slime-bats," Ari growled, glaring between Seaghdh,

Eilod, and V'kyrri as pieces suddenly shifted in her head and fell into a new pattern.

Seaghdh drew up short, desperation and fear growing in his golden eyes.

"You let me think V'kyrri was a traitor!" she shouted.

V'KYRRI burst out laughing.

Eilod shook her head.

Swearing, Ari glared at Seaghdh's cocky grin. It made complete
tactical sense. When an enemy looks for inside information, plant
someone to provide it in controlled quality and quantity. Seaghdh's
execution had been so flawless, not even Angelou had suspected he'd
harbored a double agent.

Lesson one for the newly aware telepath. Just because you're inside someone else's head doesn't mean he or she or it has any better
a lock on the truth than you.

V'kyrri regained his composure, crossed the little bay, and patted
her hand. "Very nice work, Captain," he said, his humor firmly in
place. "We'll get you some training once you're back on your feet.
First thing, we'll teach you how to shut it all off when you don't want
to read or be read."

Ari studied him, seeing the traces of long recovery in his shadowed eyes and nodded. "I didn't think I'd ever see you again, V'k. Alive or dead. Glad I was wrong."

"Me, too," he said. "It was a near thing. For both of us." He turned to go but paused at the door. "Your Majesty."

"Dismissed, Mr. V'kyrri," Eilod said. "Thank you for your service."

Service? What service? Confirming that she'd influenced and nearly destroyed a man two sectors away? Baxt'k.

Seaghdh closed in beside her and covered her hand with his.

Warmth eased through her tense body. She glanced at him. All traces of emotion had vanished. He'd shuttered his expression with a studiously neutral mask that told Ari nothing. There was so much she still needed to know.

"Ari." The caress he made of her name sent a tremor through her before he pressed even his tone under iron control. "IntCom has hounded us every hour of every day since the destruction of the two Chekydran cruisers."

She felt a grim smile on her face. "Did you let them debrief you?"

"I let them try."

Laughing hurt and made her cough, which hurt worse. She wrapped her arms around her aching ribs and gasped for breath.

"Get the doctor," Ari heard Eilod instruct.

Ari tried to wave her off.

She ignored it.

Dr. Annantra strode into the room, shoved Seaghdh to one side, and pressed a series of buttons.

Pain vanished, but so did most of Ari's motor control. She collapsed back against the bed and huffed.

"I could put you back in regeneration," Dr. Annantra threatened, studying readings and the tubes running to Ari's left arm. "Your father would love the opportunity to put in another nutrient tube. He's out of practice."

"Stop. You're scaring me," Ari grumbled, suppressing the question of just how Dr. Annantra knew so much about her father's technique.

Seaghdh's expression remained impassive but his eyes danced.

"Can she talk to IntCom?" Eilod demanded.

"Yes," Ari said over the top of Dr. Annantra's considering expression. It had occurred to Ari that the past several minutes had been a test to see whether or not she represented unacceptable risk. The Claugh needed to know whether she could be trusted. She had no way of knowing how she'd scored. Ari didn't trust herself. How could they?

She needed data. Just so happened, that was IntCom's specialty. Could she trust her own government to give her anything useful?

"One more thing, Captain," Eilod said, "before I patch Director Durante of Intelligence Command through. Captain Xiao of the *Balykkal* has asked for status regarding your investigation into the attack on Kebgra."

Swearing, Ari nodded. Yet another test of what she'd accomplished or of what she was willing to admit? "Target ID'd and neutralized."

Eilod scowled. "Angelou gave the order to murder those colonists."

"I was his target, but yes."

"I'm sorry there's anything left of him to court-martial," she growled. "I will inform Captain Xiao. IntCom on your screen in three."

"May I see my father for a moment first?" Ari hesitated. "Alone?"

Seaghdh's head came up and she glanced at him. His gaze searched her face, but still he gave her nothing to see, no hint of what he thought, what he wanted, and every tendril she sent out to sense his emotions bounced right back to her. Was that the room? Or the medications?

"Of course, Captain," Eilod said. "Auhrnok? Will you join me?"

The queen stood in the open doorway, waiting pointedly for Seaghdh.

"Ari . . ."

"Cullin," his cousin cut him off.

He blinked, pressed his lips tight, and stalked from the room.

Eilod, her expression unsettled, followed him as Ari's father strode to her side and took her hand.

Dr. Annantra smiled. "I'll leave you. Exercise some judgment, Captain, please? You are not cleared for duty. Of any kind."

"She will," her father said.

Ari rolled her eyes.

"Oh. Captain." The woman paused in the doorway. She held up a bit of round metal.

Ari couldn't identify it. Frowning in confusion, she shook her head and glanced at the woman's face for a clue. The sparkle in the doctor's brown eyes and her self-satisfied grin set off a burst of awareness.

"The transponder?" Ari breathed.

"The very thing," Annantra replied, beaming, and quit the room.

After everything, Seaghdh had authorized the removal of the last fail-safe he might have? Or did he simply not realize what she'd become?

"Alexandria," her father said.

"Sindrivik and Pietre figured out how to extract that thing safely?" she asked.

He nodded, looking pleased. "I have great expectations of that partnership."

"Extend my gratitude," she said. "I owe them my life. Twice over, it seems."

"What am I? Junk DNA?"

"There's no such . . ." Ari broke off in the midst of the rote answer to gape at her father. Teasing. He sounded teasing.

Preening, he rocked up on the balls of his feet and back down. The last time she'd seen him do that, Hieronomus had been valedictorian of his university. Ari had been five. Another flash of awareness whispered "Dr. Annantra." Ari blinked and shut it out.

"I formulated a cure for you," he said, then waved off the declaration. "Inoculation, really. The Chekydran had built a molecular capsule around an array of ancient pneumonia viruses. The capsules held them in check and embedded in the spinal column. They even gave each of them a countdown clock. When time elapsed, the capsules disintegrated and you infected everyone nearby."

Ari sighed. "Then you realized about the same time I did that this plague wasn't a death sentence."

Her father sobered. "Only for the few we lost and for you. Or so I thought."

"How'd you beat it?"

"Vaccinating against pneumonia was easy, once we realized," he said. "We vaccinated you, then I built a specialized enzyme that attacks and destroys the molecular bonds of the nanotech delivery mechanism."

She crinkled her forehead and glanced down at her body. "I'm your sole test case? I should start dissolving any moment."

"The nanotech was Chekydran, Alex," Dad countered. "I targeted my serum. We've taken a few spinal fluid and cord samples to be certain you're clean."

Clean. Free of the Chekydran from the inside out. She wondered if her dad's concoction would destroy Chekydran memory enhancements. Free of the Armada from the inside since Eilod and Seaghdh had removed the transponder. All she had left was a meaningless rank. Ari smiled and, still seeing Seaghdh's painfully neutral expression, said, "Dad. Can I ask you something?"

SEAGHDH paced the hallway outside medical, cursing as Eilod and her bodyguards watched. He'd swallowed every instinct in him that had screamed for him to sweep Ari into his arms and never let her go.

"Son, what is your problem?"

Seaghdh spun.

Linnaeus Idylle stood in the hallway, peering at him, his head tilted and his hands clasped behind his back.

"I beg your pardon?"

"I have spent plenty of time misunderstanding my daughter, Captain Seaghdh," the man said, "but this I do know. If you have feelings for her, you had better say so."

"Or I'll be your vaccination test case?" Seaghdh prompted. He shook his head. "She's had too many people imposing their will on hers. She deserves the chance to find out what she wants."

Dr. Idylle smiled. "You believe Alexandria doesn't know her own mind, Captain? After everything she's been through?"

Seaghdh sighed and rubbed a hand down his face. Anxiety made his heart tremble in his chest. He was losing her. He could feel it. Ari was slipping through his fingers.

Dr. Idylle put a hand on his shoulder. "She asked me to destroy her PhD samples."

"What?" Hope slammed breath into Seaghdh's chest.

"I'd say she knows what she wants. Do you?"

His eyes watering, Seaghdh spun to stare at the closed medi-bay door and groaned. He hadn't told her. He loved her and he'd left her, even after seeing the heart-wrenching uncertainty in her eyes, to face whatever offer IntCom would make.

"Hang your pride, Captain. If she matters to you, make a counteroffer," Dr. Idylle suggested before he walked away.

Seaghdh glanced at his cousin. "I can't do this alone."

Worry vanished from her expression. She nodded.

COMMANDER Durante, the director of Intelligence Command himself, signed off after enjoining Ari to think carefully about his offer. She sighed and leaned back. She'd be careful all right. The package IntCom had put together for her reeked of desperation. They'd made sure she wouldn't refuse. That put her back up.

"You look like you're chewing on Nurrellan lemon berry," Turrel said. "Must have been a hell of a deal."

Ari glanced at him, lounging against the wall, just inside the door. As he talked, V'kyrri, Sindrivik, Eilod, and finally Seaghdh, filed into the room.

"What is this?" she demanded. "Tag-team interrogation?"

Sindrivik chuckled. Eilod's eyes danced with suppressed amusement. Seaghdh smirked and V'kyrri flushed an interesting shade of mahogany.

But Turrel grinned.

Ari gaped, both at the sudden transformation in the colonel and from wondering if it was a sign of impending doom.

"You've seen through everything the Murbaasch Tu has tried to put over on you," Turrel said. "Straight answer is we're here to handle you."

She raised an eyebrow. "Why, Kirthin Turrel. I didn't know you cared."

Eilod snickered.

Seaghdh rubbed a hand down his face.

"Don't want to start that with me, Captain," Turrel advised, a smile firmly in place. "I'm into plural partnerships. The more participants, the merrier."

Ari flushed and held up her hands in surrender. "Call the doctor. I need something to scrub that image from my brain. They offered me command of a Kessola and its ops team."

Seaghdh and Turrel swore in unison.

"Do they think I'm stupid?" Eilod demanded. "Or that you are?"

"I'm aware it might force you to arrest me for spying after all," Ari replied. "We can be certain they didn't intend for me to tell you."

"Could we negate spying charges, get you aboard a Kessola, and let me have a look at it from inside your head?" V'kyrri pleaded.

Ari smiled.

Sindrivik choked on a sharp inhalation, then managed to exclaim between coughing spasms, "They set you up? Because of us? They won't really give you a Kessola, will they?"

"You're Murbaasch Tu, Lieutenant, but you think like a man accustomed to telepaths in the ranks," she said. "What would you do with the first telepath ever in the history of your people? Someone with proven efficacy against targets halfway across a galaxy?"

"I'd bury her in the deepest, most secretive, bomb- and assassin-proof shelter I could find and work her to death," V'kyrri said. His tone led Ari to believe she'd just heard a part of his race's early history.

He shifted and she could tell his eyes saw her again. "They do know that you were only able to do what you did because you knew Angelou?"

"Like I know the Auhrnok Riorchjan?" she responded.

"I hope not," she heard Seaghdh grumble and had to suppress a grin.

"I cannot allow them to use you," Eilod said. She met Ari's eye, her expression troubled but resolute. They both knew she wasn't talking about Ari's happiness or safety. She couldn't compromise Claugh security interests by allowing Ari to return to any kind of position at IntCom.

"I didn't risk my life or anyone else's to preserve your people and mine just to walk into another prison," Ari replied. "Not to mention some unresolved accusations against the Council regarding the genocide at Shlovkora."

"You have a lead?" Turrel demanded, his smile gone.

She nodded. "Partial. I'll get you a full report before I go."

"Go?" Seaghdh echoed. "Go where?"

"Far and fast from TFC," she replied. "Director Durante offered the Kessola as a warning."

"You got someone inside IntCom?" Turrel marveled, admiration in his voice.

"Jayleia does," she said. "Director Durante is her father."

Turrel grunted, subsided against the wall, and crossed his arms. "Here's where we handle you, Captain," he said.

"I'm not a captain anymore," Ari countered. "I resigned my commission."

They stared at her.

"So no one could order you back home," Eilod surmised.

"There's more. When I went after Angelou, I thought we were after one misguided, power-hungry man. I may have miscalculated."

Eilod's expression sharpened. "He wasn't acting alone?"

"The director hinted at indications of a larger network. We may never know, however," Ari replied, pressing her tone flat. "Angelou's sanity appears to be in question."

V'kyrri paled and closed his eyes.

Just as she'd feared. Her doing. Ari nodded, accepting the guilt.

"Unless he recovers from what I did, we'll never know if we had everything reversed," she said. "We assumed the Chekydran were using Armada. What if it was Armada using the Chekydran?"

"To build an army?" Turrel mused.

"With soldiers that never question a command," Seaghdh said.

"Are we looking at an attempted overthrow of the Council?" Eilod asked.

"Possibly." Ari stared at her pale hands, gripped together atop her green blanket. "Regardless, we'd better ask ourselves what Armada offered the Chekydran that induced them to cooperate within some kind of marginal alliance."

"Right," Turrel said, sounding resolute.

She looked at him.

"I'm recruiting you, Captain," he said. "You keep your rank. You report to me."

Ari blinked. "The Shlovkur Armed Forces?"

"Yep."

"Comprised of just you and me."

"That's right."

"Got a ship?"

"Nope."

"He doesn't," Eilod said, voice ringing, "but I do. Captain Alexandria Idylle, upon the authority and trust vested in me by the Peoples Voice Council and the Nobles Council, I hereby extend to you the rank of captain in the Claugh nib Dovvyth Diplomatic Service. Your command is to be the royal flagship, the *Dagger*."

Elation fired through Ari and she breathed a laugh. "Just before he signed off, Durante said something about how nice it would be to have someone in the Claugh ranks who understands the TFC mind-set."

It didn't matter. Too much stood in the way, yet. She'd only be a danger to everyone and everything she'd come to care about. Ari held perfectly still until the longing raking her insides died down. How could she still want so badly to belong?

She stared at Seaghdh. He wouldn't meet her eye. She hesitated. He hadn't said he loved her, had he? The words to beg for a reason to stay died in her mouth. If Seaghdh was done with her, Ari refused to pressure him. He had to want her, and not because she'd helped preserve his government or because they'd traded off saving one another's lives.

Eilod straightened and glared at her cousin. "Cullin Seaghdh, you are a brave man who has never cowered or hesitated in the face of the enemy. If you do not speak in the next several seconds, my estimation of your character will be forever damaged."

"No!" Ari snapped.

Seaghdh jerked upright to stare at her. His tightly held control fractured and a maelstrom of emotion whirled out from him. Want. Fear. Pain.

"You do nothing you do not want to do," she gasped at him.

Hurt fell out of the mix. Fear spiked and infected Ari so that her heart thumped uneasily against her ribs.

"Gods, Ari," Seaghdh burst out in a rush. "I want you to stay."

Heat raked the backs of her eyeballs.

"Here it comes," Turrel said. "You honor-bound command types are all alike. Too fond of noble gestures and ready to run off to the outer reaches to spare everyone around you. It isn't going to fly."

"Baxt'k, you, Turrel," Ari growled. "You have no idea what happened . . ."

"You were wired for more than sound with that transponder," Turrel interrupted. "So, yeah. After careful analysis, we know exactly what went on in that torture chamber."

She leaned back and closed her eyes, nausea surging at the realization that everyone in the room knew what she'd done.

"The bastard deserved to die," Turrel said.

"Three Hells!" she muttered, opening her eyes and pinning him with an annoyed glare. "What he deserved wasn't my call to make, Colonel. I had a job to do. I couldn't do it while he lived. Am I sorry the thrice-damned Chekydran is dead? Hell no. I'd happily kill him again, if . . ." She heard what she'd said and broke off. "Happily."

"I translated the hum I used to control the ship," Sindrivik essayed. "At least, I think I did. If I understood it correctly, it's a hive— er—courtship vocalization."

"Sex," she corrected, watching colorless liquid drip in the tube in her left arm.

"Yes," he agreed. "Pervasive. It shut down all but life support and passive defense systems on board. It never occurred to me that one Chekydran having a good time would cause the entire ship to participate."

"One hell of a sex drive," Turrel muttered, sounding envious.

Ari nearly smiled, but she looked at Seaghdh's wan face and pressed back feeling of any kind. "So you know I killed the Chekydran from within his own head. Did it show up on your damned sensors that I watched while he died? That I got off on his pain the way he'd spent so many months jacking off with my blood after beating me nearly to death?"

Rage fired in Seaghdh's gold eyes as he blanched an alarming shade of white.

"Still want me to stay?"

"Baxt'k," he ground out between clenched teeth. He closed the distance and yanked her to his chest so swiftly, she cried out in surprise.

"Hush," he commanded, resisting her feeble attempts to disengage his arms. "Yes, I want you to stay."

Ari subsided, relaxing into his embrace, frightened by how very badly she needed his arms around her.

"I don't understand," Sindrivik said. "You know the Chekydran language. Directly, I mean. Yet, you blame yourself for . . ." He broke off and cleared his throat before going on. ". . . Enjoying the death of the thing that tortured you, then tried to kill the Auhrnok?"

Seaghdh eased his hold to allow her the space to meet Sindrivik's eye. Her brain rolled, sluggish after so much trauma and so many medications. The pieces of data came together grudgingly. "You're saying I responded to the hum?"

"Not until Pietre and I got the playback device positioned correctly, you didn't. Physical readings remained consistent with shock and pain," Sindrivik said. "After we switched on playback, your pain reading shot up, but then, over a period of time, it changed."

"Pain sensing structures in the humanoid brain are right next to pleasure centers," Ari murmured and shuddered in distaste. "It might be possible to alter brain wave activity with something like that hum and there's no reason pain sensing in the brain shouldn't spread out to encompass pleasure centers."

She shook her head. "I don't know enough about that sort of thing. I'd have to ask Raj, and I don't think I want to explain why I want to know."

"It got to me, too," Seaghdh rumbled in her ear.

That stopped her. If it wasn't just her . . . she couldn't laugh, so she pressed tighter to him and whispered, "Thank you."

He shifted. It felt like he looked down at the top of her head. "What else?"

"What happens next time?" Ari blurted.

"Next time?"

"The next time someone presses her too hard or threatens everything she holds dear," V'kyrri clarified. "I can't tell you this will be easy, Ari. You have a new weapon in your arsenal. One you've always had but didn't understand. Give me time. I can teach you its uses and its limits."

That made sense. Ari comprehended weapons training, both the necessity and the utility. Something else gnawed at the edge of her awareness, and she struggled free of Seaghdh's grasp to peer at him.

"Mission objectives?" she muttered, uncertain she was picking up what he seemed to be trying so hard to communicate without saying the words aloud. A picture flashed into her head. She gasped and understood.

Raj had successfully extracted one of the Chekydran larva. Sindrivik and Pietre had found a way to keep the thing alive. They'd even hooked it into an isolated computer bank on board the *Sen Ekir*.

Abruptly sick and shaking, Ari fumbled for a com switch.

Seaghdh guided her hand.

"Dad," she rasped. "Dad?"

"Alex?" Her father answered, the link went video enabled, and her father's gaze searched her face. He paled. "Alex, what's wrong? Why are you awake? Are you . . . ?"

"Destroy it," she ordered.

Silence.

Then Ari heard someone shift in a chair. Her father looked over his shoulder, then back at her. "Destroy what?"

"The Chekydran."

"What?" Raj protested.

She must have caught them in the midst of experiments on the . . . Her brain cut off the train of thought.

Her father widened the video field. He, Raj, Pietre, and Jayleia were in cargo. Every single one of them stared at her.

"No! The research potential alone . . ." Raj was saying.

"It is a living, thinking, feeling creature! Don't do to it what was done to me!" Ari commanded and found her fists were clenched. "We've taken it from everything it has ever known, subjected it to tests, study, and our own form of interrogation! We can't give it back, but we can end its misery."

Pain warred with indignation on her father's face. He glanced at Raj.

"I can't believe you're accusing us of being just like the Chekydran," Raj said. From the petulant tone of his voice, she could tell she'd won.

Raj sighed and scrubbed his face with both hands.

"I had wondered," he murmured. "Our instruments can't register things like pain or pleasure in these larval forms, but there's a reading I've never been able to alter."

"The one you said looked like a scream?" Jayleia prompted, the edge of tears in her voice.

Raj and her dad traded a resigned look.

Her father nodded.

"I'll take care of it," Raj promised. "As humanely as possible, if that isn't a horrifying oxymoron."

"Rest, Alex, please," her father said. "We'll make this as right as we can."

"Thank you."

Looking unsettled, her father signed off.

Seaghdh, his expression grim but satisfied, said, "You just drew the line."

Ari scowled at him. "What?"

"You could have destroyed that creature," he said. "You know the *Sen Ekir* well enough to disrupt nutrient feed. You didn't."

She stared at him and felt some tightly shut place within her break open. *Baxt'k you, Hicci. Match to me.*

She felt elation leap within Cullin Seaghdh as if it were her own and wondered how he managed to read so much from her without being a telepath himself.

"I don't care what you think you are, Captain Alexandria Rose Idylle," he said. "I love you. I love your courage and determination, your refusal to sacrifice anyone or anything to expedience. I love the sense of humor everyone told me you didn't have. Which reminds me." He released her and straightened, a cocky, promising grin on his face. "I have something for you."

Uh-oh.

Dr. Annantra's son handed a covered tray through the door. Eilod took it from him and set it before Ari.

Still grinning like an idiot, Seaghdh removed the cover with a flourish.

The savory aroma of freshly grilled Wrate Leaf hit her. She burst out laughing but had to stifle the urge when her ribs complained.

"You are going to explain this at some point," Eilod commanded with a smile before turning away.

Seaghdh brushed a curl from Ari's cheek, his eyes shimmering with mirth, but his expression somber. "I know you think you're alone in the universe because of what your mother did, but, hwe vaugh, you have always been one of a kind to me, from the moment I saw the media shot of your very first blade win."

Ari sighed as she tasted hope again in the swelling of her heart. It wouldn't be easy. She wasn't the same person the Chekydran had captured so many months ago. Seaghdh had been right. She had an opportunity and an obligation to rebuild herself and her life. With him. They'd be starting from scratch.

She looked at the man staring into her face.

"Tell me you'll stay," he urged.

What had she said to him before flying off to beard the Chekydran in their ship? He was more than worth the risk. Maybe she was, too.

"What is the final point?" Ari demanded. "The one which binds all points into the Art of the Blade?"

Seaghdh blinked, hope, and something much warmer, kindling in his eyes. He held out a hand. "Commitment."

She put her hand in his. Her heart soared. "Commitment."